TRILON:
THE FLIGHT OF THE COATUS

DAVE CAPP

Hey Marie,

Thank you so much
for your support!

ISBN: 978-1-7338489-0-9

Library of Congress Control Number: 2019903097

Any references to historical events, real people, or real places are used fictitiously. Names, characters, and places are products of the author's imagination.

All artwork and images by Leanna Crossan

Editing and proofing by Katherine Marzullo

Printed by Kindle Direct Publishing in the United States of America.

First printing edition 2019.

Thinking Capp Publishing
PO Box 5
Bergenfield, NJ 076

For Amanda Jean

ACKNOWLEDGEMENTS

Whoa, it's finally here. I feel like Trilon and myself have formed into a singular entity over the last few years. If you were to ask me how I was doing, you could have asked how the world creation was going, and you'd probably get the same answer. It feels good to get this out to you all. If I were giving a speech, this would be the part where I'd play Queen's "We Are the Champions."

First, I'd like to say thank you for taking the time to open my book. Please continue, it gets better.

Now, there are some very special people I'd like to thank. If you feel left out, I apologize. Maybe you just weren't as important as you thought you were.

My father, for introducing me to Middle Earth.

My mother, who spared me the extra five dollars I needed to purchase The Legend of Zelda: Ocarina of Time.

My sister, who always read my seven-page stories when we were kids.

My good friends Chris Fierro, Harry Chan, Scott Puglisi, Dan Johnson, Matt Petillo, Ryan McHugh, Brian Sullivan, Jeff Shaw, Zach Heir, Genna Martorelli, Rob Dimarzo, and last, but most certainly not least, Marya Layth. You all have helped me create Trilon, and I thank you. Whether it was reading rough drafts, creating character names, helping me shape my original map, introducing me to my influences, or letting me corner you at a party to talk about the horrors of poaching, you are all a part of this.

Brook Zelcer, for showing me that the world isn't so black and white.

Leanna Crossan, for illustrating both the cover and map.

My friend and editor, Kate Marzullo, for wading through my first manuscript.

My partner and best friend, Amanda Jean, who supported me when I was at my lowest, and encouraged me when I thought I was at my highest.

TABLE OF CONTENTS

LANDS OF TRILON

TRILON: THE FLIGHT OF THE COATUS

PROLOGUE

GOJII: THE YLEWOOD

PING!!!

A sharp stone, lodged deep into a candlestick, fell onto the brass candelabra as soon as the wax covering its top melted away. The tiny flame that was barely breathing extinguished as Evore's nectar-colored eyes opened to his bedroom, faintly lit by the pale morning glow shining through a square-shaped window.

He arose from his bed; its outer frame was a tree trunk carefully hollowed before it was bleached white, and the mattress was filled with feathers. Evore reached his hands up to the short, pointed ceiling and stretched, standing upon his toes. The boy of ten loved the feeling of a morning stretch and swore that, sometimes after a good long one, he felt himself grow taller.

Still barely able to keep his eyes open, Evore's bare feet slid across the floor of his chamber to a large, coffee-colored wooden chest. While the trunk looked rather plain from a distance, a closer examination showed a curved eye intricately carved in the top. One side of the pupil had a sun and the other a crescent moon. Unlocking the brass clasp, he sleepily opened it, releasing a strong scent of cedar wood through his nostrils, which woke him up just as much as the morning alarm. The boy tossed blankets and wrinkled corsair trousers onto the floor, eventually pulling out a pair of forest green leggings that he slipped over his skinny bare legs. He wrapped himself in a sand-colored robe, fastened it with a leather belt, and made for the door.

Evore's dome-shaped bedchamber was separated from the rest of the tree hut by a thin, winding staircase that curled through the branches of the great oak it was built upon. Every story stood on a wood platform that rested on the tree's arms, each strong as steel. When his father, Onexis, the Chief of his people, constructed the bedroom, it frightened Evore. No longer could he sneak into his parents' quarters when the wind screamed through the leaves or when the branches groaned. His father told him that the trees were the guardians of the Verrativas, and just as the mortals didn't fear their armored protectors, neither should he.

"It's not the trees that scare me," he whimpered. "Just the height."

Onexis laughed heartily at this, patting his son hard on the back. "Height is the weapon of a tree. You want your guardian to wield something fierce to protect your life."

As the morning air brushed against his fair skin, he felt the wind dance through his robe and out the baggy sleeves. Most times, Evore would land at the bottom of the spiral staircase after two leaps, but not today. Today, he walked gingerly down each step, the wood creaking under his bare feet and echoing through the tree. It felt as though there were hundreds of stairs, maybe thousands.

When Evore reached the bottom of the staircase, he pushed in the circular mahogany door, which led inside to the much larger tree hut. As soon as he crossed the threshold, his mother greeted him with a smile warmer than the sun. The window, which was almost the size of the apple red wall it was cut into, let in just enough sunlight that it seemed to illuminate the woman. She began to stir a small black cauldron that hung over an open fire, its flame's skinny orange fingers tickling the sides of the pot. The abode was one large room, which had a sleeping area in one corner, a kitchen by the back door, and a study in the front.

Emery spooned a ladle of oats from the caldron into a small clay bowl and placed it in front of her son as he sat down at a round table. Evore reached into a larger wooden bowl and pulled out a handful of berries.

"How many times must I tell you to use a spoon?" Emery questioned. "I don't know where your hands have been!"

She sat at the opposite end of the boy with a steaming mug of tea to watch him eat his breakfast. Her hair was chestnut brown, the same as his, but while Evore's was curly and unruly, Emery's laid straight down her back. She was clad in a vibrant silk robe of emerald green that had a tree trunk stitched down the back. Bare branches spread from it and crept over her shoulders onto the front of the garment.

"*Eat*, child. You'll need your strength for today." Emery's voice was tender but still had a sense of urgency to it.

Evore stirred the raspberries and blueberries into his oatmeal until it was as pink as the sky at sunrise. His insides turned and his throat tightened as he swallowed the first spoonful. "I'm *not* hungry." He frowned at the full bowl and dropped the spoon onto the table. He couldn't remember the last time he didn't want his sweetened oats but knew that if he took another bite, his stomach would send it right back up to him.

Standing from her seat, Emery glided over to Evore, and with her right hand she gently massaged his shoulder. As she ran her fingers through his tangled forest of curls, Emery found her warm smile once again. "It's okay, baby, it'll all be over soon."

"I'm not a baby!" Evore whined, pulling himself away from his mother's embrace. *How could she say that? Today is my test to become a man. No, today is my test to become a*

3

true Verrativa. How many Verrativas are still called "baby" by their mothers?

Emery sat back down in front of him. "No, of course you're not! I'm sorry, love, I still see my newborn whenever I look into your eyes. Your father placed you in my arms kicking and screaming, and now you're off to take your *first* test."

Tears began to well in Evore's eyes. "What if I can't--"

"You can! You're Evore, son of Onexis, Chief of the Verrativas!"

The tears began to fall down his cheeks and he tasted their salt as they ran over his lips. "I just need to know that you and father will still-- will you still love me if I fail?" He sobbed into his sleeve, and Emery wiped his tears away with the back of her hand.

"It's not like we have much choice in the matter, do we?" she lovingly joked and watched a small smile curl on Evore's tear-stained face. "It's natural to worry about failing, child. Remember, though, thinking about failure won't help you succeed."

He sniffed and nodded in agreement. Emery took a sip of tea from her mug.

"Now, eat your breakfast."

After Evore's stomach allowed a few more bites out of respect for his mother, he knew procrastination was no longer an option. "Where's Father? I thought he would be coming with me."

"Your father is busy picking and burning shy aconite. He will meet you at the Ironash Tree."

Father is always burning shy aconite. Evore didn't respond to his mother but instead stepped away from the kitchen table and into Chief Onexis's study.

The study had always fascinated him, even before he was able to read. On top of a chair carved in the fashion of an

4

oak tree laid a book that his father would joke weighed more than Evore: *Trilon: The History and the Magic of the Three Realms.* It was open to his favorite page, the colored map of the entire world. He traced his middle finger over the Moiira Sea, which separated the Ylewood from the rest of the western realm of Gojii. *Will I ever leave the Ylewood?* As Evore wondered to himself, his eyes went to the top of the map, where Soarfrost should have been located. That was where the Oracles lived in seclusion from the rest of the world, to practice their banned magic. His father would tell him stories that, before Tanwill Embray took Trilon, the Oracles lived in the capital province Reliss and helped King Zabkar Inwar rule. Set loose upon his Kingdom, the Oracles used their power as a way to intimidate the men and women of every realm and made Trilon a world built on fear and despair.

"Rebellion follows tyranny, much like the moon follows the sun," Onexis explained. "Trilon needed a new leader, someone without the gift of magic."

Tanwill Embray gathered armies from both Gojii and the eastern realm of Aleru to put an end to the hostility that King Zabkar had created. When he approached Onexis to ask for aid in the battle, he declined at first, but Tanwill made him a promise that he couldn't refuse. Now, Zabkar was dead, the Oracles banished to the snow-capped mountains of Soarfrost, and King Tanwill ruled over Trilon. Whenever Evore asked his father what that pact was, Onexis always refused to answer but would promise to tell him "when the time is right."

Forbath was where Evore wanted to travel to the most. He wanted to go to Ghordaan, to watch the blacksmiths forge swords and shields, and eat the fresh fish from Yatorga, which he read was the most delicious in the entire world. Most of all, he wanted to go to Reliss. Not only was

Larkmour Castle there, but it was also where the Coatuses were trained.

They were magnificent winged creatures that had a scaly torso, feathered wings, an oddly long neck, and a beak that was typically striped with a sunflower yellow and an indigo blue. Altogether, there were three Coatuses, known as "the sisters", each one taking care of their own realm. There was Akupara in Forbath, who was said to be larger than Larkmour Castle; then Syaestra in Aleru, who was quick and the color of ice; and finally, the Coatus of the west, Nyteah. Evore's father had always shown him the Moon and would tell Evore to wish upon it, and every time the boy had wished for a flight upon Nyteah.

Although Evore had never actually seen a Coatus, *The History and the Magic of the Three Realms* showed countless pictures of the three sisters, which allowed him to draw a few of his own. After Tanwill defeated Inwar, he was greeted with three eggs, and when they hatched, the new King realized that these creatures could either destroy Trilon or make it a better place.

After the sisters were fully grown and trained, many other animals fled from fear, even though the Coatuses were peaceful and ate a vegetarian diet. Two men, Lorrode Allwater and Vengar Stoneburner, harnessed their aggression before setting up a Trainer's Guild in Reliss that taught a chosen three to ride the Coatuses in an effort to transport both goods and people all through Trilon. Evore would beg his father to let him come on one of his trips to Forbath so he could see the Guild, speak with Allwater or Stoneburner, and maybe ride a Coatus like the rest of the inhabitants of Trilon, but he was never able to persuade him.

A long piece of parchment which Evore hadn't noticed during his previous reads was sticking out towards the end of the book. He pulled it out and saw that it was a letter:

Dear Onexis, Chief of the Verrativas,

We have received your inquiry for a time where you can join us in Reliss and meet with King Tanwill as well as his Cabinet. We understand the relationship that you hold with the King of Trilon, and that you believe face-to-face meetings are vital to not only keep you but your entire race safe.

However, as the King's Cabinet, we believe that traveling from the Ylewood all the way to the southern realm puts your life at risk, which in turn endangers the lives of the entire Verrativa race.

For your information, the King is busy with a new breakthrough discovery by Saige Lorrode Allwater. Using science, our Royal Saige has found a way to create two Coatus eggs, one of which has already hatched. Master Vengar Stoneburner has been working tirelessly with his Trainees to assure that the Coatus will be tamed in a timely manner.

When King Tanwill finds it necessary to contact you, he will send another letter to one of the designated areas that we have discussed. Until then, please be safe, and know that our King sends his love and blessings to you and your people.

Sincerely Yours,
Brannon Broadwine
Lead Confidant for King Tanwill
FORBATH: RELISS

At the bottom of the letter was a simply-drawn Coatus which Evore assumed was Akupara.

Evore's heart fluttered like he was just given his Nascense Day present. "Another Coatus," he couldn't help but scream out loud. *This has to be a gift from King Tanwill to my father; after all, they are best friends.*

"Are you still here?" Emery squealed when she saw her son in the study. "Get out! You were late when you woke up this morning!" She pushed her son out the door, and, running down the staircase until it ended, he grabbed onto the tree's trunk to climb to the ground.

While most lands had villages with rows of cottages, the Verrativas built all of their homes in the trees. No tree huts were ever visible to the naked eye, nor were they ever built next to another. His father always told him that being hidden in plain view was the only way because your enemies would never know where to look.

The dirt path that Evore followed winded to the left and right while a wall of trees on either side made the morning seem darker than it already was. Although the road was littered with roots, rocks, and small holes, and was wide enough for two to walk abreast, the twists and turns made it seem quite narrow. As the path dipped down, part of it veered to the right, leading to a grassy overhang. Evore had spent most of his ten years at the mossy jut. Without any real friends, he would sit, his feet dangling over the edge, and imagine the world outside of the woodlands he called home. More recently, Evore would borrow books from his father's study and read at the overhang. He knew all the rules to shinty, horseshoes, and knucklebones, but never actually played any of them. Sometimes, Evore would close his eyes at the overhang and imagine boys and girls dancing and carelessly kicking dirt up into the air, calling out his name to join.

Continuing on down the small hill, the trees opened up to let in an even smaller lake, its water's open arms inviting him in for an embrace. Evore wanted nothing more than to kick off his shoes, remove his robes, and swim his worries away.

A wooden bridge was built over the middle of Lake Gheller to get across rather than wrestling with the endless sea of trees around the perimeter. The arm banisters were thick tree branches, carved and shaved down smooth and painted crimson red. Before Evore made for the bridge, he cupped both hands into the lake and drank as much as he could hold before the water trickled through his fingers. The coolness of the liquid felt soothing down his throat and gave him some much-needed energy that he didn't receive when he refused his breakfast.

Suddenly, the middle of the water began to stir and bubble slowly as if it were starting to boil. Evore ran to the middle of the bridge to get a better look when a head and shoulders popped out. The girl's hair was long and black as a cauldron. She looked up toward Evore, whose jaw was in desperate need of picking up, and she smiled the most beautiful smile he had ever seen. Although she was older than Evore, she couldn't have been more than fourteen years of age.

"Hello up there!" Her bare breasts bobbed in and out of the young boy's sight. "Are you all right?" she asked, knowing exactly what his eyes were so focused on.

Evore nodded. "I'm just going to--"

"You're going to the Ironash tree, aren't you?" the girl asked. Water dripped from her hair onto her sun-tanned shoulders.

"I am," Evore perked up. "Today is my--"

"I know who you are, Evore. Your father rules the Ylewood. It's hard not to know you," she laughed.

He tried to laugh with her, but what came sounded like a mix between a yell and a cough.

"My name is Tawanie. I live in the tallest tree near the overhang." Her yellow eyes distracted Evore. They were the same color as his, and the rest of the Verrativas, but her eyes made him forget everything that was wrong in his life. She

9

smiled again at him. "Better get going! It would be hard for them to start without you!"

Evore's head came crashing down from the clouds like a meteor. "Ni--nice to meet you," he awkwardly choked out before almost tripping over his own feet.

"You too, future Chief!" Tawanie dipped back under the water, and Lake Gheller was still once again.

When Evore hopped off the bridge and back onto the path, the trees swallowed up the sunlight, and for a mile, Evore wasn't even able to tell if it was day or night. He heard the creaks and groans from the branches, and for a split second he thought of turning around. *Trees are the guardians of the Verrativas.* He began to run, so fast he swore that his feet didn't touch the ground. *Faster. Faster. Faster.*

FWATTT!

A tree root grabbed onto his right foot, sending him flailing to the ground. As he wiped the dirt from the front of his robe, Evore realized that he had finally made it. The trees sectioned off left and right, like soldiers marching in formation to allow space for their captain.

Four hooded men stood around the base of the Ironash Tree but didn't even acknowledge that Evore had arrived. They were all clad in the same robes, green as the leaves on the tree they surrounded. Each one held a lit torch, their flames standing idle as if they were waiting on instruction.

Evore looked up at the great tree and felt goosebumps grow when he realized the top was not in sight. The tree had too many arms to count, but the boy knew that he would most likely have to use every single one. This was his time to prove he was worthy of being Onexis's heir and the future Chief of the Verrativas. If he couldn't make the climb, he could always spend the rest of eternity burning shy aconite for his father.

No. Thinking about failure won't help you succeed.

The first branch hung quite low, and Evore was able to jump up and grab it with both arms. Once he hoisted himself up and stood, the four Verrativas below began to chant together:

"Kings will rise, Kings will fall
The sands of time will cover them all
Ghosts crave blood
Potions made from mud
Shadows only lie
Fire can help those fly
But when the rest are gone
The Verrativas will live on"

Evore climbed up to the next branch, then straddled the trunk and stepped through to the opposite side. The Ironash's leaves began to swallow him whole, and the tree seemed much smaller. He noticed that the branch above him was easy to grasp, but the one above that was significantly higher and out of his reach. There was a branch straight ahead of the one that he could reach, but it was lower than the one he was already standing on. However, the lower branch had a few more arms above it that made for a much easier climb.

Reaching up to the branch above him, Evore began to swing the rest of his body to make the leap to the lower level. It took three swings for him to muster up the courage to let go, but by that time his body was moving quite fast. He went flying feet-first, smashing his bottom onto the branch, and he was falling. At the last moment, his left hand grabbed onto the branch. Dangling from the branch, he was able to grasp the other side with his right hand and pull himself up. From there, he climbed up a few more feet without any problem.

Evore still heard the muttered chant from the Verrativas, but when he looked down, he was barely able to tell there were people below. He crossed over the trunk once again and pulled himself up another branch when he heard a noise that almost sounded like the Ironash Tree was complaining.

Trees are the guardians of the--

The tree bark splintered and broke off to fall back down to the ground. For a moment, Evore's body felt frozen in mid-air, and then, as time sped up, so did he. Grabbing and clawing onto anything, Evore tried to save himself, but every handful was either air or leaves. His head smashed against a branch, sending a high-pitched whistle through his ears, and he finally grabbed onto the trunk out of desperation.

Just like that, Evore was no longer falling, and he was just as confused as he was relieved. His fingernails had grown pointy and long and stuck deep into the trunk, but when he removed one hand from the tree, it shrunk back down to normal size and shape. Evore continued this motion three times over just to make sure he wasn't hallucinating. *How have I never noticed this ability? Why would father hide this from me?*

Blood was leaking from his nose like a broken basin, but he continued his ascent to the top. It was significantly easier to climb up this way rather than hop up and guess which branch to swing to next.

It was closing in on midday when Evore realized that his new strategy may have required less thinking but much more physical strain. His biceps were on fire and his hands ached, like someone was stepping on each finger individually. He looked to the right and saw a sturdy branch where he stopped to rest for a moment. Dried blood was caked under his nose and easily cleaned off, but Evore's arms were too fatigued to continue on the trunk.

After a few more twists and turns through the Ironash's maze, he noticed a stream of light shining through the leaves. Clawing and grabbing, the boy made his way to the source and stuck his head through and felt a breeze blow hope back into his system.

"You *finally* made it up!" A voice called from beyond the layer of leaves and twigs. Evore began to push through and stepped out onto the Ironash Tree's tallest and strongest arm when he saw his father. "Thought you weren't going to make it."

Onexis pushed his son's hair out of his eyes. The man was tall and muscular with a head of long, chocolate-colored hair. He was clad in a pair of navy leggings and a honey yellow robe tied at the waist. His chest was exposed, which was tattooed with a great tree, the branches spread far along his upper body, covering every area that was visible. Around his neck hung a thin chain with a small horn attached to it.

"I fell once." Evore was still wiping the blood from his face.

Onexis laughed. "You're here now, though, son."

The boy shook his head. "Father, something happened to me. My fingers, they--"

"Your claws came out, that's good. As Verrativas, our claws come out when our lives are in danger. It's part of what makes us who we are."

Evore stared at his fingertips. "Only when we're in danger?"

"That's right," his father smiled.

"So, let's say someone was trying to-- trying to kill us. Would they come out?"

Onexis grimaced. "Who's trying to kill us?"

The boy shrugged.

"Evore, no one will hurt us here. I've made sure of that." He grabbed his son by the shoulder and walked him out to the edge of the branch. "See that sea down there? Do you know what that is?" He pointed into the distance.

"The Moiira Sea. I read it in--"

"*Trilon: The History and the Magic of the Three Realms*, I know." His father smiled at his son. "Do you know why no one has tried to cross the Moiira Sea?"

Evore shook his head. "No, I don't, but I have always wondered why no one has tried to come over from the other side. Is the seawater keeping our people safe?" Evore's curiosity was peaking.

His father nodded. "When you're ready, I'll show you the sea. Mortals want us dead, Evore, and nothing will stop them. They're a race that desires what they don't have. Mortals will even kill their own kind if it means getting closer to what they want."

"And what's that?"

"Our gift."

Evore looked out to a never-ending landscape of greens and blues. "So, how did we cross the Moiira Sea?"

"When King Tanwill asked for my aide to take Reliss, he promised me protection for the Verrativa race and flew us into the Ylewood on Coatuses. We lost a lot of good men in the battle to help the humans crown a new King, but it's hard for me to regret it because you're safe."

"Will I ever ride a Coatus like you did?" Evore couldn't contain his excitement.

"Pray that you don't, good boy. A Coatus ride for us only means danger but know that we're safe. Also know that, if we are in true danger -- not falling-out-of-a-tree danger -- King Tanwill gave me this..." Onexis grabbed the small bone-colored horn around his neck. It was small, starting out thin at the bottom and opening up wide at top. "This will save us."

Evore grabbed the rather plain, colorless horn, which looked more like a shell than an instrument that could produce any sound. It was smooth to the touch and made of what seemed to be either ivory or bone. But for a gift from the King of Trilon, it seemed rather boring. "What does it do?"

"You're more obsessed with Coatuses than Master Vengar Stoneburner, yet you don't know what a Coatus horn is?" His father stood abruptly. "There will come a time to answer all your questions, Evore. That time is not while standing atop the tallest tree in Trilon."

Evore looked down from the edge of the Ironash. He gulped anxiously when he realized that most of what he was looking down upon was the tops of trees. Squinting, the boy thought he saw the four hooded Verrativas, but they just looked like ants from this height. "I'm not sure." As much as he didn't want to let his father down, the idea of jumping made him want to curl next to his mother and sleep his troubles away.

"You're on top of the world right now, my boy. You always say you're jealous of the mortals in the other realms; how many of them have been on top of the tallest tree in Trilon?" Onexis's hair danced in the wind, grazing Evore's shoulder.

"You're right, but--"

"But nothing," Onexis interrupted. "You'll never be ready for this. No one is. This isn't about being ready. It's about conquering fear. It's about being your own Master and only relying on yourself."

Evore stepped to the very edge. "Can we ever trust anyone else?"

"Never," his father answered without hesitation.

Evore didn't remember when he stepped off the branch, but for a moment, he felt weightless. His eyes watered, but he couldn't close them, and his mop of hair flew above him and looked as if it was hanging on for dear life. The boy's arms grabbed at air and his legs kicked until he heard the low murmur from the four men below.

When his feet hit the ground, he fell immediately. A burning sensation, strong as fire, filled his chest and flew through the furnace that was his body, and Evore thought he would never stand. Then, the pain left him, and he stood up as if waking from a nap. As his eyes and ears came into focus, he saw the four hooded Verrativas and heard their chant:

"Kings will rise, Kings will fall
The sands of time will cover them all
Ghosts crave blood
Potions made from mud
Shadows only lie
Fire can help those fly
But when the rest are gone
The Verrativas will live on"

FORBATH: YATORGA

The late night was humid and suspiciously quiet outside of the Grateful Swine. The bar was a sanctuary for everyone in Yatorga, a place where they would go to forget. When the city thrived, the people would go to forget their long workdays. Now, they all went to forget the fact that they had holes in their roofs, or that they hadn't had a decent meal in weeks. Inside the Grateful Swine, after a few steins of dark beer, anyone was as rich as the King's Cabinet.

Forbath was once an area of great wealth and prosperity. From the Coatus Port of Piklorha to the capital province of Reliss, everyone who inhabited these lands bathed in gold and did not eat to get their fill but instead to get fat. Every city in the southern realm had a special trade, which allowed the highest individual earnings. If you wanted a sword made from the finest steel, Ghordaan was the town to go to, but if you wanted silks of any color, your best bet was further east to the village of Hilrode. The weather was consistently gorgeous (save for the occasional rain shower), all fruits and vegetables were ripe year-round, and the wine flowed as red as the roses in King Tanwill's garden. However, it's been said of what happens to all good things...

After everything came screeching to a halt, towns and even cities were neglected. The Mayors of the southern cities had no Baron to go to, like the other two realms, to ask for food or materials, and not a single letter to the Capital garnered a response. Some claimed King Tanwill was murdered, others that he had gone mad, but no matter the story, one fact stayed the same: all of Trilon would eventually crumble if big changes weren't made.

On a curled, skinny strip of land at the very edge of Forbath was Yatorga, which now could be considered a ruin rather than a city. While most of Forbath was in trouble, Yatorga was hit especially hard. It was once a city of fisherman who caught the meatiest herring and pike straight from the sea. This was their only export, so when the fish left their waters, the city was completely forgotten. When the people of Yatorga had their only source of real income ripped away, they lost all hope. Unfortunately, when someone loses hope and still has children's mouths to feed as well as their own, they tend to take matters into their own hands.

Past the rows of shacks on Beachwood Street that were once sturdy and whole, a strip of small stands dotted the avenue. These were once filled with busy salesmen hollering false promises to passers, such as, "Eat this pike and you'll gain powers only Oracles could dream of!" Or, "Fresh salmon! This fish will never spoil!" Now what were they? Nothing but broken-down cottages with smashed windows and kicked-in doors.

Continuing down, at the very end of the path, in the middle facing inwards, was a large building made of grey ashlar. Yatorga's strongest establishment, the only one that still stood tall amongst the heaps of charred wood and tattered banners, was a tavern.

The large walnut wooden door flew open, breaking any silence outside.

"Get da *FUCK* out of my bar!" A porky bald man dressed in a baggy, age-worn grey robe was shoved out of the Swine and fell flat on his face. Spitting up dirt, he stumbled to his feet, leaning against the stone tavern wall to regain his balance. His brown eyes stared down the ghostly row of shops and watched as stragglers shadily crept through and down back alleys looking for any excess goods that could have been left behind, or a whore to have a tussle with for three boros. Shaking his head and smiling, he reached into his weather-worn robes and pulled out a small black pipe.

"Typical," he muttered to himself.

As smoke billowed from his mouth like a chimney, his attention focused on a man who continued down the stretch and didn't duck down an alley. As the silhouette grew closer, he noticed that the traveler was not a man at all, but a young boy, wrapped in a cloak as silver as a sword blade.

"Welcome, traveler, to the greatest city in Trilon!"

The traveler walked until he was right in front of the Grateful Swine.

"Well, have a look at you," the man laughed. "A young boy with pretty orange hair. What would bring you roun' here?"

"I'm looking for a man," the traveler started, his mysterious green eyes darting all around, staring at nothing and everything.

"Sorry, boy, I was fucking with you. I don't chew on bones."

The traveler ignored this. "Sir, I'm--"

"Not every man outside a southern tavern is a Knight, ya idiot," barked the fat man.

"Do you know a man named Graybill? I was told I could find him here. Is-- is he inside?" The young boy's voice quivered.

"Don't you see I'm outside of the bar? I donno who's in there, and even if I did, why would I ever tell a scrawny little shit like you anything?" The man pulled a clump of dirt from his long ginger beard. "What's your name, boy? I see that you're wearing a silver cloak without a hood, so tell me, is it your fuckin' fault all o' this shit happened? What's a'matter, couldn't handle blowin' a horn and scrapin' bird shit off Larkmoar Castle any longer?" He smirked, but the traveler didn't respond. "Come now, boy, your secret is safe with me. I know you're not from around here, but we're not all bad. I tell you what, I'll start by telling you who I am. Name's Dink, an' that's me only name."

The traveler watched the man take a drag on his pipe and blow a cloud of grey smoke that swirled in the black sky. "Apologies, my Lord, I should have spoken with more caution. Next time I'll be sure to--"

"You really think I'd be wearing these rags if I were a Lord?" Dink yelled, showing a mouth filled with teeth as brown as the dirt in his beard.

There was a flicker of sadness in the traveler's face, and he bit his lower lip as he fought back the tears that welled up in his eyes like clouds before a rainstorm. "Most of Forbath is destroyed, and you're actually squabbling over what title I should call you? Haven't you ever heard of simply helping someone because they're in trouble? The Trainer's Guild, where I've spent almost all of my life, was destroyed, and I don't know what to do now. I've never felt so alone, Dink, and I've always felt alone."

Dink held his hand up. "Alright, boy, don't get your smallclothes in a twist, maybe I can help ya. First, though, you know my name, so it be your turn."

The boy stared down to his boots. "Kylan. Kylan Corwin," he conceded.

"And that's your real name?" asked Dink.

"It is," Kylan answered.

"Are you fucking stupid or mad then? Telling a stranger your family name when all of Trilon knows it?" Dink brought his face so close to Kylan's that he was able to smell the boy's sweat, taste the boy's fear. "Do ya have any idea what some of the real criminals here would do with you if they knew you were the Baron of Aleru's kin? And you stroll down the market strip in your Trainer's cloak like you're dressed in rags?" Dink stepped back, took a deep breath, and put his pipe back in his pocket. "Now, who told you to come to Yatorga?" he calmly asked.

"There was a man at the Euku Market. I went there to look for work after what happened, and he was very interested in me," Kylan said.

Dink was intrigued. "What'd this man look like?"

Kylan shrugged. "Couldn't tell you. He wore a black hood with a mask."

"What kinda mask?" Dink asked.

"It was skull mask." Kylan watched as beads of sweat began to form on Dink's blotchy bald head.

"You better not be fucking wit' me, boy," he said.

"Not at all. A stranger in a skull mask told me to come to Yatorga and ask for a man named Graybill at the Grateful Swine," Kylan answered. "My home is a long way off from Forbath, and I'm not even sure the door would be open to me."

"Come on, boy, let's go inside then," Dink said, uninterested in what Kylan had to say next. The rugged tone that he had when he first met Kylan had changed to a warm and helpful one.

He grabbed onto the circular handle of the bar door and started to pull, then paused abruptly.

"Take off your cloak," Dink ordered.

Kylan pulled off his silver cloak and handed it over to him. Underneath the cloak, he wore a maroon tunic decorated with burns, rips, and patches. Dink reached in his pocket and pulled out a match and, striking it against the wall, kissed the flame to the bottom of the cloak. Kylan watched as the fire swallowed the fabric whole, until there was nothing left but stray embers to dance away in the night's breeze.

As soon as Dink crossed the threshold, he was hit in the face with the roars of laughter and the stench of ale. His eyes watered with the smoke that wafted through the air, like fog on a humid summer night. The bar had sturdy walls with tapestries of moons and animals covering all of them. The largest one was draped over the center beam of the Swine and featured a large corked bottle filled with green liquid. This symbolized the taking of Yatorga a century ago. Dink had forgotten his father's face in the bottom of a bottle, but he couldn't forget the story he told him of Razzo Klessen, the Shadow who snuck in through the city and posed as a servant to the Mayor, Lord Eron Sichel.

For a full year, Klessen scrubbed privies and cleaned after every one of Lord Eron's affairs. Being that the Mayor of Yatorga at the time was quite fond of whores, alcohol, and feasts, these clean-ups occurred quite often. After the year of service, Razzo stole a small fortune from the city vault and planted it on another servant. When Lord Eron found out, Razzo revealed that he saw the servant sneak into the vaults and thereby gained the Mayor's full trust. The scapegoat servant was stoned, and Razzo Klessen became Lord Eron Sichel's cupbearer.

The poison that Klessen slipped into the Mayor of Yatorga's sour apple ale was called Stranger's Tongue, which, when brewed correctly, turns a bright green. All it would take is a single drop, and the brewer of the potion would be able to control the mind and mouth of whomever ingested it. Yatorga belonged to Klessen after that, but the people of the city never knew it. Rather than having Lord Eron sign the deed of Yatorga over to Klessen, the Shadow chose to hide in the darkness and use the poison for the power of speech. Every law, every deal, every sentence was spoken by Razzo Klessen's puppet.

Dink pushed Kylan through the endless sea of people and weaved in and out through an array of scattered stools and wooden tables.

"Could we possibly get a drink?" Kylan asked as he tried to look back to Dink. "It's been quite the journey, and I'll take anything that'll quench my thirst."

Suddenly, a giant of a man stepped in front of Kylan and stopped him cold with his enormous gut. He had a head of short black hair and a scar across his right eye, which had obviously been opened on more than one occasion. "I thought I told you ta get the fuck outta my bar, you pig-looking piece of shit!"

He shoved Kylan into a table, spilling full steins all over the barroom floor, and grabbed Dink by the scruff of his collar. The people at the table stood up in anger, and all of the merriness from the Grateful Swine changed to curiosity.

The large man pulled Dink closer to him. "What do you have say for yourself, you piss-on?"

"This boy." Dink put his hands in the air as a sign of surrender. "This boy was sent here by the Iron Skull."

There were a few inaudible whispers throughout the bar after Dink uttered those words. Kylan rose to his feet and shook his long hair out of his eyes.

"Doesn't look like much of a boy," the large man said, causing many drunken laughs from the close-by listeners.

"You're too clever, Porter," Dink said in his most flattering tone. "However, it is not me job to question the Iron Skull, nor is it to check and see if the boy has a cock."

Porter let go of Dink's collar and let the duo continue on through the bar. After many angry glances, they finally reached the back of the tavern.

A small, floppy-eared hound frolicked up to Kylan and playfully licked him on the hand. Kylan scratched the dog on the chest, and it panted affectionately then went along to look for scraps under tables.

"Follow me," Dink said as he walked down a set of steep stairs.

Before Kylan stepped down, he heard the light picking of a lute behind him. A man clad in worn blue robes with faded yellow embroidery around the collar and arms was gathering the bar together for a song. As his fingering of the strings became louder, the people around him began to drunkenly drum on their tables. One bald man even used a knife and tapped it against his stein as if it were a cymbal. The singer in blue closed his eyes and began to sing:

"The wine flows red and the ale pours brown
But we can't forget how our city burned down
King Tanwill sent his beast out in rage
To destroy the southern lands in his name
Our houses burned and our children died
Their mothers had no reason to dry their eyes
We can no longer fish, we can no longer sell
Yatorga has become our living hell
With the Coatus' flight there was no way he'd lose
But we got our King back...
WE STOLE ALL HIS BOOZE"

At that last line, it seemed that the entire bar joined in and crashed their mugs together, spilling their drinks and laughing heartily.

The stairs led to a much smaller room, with nothing to it except a large steel door and a man armored from head to toe to guard it. He wore a bronze close helm with a red stripe

24

down the middle and a breastplate that matched in color. On his armor was a scratched -- or maybe burned out -- symbol that still had an outline of a crown. His gauntlets led up to his biceps and were strong silver with golden fingertips. While the greatsword that dangled from his hip was in a sheath, the guard's right hand was wrapped around the hilt, even though he didn't even look in either Kylan's nor Dink's direction. Kylan stared at the guard, trying to see his eyes through the visor's slit.

"Pay no attention ta him, boy. He won't hurt you as long as you're with me." Dink chuckled as he knocked on the door, which was incredibly cumbersome and made from a very thick metal. Dink always thought that this door would have been more suitable for a very large vault than a dingy cellar room, but he knew the boss always had his reasons. Dink pounded the metal three times when a small latch opened, revealing two beady brown eyes.

"Yes?" a gruff voice called from inside the next room.

"Fuck off, Atrius, it's Dink. Lemme in," Dink sneered, his hand already on the door handle.

"You know I can't without--"

"Stay in the shadows," Dink cut off Atrius, his patience clearly running thin with the man.

There was a sound of a crossbar lifting up from inside the room, and the door slowly pushed open. Dink, whose hand was still firmly wrapped around the handle, pulled as hard as he could to speed up the process. Standing in the doorway was a short and skinny pock-faced man with greasy blonde hair dressed in a worn black leather jerkin that was laced down the center and matching breeches. The room was tiny and just as smoky as the rest of the Swine. Candles were placed in hollowed out Smiladon fangs, which hung from a rusted chandelier, barely giving any visibility to the empty chamber. Towards the back of the room, which was partially covered by the candle light's shadow, was a table filled with bottles of ale and crusts of bread. A man sat behind it, his feet resting next to the plates and a white pipe between his pursed lips.

Dink pushed the young man of twenty out of the way. "Why do you always have to give me such a hard time?" Atrius called out.

"I said *fuck* off," Dink yelled. "I have no reason to answer to you yet."

"Aye, but soon ya will! You best remember that, you fat stubby drunk."

Dink reached into his baggy pocket and pulled out a small dagger, which had a short but very sharp hooked blade. He pressed the knife against Atrius's groin.

"Listen 'ere, boy. I don't give a shit who your father *is*, or what your family name *was*. You're no longer a Callowat, *but* you're not a Shadow yet. Now, If you keep giving me lip, I'll cut your shit off, burn it, and make you Porter's girlfriend." His eyes were red with anger, and an evil smile crept upon his dirty face.

The hairs on the back of Atrius's neck stood on end when he saw this twisted side of him. He bit his lower lip in frustration and yielded in fear that Dink's inebriation could cause his hand to slip. Dink put his blade away and escorted Kylan through the room to the full table.

The man behind the table sat upright and pulled down the hood of his midnight black robe, revealing a pair of lilac eyes. His hair was black, longer than Kylan's, and much more tangled. He had a thick moustache and a goatee, which hung well below his chin. Blowing out a mouthful of smoke, he examined Kylan from head to toe and then clapped Dink on the shoulder.

"Please don't give Atrius a hard time, Dink." He smiled affectionately. "He'll be taking the journey to Soarfrost soon, and after that, he'll be one of us."

"He'll be one-a *you*," Dink fired back. "You'll never get me out of Forbath, let alone to the Mirrored Mountains. Ice trolls and spiders the size of wolves huntin' for human flesh."

"That's enough."

The man's voice seemed to clear the dust from the walls. Out of the corner of his eye, he glanced over at Atrius, who was anxiously wiping sweat from his palms. He smiled, looking down at Dink's large gut.

"He'll be one of us, Dink. There will always be a place for you here as long as your thirst to spill blood is as unquenchable as your thirst for ale." Once again, the man eyed Kylan and took a swig from a beige stein. "Forgive us, friend. My name is Graybill. Care for a drink? I'd offer you a bite to eat, but I doubt you'd want stale bread."

Kylan nodded, unsure of what was going on, and sat down in an unsteady wooden chair opposite of the stranger. He stared at the throne-sized seat the man sat on, which was made of rich mahogany leather. Each armrest led to a roaring wooden Smiladon head; their carefully hand-carved teeth looked sharp enough to pierce through skin.

"What's the matter?" Graybill asked.

Dink spoke before Kylan had a chance to even mutter a sound. "This is Kylan Corwin from Reliss."

"You mean from Everlid?" Graybill spoke with great confidence. His voice boomed, and when words came from his mouth, everyone listened no matter what he said. "I know your father; he is a good man. Does he plan to do anything for Forbath?"

"Not that I know of, my Lord."

Dink broke in, "You need to stop with that 'm'lord' bullshit, boy, or you'll end up in a cell or in the dirt…"

"Please." Graybill put his hand up to silence Dink. "My name is Graybill, not 'my Lord'. You're not in the Capital anymore. Best stop acting like you are." His tone hardened as he spoke. It wasn't anger, but concern.

"My father sent me to the Trainer's Guild when I was six. My older brother Elmar is the heir to be Baron of the east, so my father wanted another way to connect me to the crown. He said that there was great honor in being a trainer. Without the Coatuses, Trilon would cease to exist."

"Guess we can't exist *with* them either," Dink growled.

Kylan paused for a moment and ran his hand through his sweaty auburn hair. Dink watched as the boy stared blankly at the floor and, for a moment, thought he would fall upon it. "For ten years, I trained in the Guild."

Reaching for his drink, Graybill furrowed his brow in confusion. "So, you fled the Guild before your training was complete."

"Right. All the trainees did as well. That is, the ones that survived," Kylan said as he eyed a wooden goblet on the table. Dink took note and filled it up with honey ale. "It wasn't *our* choice to leave. Well, not really." Kylan took a large gulp from the goblet and coughed up a bit. The bitter burn seemed to breathe new life into the young boy.

"See, I told you, Graybill, King Tanwill ain't dead! He took out the three Trainers and sent the mystery Coatus for us and the rest of Forbath. Next, he's going to take out Gojii and Aleru and be the King of the fucking ashes!"

Graybill pressed his pointer finger to his lip, signaling Dink to let Kylan speak.

Draining his cup and letting out a small burp, Kylan refilled the goblet and chugged it down to the bottom. He clearly wasn't used to drinking, as his voice grew louder and his frown larger with each sip. "No, King Tanwill didn't kill anyone. Saige Lorrode Allwater found a way to create two

Coatus eggs using a sort of science, and finally one hatched. She was so cute when she would take clams straight from my hand, and on nights I couldn't sleep at the Guild, I would sneak to the training cage and cuddle up with her. Once the Coatus grew large enough to fly, our Head Trainer, Master Vengar Stoneburner, left us."

"The Head Trainer? What do you mean 'left' you?" Graybill questioned as his curiosity began to pique.

"Master Stoneburner must have used his abilities as a RoarCatcher to communicate with the baby Coatus, because she wasn't fully trained. He flew her straight out of the Guild, destroyed the Capital, as well as most of the south. Now, who knows where he is?"

Graybill's lilac eyes glimmered. "He used his Bellow, then."

"The fuck is a Bellow?" Dink asked his questions the same way he made his statements -- unabashedly.

"Like a Shadow's robe, a Bellow gives a RoarCatcher the ability to perform magic. It's a stained-glass apothecary jar that RoarCatchers wear around their neck. The Bellows hold the blood of all the creatures they can communicate with. While they wear the Bellow, commands can be given remotely, so your Master Stoneburner is most definitely in hiding." Graybill's response came with a smile of patience. "Do you know what happened to the second egg?"

"Donno, everyone seems to think it cracked when Master Stoneburner flew off." Kylan reached for the bottle again, but Dink pulled it away.

"Careful, boy. I like you, but a few more drinks and you'll be crying like a little girl. Atrius over here might want to take you to a room upstairs and have his way with you." Dink smirked at the pimple-faced man who still stood by the door.

Graybill ripped off a piece of bread and began to chew on the end. "So, you're saying that Vengar Stoneburner, the Head Trainer of the Coatus Trainer's Guild, stole a Coatus and is now running rampant on Trilon?"

"Yes m'lo-- I mean, yes, Graybill," Kylan said. "Those that have survived are going to tell the tale to their families and loved ones in hopes to stop this mad man, though it seems hopeless."

"Why didn't you go back to Aleru?" Dink asked.

Kylan grabbed a loaf of bread and tore off a chunk. The face he made after his first bite looked as if he bit into an old sponge. "I couldn't disappoint my family like that. What with the great Elmar already acting like a Lord, I'm seen as the outcast. I couldn't go back there and tell my father what happened. It wouldn't matter, no story would please him. He'd still say I committed treason. That bastard shipped me away because his war buddy sits the throne, and now here I am. For ten years, I looked forward to my Nascentem Feast, a chance to finally see my family again... instead, I get this." Kylan threw the bread behind him and folded his arms together.

Quickly, Dink snatched Kylan's goblet. "Okay, that's enough juice for you, boy."

"But what about your city?" Kylan didn't understand what was going on but suddenly seemed much more confident than before. "Where's your Mayor?" He let out a small hiccup.

Graybill grinned at the question. "Our Mayor was a man named Rean Atalay, son of Bekan. His father, another one of *your* father's 'war buddies', helped King Tanwill win the crown years ago. Bekan was a fierce warrior who, like many southerners, rode a Smiladon into war. During the battle of Hillrode, he wielded Desire's Rage, and it was said that no man even scraped his armor." Graybill sighed with nostalgia.

"Bekan wanted Rean to fight for the southern army, but he had no interest whatsoever. The boy could have been passed down Desire's Rage, the most powerful mace in Trilon, which was in the Atalay family for three generations. He had interests in fashion, and food, and, well…" Graybill trailed off. "Bekan begged King Tanwill to give Yatorga's deed to Rean. He said that if he owned land, then his inner protective warrior could be unleashed. But--"

"He's a bone-chewer," Dink chimed in.

"Did you kill him?" Kylan quickly came to his senses.

Graybill laughed. "We're not savages, boy. Our Mayor left us when your Coatus flew out of the sky and destroyed our city. Damned thing scared away any living thing that wasn't human. The dogs eventually came back, but the fish haven't. When the fish left, our people couldn't sell them, and no one outside of this city had reason to come here. Every business here lived off of the people who traveled here for the best fish in Trilon. When the other realms wanted us to send Smiladons with packs full, we charged whatever we wanted. Mayor Atalay fled when he believed that there was no chance to rebuild. Lucky for him, but not everyone in Yatorga has family in the east to run to."

"So, who runs Yatorga then?" Kylan asked.

Graybill sat back in his chair and proudly stuck out his chest. "You're looking at him. Remember this, my friend -- when things get really bad, people won't do what's right but instead what they can to get by. The Shadows have been getting by since Razzo Klessen made Yatorga ours."

"Razzo Klessen?" Kylan's head was now swimming.

Dink, who now rested a full stein on his belly, scoffed at Kylan's confusion. "Didn't they teach you any sort of history in the Capital, boy? Or were you just cleaning giant bird shits off the castle for a decade?"

Graybill's lilac eyes were caught by a candle flame giving them a slight red tint. "Never castigate someone's knowledge, for the act of learning is forever ongoing, never a competition." He looked over to Kylan. "I'm sure you're tired, my good--" He cleared his voice. "I'm sure you're tired, my good boy. Atrius, take our new friend's tunic and give it a good wash, it looks like you've been wearing it during your training sessions." He took another puff from his pipe.

"No!" Kylan wrapped his hands around his chest. "I mean, no, thank you, it's fine the way it is."

A cloud of smoke hid Graybill's face as he exhaled. "I'm sorry, I didn't mean to offend you. No matter at all, who am I to say your clothing needs washing anyway?"

"He's not fuckin' bunking with me then. I ain't gonna be smellin' shit all night," Dink said, taking a swig of the honey ale.

"I'm sure he smells bettuh than the sluts you bring to bed anyway!" Atrius saw his chance and charged into the conversation, calling from across the room.

Graybill chuckled heartily and stood up from his chair. "So, shall we get to the point then? You're here because our masked friend told you about our city."

Kylan nodded mindlessly; at this point, he was so tired that he couldn't even think of words to say anymore.

"The Shadows are a society of assassins and thieves that use the darkness to our advantage. We can manipulate it to hide ourselves and confuse our enemies. Our friend in the iron mask is a recruiter of sorts, and I think I know why he sent you to us." The man stared down at the murky stained floor. "Would you mind looking under the table?"

Kylan didn't say anything at first, nor did he move. "Is this the part where you capture me? If you're going to do it, just do it already. I know it was stupid to say my real name; you were right, Dink."

Graybill shook his head and simply pointed under the table without a word.

The boy squatted below the table and for a moment disappeared from Dink's sight. There was a low, scraping noise, and when Kylan returned from under the table, he had a turquoise stone.

No, it wasn't a stone... it was an egg.

GOJII: THE YLEWOOD

The Moiira Sea was as still and silent as a thief hiding from the King's Law, but Onexis knew what stirred below. He stared into the blanket of watery darkness, which, for all the Chief Verrativa knew, was bottomless, as if it would erupt at any moment. The sea was home to the Moiiralatta since well before Onexis's time and was feared by all men, magical or mortal. After the siege of Reliss, when Tanwill Embray and Chief Onexis were negotiating the Verrativas' reward for their efforts in battle, the King of Trilon was readily willing to give away the deed to the Ylewood, because no one had ever wanted to cross the Moiira Sea.

While the Coatuses were easily able to fly into the territory, King Tanwill was never able to convince any of his Lords to take the land, as legend told that the Moiiralatta cursed it and believed that the Ylewood belonged to her. It could have been heard at a tavern, market, or brothel, but the story always stayed the same -- those who inhabited the Ylewood were the sea monster's slaves and, eventually, her sustenance. However, even when the Verrativas lived throughout the west, they spent no time in taverns and whorehouses and always thought that the tales the mortals told were immature, filled with flare rather than substance.

After deeming it a worthy gamble, Onexis agreed to the land's deed and soon found out that the mortals couldn't have been more wrong. The Moiiralatta protected the Verrativas and made sure that no one entered their land. When the Ylewood was signed over to the Verrativas, armies from every realm marched on them as if their stories were never told, and, of course, none of the aspiring conquerors were successful. Some of the men were clad in the finest mail from Ghordaan and flew high banners from their realms, while others wore tattered boiled leather, with no allegiance to anyone or anything. No matter who the foe was, the Moiiralatta protected her land and those who made it their own.

From the Ironash Tree, the Chief Verrativa watched more times than he would be willing to admit as the Moiiralatta took body after body. Some men had quick deaths, screaming like babies being ripped from their mother's breast before the sea turned black with their insides. Others were lifted high into the sky and had their limbs ripped off as if they were bananas from a bunch. Onexis always wondered whom the men were that marched on the Ylewood. *Was it someone's Lord, trying to win glory for his village? Was it someone's father trying to help his family? Or could it have been someone's son, listening to his father's orders? Would Evore do the same for me?*

Although Onexis would have preferred to travel by day's light, he simply couldn't risk it anymore between his counselor and now Evore wanting to accompany him on every journey. While they were safe at the time, the Verrativa population was still teetering on endangerment, which meant that every life was that much more vital for the rebuild. *Evore will have friends soon and feel like a normal boy. Trovado just gave birth to a son, he'll grow up quickly.*

When Onexis slipped out of bed in the silence of the night, Emery gave a light groan but never opened her honey-colored eyes. Typically, the Verrativa never brought any sort of pack, a bet that no mortal would make. If he grew hungry, he could pick some berries or maybe find a tree with an apple or two. The Chief chose a long, midnight-colored cloak to wear over his disguise, which camouflaged him within the

35

darkness of his hut. The large bookcase in the study stood tall, almost touching the ceiling, and Onexis ran his fingers down its left side before grasping ahold of it with both hands. He pulled hard, removing the wooden board and exposing one side of the case. Placing the board on the floor, he peered inside and pulled out a skinny, pale bamboo staff. Next, Onexis flipped the board over as if to empty all of its contents, and a small dagger slipped out and clanged right by his feet. The steel was forged in Ghordaan and had a Clubsodon bone hilt. It was a gift that Onexis always felt uneasy using for anything other than cutting fruits and vegetables, but because of the size of the knife, he decided to bring it along for this journey.

He sent his letter to the Capital exactly a fortnight ago, which meant that today was the day he would venture into the mortal realm to retrieve the response. *Fourteen sunrises, I've counted each one.* Brannon Broadwine, King Tanwill's Lead Confidant, set up an overly complicated system to communicate with the Crown, but if this is what it took to stay in touch, then so be it. Lord Brannon emphasized more than once how important it was to not harm any mortals, a rule that Onexis had no issue following. The Verrativas had hid from every other race since the beginning of time to try and protect their power, so stealth was always their strength. *We are not a violent people, yet I thought war was the answer to save us. The bards don't sing of the Verrativas I commanded to march. No stories mention who spoke the banishment spell, but the mortals certainly remember our magic.*

Stepping backwards up the steep dirt hill, Onexis dug the balls of his bare feet into the ground before he took off with the grace and precision of a cat. As he picked up the pace, his strides grew longer, and he neared the edge of the sea. Planting one end of his staff into the ground, he launched himself high into the air, his long chocolate-colored hair following closely behind like a dog after its owner. Once he reached the opposite end, he knew the real task had begun. *Getting past the Moiiralatta is never easy, but not nearly as hard to deal with as mortals.*

As the path got further away from the Ylewood and transformed into the rest of the western realm of Gojii, the trees diminished in both size and quantity. While the Verrativas were able to live amongst the trees and use them as they were, Gojii needed to cut them down and use lumber to build, trade, or sell. The west was once known as the woodland realm, during a time when there were more trees than people. When King Zabkar ruled, the Oracles used their magic to strike down the trees to intimidate the westerners. This was when the Verrativas lived in Gojii, and many of the trees that were struck down were their homes. *I thought that, when we helped King Tanwill win his throne, the woodlands would be preserved.*

The dirt path that Onexis traveled down ended and one of pebbles began as he came upon a small village known as Leefside. The locked gate that stood in between two small towers had bars too close to squeeze through, so the Chief decided he would have to climb to gain entrance. Each tower was of grey stone, but unlike the front entrance to the village, both were covered in muck and moss. As far as the people of Leefside knew, they never had any visitors traveling from west of them, so this entrance remained unguarded. Onexis pulled off his cloak and hid it with his staff under the brush near the tower. The brown doublet embroidered with a green tree down the side made him look like a real western mortal, and although he didn't expect to see anyone before morning's first light, he couldn't be too careful.

Not only were the back entrance towers filthy, but the village keepers also neglected to keep the stone in proper condition. Onexis stuck his foot in a hole at the bottom of the right tower and grabbed onto a stone brick that jutted out as if it was specifically there for intruders to scale. He pulled himself up onto the brick and balanced both of his feet together after a few unstable wobbles. From there, he leaped up and grabbed the top of the tiny tower, while sending the brick he stood upon crashing to the ground, adding yet another hole in the wall. The sun began to crawl out from hiding, and the sky went from black to a pale smoky grey when Onexis jumped down and landed within Leefside.

Leefside was a quaint village with rows of small houses on the southern side, through which Onexis carefully tip-toed. In the center of town was a courtyard of multicolored cobblestones with small patches of long green grass throughout and wooden benches placed around the perimeter. The centerpiece of it all was a large fountain fashioned after a three-pointed leaf, which shot out a stream of water to a small pool filled with boros when passers made a wish. *How many of these coins came true? How many still have hope?* The north side was Mayor Emerick Callowat's office, so Onexis wanted to steer clear of there. If he was going to disguise himself as a common villager, it was best to stay away from the man who knew every face in the town. The Mayor hadn't slept much recently; at least that's what Onexis had heard the last time he visited Leefside… something about Callowat's son fleeing the village and presumed dead…

Onexis thought of losing Evore and how he would react. As a Chief, he would have to stay strong for his people, but his child was the sun that rose in the morning; without him, there would only be darkness. *Would Evore ever leave the Ylewood?* As much as he hated to admit it, his son couldn't act like a boy anymore. It was just a fortnight ago when Onexis watched his baby leap from the Ironash Tree, his stomach writhing all the while like a bear caught in a trap as Evore free-fell to the unforgiving ground. *The boy is only ten. He's growing up before my eyes and hasn't had anything that even resembles a proper childhood.*

The eastern and western sides of town were littered with shops of every shape and size. The Chief Verrativa headed quickly to the west, his bare feet silently sliding over the cobblestones, which were just being awoken by the sun's glow. The strong, red brick building looked the least decorated of all the shops in Leefside but precisely what Onexis was looking for. Above the rounded door was a poorly drawn sign that simply read "LEEFSIDE BUTCHER" in black. Removing his knife from its sheath, he jammed the blade between the brass knob and the door frame and pushed it in with the palm of his hand. The door creaked open, and Onexis snuck inside, shutting the light out behind him.

Sausages tied in twine hung from the ceiling like bats in a cave. Behind a wooden counter were great veined wheels of cheese and towards the back a round cutting table with a dull cleaver wedged deep inside. Onexis noticed that, for a butcher shop, there sure was a lack of meat, which pleased him. *I'm not too late.* The room was cold as ice as he ducked down to hide in the shadows, his yellow eyes glowing like fireflies. As he blindly groped the ground, stirring up dust into his mouth and nostrils, Onexis grabbed the handle of a forgotten broomstick when the door flung open.

TRILON

An old man with more hair on his face and arms then on his head, dressed in a stained white shirt and black trousers, entered humming happily. As the man made his way behind the counter, Onexis began to crawl, using the temporary darkness to his advantage. The old man tied an apron on, cut himself a large wedge of stinky cheese, and smiled as he sloppily munched. When he finished eating, he licked his fingers clean and patted his large gut of jelly. On top of the counter were two small oil lanterns which the butcher lit, illuminating the shop. As soon as the light flickered on, Onexis sprung up, with the broomstick in hand.

"Who the hell are you?" the butcher asked, his voice scratchy with age.

Onexis's knuckles turned white around the broom, but he couldn't bring himself to hit the man. "That doesn't matter."

"Are y'ere to kill me?" the butcher asked defiantly, as if the prospect of death annoyed him.

"No," the Verrativa shook his head.

The old man cut himself another wedge of cheese and took a bite. "Ah, then you're a robber." Bits of cheese clung to his white moustache. "I may have been cutting and selling meat my whole life, so who am I to say, but don't you think you should be hitting up shops that have money? Seems to me the shops that sold furniture would have the most in Gojii."

"I'm not here to rob you, friend."

"Oh, we're friends now, are we? If we're such good friends, how about you put down that broomstick and I'll put down this here cheese knife and we can talk things through-"

THWACK!

Onexis swung the broomstick, hitting the old man across the side of his head and sending him to the floor, unconscious.

"I'm sorry, friend, this is the only way." Onexis was just able to slip the butcher's body behind the counter when the door opened up once again. He stood up quickly and saw a man wrapped in a maroon traveling cloak carrying a large burlap sack over his shoulder.

"Damned thing is heavy," the traveler said as he slung the sack to the shop floor. His hair was a bright orange that covered both his forehead and ears. Although he was short in height, large pectoral muscles bulged through his cloak, giving him a rather stout look.

Onexis strolled calmly over to the man and smiled courteously. "I can imagine."

"Where's the butcher?"

"He told me to open today. Late night I suppose. Name's Fabian Fordwin." Onexis stuck his hand out to shake the traveler's.

"Broddi Trap." The ginger man furrowed his brow as he examined the Verrativa from head to toe. "Tree on your doublet, so you must be from Gojii, but not Leefside."

Onexis looked down at his doublet as if to check if the embroidered tree was still sewn on the garment. "What makes you say that?"

Broddi laughed. "Those clothes are too fancy for Leefside."

Damnit, Tanwill. "You're right, friend, good eye."

"Can't fool a westerner." Trap took off his traveling cloak, revealing an apple-red tunic almost as bright as his hair, black leggings, and a pair of worn leather boots.

"I'm from Rutherfall." Onexis knew enough about the Capital of Gojii to fool a mortal.

Broddi lifted up the sack, his biceps tightening as he brought it to the back table. "Ah, fancy doublet for a fancy Lord. Do you ever see Lirum Rhygell?"

"He's too busy drooling over the Knights of Rutherfall to deal with us, fancy doublet or not." They laughed together. The young man couldn't have been more than 20 years old, judging by the patchy, uneven scruff he had under his lip and around his jaw line.

Opening up the sack, Broddi rubbed his hands together in delight. "This is the best beef in all of Trilon, let me tell ya. Xxafulok is where the real cows are; there ain't room for them in the east or south. There are too many fucking mazes that either lead to small village towns or cities. No, cows need to graze in an open meadow and grow strong on healthy grass. In Xxafulok, farmers even feed their cattle ale to fatten 'em up." Broddi reached into the sack and pulled out a thick pink steak. "You see how it's marbled all through the inside? That's where the flavor's at!" The young man pointed at the thick lines of fat and licked his lips as if he would take a bite raw. "Some cuts in here would be better dried out and salted, amazing for long journeys. C--could you grab me my cloak?"

Onexis walked back to the entrance of the shop and picked up Trap's cloak that was tossed on the floor and brushed away some of the dust that clung to it before bringing it to the cutting table. Broddi put his hand in its side pocket and pulled out a small bag filled with thin strips of dried beef. "It's really good," he said as he took a bite. "Wanna try?" Specks of meat flew from his lips as he spoke.

"No, no, thank you." Onexis shook his head, his mane of long hair swaying.

Swallowing the bite of beef, Trap finished the strip and reached in for another. "So, you're training to be a butcher?"

"I'm certainly thinking about it."

Trap's grey-blue eyes lit up. "I can tell you from my training in Xxafulok that, if you like to eat, there ain't a better profession. Some say to become a cook, but I say fuck that. Let the women heat our food, we'll do the cutting, am I right?" He slapped Onexis on the chest with the back of his hand.

"Couldn't agree more." The Verrativa was growing impatient, but he couldn't let the mortal know.

"I'll tell you, though, Fabian, you're lucky to be learning from Mason Stillwell. He's one of the best butchers in the west. What people don't realize is that cutting is an art." Broddi took out a fresh piece of dried beef and chewed on one end, sucking out the salt.

Onexis faked a smile. "Yes, Master Stillwell has been a pleasure to work for. That's a rare thing to say nowadays."

"It is, you're right. Only..." Broddi wrapped his fingers around the hilt of the cleaver. "Mason Stillwell isn't the butcher in Leefside." He ripped out the cleaver from the table sending pieces of wood into the air. "So, who are you? Careful what you say now."

Startled, the Verrativa stepped back into a defensive stance. "I'm no threat to you, friend, I promise that."

The ginger man tossed the heavy meat axe from hand to hand as he walked around the table to get a better look at Onexis. "Where are your fucking boots? What kind of man doesn't wear--" His eyes met the Chief's yellow ones and his grip tightened on the handle. "You're a fucking Verrativa!"

"A what?" Onexis didn't know what to say. How could he have been so careless?

"If you're a mortal, untie your doublet and show me your chest."

"My friend, I--"

"Do it, or I'll bury this axe between your cat eyes!"

Onexis undid his garment as slow as possible. When he opened up the doublet, revealing his chest covered in tree branches, Broddi gasped. For a moment, they both stood frozen, as if each one was waiting on the other to move.

Trap charged violently with his cleaver, swinging madly with no technique whatsoever. The Verrativa leaped backwards out of the mortal's reach. The second attempt was directly for Onexis's head, which he dodged. When Broddi tried to deliver the finishing blow, the Chief barrel-rolled out, causing the axe blade to land firmly in the shop floor.

"I have no idea what you're doing in our land, but I'm going to cut out your guts." Trap pulled the cleaver out and once again tossed it from hand to hand.

"Please, you're making a mistake." Onexis jumped out of the way of another strike. He was able to grab hold of Trap's shoulders and fling him back into the wall.

Broddi shook his head to regain his composure. "So, what's your plan, Fabian Fordwin? Take over this village so your people can move in? Are you going to send the Moiiralatta through Gojii?"

Onexis danced away as Trap swung again. However, as he dodged the blade, the Verrativa lost his balance and slipped to the floor, causing the back end of the axe to kiss his ribs. Although he was able to recover from the fall quickly, blood began to flow from the cut and ran down like a stream, staining his grey breeches to a murky black.

The ginger man smiled at the contact he made with his foe. "You're going to die, time stealer. I'll kill you and then I'll find a way to take out your shit race. Your family, everyone you know will be murdered, and you won't be able to do anything to protect them. How does that feel?"

"My family?" Onexis said quietly. "*My family*?!" he screamed. His voice was a blow from a hammer.

Pulling his dagger from its sheath, he threw it directly at Trap's throat, sending him backward into the table. There was a look of confusion in the young man's eyes as he wrapped his hand around the dagger's hilt, the blade lodged halfway through his windpipe. Coughing up thick red globs of blood, he dropped the cleaver and then fell to his knees.

Onexis stormed over to him and, grabbing a hold of Trap's hand still wrapped around the dagger's handle, knelt before him. "You did this. Mortals can never leave anything alone, especially things that don't concern them. You threaten my people and my kin as if you know them, but you know nothing. None of you know anything. Without us, the time stealers, you wouldn't exist."

With that, Onexis pushed the rest of the blade through his foe's throat, and after a few blood bubbles watched as the blue left his eyes and transformed to a stone grey.

Onexis brought the lifeless body gracefully to the ground and wrapped both of the mortal's hands around the Clubsodon hilt of his dagger. *He took his own life.* Jumping up, he opened the sack of meat and began to rummage through it. The beef was squishy and turned his hands damp, but when he got to the bottom of the bag, he found what he needed. The Verrativa grabbed the rolled up piece of parchment stained with grease and stuck it in his breeches. Before he left, he tore the top off the burlap sack and wrapped it around his bleeding wound. His anger was still boiling, which caused him to slam the butcher shop door as he entered the sun's morning light.

When he reached the rows of houses, a man plainly dressed in a undyed tunic was going from house to house banging on the doors and yelling, "Rise and shine!" and "Sun's up, time to wake up!" Onexis spent more time than he would have liked in Leefside, but at least the common villagers didn't make it outside yet. He climbed the nearest house and, jumping from rooftop to rooftop, made it past without any trouble.

As he scaled the short tower, regret began to overcome him. *Was there another way? Did I take someone's son?* Onexis jumped down, ripped off his doublet, threw it in the brush, and picked up his other items he had left there. The cloak felt good on his chest, much less constricting than the tight leather doublet. Verrativa males almost always wore a sort of cloak or robe tied at the waist, exposing part of their chest to show their status, which was determined by how tattooed they were.

It was past midday when Onexis made it back to the Ylewood. He was out of breath as he charged up the hill that led down to the Moiira Sea but continued, nonetheless. The cut on his ribcage was stinging quite badly now, and the Chief knew it was past time to change the bandage. Untying his cloak, he pushed the cut with two fingers and saw that the bleeding had subsided for the time being. As he ripped off the bandage, he realized that the laceration was deeper than he originally thought, but he kept walking as if it was fully healed. *The renewal moon will rise soon.*

The Ironash Tree was a welcomed sight for Onexis, its trunk as inviting as a smile from Emery. Rubbing his hands across the bark, he remembered when he made the jump at ten years old, the Order chanting all the while. He closed his eyes and saw the look of uncertainty that Evore gave him before he jumped. *Did I have the same look on my face?*

The base of his staff hit the tree, one, two, three times, and an outline of a door formed in the Ironash's trunk. Sliding to the side, the entrance revealed a long set of cement stairs. The mouth of darkness swallowed sunlight whole as Onexis carefully stepped down underground.

A long, dank corridor of dirt stood before the Chief when he reached the bottom of the staircase. Using his staff, he walked through the silence below Trilon, which had a darkness that made Onexis feel as if he was walking in place. After about a mile, and as his mind started to clear of his endless guilts, he began to hear a low murmur. The murmur began to take shape into the Verrativa's words, and it filled Onexis with pride. *This is what we fought for, what all of our people died for.*

> *"Kings will rise, Kings will fall*
> *The sands of time will cover them all*
> *Ghosts crave blood*
> *Potions made from mud*
> *Shadows only lie*
> *Fire can help those fly*
> *But when the rest are gone*
> *The Verrativas will live on"*

Darkness opened up to an enormous dungeon-like room lit with rows of torches hung from chains. One hundred Verrativas, male and female, swayed in a circular pattern chanting in unison.

Directly in the middle of the crowd was a bald, shirtless Verrativa, his chest tattoo small, but he had a number of other pieces of art throughout his body, including a piercing through his neck. In his hand was a long black needle as skinny as a blade of grass. Sitting in a wooden chair in front of him was the small boy with nectar-colored eyes. *If he's safe, that's all that will ever matter.*

Onexis took off his robe, exposing his upper body fully and the tree tattoo with branches of accomplishments covering every inch of his torso. He walked through the circle to join Evore and the rest of the Verrativas. When his son's eyes landed on Onexis's, he inhaled deeply, and let out a sigh of relief.

The chant stopped when Onexis opened his arms to his people. "Thank you, friends, for coming to witness a new age for our race." Every muscle looked as it were chiseled by a stonemason as he paced back and forth, looking at everyone who came to celebrate with him and his son. Every single one of them had eyes locked on him -- all except a young girl with long black hair who stared at Evore.

When Onexis found Emery, he smiled and gestured for her to join him in the middle of the circle. She was clad in a magenta robe, tied together tightly, with a picture, half of day, half of night, stitched on the back, its white sun and crescent moon glowing in the torch light. When Onexis closed his wife in an embrace, their lips locked and all the Verrativas cheered proudly. There were cries of "Ylewood!" and "All hail Chief Onexis!" as well as "Thank you, Emery!" As the two opened their eyes, they turned their attention to Evore, who wore pale leggings and his sand-colored robe. *This is all I would ever want. This is all that I ever need.*

Damn anyone to a Moiiralatta death who would try to take this from me.

When Evore undid his robe, exposing his skinny stomach, shivers crawled up Onexis's spine as he watched his son twitch in the chair. *The boy is so little, I must make sure he eats more.* Everyone was silent as the bald Verrativa stood in front of him, the thin needle squeezed between his thumb and forefinger. He pressed the needle deep into his inner pectoral muscle, drawing a line of black, and trickles of blood began to flow. The tattoo artist reached into his rags and found a large leaf to wipe up the blood, its healthy green color turning to a death red. Onexis watched his son receive his mark of eternity, a great day for the entire Verrativa population, but all he could see was the blood. As it flowed like tears, the Chief felt his head spin. *I'm no better than any of them. I spilled the blood of the innocent, just like they do.*

"What's the matter, dear?" Emery whispered in his ear.

"It's nothing," he muttered back.

Emery kissed him on the cheek and pressed her head into his chest. "It's an emotional day for us. He's growing up so fast, Nex. Soon he'll be fighting beside you."

"I'm not looking forward to that day. He should be with friends, with children."

Emery nodded. "Maybe in another lifetime, my love."

It ended just as quickly as it started. Evore stood from his chair with a giant tree trunk tattooed between his chest muscles. His skin was puffy, red, and raw, but he beamed, nonetheless. The entire room cried out merrily, and it was the happiest that Onexis had ever seen his son. His people chanted as loud as ever, "Evore! Evore! Live forever! Evore! Evore! Live forever!"

When the room began to file out, Onexis turned to see Evore still sitting on the chair in the center with his eyes glued to him. "How did I do?" he asked confidently.

"Couldn't have done it better myself." Onexis laughed, messing up his son's hair.

Evore swatted his hand away, playfully. "I thought you weren't going to make it."

"I wouldn't miss this for anything, you know that!"

Evore shuffled his feet. "I know, it's just when I came down this morning, you weren't there again, so..." Onexis pulled his son in and embraced him tightly. "Father, can I ask you something?"

"Anything, my boy." His voice shook lightly.

"Why can't we trust anybody else?"

Onexis was lost for words. "There are others who-- There are others who want to kill us."

"All of us?" Evore questioned.

"All of us," Onexis said as he stood.

Evore looked up to his father. "But you'd protect us."

"That's right. And someday. everyone will look to you for protection." Onexis began to walk toward the exit.

His son followed closely. "Have you ever thought that maybe everybody else isn't bad? Maybe someday we can leave the Ylewood?"

"I have, many times. You could be right someday."

"Have you..." Evore trailed off.

Onexis halted. "Have I...?"

His son's nectar eyes fell to his feet. "Have you ever protected us?"

The Chief sighed. "I have."

"Was it hard?"

As his voice tightened, Onexis saw Broddi Trap struggle for his last breath. "It's the hardest thing to do." He reached into his breeches and pulled out the grease-stained piece of parchment, the wax seal of a Coatus still unbroken. "Let's read this together."

Evore took the letter from his father, broke the seal, and unraveled it.

FORBATH: RELISS

Sunlight crawled through the openings of Larkmour Castle's covered parapet walkway as Prince Tycho stepped briskly down a path of granite. Midday's glow had filled the courtyard by the time he made it outside for his sparring lesson. When Tycho walked through the entrance to the yard, to a large, rounded doorway of grey brick with its protective iron gate pulled up for the daytime, he was greeted with the sounds of wooden sparring swords clanking against one another and the thumps of arrows whizzing through the air and landing in their targets. The shortly-cut green grass bounced under the soles of his leather strapped boots as he made his way to the middle of the yard.

"My Prince," said a chubby man dressed in a black tunic that stretched over his belly, the neck striped with a thick line of forest green. He knelt down to one knee, the blade of his sparring sword in the ground while his shin guards looked as if they would unbuckle any minute.

Tycho shook his head. "Stand, Sir Ryker."

The fat man, who had no hair on his head save for a thick black handlebar mustache salted with grey, stood at once, using his sword to push himself up. "As you say, my Prince." He mopped his bald head, which had a number of long scars along the top and sides, giving it the appearance of a hastily-drawn road map. From the looks of it, one would have thought the Castle's Battle Master had been sparring for hours, but in reality, the plump Knight didn't need an excuse to be red in the face. Some of the squires even joked that he would get winded from shelling a hard-boiled egg.

Sir Ryker Tygurnach grew up in the blacksmith village of Ghordaan and spent his teen years into his twenties as an apprentice, until his Master sold him to the current Lord of Windrip and former Lord of Ghordaan, Bekan Atalay. At first, Ryker became Lord Bekan's personal blacksmith and forged the finest weapons made from Ghordaan steel. Lord Atalay was pleased with the first-time smith, heaping praises on him and the Master who trained him. Atalay always said, "A man's strength can be measured by the weapon he swings," a quote that his father taught him when he was much younger, on the day he passed down Desire's Rage to him.

It wasn't until a raid attempt on Windrip when Ryker Tygurnach showed his abilities as a warrior. Lord Bekan watched with his own eyes as his blacksmith took three men's lives, all with different weapons. The first and the quickest was a stab to the heart of a skinny ginger man with a longsword; the second he landed an axe blade into a boy's neck, which caused him to silently bleed out. Lastly, Ryker buried a mace in a fat bearded man's head and flung chunks of blood and brain onto the raiders.

From that point on, Bekan Atalay thought the world of Ryker. Not only could the man forge weapons as good as anyone in Ghordaan, but he fully knew how to use them, which, as far as Bekan knew, was as rare as red gold. After that, they fought side by side, and when they emerged victorious, Tygurnach would restore the weapons damaged from battle.

He had an aggressive and fearless style on the battlefield, which Bekan admired and told everyone about whenever he was given the chance. "Tygurnach stalks his prey and goes in for the kill like no man I've ever seen," he would say at feasts to any Lord, Lady, or servant who would listen. "In fact, I wouldn't be surprised if he has tiger blood running through his veins." The singers and writers who were told this gave Ryker the nickname "The Tiger", one that caught on quite quickly throughout the other realms.

"We've got some good competition for you today, my Prince."

"Please, call me Tycho." The Prince clapped Sir Ryker on the back as they walked through the field.

The Tiger let out a small cough. "As you say, my--er–Tycho." It was hard to tell if Sir Ryker was blushing or if he was still out of breath from standing up.

"How many are sparring today?" Tycho looked out in the distance to see a number of young boys parrying in mismatched armor.

"Four. The best that we have to offer." Tygurnach huffed and puffed as he tried to keep pace with the sixteen-year-old Prince.

Tycho Embray was tall and handsome, with golden hazel eyes and a head of short brown hair that was kissed with streaks of red. He wore a studded, sky blue gambeson with grey breeches and long brown boots that led almost to his knees. A leather belt decorated with silver rings was fastened tightly around his waist, and crimson fingerless gloves covered his hands.

Prince Tycho pulled his freshly-sanded wooden sword from the scabbard that laid across his back. "Let's get to it then." He gave the sword a light swing.

"As you command, Tycho." The old Tiger smiled before he spun around to face the squires. "Come on, ya sacks of meat an' blood," he called out to the practicing squires. "Your Prince is here, start acting like it!" Sir Ryker's scratchy voiced bounced off the Castle walls and echoed through the courtyard.

At once, two of the boys got down on one knee and averted their eyes to the ground. The archers followed hastily, but the other two sparring squires continued as if they didn't hear anything. Back and forth they went, neither one of them letting up any ground. One of the boys was tall and looked underfed, while the other one was equal in height but had a muscular build with tree trunks for both arms and legs.

The skinny boy was significantly quicker than the bulky one and chose a defensive approach to the duel. He danced out of the way from slashes and hacks, his feet light as silk as he bobbed and weaved. Then he blocked a thrust attack, and their wooden blades were engaged. The muscular squire pushed off and followed up with a backhanded blow that broke his opponent's sword, wooden splinters fluttering across the courtyard in every direction like birds flying out of a tree. He took the pommel of his blade and smashed it into his foe's mouth, sending him relentlessly to the ground. As the skinny squire spat out three teeth, blood from his mouth began to paint the green grass red. That was when the victor threw his sword down, pounded his chest once, and finally knelt for Prince Tycho.

"Fucking Quist," Sir Ryker boomed as he stormed across the courtyard. For that moment, he wasn't the aged Battle Master but a tiger zeroing in on its target. The Tiger raced to the squire and, pulling the boy up by the scruff of his collar, brought him in so close that their noses almost touched. "I'm not sure who you think you are, but when I say you stop for your Prince, you stop. Ya hear me?" Sir Ryker's bushy mustache grazed Quist's face as he spoke.

"Edwyrd didn't stop eitha," Quist cried out defensively as he pointed to the barely-conscious boy sprawled out face down in the grass.

Tygurnach let go of Quist, shoved him to go kneel with the other anxious squires, and reached for a fistful of the skinny boy's dirty blonde hair to examine his mouth. "Serves you right for dancing like a tavern slut tryna make a couple boros from a drunk." He let go of Edwyrd. "Go see Saige

Lorrode and get cleaned up. Your three missing teeth will forever be a reminder of the day you could have sparred with the Prince of Trilon."

The skinny squire stumbled to his feet and made for the Castle.

Sir Ryker began to walk in a large circle around the rest of the kneeling boys, looking at all of them and none of them. "All of ya, listen up. The reason you're out here today is because you're the most promising squires in the southern realm. Today, you fight Prince Tycho Embray, your future King! Those who compete valiantly will be well on their way to Knighthood, while those of you who don't will find it much harder to trade in your boiled leather for chain and mail."

Sir Ryker lumbered back to Prince Tycho to introduce his competition for the day. He beckoned the first boy to stand.

"This young man is Toby Vaino, originally from The Moondown Lands in Aleru. I would say that his strengths are on offense, specifically his backhand attacks, while defensively he comes up short. He has a hard time back-peddling, which causes him to trip over his own feet more often than not. Most of his defeats have come from yields."

The boy wore weather-worn boiled leather, matching brown breeches, and scuffed boots, all of which were too large for him. Toby's orange hair, which glimmered in the sunlight, covered his ears and part of his sapphire blue eyes. His once fair and freckled skin looked so burnt that Tycho wouldn't have been surprised to find blisters on the boy's cheeks.

Tycho placed a gloved hand on the young boy's shoulder. "It's a pleasure to meet you, Toby. I hope that I can help you on your way to Knighthood."

"Thank you, my Prince," Toby squeaked. As he bowed graciously, his boiled leather armor shifted and almost went over his head.

The Prince of Trilon turned back to Sir Ryker. "Can't you get the boy armor that fits?" He whispered, "It's no wonder he's always tripping over himself."

"Yes, my Prince--I mean, yes, Tycho. I'll see to it as soon as possible." Sir Ryker wiped a handful of sweat from his head. "Next, we have Molte Holten, originally from Leefside in Gojii. He's a well-rounded fighter who has a good catalogue of moves but isn't elite in anything specific. Defensively, he's the best squire that I've trained, though." Drops of sweat fell from the Tiger's salted mustache as he spoke. "Problem wit' him is, he's a bit too defensive and sometimes hesitant to attack. Got a great reach, though, an ideal length to be deadly with lunge attacks."

It was true, Molte Holten had abnormally long arms for a boy that wasn't particularly tall. He had a shaved head and a skinny, almost gaunt face with bits of hair under his lip and on his chin that made it look like he needed a wash. His brown wooden armor matched his eyes in color, and although what he wore wasn't too big for him, the breastplate had seen better days. A large crack down the center would surely split in two with a direct hit from even a sparring sword.

"I know a great lunge technique that I'll be sure to show you, Molte." Tycho smiled. "Remember, defense is important, but no one ever won a fight without swinging their sword."

Molte nodded in agreement. "Yes, you're right, my Prince. Thank you--my Prince."

The Tiger spat before he introduced the last squire. "There was supposed to be two more for you to fight today, but--"

"I saw, Sir Ryker. Boys will be boys." Nothing ever seemed to bother Tycho. Whenever someone was angry or anxious, he always had an answer or a solution.

"Yes, of course, boys will be boys. This last one is Forym Quist." He pointed to the tall muscular squire who had small droplets of blood on his leather armor; whether it was his, Edwyrd's, or someone else's, Tycho didn't know. He had a thick head with short black hair, small watery eyes, and wore a large scowl.

"Hope you're better than your squires. If not, Trilon is in a lotta trouble." Forym's burly arms were folded over his chest.

The Tiger's face grew crimson with anger. "Shut your hole, boy! If you must speak, then mind your damned courtesies."

"Why?" he objected. "He's no different than any of us. What, are we supposed to wipe his ass every time he takes a shit? You want me to chew up some meat and spit it in his mouth too?"

Sir Ryker's face turned a milky white. "Please, excuse him, my Prince, I fought beside his father and he begged me to--"

"Don't worry, Sir Ryker," Tycho laughed. He walked up to Forym. "I saw you fighting out there. You're aggressive, that's good. Who taught you how to fight?"

"My grandfather, Sir Thamos Quist," Forym snapped back.

"I've heard of him, and your father, Sir Thorlak. They were both legendary Knights, both just as ferocious as they were chivalrous. Did you know that Sir Ryker and your sire fought together years ago?"

"Yes, he always reminds me when I do something wrong or get angry. Sir Ryker always tells me that, if I wasn't my father's son, he would launch me with the catapult all the way to Soarfrost."

Tycho patted him on the back. "A bit of tough love never hurt nobody, right?" He turned back to the Tiger and gave yet another smile. "Let's get started while it's still light out. All the way to Soarfrost, huh?" He muttered under his breath to the Tiger. "Is he that bad?"

"You have no idea, my Prince," Tygurnach mouthed back. "Alright, lemme get Vaino and Holten up front. Grab your sword, Holten!" The two boys hustled up with their sparring swords and stood ready to duel. "Prince Tycho, do you think you can take both of them on at once?"

"I'm not quite sure, Sir, they do look like fierce warriors." The two boys beamed at one another when they heard that from their Prince.

The Tiger chortled, his great belly jiggling along as if it was laughing with him. "They sure do! Come on now, boys, show your Prince you're worthy to be Sirs!"

Vaino led in with a sharp cut to the Prince that he quickly blocked then side-stepped. When Tycho batted the attack away, the ginger squire left his ribcage wide open for a slash attack, but instead he shoved the boy, sending him to the ground. He decided to let the young squire regain his composure and set his sights for Molte Holten, who froze as soon as he saw Tycho's eyes land on him. First, he led in with a thrust that Holten blocked away but didn't deliver a counter-blow. The Prince hacked down, aiming for the boy's armored shoulder, but he ducked and spun out of that just as easily as the first attempt.

"Swing your sword!" Sir Ryker boomed from behind.

Tycho turned his head just in time to see Vaino's charge, his hair a matted fluffy flame that rippled in the sunlight. As the boy lifted his sword back without any sort of discipline, Tycho spun out of the way, and when Toby brought his

59

sword down, he connected with Molte Holten, splitting his wooden breastplate in two.

"Holten, you're done!" Sir Ryker yelled out. The boy stormed off, pouting with every step.

Then, Tycho led in with a blow, which was originally meant for Toby's chest, but was deflected quickly. The Prince saw that the block had made the boy weary and went in for the charge. As they parried back and forth, Toby back-peddling as best as he could, Tycho rained down with a series of light jabs, in complete control of the fight. When he went in with a sharp thrust, the squire fell to his feet and dropped his sword. Kicking it to the side, Tycho pointed the wooden blade to the boy's neck and smiled just as he did before.

"I yield, my Prince." Panting heavily, the boy shook the untamed mess of hair from his eyes, which stuck to his forehead with sweat.

Tycho reached down and pulled Toby up to his feet without even a deep breath. "You fought well, future Sir. If you continue on your path, I would be honored to have you fight by my side someday."

"Thank you-- Thank you, my Prince." Toby grabbed his sword and joined Molte on the side.

Quist clumsily stepped up to face Prince Tycho. "Is it my turn yet?"

"It would seem so." Tycho leaned back in his defensive position.

The Tiger spat as he watched Forym Quist crack his knuckles. He walked up to the squire gingerly and put his arm around his shoulder. "Now listen, Forym, rememba this is the Prince," he whispered. "*Your* Prince."

"I intend to beat him. I'm not like the other bone-chewers who were too scared to land a blow." Quist didn't match Sir Ryker's tone at all, allowing Tycho to hear every word that he said.

Sir Ryker shook his head and walked off to the side to watch. He could only hope that Prince Tycho could end the duel quickly before any real damage could be done.

"Are you ready? Or should I have the cook prepare us some lunch?" Tycho jawed playfully. He noticed that the boy's boiled leather was too small for him and his chest didn't allow it to be tightly strapped. His breeches were ripped on either leg, exposing both calves. Instead of being equipped with a broadsword like Tycho and the rest of the squires, Forym wielded a longsword, both of his hands wrapped tightly around the hilt.

Charging with a scream, Quist led in with a cut that was blocked quickly by the forte of Tycho's blade. Even so, the Prince felt the vibrations of the attack ring up his fingers, through his chest, and up to his teeth. He countered with a thrust that was deflected, and Forym answered with a punishing backhanded blow that almost grazed Tycho's stomach. Quist then aimed for Tycho's right side, seeing that he fought with his left hand. However, the Prince quickly switched his sword hand and blocked the attack with the outside edge of the blade. In a desperate attempt to get the sword back into his dominant hand, he kicked Quist in the stomach, sending him backwards, but not to the ground.

Next, Tycho led the attack, trying to bring the duel back in his favor. Parrying, the two fighters moved further and further from the middle of the courtyard until they were feet away from the Castle's eastern wall. He pushed and pushed the fight until Quist's back was against the wall. That was when Prince Tycho unleashed his lunge attack for the first time. As he bent down to one knee to bring the blade up, he was shocked to see that Quist had no trouble at all stonewalling the blow. He had to recover quickly and was able to deliver a half-powered cut, which the squire sidestepped, causing the wooden blade to clank against the Castle.

When Quist led in with a glide, trying to disarm the Prince, Tycho was impressed. Clearly Forym saw that his opponent was growing tired and impatient, which is the best time to take away a weapon. However, Tycho countered with a volte, sidestepping the blow, and finishing with a thrust. The squire grunted in frustration and decided his best chance was to win with power, so he tried to bind the Prince. He made Tycho's blade go left, then right, then left again, and soon they were back in the middle of the courtyard. Sweat was pouring from both their faces when they engaged. Both blades pushed against each, neither one wanting to give an inch, until Forym pushed through, breaking Tycho's sword and sending him flying back towards Sir Ryker, the other squires, and the archers.

Prince Tycho exhaled and let out a laugh of relief. "Quite the fight!"

Forym grabbed him by either shoulder and head-butted him, breaking his nose, and threw him down to the ground.

"What the fuck is wrong with you, boy?" Sir Ryker screamed out in anger.

Tycho got to his feet and wiped the blood from his nostrils, making his gloves a darker shade of red. "Now that's what I expect from someone who wants to fight by my side. A relentless effort, my friend!"

Quist stepped back, amazed at the Prince's reaction. "I'm sorry, my Prince! Sometimes I just get so-- I get so angry and I can't stop. I didn't think that it would happen, but it did and--"

Smearing his blood on the front of Quist's armor, Tycho grinned, his teeth stained with the blood from his nose. "Everyone needs to get their ass kicked from time to time, even princes. There," he said, "More blood to add to your armor."

When Forym removed his boiled leather, revealing a white long-sleeved undershirt, Tycho clapped him on his muscle-coated shoulder. Together, they walked back towards the spectators.

"If you can just direct that anger towards your enemies-- Pardon me, I should say *our* enemies-- you'll be unstoppable."

Just as Sir Ryker was breathing in deep to curse out Quist, Tycho stopped him.

"I spoke with Forym. Do not punish the boy for fighting without fear. He's exactly what we look for in a Knight."

After all the squires and archers left the courtyard, Tycho noticed that there was another spectator, one that he didn't notice before.

"Brannon!"

Brannon Broadwine walked up to stand with both Prince Tycho and The Tiger. "A valiant fight, my Prince. One that your father would have been proud to witness." The man was tall and skinny with high cheekbones and slicked-back blonde hair that was graying on both sides. He wore a golden-studded doublet that was decorated with navy blue stripes. Brannon's boots were just as fancy, with the leather dyed blue to match the rest of his outfit. "After both of you wash up, come to my solar for our meeting."

Sir Ryker looked at Tycho's crooked nose. "Make sure Saige Lorrode fixes your nose. You don't want to get blood all over Brannon's fancy table that no one's allowed to eat on."

"You could use to skip a few meals anyway!" The Prince slapped the Battle Master's belly.

Tycho entered the Castle the way he came out, but instead of walking back down the long granite corridor, he stopped at a thick wooden door with a brass ring handle and pulled it open. As he stepped cautiously up the spiral staircase, the smell of smoke and the sounds of bubbling liquids filled his senses. The room was dank and was only lit by the fires that burned under the many cauldrons and beakers, each filled with different colored potions. In the middle of the attic was a large table, black with mold and burn marks, that had a number of books haphazardly thrown on top.

A door on the opposite wall flew open and a very short, white-haired man looked through and anxiously scratched behind his ear. "This had to be Forym Quist again." Lorrode Allwater's voice was scratchy and barely audible over the bubbling potions. "I'm going to try to make a few fake teeth for Edwyrd out of a Tantae horn or a Smiladon tusk, but I'm not sure how they'll turn out. If it were a molar, it would be easier, but because they're upfront, it makes it much more difficult and significantly more painful for the boy."

"What's Edwyrd's family name?"

The old Saige pulled on the grey hairs that were growing from his nostrils. "Hendryx. His father is a Steward to Lord Xalvadore Corwin in the east." Lorrode pulled out a pair of magnifying glasses from his baggy robe pocket, which made his smoky blue eyes look absurdly large.

"What can you tell me about Forym Quist?" Tycho asked as he tilted his head back to let Lorrode examine inside his nose.

"His father, Sir Thorlak, was a great warrior who fought for Bekan Atalay during Zabkar's reign." Lorrode Allwater spoke as if he was reading text. "Of course, when the Tiger left Atalay to serve under Zabkar Inwar, he wasn't happy. After Thorlak found out that Tygurnach was knighted by the King of Magic, all he wanted to do was kill him. I remember," the Saige cackled at the memory, "I remember Sir Thorlak sustained an injury to his calf before the battle at

Hillrode, and all he could talk about was getting healed up for when he followed your father into Reliss so he could kill the 'pig belly traitor'."

Tycho felt some tension as Lorrode pressed on his nose. "And what happened?"

Lorrode reached for a white rag and dipped it in a boiling cauldron behind him, turning it a black-purple. "Your father sentenced him to death for treason."

"I'm well-aware that there is still much to be learned before I could consider myself ready to rule, but I need to keep a focus on the laws of treason. I'm still not certain--" Lorrode seemed to unhinge Prince Tycho's nose from his face with the rag and proceeded to knead as if it were made of clay. Tycho continued like nothing had happened. "I can't seem to understand how Sir Ryker wasn't punished for treason, but Forym Quist's father was put to the sword."

Lorrode crunched Prince Tycho's nose back in place, and for a moment Tycho was unable to see, but still it didn't bother him. "Sir Ryker was knighted by Zabkar Inwar, a King. Your father was nothing more than a rebel who was trying to end the reign of Inwar and the Oracles. When a man is knighted by a King, he must serve the *King*. Your father wasn't King, not yet." Saige Lorrode's tone was condescending but still warm like a little boy speaking to his younger brother. "He did the lawfully right thing by listening to Lord Bekan's council."

There was a sizzle to one of the cauldrons that bubbled over, putting out one of the flames in the brazier below it. Even though the flame that extinguished was small, Tycho still felt the darkness grow around him. "What are you implying when you say 'lawfully right'?"

"Well, my Prince, I do suppose you need to hear these things, considering the circumstances surrounding King Tanwill. There have always been those who call Sir Ryker a traitor for leaving Lord Bekan to join Inwar. Others believe he did no wrong and was simply taking an opportunity to be knighted. You have to realize, Zabkar knighted the Tiger before the King of Magic showed his true colors. Those who call him traitor wonder if he would die for the King, for *Trilon*, considering he didn't when given the chance to for the previous regime."

Tycho thought for a moment before he spoke. "Well, why didn't he die for his King? Why didn't he go down by sword or get banished to Soarfrost?"

"Your father gave specific instructions to his men to not harm Sir Ryker under the guidance from Bekan Atalay. No one knew the Tiger better than Lord Bekan Atalay, and he promised your father that the newly knighted Tiger was worth keeping alive for his expertise in weaponry alone."

"So, Sir Thorlak didn't obey my father's command?"

Lorrode shook his head. "No, my Prince, he didn't. Lord Bekan was able to cage the Tiger before Quist could get to him, but the man still tried to slit Tygurnach's throat while he was unconscious. When the guards brought him to Tanwill, your father our King wept. He was crushed that Sir Thorlak would disobey his order, not because of his superiority in rank but because they were as close as brothers. Still, your father did the noble thing and swung the sword himself."

The only stories that Tycho heard of Sir Thorlak Quist were of his valor, not treason. It hurt him to hear the Saige's tale, one that wouldn't be told at The Fox and The Hound, but he knew that, if he was to someday be King of Trilon, the painful stories were necessary to hear. Prince Tycho was constantly being protected from the dark truths of his land. When Vengar Stoneburner flew the untrained Coatus from the Guild, Lord Brannon's only words were, "A Prince should have no worries, except what woman will warm his bed and how they will get rid of the wench in the morn."

Saige Lorrode showed him enough respect to tell the truth and not inflate his ego in an attempt to distract him as to what was actually happening. It gave the Prince a boost of confidence, one that he would surely use later in his meeting with the King's Cabinet.

Saige Lorrode examined both of Tycho's nostrils and nodded. "You're all set, lad. If you must fight, please wear a helm."

After Prince Tycho changed in his quarters to a high-collared forest green jerkin with leather buckles down the middle, he made his way down a marbled hall on the western side of the Castle with golden-framed pictures of every Embray Lord dating back centuries. The sunlight that snuck through the windows on the opposite end of the hall lit up their faces as if to say that these great men were still with him. Smells of pumpkin, nutmeg, and cinnamon wafted through this section of Larkmour Castle, as the chef's corridors were nearby. These smells were synonymous with autumn to the Prince of Trilon since he was a child.

When he reached the end of the hall, there was a stuffed wooden bookcase. Tycho reached for *Trilon: The History and the Magic of the Three Realms* and pulled it back slightly. Suddenly the bookcase pushed backwards and fell out of sight, revealing a lift with a rope pulley. Tycho hopped in and pulled himself for what seemed to be ages until he arrived at Brannon Broadwine's Solar.

While the room was small, it was heavily decorated with shelves and cases. They were all covered with thick glass protecting the expensive jewels or ancient knives forged in Ghordaan that Broadwine liked to show off whenever he could. Two tapestries draped the eastern and western walls of the room. One was of King Tanwill riding Akupara, the Coatus that the commoners named "The Queen", her feathers striped with navy and sunset gold. Underneath the Coatus was a horde of dead Oracles, their cloaks drenched in a sea of blood. The other tapestry was also an illustration of the King bringing down a blade to end the evil Zabkar Inwar's reign in Trilon. Tycho looked at the tapestries and heard his father's complaints from previous meetings in Lord Brannon Broadwine's solar.

A carpet sewn in the fashion of Trilon's map covered the floor, and on top of it was a great mahogany table with four matching seats, all of which were heavily cushioned. Two of the seats were already filled by Brannon Broadwine and Sir Ryker Tygurnach. Broadwine wore the same outfit as before, while the Tiger had changed into a long, red silk robe that hid his belly significantly better than the tunic. Down one side of the garment, a yellow sword was sewn and a shield on the other. Sheathed at his hip was Ripple, the longsword that he forged himself during his time serving Lord Bekan Atalay. A rounded red cap with a yellow brim covered his badly-scarred head, and a goblet filled with dark brown ale was clenched tightly in his hand.

"My Prince. I mean, Tycho." He lifted the glass to Tycho, spilling beer all over the carpet.

Brannon sat at the head of the table in King Tanwill's chair, which was made of rich, chestnut-colored leather with a white wooden frame. "How does your nose feel?"

"Not bad, and it's a hell of a lot better than getting my teeth replaced." Tycho laughed as he poured himself a goblet of ale.

Sir Ryker coughed. "That Forym is quite the fighter, but that temper!"

"I suppose growing up without a father will do that," Tycho answered quickly, and the Tiger took a gulp of ale.

Brannon pulled out a stack of documents from the table's drawer and rifled through them, cutting the pile into two. "Before we start, I'd just like to thank you both for keeping

King Tanwill's condition a secret. As of now, only we three, Lorrode Allwater, and Lord Bekan Atalay are aware, and I'd like for us to keep it that way."

Tycho cracked his knuckles anxiously and then shook out his fingers. "I just don't understand why we're keeping it a secret from Trilon. I mean--"

"You're rightfully suspicious at this course of action, my Prince," Brannon said. He didn't make eye contact with Tycho but instead picked at a stubborn piece of lint that clung to his doublet. "Let me just say, our world has been built on bloodshed. During your father's rebellion fifteen years ago, we ripped through Inwar's men, painting all of Trilon red, albeit heroically. My point is, deep down, we're all violent; it comes with being warm-blooded. If we were to divulge the King's secret, who's to say that a new group of rebels won't emerge? Imagine the armies that Lords Xalvadore Corwin or Lirum Rhygell could put together if their thirst for power grew, if they saw a chance to become King..."

"Right, I suppose that does make sense." The doubt wasn't masked in Prince Tycho's voice at all. "Why did my father have Inwar and the Oracles banished anyway? I've read the tales and heard all the songs of how Inwar was banished to Soarfrost, but why? If the King of Magic and his followers were so evil, why didn't my father kill them all?"

Sir Ryker grabbed at Tycho's shoulder and gave it a few kneads with his fat fingers. "Your father is a man o' mercy, a man o' sense. You have to understand that there were still plenty of mortals that supported Zabkar. If your father had him put to the sword, then another rebellion would have been imminent. It was a controversial decision at the time, one that received little support, but it looks like he had the right of it."

"Seems like my father made many tough decisions when the rebellion was won," Tycho answered as he eyed the Tiger. "How did we actually perform the banishment spell, though?"

"You have enough on your plate, Prince Tycho. There's no need to worry about things that happened fifteen years ago," Brannon cut in quickly. "Now, our priority should be on finding Vengar Stoneburner and the Coatus that he stole from the Guild. He informed me a fortnight ago that he added the blood of the recently hatched Coatus to his Bellow, giving himself full control of her body and mind. While he claimed it was for precautionary purposes, his true intentions are now apparent. The RoarCatcher has already destroyed a section of the Capital and Yatorga."

"The fisherman city?" Beer leaked from the Tiger's moustache.

"Yes, Sir, although many will call it the Shadow City. Now that their home is destroyed, they're in a vulnerable position. This could in turn cause a slight increase of robberies through the south, but we need to not worry about that just yet. First, we--"

"We should send them gold, then. Give them no reason to steal from anybody!" Tycho spoke with great confidence. He saw this Royal meeting as a duel and, as always, wanted to win.

"In due time, my Prince. First, we have to find Vengar Stoneburner and bring him to justice," Brannon repeated emphatically.

Sir Ryker nodded once. "So, what's your plan?"

Brannon folded his hands together. "We call upon the Knights of Rutherfall, and then you begin the hunt through Trilon." He grinned at Tygurnach like a child.

"Aye, that's what I like ta hear," Sir Ryker's voice picked up. "I'll break the RoarCatcher's Bellow over his face."

"You'd have an easier time trying to use the Bellow than destroying it, Sir Ryker. The glass that the jar is made of is stronger than steel and can only be destroyed by the Frost Hammer, which has been lost for over a century. Until the RoarCatcher is found, we will tell Trilon that the Coatus Saige Lorrode bred was done so to defeat King Tanwill's foes."

Tycho frowned. "My Lord, forgive me, but that sounds an awful lot like Trilon's last ruler. It seems to me that you're attempting to create a sense of uneasiness through Trilon, but with *science* instead of *magic*."

The silence that followed those words was only heard in a crypt. "My Prince, the tyrant Zabkar Inwar used magic to take lives with no judgement whatsoever. Whether you were noble like a Knight, or conniving like a thief, if he wanted your life, 'twas his. The Shadows are an enemy to Trilon, a leftover cast of misfits from the previous reign who fought against our cause. They didn't even have the courage to receive the banishment spell like the Oracles and chose the craven way of using their abilities to skulk back into the darkness. Yatorga had been overrun with them for quite some time; the people will appreciate this tactic. Some may even call it courageous. We need everyone to stay away from the Capital to buy time, and this tale will allow just that."

"Well, what about the survivors of Stoneburner's attack? The ones who don't need stories right now? Shouldn't we focus at least *some* of our efforts on helping them rebuild their lives? We could build food shelters, or--"

"Always thinking with an open heart, that's why you'll one day be *our* King! You're right, though, our people need to heal. It isn't all about revenge. I will speak to Lord Aiken Pritchett to see what the crown can spare. Hopefully, in due time, this event will be remembered not as a time of despair but for Prince Tycho's generosity." Broadwine put the document aside and picked up the second pile. He shuffled the stack and cleared his throat. "I have also reached terms with Lord Bekan Atalay."

"Lord Bekan!" Sir Ryker roared affectionately. "This one's ta him!" he said before draining his goblet.

Tycho shifted in his seat. "You do owe him quite a lot, don't you? What are these terms?"

Brannon frowned at Tycho's answer. "As I'm sure you know, Lord Bekan is a large reason why we're all sitting here today. A ferocious warrior in his day; age has taken a toll on his body but not his mind."

"Ferocious is an understatement. They don't make 'em like Lord Bekan anymore," Sir Ryker cut in. "The man was so fearless that he rode a Smiladon pack leader into battle. Tela, he named the beast, and he claimed to love her more than his own wife." Sir Ryker laughed so hard that he let out a loud, phlegmy cough. "As loyal as a dog she was to him, 'til Cellyadure took her life." He trailed off as he refilled his goblet.

Nodding, Brannon began to read the parchment. "Because Lord Bekan cannot fight for his King and friend anymore, he has insisted on sending one of his own Knights to help protect the Capital. Sir Anurd Kincaid will--"

Sir Ryker slapped a hand down on the table. "The Nightmare himself? I've heard stories that the Nightmare is the only squire that Lord Bekan has ever trained completely on his own. I shouldn't be surprised that our Master negotiator was able ta pry him away, though." He elbowed Tycho playfully. "We should have him protect King Tanwill."

"No," Brannon said immediately. "What I mean to say is that coming from the rolling hills of Windrip to the city streets of Reliss will be a shock to his system." He sipped at his cup. "Sir Anurd should arrive by the morrow and will be appointed Captain of the city's watch until he has gotten used to his surroundings."

"I'd sure love ta see Lord Bekan again," the Tiger sighed.

Tycho took note of the look on Tygurnach's face. "Then you shall travel with the Knights of Rutherfall to see the man who hand-picked each of them."

Brannon chose the next document, squinted at the writing for a moment, then took a deep sip from his goblet. "Excellent idea, my Prince. There are ten stationed in Reliss, and another twenty in Ghordaan. If we combine them with the hundred in Rutherfall who stayed under Lord Raylon Tarbuck's command, it would be quite the host to present to the Lord of Windrip."

"I'll write a letter to Lord Bekan and make sure that Lady Rayne Blackwood clears Akupara's schedule for you to fly out," Brannon said to Sir Ryker. His lips were pursed tight as if the letter he just read was making him nauseous.

Tygurnach fingered Ripple's pommel uncomfortably. "That, uh, won't be necessary. Lady Blackwood shouldn't take the time ta fly my company to the east. We'll ride. It's too dangerous to fly with Stoneburner controlling the untrained Coatus. Last thing we want is to lose Akupara," Sir Ryker answered, trying to sound enthusiastic.

Brannon lifted his gaze from the letter. "I will not compromise on these matters. Time is of the essence, and that means you will fly to Aleru." Sir Ryker backhanded his goblet off the table and spat. "Try to stop me from riding, and we'll see if you actually know how to use any of these weapons you've collected."

Broadwine looked calm and collected as he ran a hand through his slicked-back hair. "Are you threatening the King's Lead Confidant, Sir?"

"You bet your fucking ass I am!" Tygurnach stood up and unsheathed Ripple. The sword had a silver hilt with a rounded pommel that was striped with yellow and black. Its blade was almost large enough for a great sword and was said to ripple like water if looked at in the right light.

Tycho stood up, knocking his chair over. "Both of you, stop, I command it. Sir Ryker, if you wish ride, please go see Lord Aiken Pritchett after our meeting to gather supplies for your party. Lord Brannon is right, time is of the essence, but I will not have fighting within my father's Cabinet. Is that understood?" Both Sir Ryker and Lord Brannon nodded without making eye contact with one another. "Good," Tycho said, lifting up his chair and sitting back down.

The Tiger sheathed Ripple, his face purple with anger. Tycho eyed the blade and cleared his throat. "Sir Ryker, you threatened a member of my father's Cabinet, and that cannot go unnoticed. From now on, you cannot wear Ripple while inside Larkmour Castle, unless we are under attack. I will permit you to wear it on the grounds outside but consider that your punishment." Tygurnach nodded, unstrapping the sword and letting it thump to the floor before taking his seat. "Now, Lord Brannon, what is written on that piece of parchment that has you so distracted?

"This is from my Lord Callowat in Leefside. There was a death in the Butcher's shop. Supposed suicide."

"Suicide? Was it a hanging?" Tycho asked.

"Stabbed himself through the throat with his own knife," Brannon said, without lifting his eyes from the parchment.

"There's no way a man would stab himself through the throat with a knife. That's a murder if I've ever seen't," Sir Ryker objected, his voice heavy like he just awoke from a good night's sleep.

"It says that his hands were wrapped around the hilt of the blade."

Sir Ryker let out a small burp. "The murderer is smart. He's far away from the crime, probably in Yatorga now with the Shadows while we're sitting in our comfy chairs just reading about it."

Tycho grabbed his nose to see if it would move. "So, what should we do about this?"

"Nothing for now." Brannon spoke softly as he put the piece of parchment back in the drawer. "I may be called upon for investigation purposes, but obviously I have to decline."

"Why's that?" Tycho asked aggressively as if the statement offended him.

Brannon bit his bottom lip. "Well, if Sir Ryker leaves for Aleru and I leave for Gojii, that would leave you as the sole member of the King's Cabinet present in Reliss."

Tycho drained his cup, thinking of the right words to say. "I'm to be King someday. I can handle a few days running things alone. Think of it as practice for when you're both retired," he said with a hearty laugh.

"Very well," Brannon said through the same smile which looked painted on his face at this point. "That'll be it for the day. Prince Tycho, please stay behind if you'd be so kind."

Sir Ryker gave a single nod, picked up Ripple before making his way over to the lift, and, after hitting his head on the top of it, crawled inside.

Brannon stared at Prince Tycho for a moment then took a deep breath. "Tycho, I've known you since you were born, and since then I've recognized your strength. You're a natural leader who's adored by his people, and you excel at making decisions both in combat and office. Today made me realize you've grown into a man, and we cannot keep you blind to anything anymore. Saige Lorrode has confirmed that your father hasn't come down with sickness but something much worse. His blood was leeched and tested positive for

75

Silent Bite, a deadly poison. Stoneburner dosed him before he fled, my Prince, and now we must seek vengeance, seek blood." He stood up. "You could become our ruler sooner than we all anticipated, but I know you'll be a great King just like your father. Follow me, my Prince." The King's Lead Confident pulled out a large silver key from his breeches.

Tycho stood up, confused and afraid. It had been a month since his father came down with "sickness", and he had seen him just once since then. It started as just a faint cough, which led to nausea, but in a week's time, the sickness paralyzed him. Lorrode Allwater had brewed every potion he knew of and was still working day and night to help his King, but nothing seemed to remedy him.

Brannon led the Prince, who was transformed from a strong young man into a baby boy, to a door next to the Coatus tapestry and, sticking the silver key in a great lock, opened it for his Prince.

"My Lord father once told me that the man who shows his enemies mercy is just, but the man who shows his enemies a blade has no enemies."

The darkness inside the small chamber was only fought off by one candle on a nightstand next to the King's small bed. There was a window, but thick curtains were drawn, blocking out any of the sun's happiness. The smell of shit punched Tycho in the nose as he stepped closer to the King, but it didn't faze him in the least bit. He bent over, kissed King Tanwill on the head, and wiped away a few beads of sweat from the bags under his eyes.

"Father?" the Prince asked as if he wasn't sure who this man was.

King Tanwill was gaunt; his golden-hazel eyes stared up at the blank ceiling. Thinning white hair covered his pink scalp but also most of his pillow. When Tycho touched his skin, it was burning hot, but his father shivered as if he was

76

naked in the middle of Soarfrost. A number of quilted blankets covered his body, but his emaciated arms were on top of them all. His hands were cold and clammy with gnarled knuckles black from disuse. Tycho examined his father's forearms, which were nothing but bones covered by a thin layer of skin, when he spotted a number of leeches feasting and growing fat off his blood. All he wanted to do was rip them off and stomp out their lives one by one.

The RoarCatcher's life will be mine to take, and I will enjoy watching his eyes turn to stone. By poisoning my father, he stole my soul, consuming me with a darkness that will never go away.

FORBATH: YATORGA

The smoke from Dink climbed up through the air after escaping his mouth of rotten teeth, only to be cut off by the ceiling of the Grateful Swine. Sometimes, after a deep drag from his pipe, he would blow out a cloudy ring and follow it with an arrow through the center. While the tavern was overcrowded with the sounds of laughter and curses, Dink sat in the back corner and drank his tankard of ale alone. A small brown hound with oversized floppy ears pranced through the throng and squeezed to the back to give the man some much-needed company. When the dog sat square on Dink's foot waiting for a treat, he smiled. "If I had food, I'd fucking eat it. Here..." He took a long pull of his pipe and blew out a large circle that the hound nipped at playfully. When Dink blew out the arrow of haze, he missed his target and instead landed the blow harmlessly on the dog's paw. "I guess I've drank my fill," he chuckled heartily as he scratched the hound behind its ear.

Dink's eyes followed the dog as it left his side and disappeared in the crowd when he spotted Atrius weaving through to the back of the tavern. The young boy was stopped by a shoulder grab from the fat bartender, Porter, who proceeded to angrily scream in his face. After a few apologetic nods, Atrius Callowat continued until he spotted Dink, his eyes widening to the size of saucers when he noticed the chubby drunk.

"I've been looking for you everywhere," Atrius yelled, stumbling through the inebriated flock.

"I'm not trying to be found, especially by a little cunt like you!" Dink said before he took a drag from his pipe. "Get me another tankard, boy," he laughed as he blew a mouthful of smoke into Callowat's face.

Atrius was clad in a crimson cloak with yellow buttons down the center that was tied together at the waist by a rope, his hood drawn up. "Graybill is looking for you. He wants you and Kylan downstairs," Atrius answered with a cough when he tasted the black cloud that was blown in his direction.

Dink drained his tankard. "Well, where's Kylan?"

Atrius took down his hood and sat on a wooden stool next to Dink. "Not sure, maybe he's sleeping. It is late," the boy shrugged.

"Did I tell you to sit?" Dink spat. "And why didn't you go upstairs and get the boy?"

"Graybill said--"

"Don't you fucking blame Graybill!" His face was as red as an apple now, whether from anger or alcohol, not even he could say.

Atrius gulped nervously. "I'll-- I'll go get him now." The young boy ran his sweaty hands through his matted blond hair.

"No, now you stay here." Dink stumbled to his feet. "The only thing you're good for is growing pimples." He took a second to gain his balance as well as his vision and headed over to the staircase leading upstairs, which was directly next to the one that lead downstairs.

Dink walked up carefully, putting all of his weight on the oak rail to the left side, while each step groaned as if to complain of the man's weight. When he finally made it to the top of the staircase, he was huffing and puffing. The long corridor was lit like the rest of the Swine, with hollowed-out Smiladon fangs that held candles, but most of the flames were put out. Passing through the doors of small quarters, he heard a woman's loud moan of pleasure followed by the back and forth creaking of a wooden bed. "Sounds like Saria," Dink laughed. "Haven't had her in a while."

When he arrived at the third door, he gave it a swift single knock but then heard another scream from the last door in the corridor. This one wasn't of pleasure but of anguish, and it turned Dink's blood cold. The scream sounded like his own back when *he* was still alive. He couldn't wait any longer for the boy to answer and made the snap decision to burst through the door.

"Kylan! Graybill needs to--"

Were his eyes deceiving him? Had he really drank that much downstairs? Those couldn't possibly be...

"Tits?!" Dink's mouth dropped. "Please tell me I didn't see what I just fucking saw." Kylan quickly buttoned up her maroon tunic. "So that's why you wouldn't let Atrius take your tunic to wash?"

Kylan shrugged. "I didn't mean for anyone to find out."

Dink slammed the flimsy door behind him and punched it as hard as he could, leaving a fist-sized dent. "It's a little fucking late for that, don't ya think?"

The girl smoothed down her curly auburn hair. "Are you going to tell Graybill?"

"No, I won't say anything. The second son of Xalvadore Corwin isn't worth much, but his daughter is." Dink began to pace back and forth through the tiny chamber. There wasn't much in it except a straw mattress, a tall mahogany-colored chest filled with knife gashes throughout, a single Smiladon candle on top, and a partially shattered mirror placed on the wall opposite of the door. Dink looked into the mirror for a moment then back to the girl. "Graybill will sell you to the highest bidder to deal with your father."

"He won't just ransom me to my father?" Kylan asked.

Dink laughed. "And have the Baron of Aleru think he kidnapped you? He'd have Graybill in chains before the fucking sun was over this shithole of a city." He walked over to Kylan and grabbed her gently on the shoulder. "Keep your mouth shut tight. Who's to say what the people here would do if they knew who you are?"

"I'm not her anymore," Kylan answered quickly. Dink nodded in agreement. "Should we cut my hair?"

Dink pulled out the dagger from his tattered grey robe and grabbed a strand of the girl's hair. Just as he brought the blade up, he paused. "No, keep it. You came here with the hair." He put the blade away. "Now come on, Graybill's waiting."

They crossed the threshold to hear Saria's moan, but this time Dink didn't so much as crack a smile. He wiped the sweat from his brow then made for the stairs, halting on the first step.

"Don't even make fucking eye contact with anyone," Dink said as he scanned the crowd.

"Well, if it isn't Graybill's piss-on and his little bone-chewer," the fat bartender, Porter, yelled out from behind the bar once they reached the bottom of the staircase. His one eye was bright with amusement, while the other eyelid battled with the red scar that held it back like a wall. "Tell me, boy, is his cock as small as all the whores say?" He chortled loudly, which caused a bunch of heads to turn.

Dink forgot his attempt at stealth. "My cock is big enough to please the only whore who warms my bed at night -- your mother!" he fired back, silencing Porter. That jape got a few laughs from the people who were listening to the quarrel. "I'll be back soon. Make sure you have a cold tankard of black ale in my corner seat when I return."

When they finally reached the cellar, Graybill was counting a bag of boros, the copper coins spread out on the table in front of him. Atrius carried over another burlap sack from the corner that had two more, both of them completely filled. His lilac eyes studied the coins in front of him, and the tangled mane of black hair was tied behind his back. He didn't look at either Kylan or Dink, who had been standing there for over five minutes, but instead muttered numbers to himself like he was in the room alone. Kylan stared at the wooden Smiladon carvings on the armrests of Graybill's leather chair as if they were going to come alive at any moment.

"Unacceptable," he spoke to no one and everyone. "This is what you come back with?" Graybill's eyes met Dink's. "Four sacks of boros?" He sat up in his seat, his black robe brushing the dusty floor. "We have a city to feed, Dink, as well as countless repairs."

Both Dink and Kylan still stood. "The raiders I brought with me to Piklorha were green as grass. All they wanted to do was rape and--"

"Why are you trying to hit Piklorha?" Graybill asked, the annoyance in his voice growing stronger by the word. "We sold the fish our city caught for them to resell. They have nothing without us, and we have nothing. Now the entire village will come to the nearest city, which is what?" Dink didn't respond. "Kylan, do you know?"

"Yatorga." Kylan looked at Dink, who could only stare at his worn boots.

Graybill reached into his deep pocket and pulled out his pipe. "The boy knows more than you, Dink, and he wasn't even on the heist." He grabbed for a small drawstring bag in the top drawer and opened it up to pull out a coin-sized amount of dried black leaves. "You have to get out of this area, Dink. We need to hit cities further up, ones that weren't affected by the Coatus yet." Graybill packed the bowl and brought the pipe to his mouth.

"All of Forbath is fucked right now," Dink argued. "If only some could leave the south, we'd make a killing in Gojii or Aleru."

Graybill nodded. "Well, that's why we have our friend here." He glanced at Kylan. "Tell me, *friend*, you've been here close to a fortnight... What do you think of *our* egg?"

Kylan looked under the table. "Well, it's definitely a Coatus egg, if that's what you're asking." Her voice quivered as she tried to make it sound manlier.

"That's well and good," Graybill chuckled as if Kylan had just finished telling a joke. "We knew that one already, though. I meant, do you think it will hatch?"

Kneeling down beneath the table, Kylan touched the turquoise egg. Upon closer examination, she noticed small crimson spots that looked smoother than the rest of the shell. She rubbed her hands together as if the egg was made of ice. "It's absolutely freezing. Allwater's other egg was incubated before it hatched."

"This one wasn't, then?" Graybill asked.

Kylan sat down, and Dink followed. "It wasn't. Master Stoneburner said four Coatuses were enough to deal with. We were planning on selling the egg to the highest bidder once time took its toll on the unhatched Coatus's life. The money would be used to fund the Guild."

"Killing an innocent creature seems so... barbaric," Atrius answered quickly from across the room.

Dink's nod was painful, as it hurt him to agree with Atrius Callowat. "You have a whole Guild dedicated to Coatuses, yet you decide to kill one off before it can even take a breath. Why even have a Guild?"

Kylan looked offended at the question. "*Everyone* grows old. We were supposed to be the replacements for the current Trainers after they chose to retire from their duties."

Graybill puffed on his pipe, covering his face in a shroud of smoke.

"I know how it may sound, but they're so hard to manage, so hard to train," Kylan continued. "There were days when I wished they never appeared from wherever they came from."

"You don't know where the Coatus eggs came from? The three Coatus eggs all fell from the same place after King Tanwill defeated Zabkar," Atrius said in a boyish tone as he sat next to Graybill.

"And where's that?" Graybill asked, intrigued at the boy's excitement.

Atrius smiled. "Hybernia, the city in the clouds!"

Dink curled his hand into a fist. "Right, the same place that Daymon Stringfellow, the Halfling Bard, comes from."

"Exactly! I'm surprised you--"

"If you keep talking, I'm going to cut you open, gut you, and wear you as a fucking pelt," Dink screamed, his face flushed from rage.

"Children's stories, Atrius, but amusing nonetheless." Graybill patted the boy on the back affectionately. "So, Kylan, what is this incubator?"

"It's a device that the Larkmour Castle's Saige invented, Lorrode..."

Graybill nodded. "Lorrode Allwater is a very smart man. A genius, I'd say. No wonder he was able to create something of that caliber." He placed his empty pipe on the table on top of the boros. "How big is the incubator?"

Kylan thought for a moment. "It's smaller than you would think. At least it was smaller than I thought it would have been."

"He's asking, is it small enough to steal?" Dink spat on the floor.

Kylan's mouth opened, unsure of what to say. "Oh," she yelled out. "I would say yes, but I'm not sure if it's in one piece. Our tower was destroyed by Master Stoneburner, and I would have to assume everything inside is long gone too."

Graybill stood up swiftly and handed Dink a small leather pack. "Well, there's nothing like trying. Dink, take Kylan and head to Reliss. Steal anything you can that's not copper-colored. Silver and gold, boys, silver and gold." He looked at Atrius. "Would you please fill up four goblets of red? Let's toast this job for good luck."

Without the slightest hesitation, Atrius went to the opposite side of the room where there was a large wooden cask surrounded by used goblets, steins, and tankards. He brought four filled cups over and handed them out, Dink snatching his before anyone else had the chance.

"To Yatorga," Graybill smiled.

The parties brought their cups together for cheers and then were silent as they drank down the deep purple wine. Just before the meeting dispersed, Graybill grabbed Kylan by the arm gently, handed her a tiny leather pack, and winked one of his lilac eyes.

There was the typical congestion of people outside of the Grateful Swine, with the sober trying to come in and the drunk stumbling out. The row of shops that led up to the bar was still decrepit, but as they made their way down the strip, Dink noticed a small stand that had just been built. It wasn't anything more than a wooden table draped with a checkered cloth and a painted sign overhead that read "Yatorga's Finest Jewelry", but it still made him smile.

"You see that? Yatorga will be back soon enough, just you wait." He clapped his hands together.

They continued on past the alleys where they heard both yells of pleasure and pain but paid heed to neither. Dink didn't have to say anything to Kylan; once she saw him grab the hilt of his dagger, she knew not to ask any questions.

When they turned down Beachwood Street that headed right, Dink quickened his pace. Not only were the unsavory out and about at this hour, he also never wanted to be seen during a job. That was the Shadow way, and even though Dink wasn't exactly part of their underground Guild, he still tried to emulate the manipulators of darkness. Of course, he was nowhere near as gifted, but the Shadows had the unfair advantage of magic in their blood.

The small shacks and cottages that stood on either side of the paved road all seemed as though something as light as a storm's wind would knock them over. One house on the right had a number of holes in its brown roof, while another on the left had a door missing its top half. The rest of the abodes were ruins that offered no protection whatsoever except for the memories of when they were whole. Dink was relieved that no one was strolling the streets tonight, and Kylan noticed that by the slight grin of victory that he wore when they reached the end of the street.

"Do ya member when you said you're always lonely?"

Kylan nodded as she stepped closer to Dink. The warmth from her body made him feel alive, gave him purpose. "Yes, of course. It's like nobody cares whether I live or die."

"Well, I don' fuckin' know about that," he answered shortly. "What I do know is, if you do feel lonely, just look at the moon."

"The moon?"

"Aye, the moon." Dink's voice deepened as he grew more embarrassed. "The moon will always chase you no matter where, so you'll never be alone."

The entrance to Yatorga was a gigantic stone archway with thick banisters on either side that connected at the top by intricately carved wood and a Smiladon head. When they exited onto the grey-pebbled Dearborn Road, Kylan saw Dink loosen the grip on his blade.

"How was the city before?"

Dink halted, the tiny rocks scratching under his boots. Looking back to Yatorga, he delicately grazed the gate with the back of his hand as he would to a departing lover. "No better city in all of fucking Trilon. I wasn't kidding when I said that. The laughter, the smells of fresh fish and bread, the fucking tavern sluts... We lived like Kings. Even the bone-chewer Mayor didn't fuck with us. Now what are we?" He kicked at the gravel. "Nothing but a bunch of raiders stealing from the poor. I can't even remember the last time I ate a good piece of meat."

"Trust me, there's still meat in the Capital." Kylan smiled warmly.

Dink laughed. "You're right about that. I'm not trying to spend any extra time where I'm within a mile of the fucking King, though."

They began to walk north up Dearborn Road, the stars sparkling to guide them and the moon shining down on both of them. The path ahead had both tall trees withering over and grey boulders on either side, which gave it a ghostly feel. When the path sloped upward, the smell of salt air that permeated the city finally dissipated. After a few days in Yatorga, the smell made Kylan queasy, and between that and the smell of vomit in the Swine, fresh air was heartily welcomed.

After the slight incline leveled out, Kylan and Dink reached a fork that had three brown boulders beside each individual path. The far right one had "Piklorha" carved in it, with an arrow pointing east. On the path going left, the rock had "Craven's Bog" etched in the middle, with mold caked in the grooves. Without hesitation, Dink continued straight past the rock that read "Reliss ahead".

Pinks and reds of dawn's light began to creep in through the sky, and Dink quickened the pace. "We need to hurry."

His voice quivered with exhaustion. "Soon the sun comes up, and we need to be inside the Capital's gate by then." He looked up ahead and screeched to a halt. "You have to be fucking me."

Straight ahead was a large, grey stone tower. At the bottom there was a great oak door with a heavy brass handle and up top one lonely window with a small candle glimmered through the fading darkness. Other than that, the building was rather plain, with nothing distinct about it except the stains from both weather and time.

"Why the fuck didn't you say there was a toll tower?" Dink hissed at Kylan.

"You didn't know?" Kylan snapped back.

"The point is to not get seen. Didn't you fucking think to say that we would have to run into at least one person on this job?"

Kylan tossed back her hair. "They don't care about us. I got by no problem before!"

She began to walk forward when Dink grabbed her by the elbow and twisted her back. "You were leaving Reliss before going to the scummiest city in the south. They want people coming out of the Capital, not going back in, especially from Yatorga!"

Kylan swallowed when she realized that her companion was right. "We have to go back." Her voice transformed into a whisper. "We can head to Piklorha or Craven's Bog."

"Craven's Bog? Are you as stupid as the shit you say?" Dink scoffed.

Kylan shook her head of auburn hair. "They could take us in for--"

"They ain't taking us in for shit, girl." Dink stormed ahead, dragging Kylan by her arm. "Just let me do the fucking talking."

The door flung open and a tall, skinny man strolled out without a word. When he stopped in the middle of Dearborn Road, he put both his hands on his hips. A patchy brown beard salted with grey covered his clenched jaw, and his nose was very long and thin. The hair on the toll collector's head matched in both color and patchiness, and his eyes were a mysterious blue. "Coming from Yatorga?" The man's voice was higher and cold.

"Piklorha, my friend."

He eyed Kylan then Dink. "And what would you two be headed to Reliss for?" The tollman's voice was nasally, his large nose no doubt the culprit. "Couple of street rats come to beg the King?" He looked directly to Kylan again.

"Going to work good, m'lord. Pieces of shit from Yatorga stormed our walls and raided us."

The tollman spat on the ground. "Fucking raiders. Those scumbags will do anything to not work." He clenched his hand into a gnarled fist and then reached into the pockets of his breeches. The man's leather jerkin hung off his body, its laces tied loosely as if slipped it on over his head. "The toll is five boros, even though I should just let you two pass by for free." Once again, he made eye contact with Kylan. She looked down at her feet without trying to be too obvious.

"Why's that?" Dink asked.

The Tollman shrugged. "Why should I collect money to give to a King who hates his cities? He's the one who sent the Coatus to Yatorga. Can you believe his li'l Saige bred a Coatus as a weapon?" The Tollman kicked up pebbles in anger. "Tried to kill the Shadows, our King did, but obviously he fuckin' missed. King Tanwill pardoned the lot after his rebellion instead of putting them to the sword and now decides to attack them when they're amongst us normal folk."

Dink reached in his pocket to pull out five boros and pressed them into the man's palm. "You still need to do your job, though." The Tollman nodded in agreement.

FORBATH: DEARBORN ROAD

"And what's your name, girl?"

Kylan felt as if her tongue doubled in size when she heard this question. A swift breeze fluttered across her face and the trees that surrounded Dearborn Road began to sway, even though there was no sign of a storm. "We have to move," she yelled.

"Oh no, you ain't gonna dodge my questions 'cause a little rain is a comin'!" the Tollman said, puffing his chest out. "Now *who* are you--"

Suddenly, a loud *BOOM!* interrupted the man, and all of Trilon. It vibrated through each of their bodies, sending them all to the ground.

"What the fuck was that?" Dink yelled out as he failed to stand up, the ground still rumbling like it would break apart at any second.

Kylan had hit her head hard on the rocky path when she fell and couldn't hear anything except a high-pitched ring. Dink was mouthing something to her, but she couldn't read his lips with her vision blurred from her fall.

When Dink was finally able to get to his feet, he lumbered over to her and picked her up. "I said, are you alright?"

She nodded, her hearing still hindered by the ringing throughout her head. Kylan wiped away a handful of pebbles from her mouth and looked up to the sky just in time to see wings flapping.

The Coatus looked magnificent from a distance, its purple and black feathers mixing with the early morning pink sky. As the beast got closer, the elegance and grace with which it flew quickly changed to horror and despair. Her wings created tornado-like winds that were so strong that the trees around them were ripped from the ground like weeds from a garden. One trunk smashed into the top of the toll tower, forcing Kylan and Dink to leap out of the way. The Tollman, however, was not as lucky -- his right calf was lodged deep under the great tree.

"Help," he cried. "I--I have money! I'll do anything! Don't let Reaper take me life!" The man twisted and pulled but couldn't get free. "Please!"

Kylan jumped up, her head still spinning, and began to run to the man's aide but stopped when she saw the Coatus had landed. Dink grabbed and pulled her down by the sleeve behind one of the fallen trees. Kylan wished she had her horn, then she could save the man. The winged creature wasn't as large as the trained Coatuses, but she still stood taller than the tower and any tree she knocked down.

When the Coatus spotted the tollman stuck under the tree, Dink put his sausage-like pointer finger to his lips, as if Kylan needed telling to be quiet. The creature's sunflower yellow and indigo blue beak brushed against the man, and he began to weep uncontrollably. With one flap of its wings, the Coatus brought the toll tower tumbling to the ground on top of the man and took flight once again.

"It's headed east!" Dink said. "Maybe it'll leave Forbath for fucking good"

Kylan stood up slowly. "So Graybill was right then. Master Stoneburner is using his Bellow to control the baby, because he certainly wasn't riding her."

"Is there a reason you're still calling Stoneburner 'Master'? The RoarCatcher betrayed you and all of Trilon, he don't deserve the title," Dink said as he pulled a fistful of mud from his beard. "Of course, Graybill was right, Graybill is always right. He's the most trustworthy person I've ever met, an' with all the people I've met, that's sayin' something. The man has done more for me than you'll ever know," he continued as he wiped his muddy hands onto his robe.

"We need to find a way to break his spell then. The baby must be set free!"

Dink looked over to the tower, so easily brought down by the Coatus, and shuddered. "Forget the fucking Coatus. Look at what the beast just did! Let's go see if we can help the poor man out."

"It wasn't her, it was Stoneburner!"

The white-pebbled road looked as if it was painted red around the tower, and Kylan fell back to her knees when she saw the Tollman squashed underneath the grey bricks.

"What's the matter, girl, you've never seen brains before?" Dink laughed sadistically as Kylan began to dry-heave. "Come on, let's get these bricks off of him and see if the bastard's got any loot."

Piece by piece, they pulled off the broken bricks until they were rewarded by the sight of the skinny Tollman's long twig of a nose snapped and his head completely caved in.

"Come on," Dink said as he struggled to get a large brick off the man's torso. Kylan grabbed a hold of the other side and saw bits of brain and skull stuck to the end. She stopped trying to help, grabbed her stomach, and this time her heaving wasn't dry.

Dink was able to flip the brick over himself, revealing the Tollman's body broken in two. He reached into the corpse's breeches and pulled out a small burlap sack and opened it. "Fuck yes," Dink yelled as he pulled out a handful of gold and silver coins. "Let's get the fuck out of here. The King's Law will be here soon." He stuffed the sack into his leather pack and began to walk east off Dearborn Road into the brush of scattered rocks and fallen trees.

"Where-- where are we going now?" Kylan asked as she followed him, wiping her mouth clean.

Dink stepped over a thorny vine and slipped under a fallen tree that was being held up by a strong boulder. "You were right before; too many fucking eyes on the path. We're going to the swamp."

"The swamp?"

"Craven's Bog, girl. The only place dirtier than Yatorga." Dink spat and stepped into a bush. "Ah, watch that bush, there's thorns there too," he said as he pulled his grey robe free.

Kylan hopped over the bush and hurried until she was walking stride for stride with Dink. "But you said--"

"I know what I fucking said," Dink fired back. "I said it! But if my choice is going to jail for murder and wading through shit, bring me a fucking paddle."

They continued through the brush until they were on the edge of a rotten-smelling swamp, its water a swirl of murky brown and moldy green. Dink slid into the water and reached out his hand to help Kylan down. "Come on in, the water's fine!" he laughed as he swatted at the flies buzzing around him. Kylan jumped in and felt her boots stick to the muddy bottom as if it was quicksand.

Tall, leafless trees hung over the edge of the swamp, their branches like hands trying to grab those who ventured too close to either side. The air was sticky, and the fog that swarmed around them was thick enough to cut with a knife and spread over a chunk of bread, but they continued on.

"So, what's your plan?" Kylan asked as she struggled to lift her feet through the waist-high muck.

"We get the fuck through here and sneak into Reliss through the eastern gate. Shouldn't be too hard if you keep up." Dink felt his boot loosen and stomped it back into place.

"Seems like you're having a bit of trouble yourself," Kylan giggled. She looked to the right side of the swamp and noticed a small, run-down hut. The sides of it were made of sliced tree trunks, and the roof was bark and mud. There was no door, so Kylan was able to peer inside and see that it was abandoned. "Wonder who lives there."

"Probably some stinking old fucking hermit," Dink scoffed. Once again, he felt his shoe loosen in the mud, except this time, when he went to kick it back into place, it fell off, forcing him to reach into the water. "I can't fucking reach it," he said as he tried to find it without dunking his head under the swamp. Finally, he conceded and disappeared into the murk. When he came back up, his was face covered in mysteriously-shaped and colored scraps, and brown water dripped from his ginger beard. He looked at Kylan victoriously, but her gaze was stuck on something ahead. "What's a'matter?" Dink asked.

Kylan took a step to Dink, shaking with fear. "Eyes."

"Who's fucking watching us?" Dink pulled out his dagger.

"Not who. What." She pointed to a pair of yellow eyes staring at them through the trees.

"Oh, what the f--"

A Smiladon jumped out of the darkness, cut through the mist, and leaped into the swamp. The cat was enormous but just seemed like a blur of yellow that tackled Dink into the water. Back and forth they wrestled, with the beast clearly winning as it pinned the porky man beneath the water. Bubbles began to rush up from the bottom fast at first, but they steadily slowed as Dink's life was being taken from him. The Smiladon opened up its mouth of sharp teeth and aimed to dig one of its fangs deep into Dink's neck when Kylan yelled out. For the instant that the cat was distracted, Dink was able to push himself out of the water and drive his dagger right into its chin and let it fall limp into the bog. He stood up panting.

"You see? That's how it's fucking done! I need a drink after that one."

With a splash, the Smiladon rose again, knocking the blade from Dink's hand, blood spurting from its jaw as it went in for the kill when it fell back down, dead.

"I knew I fucking killed it!"

"Um, not quite." Kylan pointed to a long, feathered arrow that was lodged deep in the Smiladon's skull.

"What were you trying to do, show your friend how to not kill something?" a voice cried out from behind them.

They turned around to see a woman standing on top of the hut they had passed before, a wooden bow with red jewels encrusted in it firmly in her grip. She jumped down from the roof, rolled before she got to the ground, and jumped back up to her feet.

"Are you two hurt?"

"We're alright!" Kylan yelled back. "Good shot!" She smiled back at the woman. Dink began to pull the Smiladon to the side of the swamp to take anything he could from the beast.

The woman walked over and reached out a hand to help Kylan up out of the swamp. "You sure you're okay, love?" Her accent was like nothing Kylan had ever heard -- the Us were short and the Os were long. "How about you, big boy? Need any help?" She had a thin face with fair skin and brown doe eyes. While her hair was black and fell only to her chin, she had bangs that came together to form one longer strand that was down to her chest and dyed a fire red. "I'm Cyleena Manarusturo, but you both may call me Manx." Manx wore a leather vest dyed green with matching leggings, a thick belt that had a number of trinkets attached to it, and light grey slippers with iron buckles on their sides.

Dink shook his head. "I'm fine, thank you, Manx."

Kylan beamed at the woman, who was around eighteen years old. "I'm Kylan and that's Di--"

"Would you shut the fuck up?!" Dink yelled as he found his dagger and began to cut open the Smiladon.

Manx chuckled. "Relax, I'm not the King's Law!"

"I fucking know that!" Dink began to gut and skin the cat.

The woman strolled over to him and grabbed a hold of her arrow that was wedged the Smiladon's skull. "These things are hard to make!" She pulled on the shaft, dipped the bloody end in the swamp water, and threw it into the quiver behind her back. "Good as new!" Manx furrowed her brow when she looked down at Dink. "What the hell are you doing?"

Dink was butchering the cat and placing the slimy cuts of meat into his leather pack. "What's it fucking look like?" he snickered.

"It looks like you're trying to die on the road. Can't you feel how hot it is out? That meat won't stay!"

Dink ignored her and looked over to Kylan. "Come here for a sec!" he called out.

"Fine, don't say I didn't warn you!" Manx jumped onto a boulder and pulled out a stick from her quiver, a knife from her belt, and began to carve out an arrow.

When Kylan crouched down to talk to Dink, he was removing the cat's teeth. "Don't look at her," he whispered. "I know bitches like her; she's a nomad."

"A nomad?" Kylan asked, trying to keep her eyes away from both Manx and the dead Smiladon.

"Shhh," Dink whispered. "She's going to try to kill us and take our gold."

Kylan stood up. "What? No way! She saved our lives!"

"That's how these people do things. They make you think they can be trusted but then they put a fucking arrow through your heart. Well, not me!"

"So, what's your plan?" Kylan asked as she watched Dink skin the cat.

Dink folded up the pelt and stuffed it in the pack. "I'll kill her before she has the chance to do anything." He stood up.

"What'd you skin the cat for?" Manx asked as she hopped off the tree, her bow now behind her back with the quiver.

"Fucking wear it." Dink laughed at the question.

Manx began to crack up. "You're going to wear the pelt of a beast you didn't kill?"

"I pretty much killed it!" Dink fired back.

"Manx killed it, and you know it! She saved our lives," Kylan chimed in.

"The girl's smart." Manx smiled at Kylan. "Come on." She walked towards her hut. "Let's eat something before you two go. I don't particularly care about you--" She looked at Dink. "--but I don't want this girl getting sick eating spoiled Smiladon meat."

The hut was one large room with a feather sack in the corner -- which could only be seen as a bed -- a table in the middle with a long white arrow on top of it, and a few sacks of dried meat near the entrance. Although the floor was soil, and the walls were caked with mud, the abode smelled surprising sweet, as if it were scented with some sort of flowery oils.

Manx noticed Kylan eyeing the arrow when they entered. "You like that?" She picked up the arrow, which was as tall as she. "Ghordaan steel tip, Tantae horn shaft, with a feather from Akupara at the end. This is a masterpiece, if I do say so myself." She lifted her bow from around her body, loaded it, aimed it out the entrance, then placed them both onto the wooden table. "Here," Manx said as she walked over and picked up the sack by the door. "It's not much, but the beef is good, and all the way from Xxafulok."

"How the fuck did you get beef from Gojii?" Dink scowled.

Manx grinned. "Don't you worry about that, big boy." She grabbed a slice of beef, bit into it, then dropped the bag into Kylan's arms.

When her back was turned to him, Dink pulled out his dagger and crept up behind her.

"I have no idea what you think you're doing, but you should stop while you're slightly behind," she said as she faced Dink. "I save your life and bring you to my home, and you're going to kill me? For what, being too hospitable?"

"You're a fucking nomad," Dink screamed.

Manx shrugged. "Yeah, and?"

Dink's frustration finally spilled out from his mouth. "You're going to kill and rob us!"

"Oh, yeah, I really want your spoiled Smiladon meat. You caught me," she scoffed.

When Dink charged at her with his dagger, Manx looked as calm as the sea. As he reached back to thrust his blade into her chest, she ducked and with both her hands pushed him, sending him back into the opposite wall. From there she somersaulted across her floor, snatched her bow, and with a *THWACK!* loosed the long arrow, landing the tip through his hand, pinning him to the wall.

GOJII: LEEFSIDE

"Water," the old man cried into a wall of darkness. "Please," he continued as he struggled to his feet. "I just need a sip, I--I can't breathe!" As the man limped to what he believed to be the front of his cell, he smashed into the tiny chamber pot left for him to relieve himself and fell forward, smashing his face into the cold iron bars that held him captive. When he pulled himself up, the smell of shit filled his nose and he began to sob uncontrollably. "I'm an innocent man! I'm inn--"

"Would you shut that hole in your face?" a voice answered. Whether it was real or in the man's head, he couldn't tell, but there were many things that the butcher was unable to distinguish in his cage. Was it day or night? How long had he been in this shit-filled hole? Were his eyes open or closed?

"Who--Who's there?" the butcher called out, and a lantern flickered on, blinding him for a moment. When his eyes refocused, a tiny young man stood in front in him, plainly dressed in a leafy green doublet and matching breeches, wearing an obvious smirk.

"Look at you, old man, crying like a bitch, covered in your own shit." The guard let out a high-pitched laugh as if he expected others to join in.

"I'm telling you, I'm--"

"Innocent. I know, you've been yelling it out for a fortnight, trust me, we've heard. And no one believes you." The guard grabbed at a pair of rusted shackles from a peg on the stone wall and replaced them with the lantern. When he pulled out the brass-colored key from his breeches, his eyes met the old butcher's. "If you try to escape, I'll cut your dick off, shove it in sausage casing, and force you to eat it."

The old butcher tried to spit onto the ground at the guard's jape, but his mouth was too dry to produce anything but a sound. For a moment, the prisoner saw a chance to escape when the cell was first opened, but then what would he do? Even if he made it outside of the prison, he'd be an outlaw, and the King's Law would surely find him.

When the rusted shackles were fitted tightly around the old man's wrists, the guard shoved him out of the cell and grabbed the lantern hanging on the wall. "You know, old man, you did it right," the tiny guard said as he directed his prisoner up a flight of dusty stone steps. "If you're going to commit a crime punishable by death, you might as well do it when you're an old bag of bones who's going to die soon anyway, right?"

At the top of the stairs, the exit gleamed, and for the first time in days, the old butcher felt the morning sun's embrace. Just as the man felt the wind brush against his face, two guards armored in steel grabbed him, one in each arm, and escorted him through the village. The prison was on the western side of town, so when they passed the Leefside Butcher, the old man began to cry once again. Each of the silent guards showed no signs of sympathy, their faces hidden by their iron helms, while the tiny guard couldn't help but laugh at the man's misery.

"Don't worry, we'll burn the place down once we're done cutting off your head. Ain't that right, fellas?" Neither one of the armored guards answered but continued on as if the tiny guard was nothing more than a hound nipping at their heels.

The old man was almost relieved when they reached the northern part of Leefside. There was nothing more embarrassing than being dragged through the town in which you've made a livelihood for a half a century covered in your own shit to be brought before the Mayor for sentencing, and during that moment, the prospect of a beheading didn't seem so bad. If Mayor Emerick did indeed decide to remove his head, at least the butcher would be relieved of the financial hole that his shop had dug over the past few seasons, a burden that plagued his mind and caused many sleepless nights.

Mayor Emerick's office was positioned in the center of the north side of Leefside, so as to be the first building seen when entering through the Sycamour Gate. Rounded green shrubs stood in lines down both the back and sides of the office but broke apart for a beige granite walkway that led to the archway door. Both of the guards grunted as they pushed the cinnamon-colored door open, leading to a hall that was significantly too decorated for its size. While the tiny guard didn't follow the rest of the party inside, he made sure that the old butcher remembered him with a swift kick to the back of the calf. A rich red carpet led the way through a forest of old battle-worn armor to a small green door with a brass knob.

While the hall that led to Mayor Emerick's chamber was brightly lit with candles and lanterns evenly spread down the corridor, the room itself was not, with barely enough light to study the lines on someone's face, let alone read a document. There was a long table of rich mahogany which was expertly crafted by the Carpenters on the east side of town but hadn't been cleaned in quite some time, judging by the thin layer of dust that covered it. Heavy trunks were on each side of the table, and a tiny bar was situated in the back corner which had way too many bottles for a place of court.

The Mayor of Leafside sat at the far end of the table and watched as his two guards brought the old butcher before him. He was an average-sized man dressed in a light green tunic with brown sleeves that had leather lacing down the sides, which matched the front of the garment. A slight belly had grown with age, as well as thick, smoky-gray mutton chops, as opposed to the once lustrous blond ones he had as a younger man.

Emerick Callowat had been the Mayor of Leefside for close to a half-decade now, after he received the title from Lirum Rhygell, Baron of the west, for his capture of the pirate Traetark the Blind during his time as a member of the King's Law. The Mayor always ruled with strict justice and was often considered a tad harsh with his sentencing, but because of that, Leefside boasted one of the lowest crime rates in the west.

Once, after his son Atrius had mysteriously left Leefside, a messenger came to him with a tale that the boy had died somewhere in the south, and Emerick had his tongue removed before he was beheaded so that he couldn't "spread that filth to the worms in the hole he'll be buried in." However, after a few months of unsuccessful searches for his son through Gojii, Aleru, and Forbath, the Mayor had changed, oftentimes letting fits of depression take over him. Emerick would still revert back to his old ways after drinking benders that typically lasted days, but even then the townspeople knew he was releasing his pent-up internal rage.

"Adley Roundtree, it's a shame to see you here like this," Mayor Emerick said, his words slurring together in a bourbon-induced accent.

Roundtree's puffy eyes met the Mayor's, and he did his best to harden them. "My Lord, please." The old Butcher's raspy voiced struggled to squeak out of his mouth. "I'm an innocent man. I never even saw that Trap boy from Xxafulok; how could I have taken his life?" His hands shook as he brought them up to his forehead, the rusty shackles clinking anxiously.

A small smile crept out of Emerick's pug-like jowls. "How has the shop been, before all--" His nose twitched once he smelled Adley. "What on Trilon is that smell?"

"My Lord, I--I tripped over the chamber pot and--"

Mayor Emerick looked back and forth to his guards, who stood on either side of the old butcher. "Why does he smell like shit?"

"My Lord--" one of the guards stuttered through the visor of his helm.

"How many fucking times do I need to hear 'My Lord' before I get an answer? Why does he smell like shit?" Callowat smashed his fist down onto the table.

The second guard lifted his visor, revealing a rough red face. "It wasn't us, Mayor Emerick. Blame Sermi, he brought him to us like this."

Emerick stood to his feet. "Is this true?" His eyes darted to the other guard, who was still too afraid to lift his visor. He nodded, clearly willing to agree with whatever would keep him out of trouble with the Mayor.

"Then I want you both to leave, find Sermi Blackwood, and remove his head."

The red-faced guard's mouth opened for a second before he found his voice. "My Lord?" he asked as if he misheard Callowat.

"I know I didn't stutter. Leave here, bring me the head of whoever made my office smell like a pot of shit, and if you don't, I'll have both of yours on spikes at the top of the Sycamour Gate!" Without another word, the two guards left, leaving the Mayor alone with Adley Roundtree.

Emerick stumbled over to the bar and splashed a goblet with dark bourbon and took a swig. "How has the shop been, before all of this?"

Roundtree's frown was so long that even his great beard couldn't hide it. "I know what it looks like. Business has been spiraling down for the past two springs."

Emerick's eyes widened as he examined Adley, who had always been a chunky man but visibly lost some of his fat after a fortnight in the dungeons. "Meat in the west has certainly tasted better; most butchers in Leefside's surrounding villages have been buying theirs from Aleru for quite some time."

"The ones who could afford it," Roundtree snapped back, half to himself.

The Mayor filled a warped and unevenly-carved wooden cup with water and, placing it onto the table, slid it down to Adley, who caught it despite the fact that his hands were still bound. As he gulped down the water, letting some of it wash over his shit-stained beard, Emerick made his way back to his seat. "Xxafulok sells their meat for much cheaper, though, and theirs is imported from Aleru. The ones who can't afford the trip to the east on their own can still reap one of the land's benefits. Did you know that the Trap boy who was murdered was Mason Stillwell's apprentice?"

"Aye, I did," Adley confessed.

Emerick leaned back in his chair. "So, you knew the boy was coming from Xxafulok then?"

"I did, my Lord. I was waiting for the damned shipment from him and was planning on spending almost all my savings to try and save the shop, or at least try to clear some of its debt. An old man should be able to die in his bed with a belly full of food and wine instead of headless in front of an audience."

The Mayor scoffed at that. "A desperate man is a dangerous one." He scratched at one of his mutton chops and bits of grey hairs fell onto his wool breeches. "I'm going to be honest with you, *old man*. I informed Lord Lirum that the boy's death was a suicide, who in turn passed on that message to the Crown, but the truth is obvious. The last thing this town needs is extra eyes to scare the villagers into doing something rebellious, so I'm fully taking matters into my own hands."

"You're making a mistake! You have to listen to me!" For the first time during their conversation, the old butcher raised his voice loud enough to take control. "I was knocked out the morning of the boy's death, and when I came to, members of the King's Law were dragging me out of my shop as a prisoner!"

Throwing his head back with a hooting laughter made Emerick's jowls jiggle. "I've heard this tale! You really expect me to believe it?"

Adley scowled. "Aye. You haven't heard the entire tale, though."

"Go ahead, old man, see if you can be the first criminal to convince me of his innocence." Emerick spoke with a sarcastic tone as if he was appeasing Roundtree.

"My Lord," Roundtree started, "I was knocked out by a man in a doublet that was way too fancy to have lived around here. While I didn't realize it at first, the darkness of my cell sparked a memory from that day."

Mayor Emerick sat back up in his chair, and Adley was able to smell the bourbon on his breath from across the table. "Which is?"

The old butcher twisted his wrists back and forth, which had both gone numb from the shackles. "His yellow eyes."

"So you're saying--"

"The murderer is a time stealer!"

Emerick stood once again to take a drink of bourbon, this time straight from the bottle. "That's a bold statement right there, but like I said, a desperate man--"

"You could kill me if you must, but Leefside is now facing a much larger problem than a simple murder of a butcher's apprentice! Time stealers will take out every mortal man, woman, and child, until they rule all of Gojii! We can't attack the Ylewood because of the Moiiralatta, but they can come and go from our lands as they please!"

Draining the bottle and slamming it down, Callowat let out a cough before wiping his mouth with the back of his hand. "That's enough. I'll take you back to your cell now."

After bringing the old butcher back to his cell and commanding the new guard on duty to get his prisoner a change of clothing, Emerick's curiosity began to percolate, and he decided to venture to the south side of town to investigate on his own.

His arrival to the residential area of town was met with smiles and bows from the villagers coming and going from their humble brick houses. All of the abodes seemed to be identical, with the same red bricks and green roofs and nothing but brass numbers on their wooden doors to differentiate them. The sky was a comfortable blue, with soft clouds spaced out just enough to let the sun shine down on the western town, which almost inspired Mayor Emerick to smile for the first time in half a year.

"Good day, my Lord," a voice called from on top of a roof. The man, Opoku Darkwa, was balancing himself on the almost-complete cobblestone roofing of his house, a renovation that he had been working on for quite some time. At first, when the man asked if he could reconstruct his roof, Mayor Emerick was wary and thought it would open a can of worms to the rest of the villagers. But now, after seeing all the identical brown shackled roofs, Darkwa's cobblestone project was a welcome change.

Opoku climbed down a makeshift wooden ladder held together at the rungs with twine to greet his Mayor. The man was tall, black-skinned, and burly, with a gigantic stomach that seemed hard as stone. His roughspun tunic was filled with patches and tears, but he stood before Emerick with his chest out as if he was dressed in a surcoat made of the finest silk Hillrode had to offer. Darkwa's dark hair was short with a small bald spot opening from the top, and his beard was closely shaven, covering his square jaw. He held out an oven mitt-sized hand that was filled with scabs, calluses, and blisters. Emerick hesitantly shook it, not wanting to get too close so the man could smell his breath.

Emerick looked up at Darkwa's roof and let out a small burp. "The roof certainly looks nice. Excellent work, Opoku."

"Thank you. It's coming along. I didn't realize that cutting the stone would be such a pain in the balls..."

Whether it was the alcohol that was clouding his mind or the fact that this common villager didn't shake when he spoke to him, Emerick laughed as if he never had before. "Well, you seem up for the task! Tell me, my good man, what do you do for work?"

Opoku looked down at his age-worn boots. "Nothing now, my Lord. I was down south for a year in Yatorga working as a fisherman, but after the Coatus attack, I came back to Leefside to be with my wife. Our children are at The Mind training to become Saiges, so I was trying to make as much gold as I could to pay for their education. There was nothing to do there but dig for boros after the Coatus ruined the city, and that wouldn't even buy a pint at any inn. It's still so hard to believe that King Tanwill would attack Forbath, though. Some say he was trying to kill the Shadows, but I think he's gone mad."

Emerick patted Darkwa on the back, trying to comfort him. While he didn't want to comment on the affairs of the

King with a common villager, the man did have a point. "And your wife, does she work?"

Spitting on the ground, Opoku's eyes narrowed with anger. "She does, but her profession is too embarrassing for me to admit. I'm sure you understand."

Emerick nodded, not wanting to push the issue, even though he thought to himself that the information would be worth pursuing in the future, even if only to see if the woman was committing any crimes. "Come with me, Opoku, I need to check on something."

The dark-skinned man followed, casting a giant shadow over Emerick. They continued through the rows of houses as many nosy men and women watched them walk towards the southern Gate.

"May I ask you something, my Lord?" Darkwa asked, stepping up to walk next to Emerick.

"You may," Emerick said, faking a smile but knowing he would regret his answer.

Opoku inhaled deep and shrugged his shoulders up for a few seconds then back down. "Do you believe that Trilon is in danger of repeating history?"

"In what way do you mean?" Callowat never liked answering a question with another question, but he didn't want to say the wrong thing.

Both men slowed their pace as they spoke. "Do you remember the firestorms that *they* used to cast? To this day, I can't take a deep breath without tasting the black smoke from *my* village. The drops of burning flames would explode upon impact and multiply, burning anything they would touch, until there was nothing left but a graveyard of bones and ash."

"Of course, I do, friend, but all of the Oracles were banished." Emerick hoped that would end the conversation.

Opoku, on the other hand, chose to dig deeper. "King Tanwill now has a Coatus, which many southerners have given the name 'Reaper'. He was bred to attack enemies of the Crown. Doesn't that seem like too much power for any man?"

Mayor Emerick was at a loss for words. "I have heard of this Coatus and believe in King Tanwill's strategy. Those who practice magic have an unfair advantage on the vast majority of Trilon, and this will be a way to dispose of them." He was angered by this conversation and the disrespect a lowly commoner could show for his good friend.

"You're right. I suppose I'm just scarred by the Oracle attacks."

Emerick faked another smile. "We all are, my friend. Scars that can't be seen often take the most time to heal. "

When the path on which the men walked ended, they stood in front of the southern Gate, which was completely unguarded. As the Mayor flung open the faded wooden door to the tower on the left, the smell of dust and mildew punched him in the face, causing him to gag and almost throw up his bourbon. There was a small table in the room, a homemade fireplace filled with black logs, and a number of empty wine barrels. Emerick kicked over the barrels in anger, causing them to topple down on one another, and proceeded up the winding staircase. A crossbow and several dozen arrows leaned against the grey stone wall of the top floor, which could hold one man at a time.

"M'lord? Should I come up?" Opoku called up the stairs, but Emerick ignored him. Instead, he loaded the crossbow and aimed it out the window towards the path which led to the Ylewood.

A number of trees were on either side of the path, their healthy leaves inviting to the eye, as he followed it until he couldn't see anything but a green blur. Emerick fired the crossbow out into the distance then threw it down to the floor in anger.

Without another word, the Mayor ran down the steps and, brushing past Darkwa, kicked open the door to go back outside. The southern Gate itself was rusted and seemed like, if an attack party had enough members, it could be knocked down with force. Both of the towers were covered in dirt, moss, and age marks. If a part of either tower wasn't covered in some sort of earthly stain, it was because the bricks were missing, the holes giving them a strange resemblance to a honeycomb. Emerick ran his hands over one tower and then the other. Grabbing at the craters and tracing the cracks with his pointer finger, he bent over to throw up, turning the dirt path into mud.

"M'lord..." Opoku rushed over, but Emerick stuck out his hand, signaling to not come any further.

He wiped the puke from the corners of his mouth, cleaned his hands with his breeches, then stood up straight. "We must prepare for Lord Brannon Broadwine's arrival. Unlike our enemy, time is not on our side."

FORBATH: CRAVEN'S BOG

The Smiladon steak roasted over the open fire as droplets
of grease trickled from it like rain at the beginning of a
storm, each drop causing embers to fly up into the misty air,
only to be extinguished by the damp grounds or the swampy
waters of Craven's Bog. The flames were strong and even,
thanks to Manx, who had started it with a number of
matches, which she claimed she stole from a tiny town in the
west.

Dink and Kylan sat on two rocks placed around the fire,
which some would say was dangerously close to their host's
hut. The nomad, however, insisted that she cooked her food
in this spot almost every night and that there was no need to
worry. Manx strolled out of her abode clad in a stolen
leather jerkin that had a number of straps held together with
brass clasps, and a tight pair of black leggings. She sat down
on a square-shaped rock next to Kylan and began to weave
together a thick spool of grey yarn without a word, as if she
were alone.

Dink reached down to the ground and pulled a crooked
stick from the mud. "We gotta flip it over. The top is as pink
as a baby's ass," he said, poking at the spit that held the meat
over the flame.

"First time cooking?" Manx laughed as she stood up. The
young woman's body was hard, her arms slim, but her
athletic build was accented with curves which she chose to
highlight with tightly-fit clothing. She grabbed ahold of the
end of the spit and flipped over the steak. When the top of
the meat was grabbed by the flame's fingers, the sizzle made
Kylan's mouth water.

Kylan, who had witnessed more than one fight break out between her other two companions, always noticed that, when Dink was arguing, his eyes always started at Manx's doe eyes but eventually floated down to her bosom or legs. Even after what happened when they first encountered the nomad, Kylan had to admit that she felt much more comfortable with Manx than she ever did with Dink. Firstly, she didn't have to wear the itchy tunic buttoned up to her chin to hide the fact that she was a girl. The woman had given Kylan the green vest she wore the day she saved their lives, as well as a pair of leggings that were a little on the baggy side but still snug enough that she didn't need a belt. Secondly, Manx was the first woman she had seen since arriving in Yatorga that wasn't a whore.

"I've been cooking meat since before your father squirted you into your back alley gypsy of a mother," Dink yelled back. Pushing down on the spit with both her hands, Manx sent embers up to land in Dink's bushy beard. "What the fuck?" He patted out the fire kisses that landed in his ginger beard, which was looking a bit more grey since his journey to Reliss with Kylan began. Unfortunately for the man, danger's reaction took over, and he went to put out the flames that were crawling up his face like men scaling a mountain with his right hand, which was heavily bandaged with different-colored leaves and a mud-based paste. "Aaahhooow!" Dink grabbed ahold of his injured hand as if pressure would stop the pain from the hole in his palm. It didn't.

Manx's smile was clean and white, but her smirk made her look sly, like she was always up to no good. "Don't ever say a thing about my family. I would think that the hole in your hand is enough of a reminder that I'm the wrong person to mess with." Her voice snapped like a whip. "And don't touch it! You'll start the bleeding again. You already stained my wall."

"Your *wall*? Your wall is made of sticks and shit. I'm a cripple now!"

The nomad walked into her hut without a word and returned with a large wheel of cheese. "Better to be a cripple than dead, no?" For three days, Manx had hosted Kylan and Dink, even though the latter had tried to kill her out of paranoia. They feasted on her dried meats, but Dink had finished off the sack when the two girls went to sleep the second night. He claimed that it wasn't him, that the fever from his injury caused him to "sleep-eat", but neither Kylan or Manx believed that. "From the looks of it, you must sleep-eat every night!" Manx's voice was as a stab from a sword when she spoke to Dink but a soft motherly embrace when she conversed with Kylan. Finally, guilt took over Dink, and he offered to cook up the Smiladon he had slayed. This, of course, sparked the recurring fight as to who killed the beast, but Kylan yelled and told them that knowing who killed it wouldn't fill their stomachs.

When the meat was cooked, and as the three rebels waited for it to cool down, Manx grabbed Dink's knife from his pocket, wiped it on her pants, and began to cut the cheese, giving Kylan the first piece. Kylan ate her wedge of the yellow cheese in two bites, her eyes closed in ecstasy as the flavors danced on her tongue. Next, the nomad cut herself a slice that was smaller than Kylan's, which she took her time to chew. Dink's impatience boiled over as he stood up, snatched his knife with his injured hand, and, biting his lip in agony, cut himself a wedge thicker than the other two combined. His first bite was the most pleasure he had felt since Yatorga was destroyed, the cheese tasting as sharp as the arrow that shot through his hand.

"I'd slit King Tanwill's throat for a stein of ale." Dink leaned back on his rock, bits of cheese flying out of his mouth and into the flames.

Manx laughed. "You and me both. Maybe we'll get our chance."

Dink shook his head. "We're not going to kill the King." He took another bite of cheese and this time savored each chew.

"Then why are you two going to Reliss? I thought your plan was to take him out before he could command any more cities to burn."

Kylan stared at the meat. The charred skin was the most beautiful thing her eyes had ever feasted upon. "It's not the King who's doing this; it's Master Stoneburner. He's the one destroying the south. We had no idea that this was his plan."

Manx furrowed her brow. "We?"

The fire caused Kylan to sweat, and she brushed away a strand of her auburn hair that stuck to her forehead. "I was in the Trainer's Guild before Master Stoneburner set the Coatus free, killed most of my fellow trainees, and claimed the south for his own to destroy."

"Well, someone has to do something. Who knows how many lives have been taken?" Manx spat. "Tanwill's entire reasoning for banishing King Zabkar and his armies of Oracles was because of their slaughtering of the so-called innocent."

Dink frowned. "*King* Zabkar? 'So-called innocent'? You really are a treasonist bitch, aren't you?"

"Oh, Tanwill is so much better?! He allowed someone to steal a creature the size of a small city and use it as a weapon. Who knows, maybe *he* ordered *your* Master to destroy Trilon bit by bit. Was King Zabkar overly stern at times? Yes, but at least he didn't hide his agenda. How often do you even hear a course of action from *your* precious King?"

"King Tanwill could be dead for all we know." Kylan spoke softly, but both Dink and Manx stopped their clamoring as if she screamed over them.

Dink rose, grabbed a long pointy stick, broke it into three parts, and, keeping one for himself, handed the other two to Manx and Kylan. "What makes ya think the King is dead?"

Kylan looked up to Dink. "The Trainer's Guild would meet with the King and his Council once a month, so to see our progress. We would use the Coatus horns to call them, make a run, and even show the growth of the baby Coatus. King Tanwill didn't come to the last meeting, though; only his Lead Confidant, Lord Brannon Broadwine." The fire was now dying, as there was nothing to keep it going. Still, under the brush of a splintered stick, a single flame was gasping for help. "The next morning, Master Stoneburner was missing. He must have--"

"Flew that black demon over to my city," Dink interrupted her. "Luckily, Graybill was hosting a meeting at the Swine when Yatorga was attacked. He saved way more lives that day than that fucking bone-chewer of a Mayor who abandoned us at our time of need."

Grabbing the spit and taking the steaming Smiladon meat off the fire pit, Dink chopped it into three sections on the rock where he sat and stabbed an end piece with his pointed stick. Once he was done preparing his meal, he sat on the ground, while Manx and Kylan used their sticks to pick up their shares. It took Kylan a few tries to get the pointed end through the tough flesh, but once she did, the only thing that could stop her from drooling was to take a bite. The company sat in silence while they enjoyed their meat, Manx being the first to finish. Dink and Kylan, on the other hand, were determined to eat every morsel, whether it be meat or gristle.

Leaning back on the rock, Kylan took off her boots, exposing her blistered and cracked feet. The swamp in front of them was haunting, its waters a little too calm, even for a bog. The trees were all dead, most of them drooped over, but some surrendered all their strength to the ground. She threw the greasy stick into the swamp and watched as a ripple opened, giving the water some life. "So why is it called Craven's Bog?" she asked.

Manx had once again resumed her yarn weaving. "It's a horrible name," she answered as she shook the long strand of red hair out of her eye. "A name that those who feared King Zabkar created to further insult his greatness. This was his fortress during the taking of Reliss."

"That's right," Dink chimed in. "He let his band of Oracles and Shadows do all the fighting for him!"

Kylan met Dink's eyes. "Shadows?" Dink shook his head, signaling Kylan not to say anything more. "It does sound like he was a coward, though."

"King Zabar was not a fighter, that is well known, but obviously Tanwill agreed with his strategy, as he still rules Trilon as the only King!" Manx said, her teeth clenched together. "Before Zabkar took over Reliss, three Kings controlled Trilon." Manx continued, giving Kylan the other side of story for the first time. "Inwar had no desire to be the King of the south but instead saw an opportunity to seize control of every realm."

"With the help of magic," Dink added. "First, Zabkar went to the Tsumari, a race of fire barbarians located on a tiny island off of Forbath, Ofrea, with his proposition."

"Don't you call them barbarians, you scumbag." Manx's eyes narrowed in anger. "While they believed in his cause, the Tsumari could not justify fighting with their population just above endangerment, even though their hatred for mortals was documented by every Saige in every realm. The

117

Oracles, on the other hand, were very willing to fight, after Zabkar gave them permission to do as they pleased once he took his throne as King of Trilon.

"After the Oracles were able to form an alliance with the Shadows, their preliminary meetings were held in Yatorga, which at the time was a busy city -- it was hard for the Law to keep track of anyone, let alone a group of unknown rebels. Being a paranoid man, Zabkar demanded that, when they carried out their attack on the King of the south, Celux Abale, he would be protected in a sanctuary that was guarded by a force stronger than steel. He had created a long list of enemies along the way to becoming a man of power, which included the Verrativas, who, although they had magic in their blood, were still attacked by Inwar and his followers. I never agreed with his views on the Verrativa race, but *my* King wanted to live and rule forever." Manx stared into the fire's last gasp and let out a deep sigh when it finally died.

"Led by the council of the two most powerful Oracles, Cellyadure and Syrah the Creator, Zabkar found the abandoned bog to hold refuge. Syrah created the secret passages, the most important being the one from the swamp to Reliss, while Cellyadure spoke a number of enchantments that protected it from all magical attacks. Inwar stayed there while his armies stormed Reliss, and when the battle was finally won and his forces returned with Abale's head, he claimed Reliss as the Kingdom of Trilon."

"Don't forget that he had Tidas Rhygell and Deryk Staley assassinated!" Dink said, waving both his hands as if Kylan and Manx had forgotten he was there. "Zabkar didn't want to deal with no Kings of the east or west. Though, I guess you're right, nomad. King Tanwill named Lirum Rhygell and Xalvadore Corwin his Barons."

Manx didn't respond to Dink but gave a nod of acknowledgement. "Years later, when Tanwill Embray took

Reliss, his forces located Inwar hiding in the swamp, and after banishing him and his armies to Soarfrost, named the area Craven's Bog."

An awkward silence fell over the company, and Kylan felt a cold shiver creep up her back -- one that she hadn't felt since she lived in Everlid.

"Enough of the fucking story time! How do we get through here, nomad?" Dink growled as he grabbed his pack and flung it over his back. A blanket of darkness had hidden all the stars in the sky, and Dink determined there would be no better time to travel.

Manx smiled. "Well, that depends."

"On what?"

"Tell me why you're going to Reliss!"

Dink ignored the nomad and instead nudged Kylan. "Open your pack, girl, take out anything that you don't think you'll need on the road. I mean to fill up on gold in the Capital."

Kylan opened up her tiny moleskin pack that Graybill had given her before they left Yatorga to reveal a number of women's silken smallclothes, and she began to laugh.

"What's so funny?" Dink waddled over to Kylan and his eyes widened when he saw the undergarments. "You have to be fucking me." He clapped his hands together, letting out a grunt half of anger, half of pain. "Am I the only one that didn't realize you were a girl?"

"You thought she was a boy?" Manx bursted out in laughter. "Makes you wonder how many men chewed your bone over the years, don't it?" She continued shaking her head.

Dink threw down his pack. "I'm no bone-chewer, you vile little bitch! I've never even given a man a hug."

"That you know of, at least." Kylan couldn't help but join in on the fun.

After a few minutes of Dink sulking, Kylan pulled on her boots and opened her mouth, unsure of what to say. "We're going to the Capital to steal an incubator from the Trainer's Guild," she said to Manx, waiting for Dink's next outburst.

"Oh, what the fuck," Dink roared in anger. "Did you have to tell her that? Can't you see behind her mask? She's a fucking nomad, girl!"

Manx's eyes widened in excitement. "Now why would you two need an incubator?" She began to pace around Dink and Kylan. "I heard that an egg was missing from the Guild when the Coatus fled, but the townspeople say it was crushed. Some go as far to say that they saw the unborn Coatus head on the streets near the Trainer's Tower."

"And where did you hear these rumors?" Dink asked as he scratched some meat out of his beard.

Manx went back into her hut, and instead of cheese she brought with her a strange device made of steel that held a long rope with a sharp, pointed, three-prong spear at the end in one hand, and an unlit torch in the other. "You've heard enough stories to know that a nomad never shares a secret." She strapped the steel contraption to a buckle on her belt. "And, I've heard enough to know that I'm coming with you two."

"Yes!" Kylan squealed like a pig rolling in shit.

"No. Absolutely not," Dink boomed. "Come on, girl, if we can't find a way out, we'll go back the way we came."

Kylan stood up and inched closer to Manx. "You were right three days ago. Dearborn will be swarming with the King's Law, and they'll be questioning any travelers!"

"The girl has a point, Dinky-poo." Manx put an arm around Kylan's shoulder. Dink's eyes narrowed at the two girls, and then he nodded begrudgingly. "Stick with me, I'll show you the way." The nomad stepped off the edge and into the murky swamp.

While Kylan followed close behind Manx after putting her boots back on, Dink kept his distance, muttering curses with each step and swatting at the flies that buzzed around him.

The bog water was lukewarm, like soup that had been set aside to cool for a minute too long. As they started through the sludge, the trio came upon a number of mossy overhangs, some of which were so high that the misty air covered their tops, while others were so low that Manx was able to climb onto them and hop back into the swamp without any sort of problem.

Dink, who was still a good distance away from the girls, began to pull out handfuls of muddy reeds from the water and throw them down like a frustrated child. "So where exactly are you taking us?" he yelled up to Manx.

The nomad turned around. "Oh, you'll spoil the fun," she yelled back to him. "Don't you trust me yet?"

Unlike Dink, Kylan had confidence in Manx but began to question where she was taking them when the tree branches connected on either side of the bog braided together to form a natural archway that almost completely drowned out the sun, causing the water to go cold and black. The young girl felt goosebumps rise up her thighs and forearms when she took the first step into the dark pool but was unsure if she should say anything to the nomad, who wasn't bothered in the least bit by the temperature change. As they ventured deeper through the covered area, though, the braided branches grew tighter, making it impossible to see anything.

"Manx? I can't see anything at all," Kylan said in half a whisper. She stopped walking and for the first time let out a sigh of relief when she heard Dink's heavy breathing behind her.

"What the fuck is this?" Dink said, grabbing Kylan and pulling her back towards him. "Don't go any further, girl. We're turning around right now." He pulled out his knife with his good hand and stepped in front of Kylan. "Fucking nomad!" His voice filled the tunnel, and just as it echoed back, the darkness in front of them was overpowered with a bright orange glow. Manx stood at the far end near a grey stone wall with the lit torch clenched in her hand.

"Come on," she cried out. "Hurry!"

Kylan was quicker to the command than Dink, but they both splashed on through the cold water to the stone barrier.

"Hold this!" Manx thrust the torch into Kylan's hands and placed her hands on the wall.

Kylan shined the fire on the branches above her head and realized that the channel she and Dink were so frightened of was eerily beautiful. The braided branches had an apple-red inlay on which hung many purple and blue berries that she could only assume were poisonous.

"Here, shine the light on the left side," Manx said as she studied the plain stone. Kylan brought the torch to the wall when she noticed a block of stone that was a dirty brown. "There it is," Manx muttered, and she pushed in the stone square with both her hands. She was elbow-deep into the stone when there was a loud clicking sound that ended in a fizzle.

Red and purple raindrops began to trickle down, coloring the swamp water and staining the company's clothing. When Kylan looked up, she realized that the tree branches above them were untangling themselves, and the berries were what was falling on top of them, exploding on impact.

"What's--what's happening?" she yelled out to Manx.

One by one, the trees stood up straight, and once again the sky was above them. The branches, however, didn't stay idle and began to reach down below to the swampy water. Manx stepped up onto a branch, so Kylan followed and noticed that the trees were once again braiding together underneath them.

Dink tried to jump up onto one of the branches, but his foot got caught in a knot and he toppled over onto his belly.

Dink rolled over, and Kylan gestured with her hands to help him back onto his feet, but he stood up on his own. "So, this is the different side of Oracle magic?" His eyes widened in amazement. "Strange."

"What's that?" Manx asked.

"No, nothing. I never thought they were capable of something--"

"Beautiful?" the nomad finished.

There was a dripping sound underneath their feet that was steadily becoming louder and stronger, until it sounded like a flowing stream. Manx began to walk across the braided branches to the wall, and in place of the brown stone, there was a wooden wheel.

"Let's hope I remember this." She grabbed a hold of the wheel and turned it to the right. "One to the right," Manx panted, "and two to the left." After the third turn of the wheel, she hopped over to Kylan and smiled. "Hold on, love."

When the branches began to untangle again to reveal the black that had replaced the swamp water, Kylan gulped. Thoughts raced through her head like flies on a decaying corpse. Where was the swamp? Should she try to run back? Where would this freefall of darkness lead?

Manx grabbed her arms together and brought her in for an embrace. "Stay with me! It'll be better together!"

The abyss was chasing them, hunting the trio like a Smiladon, and soon it would consume them. As the branches that they stood upon began to loosen and groan like an old man on his deathbed, Kylan tightened her grip on Manx's vest.

Dink, who was standing on a farther branch, started to back up and looked toward the exit. For a split second, he thought about running off of the tree bridge and back into the bog, but then his eyes narrowed. This was his job -- to go to the Capital, retrieve the incubator, and return to his friends. "Fuck that," Dink cried out. At that moment, he dug deep, spat in failure's face, and jumped onto the branch with his two companions, hugging them together.

The fall seemed to last minutes, but when you can't see what's around you, does time even exist? Kylan tried to yell out, but her voice was ripped from her body as if the Oracles had stolen it. When the trio finally separated mid-air, they felt the full-forced punch of ice, and they were underwater.

"Dink?!" Kylan yelled out, spitting the icy water when she took her first breath of air. "Manx?!" The girl began to vomit, unwillingly purging herself from the water that had forced its way into her stomach.

"I'm here, girl," she heard Dink's yell as he let out a wet burp. "Come towards the sound of my voice!" His beard felt like a wet rodent rubbing against her face and smelled like one too. Dink grabbed Kylan as they both frantically treaded water in the pool. "I wonder how far we fell," he said as his teeth began to chatter. "I've got to get out of this fucking water! I can't feel my hand!"

Suddenly, a pale light shone from the opposite end of the cavern. Manx stood on top of a stone platform that was held up by wooden beams, grinning at her discovery of the exit. A boulder was pushed to the side of the escape, allowing the light through, giving sight to the blind.

"You couldn't feel your hand well before this," she yelled out. "Now quit your bitching and get up here!"

While she had lost her torch during the plunge into the ice water, the light that crept out from behind the boulder seemed strong enough that it was no longer necessary. The wooden beams had a criss-cross pattern on either side, which made for an easy climb for Kylan; Dink, on the other hand, had trouble stretching his legs to step onto the beams, so he resorted to using his upper body to pull himself up between levels.

Manx reached out a hand to help Kylan up to the top, and the girl gave the nomad a hug when she stood back on solid ground.

"I did it!" Kylan smiled wide as she grabbed a handful of her auburn hair and twisted the water out of it.

"You sound surprised," Manx answered. "You can't see how strong you are, love, but your eyes will open soon enough." She glanced over to Dink, who was pushing himself up and rolling over onto the stone top. "You okay there, big boy?"

Dink huffed and puffed as he laid on his back. "My fucking hand is killing," he said as he showed the nomad his injured palm, naked, without the medicated wrap she had made back at Craven's Bog.

Grabbing his hand and bringing it close into the light from the hole showed the severity of Dink's injury. Blood and yellow puss seeped out from either side of his hand, and the edges of the puncture had grown a mossy green color.

Manx opened up her leather jerkin and tore into her undershirt, exposing her stomach. "It's infected," she admitted. "This won't help that, but we need to stop the bleeding." She wrapped the white cloth around it, which was a crusty red by the time Dink stood up.

"Fuck it," he said as he stared as his hand. "I've gotten worse from the whores in Yatorga."

Both Manx and Kylan chuckled at that, which made Dink smile.

"Come on through here!" Manx pointed to the hole in the wall that was just large enough to crawl through. Inside was dry and musty-smelling with a dirt floor that caused the trio to cough and spit every few feet as they tried to make their way back to the outside world.

"How long do we have to crawl for?" Kylan asked as she followed Manx's lead, shivering from the soaked vest that clung to her body.

"Not far at all," she answered. "In fact, …"

The tunnel had opened up so they could all stand up together, but the path had ended. Without the light, it would have seemed like a dead-end, but with it they were able to see a number of rusted iron ladder rungs leading up the pale wall.

"Slow and steady as you climb." Manx smiled as she squeezed Kylan's shoulder. "That goes double for you!" The nomad looked back to Dink before she began to climb.

Dink groaned as he stepped up behind Kylan. "How am I supposed to grab anything with my hand bleeding worse than a woman on her monthly course?!"

"Oh, you're a tough guy," Manx yelled back, the metal contraption strapped to her belt clanking against the iron rungs. "Would you rather hug us all together again?" Her laugh was full of love.

Kylan climbed the ladder slowly, making sure both of her feet were securely on each rung before advancing to the next. She felt bits of rust peel off in her hands as she made her way up and couldn't help but wonder if a rung would disintegrate if she grabbed it too tightly.

"Only a bit further," Manx called down.

Taking deep breaths with each step, Kylan repeated that phrase to herself: *Only a bit further… Only a bit further…* As she continued up, though, she felt the walls close in around her, as if they wanted to trap her, strangle her, kill her. "Manx?" The girl looked up, but the light blinded her. The warm glow that beckoned them out of the darkness had become so bright that the only thing Kylan could do was close her eyes and hope Manx was telling the truth. When she reached for a rung and felt nothing but air, she opened her eyes and realized she was no longer in a skinny, neverending shaft but instead in a wide open room. A hand grabbed at her and pulled her up off the ladder and behind a large stone pillar.

When Dink arrived, Manx grabbed him too and signaled for them to be silent. The room was round with a high glass ceiling that gave a full view of a pomegranate-colored sky. Different colored jewels of every shape and size decorated the walls, and the floor was a mint green marble speckled with bits of black. When looking at the walls, Kylan noticed that there weren't any sort of torches and was confused by where the white light was coming from. It was close to night, so the sky couldn't have created such a strong light, though there was no doubt that nature's glow could have lit the room if it were midday.

Kylan and Dink both sat with their backs against a pillar, facing the jeweled wall. Greens, blues, and yellows glimmered as the pale light ran its skinny fingers over each color, bringing them to life. The pillars were thick and wide enough so the trio could all sit next to each other and still not be seen. At first, Kylan thought they were made of bleached stone, but it was shockingly smooth to the touch. There were three altogether, and each featured their own designs etched into their inlay. The trio hid behind one that had a large eye carved in the middle, with a sun on one side of the pupil and a crescent moon on the other. The next had flames that started at the bottom and rose all the way to the top. On the opposite end, the third pillar showed a man being stabbed in the back, without anyone holding the blade behind him.

"Why do we need to be quiet?" Dink whispered to Manx, which wasn't so much a whisper but not quite a yell.

Manx scowled and gestured for him to be quiet once again. Kylan, on the other hand, sat in the middle almost holding her breath, debating whether or not to close her eyes. The nomad peered over the side of the pillar, her one long strand of fire-red hair dancing behind her, and quickly came back. "We could be in some trouble," she whispered back to her companions.

Dink shook his head in disbelief. "Come on, how fucking bad could it be?" Like Manx, he looked beyond his side of the pillar, and that was when everything came into focus. Crudely carved into the marble floor was a square that clearly wasn't created with the same precision and care as the rest of the room. Inside were a number of hooded and faceless creatures, all of them seemingly unaware that they weren't alone. Motionless, they hovered over the marble without any visible hands or feet, staring at each other as their cloaks let off a pale, ghostly white glow. There must have been close to fifty of them in the square, but not a single grunt or cough could be heard.

The trio stood up silently after Manx gave the signal. Kylan, who was still unsure of what was going on in the center of the room, felt her eyes well up when she saw the fear in both her friends' eyes. She wiped the tears away and mouthed to herself, "Only a bit further..."

"We have to find a way out right fucking now," Dink whispered as he stared at the shadowy area at the bottom of the wall. "Can you get her out?" he asked Manx. When she nodded, Dink put his hood up and pulled a dagger from his pocket. "I'll be in the shadows." With that, he stepped away from the pillar, turned towards the jeweled wall, and was gone.

There was a large oak door at the top of a grey stone staircase on the opposite end of the room, but the company was still very far away from it. Manx grabbed a hold of

Kylan and brought her ear in close. "Don't look to the center, love. We need to get to that door. Do you think you can do that?"

"I--I think I..."

Manx gave Kylan a swift shake with both her hands. "That's not the answer I want to hear. You need to do this!" Her whisper was loud enough to show Kylan the severity of the situation. It was the first time she had not spoken to the girl with any sort of endearment, which seemed to scare her more than anything. "On the count of three, run to the next pillar." Manx pushed Kylan in front of her and when she said "three" saw the girl sprint to the second column. The nomad followed shortly after, her strand of red hair slapping against the flames of the pillar as she stopped next to Kylan. "Okay, now we have to be more careful. We're going to crawl against the wall to the stairs."

Kylan was able to get to the wall as silent as a kiss, but when Manx pressed her back next to the young girl, her metal contraption crashed against a jewel, clanking like a steel bell that echoed through the room. At first, nothing happened, and the two girls thought they were safe, but then the ceiling began to boil in anger. The calm purple sky above them mixed with the rage of whatever was inside, turning it to a blood red. As the room turned from a pale white to a red tint, the creatures in the center began to moan in unison, at first in a low pitch, but it became higher and higher.

For a moment, they stood frozen against the wall, but when Dink appeared a few feet away, they frantically ran to him. Once the trio was finally together, the hooded army spoke as one, each word echoing off the walls.

"Dyson..."

The voice was a slithering snake that wanted to squeeze the life from them.

129

"Dyson Warwink…" it continued as the ceiling grew darker until it was near black. "If you thought I was gone, I am not. If you thought I forgot, I have not. You will pay. Everyone who wears the robe will pay."

With that, red drops began to trickle from the ceiling, but this time it wasn't falling berries.

As a storm opened up on the company, the ghostly figures began to shriek and looked up, drinking down the blood in bliss. Manx unhooked the metal device from her belt and aimed it towards the door. "Grab a hold of me, Dink! Kylan, jump on Dink's back," she yelled as she spat out bits of blood. She fired the device, landing the spear into the door, the long rope stretched tight. "Jump!"

When their feet left the ground, they went flying across the room, landing on the middle of the staircase, with Kylan slipping and falling over Dink's back from the sudden stop. They ran up the rest of the way, Kylan using her hands to help propel herself up quicker, and after Manx pulled out the spear from her device, they charged together through the exit and found themselves outside.

When they went to slam the door behind them, there was nothing but a large tree trunk, and while Dink and Kylan were surprised, Manx acted as if nothing was out of the ordinary.

"Where's the door? Where's the room?" Kylan stuttered.

The nomad put back together her steel device, coiling the rope and locking the spear back into place. "Oracle magic, my love," Manx said as she pulled off her red vest that was spotted with bits of green and tossed it into the brush.

Dink was trying to wipe the blood from his beard but stopped once he realized his hands were also covered and he was only adding to the mess. "Those weren't fucking Oracles!"

Manx looked at the path ahead, which wasn't so much a path but a zigzag of stones and bushes. "Of course not, but *those* weren't even alive. That was the work of a Maherang."

"A Maherang?" Kylan asked, her head swimming in a sea of blood and confusion.

The night was warm, but the entire trio shivered as if they were lost in Soarfrost. "A Maherang is a conjurer of the dead. Because it wasn't properly put to death, it was given a choice to die or become a Maherang. They conjure spirits from the underworld to release a specific message but can only return to their physical form with the blood of the enemy that put them in the ground."

There was a small hill off of the path that had tall skinny trees poking up from it. "So, why would these Maherangs come back? What are they capable of?" Kylan asked as Manx stopped in front of the hill.

"They'd come back for revenge, my love. Did you bury anyone alive?"

"N--no, of course not."

Manx smiled. "Then don't worry about Maherangs." She glided down the hill and grabbed a tree on the left side of the hill, stopping her momentum.

Kylan sat on the hill and slid down slowly over her bottom, crawling up to a tree on the right side. "They need the blood of their enemy to get back to their *physical* form?"

"Yes, and if they reach their physical form, they can conjure an army of the dead, but like I said--"

"An army of the fucking what?" Dink yelled from the top of the hill.

Manx sighed. "The dead, Dink. Did *you* bury anyone alive?"

"When I kill, I *fucking kill*," Dink answered as he put his dagger away in his cloak.

Manx looked over to Kylan. "I'll take that phrase to apply to men and not beasts."

Dink looked down the hill and squinted as if he was planning the perfect foolproof plan.

"Take it slow, Dink, it's steeper than it looks," Manx said with a smirk.

Dink started to step down the hill, picking up speed as the steepness grew. "You don't have to teach me how to run down a fucking hill!" With that, a root pulled him down to the ground. He grabbed a hold of a tree trunk as he rolled, but it was with his injured hand, which caused him to release it and let out a wail of pain. He stood up at the bottom of the hill and the trio all began to laugh together. "Some shortcut, nomad," Dink snorted.

Manx was laughing so hard she had to hold her stomach. "Come on now, Dink, when was the last time you laughed like this?"

Dink spat out a mouthful of his own blood. "Never in my life."

Getting through twisted woodland was easy enough, and when they found their way out, they were at the western side of Reliss, with the Trainer's Gate right in front of them. That was when Kylan realized what Manx had truly done by showing them the way on their journey. By taking Dearborn Road, they would have arrived at the Gate of Victory, which was in the northern part of the city and the most secured. Once the trio finally got through the gate, they would have had to deal with sneaking to the west side, but the Oracle's shortcut brought them right to their destination.

It all seemed too easy -- until Dink felt an arrow whiz past his head and land in a tree trunk next to him. While he and Kylan ducked out of the way back into the brush, Manx rolled and spotted an archer's tower. She shot her contraption, heard a yell, and pulled. A lifeless body fell to the ground armored from head to toe with a gold crown on the breastplate, but the spear had gone through -- metal, flesh, bone -- its three prongs stuck in the ground.

"He must have left his bow up there," she muttered to herself and looked up the wooden tower.

"What the fuck is that?" Dink called out when he saw the body drop.

Pulling out the spear with both hands, she reloaded her weapon as blood spurted out of the hole in the archer's chest like a fountain. "It's a hookshot! I guess you could call it a do-it-all device. Here..." She handed it over to Dink.

He looked down at the hole it had put in the guard's chest and handed it back to the nomad. "Where'd you swipe it?"

Manx puffed out her chest proudly. "Swipe it? You mean how'd I make it?"

"Impressive! Fucking impressive!" He smiled as he held Manx's tool with his whole hand. "How did the rope carry us through the underground hideout?"

Taking aim back at the archer's tower, Manx fired the hookshot, exposing the long rope. "See here?" she said as she held it tightly. The rope was wrapped in a swampy-colored layer that was translucent, showing the hemp rope inside. "Craven's Bog has a type of seaweed that, when dried out for five months, becomes stretchy." When her feet left the ground, she shot up into the night air and landed in the tower. Dink watched as the nomad picked up the guard's bow and fired off several arrows. Manx climbed back down gracefully with the bow and one arrow, which she strapped to her belt.

"One arrow, huh?" He looked at her belt and then at her exposed stomach.

The nomad shook her head and looked over near the brush where Kylan was hiding. "Come on, love, the coast is clear!"

Kylan emerged slowly with her hands raised, and that was when Manx realized she wasn't alone. Another guard had a sword pressed against her back and pushed her towards the nomad. Manx pulled out her bow and drew the single arrow, but the guard showed no sign of surrender. His black, flint-like eyes and smile of yellow chipped teeth were seen through his iron half-helm. He was armed with a shortsword that was pressed so close into the small of Kylan's back that he could have cut through her with just a bit more pressure to her unprotected body.

"Put the bow down and surrender and the bitch lives!" The guard's voice was scratchy and sounded as if it pained him to speak.

"You put down that blade and I'll let you live, shitbag!" Manx yelled back, closing one eye, getting ready to fire her shaft.

The guard laughed. "Go ahead, shoot! See if the arrow can pierce King's armor!" His smile was so wide that he almost looked manic.

Tears began to fall down Kylan's cheeks one at a time, but she was careful to make no sudden movements as even a deep sob would cause the blade to piece her.

"How can you even call yourself a man? Hiding from the real fight and slinking around to take a little girl? You're no Knight," Manx said, still aiming her arrow.

The guard grabbed Kylan with his gauntlet-covered hands and put the sword to her throat. "Don't test me! Put down the bow, or I'll toss you her head!"

Manx looked for a second, lowered her bow. "The half-helm was a bad idea."

Suddenly, Dink appeared out of the darkness behind the guard and buried his dagger deep into the man's bare throat, before he even had a chance to pull his sword back. When Kylan fell safely to the ground, Dink gave the guard a second smile, grabbed the top of his head, and pulled up, allowing the thick red drool to dribble out. When Kylan realized she was free, she ran over to Manx and fell into the nomad's arms.

As the guard dropped his sword, and gasped for air, Dink kicked out his legs, bringing the man to his knees. "Fuck with one of us, you fuck with all of us," he whispered, and dropped the man face down to his death. "Look at this!" He picked up the dead guard's blade and gave it a swing.

"Leave it!" Manx called back as she ran her fingers through Kylan's hair. "It's bad luck to take a man's blade!"

Dink threw down the blade and muttered a curse when Kylan raced over to him, wrapped her hands around his neck in a tight embrace, and began to bawl uncontrollably into his chest.

"It was nothing, girl," he said softly as he patted her on the head. The happiness that flooded his veins was a feeling he had never felt in his entire life.

"Uh, guys?" Manx spoke in a tone of confusion.

When Dink and Kylan turned around, they saw that the Trainer's Gate was open, and standing cross-armed in front of it was the Iron Skull.

GOJII: THE YLEWOOD

Dear Onexis, Chief of the Verrativas,

Once again, King Tanwill's Cabinet appreciates your concerns as well as your opinions. Your heroic actions that saved Trilon from crumbling at the hands of Zabkar Inwar and his army of Oracles will never be forgotten. We are forever in debt to you as well as the Verrativas that fought for our World to regain a state of peace. Unfortunately, as I'm sure you understand, trauma can leave scars.

When the Oracles used their powers to destroy our lands and intimidate our people, many became weary of those with magic in their blood, as well as those who practice it. Some find it hard to believe that there are races, such as the Verrativas, that are peaceful, with no desire to reign over Trilon, and in turn are defensive. The common folk, especially in Gojii, have labeled your people "time stealers", but please do not hold that against them.

That being said, we are not all trying to take out your race. None of us, King Tanwill included, had any idea that the Ylewood was infested with shy aconite when we offered the land as a reward for your great valor during our uprising. Your accusation is offensive and could be considered treason.

I have consulted Saige Lorrode Allwater on the removal of the poisonous plants, and he insists that setting them to fire is the only way. While we appreciate that you would allow our Royal Saige to enter your land if he brings a potion that would make this task easier, there is simply nothing to be brewed.

This will be the last letter from me for quite some time. If I or King Tanwill find it necessary to contact you, we will make special arrangements, but for now stay away from our lands. The Moiiralatta will continue doing her job in keeping our people out of yours.

Sincerely Yours.
Brannon Broadwine
Lead Confidant for King Tanwill
Forbath: Reliss

GOJII: THE YLEWOOD

To most, dreams are storybooks that cannot be opened while awake. They're portals to one's deepest desires and fears. My dreams are ghosts from the past who are determined to haunt me for an eternity...

The screams of agony from beyond the flimsy door were like sword slashes to the Verrativa, each cut aiming directly for his heart. Onexis anxiously limped around the large smoke-stained table in the center of the room, its surface covered with opened books and glass jars filled with different colored liquids. The heat that made Onexis consistently wipe handfuls of sweat from his brow came from the back of the laboratory, where a black iron cauldron bubbled angrily. Occasionally, the contents of the pot would grow so violent that foam would fizzle up over the edges and splash into the brazier, causing the flames to rise up like the hand from a drowning man reaching for air. The beakers all around the lab would occasionally puff up plumes of grey smoke as if they were glass chimneys that wreaked of death, but when Onexis heard the yell of "forgive me, mother," he realized that the stench might have come from beyond the door.

Darkness was the laboratory's cloak, and it was worn well, but that didn't affect the Verrativa like it would a mortal. His cat-eyes were focused on the door, as if his stare could open it, when finally, after the tenth lap around the table, he saw the brass knob turn. The door flung open, and the volume of the screams peaked before a small man dressed in a baggy grey robe crossed over the threshold. Smoke may have stung his eyes and throat, but it was impossible to tell by how he inhaled deeply to get the taste of blood from out of his mouth. He took no notice of Onexis when he entered but instead hobbled over to the roaring cauldron, breathed in the smoke, and spat a mouthful of phlegm onto the floor.

Onexis froze as he watched the little man fill up a vial from his pocket and pour a drop of the potion onto an open book. The pages began to curl and shrivel up until they disintegrated to nothing, leaving only the front and back covers behind. After a single nod of approval, the man corked the vial and held it up to his face for a closer examination.

"Well?" The Chief's tone was awkward, as if he were almost confused as to whether or not the man could see him through the darkness and smoke.

"He's still dead," the little man answered coldly as he scratched madly behind his ear. His eyes were glued to the potion in the beaker that Onexis saw was now glowing yellow in the darkness like a lightning bug was caught inside.

That was not what the Verrativa wanted to hear, nor was that the way he wanted to hear it. Onexis slammed both hands down onto the table, causing the little man to jump. "Look at me, Lorrode." His voice filled the laboratory.

Lorrode Allwater's eyes floated up to meet the Verrativa's and then narrowed in anger. "I specifically advised you not to bring the boy back here. He had no heartbeat in the field. It was stupid to waste a seat on the medical wagon on someone who was already deceased!" Allwater looked to the potion then back to Onexis. "The boy took a direct hit from a Burrato bomb, he had no chance of survival," he continued, his tone becoming more sympathetic.

"And what of Buldoc's father, Trovado?" Onexis asked as he ran a hand through his thick chocolate-brown hair. *If Trovado survived, then I'll have to explain to him that I marched his son to death. Trovado begged me to let him stay with Buldoc, and I refused.*

"Your Rajihn is healing just fine," Lorrode said in almost a whisper. "He'll make a full recovery, I'm sure of it." Allwater gave the potion a quick shake then looked back to the Verrativa. "Are you still hurt, Chief?"

Onexis didn't even realize it, but as his anxiety increased during his conversation with the Saige, he once again began to limp around the room. "It's nothing to worry about. Take care of the ones who need your help."

The Verrativa wore a leafy green doublet that had yellow crescent moons embroidered down the left side and sunbursts down the right, with silver triangular buttons that held it all together. It was a beautiful garment, made from the finest silk in Hillrode, a gift given to him by the newly-proclaimed King Tanwill Embray after their defeat of the tyrant Zabkar Inwar. Onexis still felt incredibly awkward wearing it and wondered in the back of his mind if the mortals were trying to transform him into one their own. His earthy brown breeches, however, told a much different story, as the entire left leg was stained a dark crusty red.

It had been three days since the battle at Stone Break Valley, two days since Reliss was taken and Tanwill Embray named himself King, uniting all three realms together, and one day since Onexis spoke the banishment spell. One day since the new ruler cut down all the hanging bodies from the gates. Some of the corpses were charred like over-cooked meat, while others were icicles, so frozen that the ropes tied around their necks were stiff as steel. The slash to the thigh that Onexis received at Stone Break Valley didn't seem to concern him at the time, but after three days, the wound had festered. While the Verrativa was almost certain that the Shadow who cut him didn't use a poison-dipped blade, the fact that the wound was getting worse by the day definitely made him wonder.

"Why didn't you come to me earlier?" Lorrode asked as he pulled out a knife from his pocket.

Onexis sat on top of the large black table and instantly felt the pain go down as he took the pressure from off his leg. "I wanted to make sure my people--I mean to say, I wanted to make sure our people were okay."

Lorrode violently scratched behind his ear. "No one can question your honor, Chief, but without you, *your* people won't survive." The old man began to cut at Onexis's breeches and slowly peeled away the left leg to reveal a large gash in the Verrativa's thigh.

My people. My people will finally be safe.

The cut was so deep that part of the thigh bone was visible. The top and the bottom of the wound had begun to scab over, but the inside was swollen and smelled like rotten cheese.

"This is no simple wound, Chief," the Saige said, shaking his head as he fingered the vial filled with the mystery potion. "How would you like to be my test subject?" Lorrode gave a half-smile. When the old man grinned, there was not a single wrinkle; other than the sunken black bags under his eyes, he didn't have any other lines on his face. In fact, if it wasn't for his dusty grey hair, Lorrode Allwater would have looked like a man half his age.

First their clothing, now their medicine. "Why not? Thank you, Saige."

Allwater laughed. "Oh, we don't have to worry about such... formalities... Chief."

If that's so, then why do you call me "Chief"?

The Saige uncorked the vial with a loud pop, as if it were a bottle of ale, and gave an uneasy look as he drizzled three drops onto the wound. At first, the liquid eased into the cut and made the red flesh glisten, but the potion then started to sizzle up, and Onexis's leg was on fire. He went to grab at it in reaction from the pain, but Lorrode grabbed his hand before he could reach the wound. Onexis screamed like he had never before, joining his fellow "victors" beyond the door.

The spiral staircase at the opposite end of the laboratory began to rattle, and Lorrode stood up quickly when Brannon Broadwine entered. He looked immaculate as a painting, his dandelion-yellow hair slicked back with a coarse beard that accentuated his high cheekbones. Brannon wore a silver doublet that had a red inlay along both arms, with sharp silver studs on both shoulders. The cape that was draped around his neck matched in color and had a clubbed tail stitched in the middle, a symbol of his hometown, Tulrose.

"Saige Lorrode," he smiled, his lips barely visible through his beard. "Chief Onexis, how are you, my friend?" Onexis shimmied his body to stand up, but Brannon waved his hand. "No, no, please don't stand."

"He's right. If you were to stand now, it would be... errr... detrimental to your injury," Lorrode mumbled.

Brannon placed a hand on Onexis's shoulder but looked directly at the little old man. "Saige Lorrode, let me ask, what do you know about meteors?"

Suddenly, Onexis felt his wound grow strangely cool, like someone poured water over it. At first it felt nice and soothed his skin, like a soft kiss from Emery, but the coolness became more and more intense until it felt as if the wound was covered in ice. His entire leg went numb before it spread to the other side, went through his calves to his bare feet, and shot up to his stomach, consuming him like a man being swallowed by quicksand. All he could do was close his eyes tight and beg for the burning he felt before to return...

When he opened his eyes, the Chief of the Verrativas was in the Ylewood. Wiping the sleep from his cat-eyes, Onexis sat up, naked, and ran his fingers over the pink scar on his left thigh then grabbed the tiny horn that hung from his neck, resting on the tree trunk tattooed in the center of his chest. He looked over to the opposite end of his bed, which was one thick circular mattress stuffed with feathers and leaves, and noticed the indent left by Emery. *Did she hear my screams?* His staff laid between him and where Emery slept, as if it were Evore hiding away from a bad nightmare. Onexis had been sleeping with his staff for over a fortnight now, ever since his encounter with the mortals at Leefside. *I can protect myself, but can I protect my people?*

The vest that he chose was thin, made from a comfortable cloth and green tree leaves. He wore it without any undershirt, which not only showed his tanned muscular physique but also the tattooed tree branches that covered his entire upper body. Slipping his grey breeches on as he made his way to the back of his tree hut, he grabbed a handful of berries Emery had left behind before opening the mahogany door to the staircase that led up to Evore's bed chamber.

A pale sun had barely risen when Onexis climbed the stairs that weaved in and out through the tree branches, as a blood orange sky filled with fluffy blue clouds loomed over him, watching his every move. Guilt grabbed him by the throat and squeezed when he entered Evore's bed chamber and saw the hooded figure sitting on his son's bed, the one that he had built in the fashion of a mortal's. Evore had begged and pleaded with Onexis for a "normal bed", and while at first, he refused to give in, the Chief eventually caved when his son sobbed that all he wanted to be was "a normal boy." *Am I an enabler?*

The Verrativa took down his green hood when he saw Onexis, stood up, and bowed deeply. "My Chief." His voice was high and unfriendly, and sounded as if he was meeting the Chief of the Verrativas for the first time, but Onexis smiled and brought him in for an embrace.

"Trovado. How was the journey to Halftop Hills?" Onexis asked calmly.

"Always long, never dangerous," Trovado answered. The Verrativa was pale-skinned and his cat-eyes were close set. While the sides of his head were clean shaven, long, thick vines of black hair sprouted from the top and fell down to his shoulders.

Onexis took notice of his friend's staff, which looked quite different from his own. While the Chief's staff was a smooth brown shaft with rounded edges on either side, Trovado's was black as a secret, with the head of a morning star on top. "How was Acconi's upgrade?"

Trovado let out the first sign of a smile since Onexis had entered Evore's chamber. "It's more than I could have ever asked for. Thank you, my Chief, for your approval."

Make sure I don't regret it. "I shouldn't have made you wait so long, my friend." Onexis looked down to his bare feet as if he were ashamed. "May I see it?"

Both of Trovado's hands were on the staff, one near the top and the other almost all the way to the bottom. He twisted each hand in opposite directions, which separated the weapon into two parts, while a thick steel chain was revealed that kept the ends connected. "Acconi remembered my first upgrade and decided to complete the transformation, making it a morning star significantly more powerful than any single one owned by a mortal." Both of his hands were now on the bottom part of the staff and the top on the floor. His cat-eyes had the excitement of a child, as if all he wanted to do was give his new weapon a swing. "Ghordaan steel chain, just like the morning star on top."

One of the terms that Onexis demanded when he and the Verrativas fought for Tanwill Embray was that they would be given a supply of Ghordaan steel, the strongest in all of Trilon. A strangely light material, Ghordaan steel was first mined and enchanted in the south by the Oracles. It was used by Zabkar Inwar and his armies, but before they were banished, King Tanwill claimed all of the steel with the intent to use it for weaponry and armor for only his strongest allies and followers. Without the Oracles, the specific iron ore was not only impossible to find but the magical spell that was used to strengthen its ability could not be cast, which in turn made the steel that much more rare.

As the Capital was only able to confiscate a limited supply, most of King Tanwill's Cabinet -- which included both Brannon Broadwine and Sir Ryker Tygurnach -- advised that they keep all of it for themselves, but the King consented to Onexis's terms. For the past fifteen years that King Tanwill had ruled, countless merchants claimed to be selling Ghordaan steel blades, but they were mostly counterfeits. Today, the only places to get true Ghordaan steel would be from the actual city from which the material was given its namesake, from King Tanwill's approval, or from the Ylewood. While it was said that the city still had a large supply of the steel, others believed that most of what was forged there nowadays was either counterfeit or cut with weaker steel.

Onexis watched beads of sweat race down the bald sides of Trovado's head as he carefully put the two ends of his weapon back together, which seemed an incredible inconvenience. *Ah, there is the downside. Once his staff becomes a morning star, he has to continue to fight with it in its transformed state. It would be near-impossible to get that chain back into the staff during battle.* "I--I have to admit that I didn't request your presence to admire your new weapon." He turned away from Trovado.

"I didn't think so, My Chief," Trovado said when he finally put his staff back together. "When Lanoria gave me your letter, I assumed it meant, er... bad tidings."

"How is your wife? And your newborn?" Onexis asked, his lips tightening.

Trovado wiped the sweat from the sides of his head and cleaned his hands with his green robe. "Lanoria seems to be doing just fine, and Waliu gained five pounds since I set out for Halftop Hills," he said with a glimmer in his eyes, but neither of the Verrativas looked at each other during the exchange. "Lanoria tells me that Emery has helped her so much since Wailu was born, so I thank you for that."

Onexis turned back around. "I'm very lucky." *Lucky I burned all the shy aconite last night.* He smiled. "She's out with Evore, gathering necessary supplies." *They won't find a single petal.* "Her duties have become that much more important now that more and more women's bellies are swollen." *We need to be able to feed the future of our race.* The Chief breathed in deep and exhaled slowly. "I made a grave mistake. A mistake that could cost me... everything." The Chief looked back out Evore's window at all the trees staring at him, watching as he admitted his crime. "My anger led me up a tree I never intended to climb. My acts could lead to severe consequences that could bring me away from here. From our people." Onexis turned and looked Trovado directly in his cat-eyes. "As my Rajihn, I need you to know everything that I know." He walked over to Evore's coffee-colored chest, placed his staff against it, and pulled out a wrinkled piece of parchment from his breeches.

"Well, what are these acts? Did anything happen to the Moiiralata?" Concern began to percolate in Trovado's voice.

Onexis picked up his staff anxiously. "No, our protector is fine." He re-read Brannon Broadwine's letter and then crumpled it. "Every single time I've requested a sit-down

with King Tanwill, it's been granted. Every single time."
The Chief's voice boomed. "Now, all of the sudden, I can
only speak with Brannon Broadwine? The man isn't even an
Embray, damn it! At least let me speak to the Prince!" He
threw the letter onto the floor.

"I hear he's a good young man," Trovado commented
without raising his eyes from the parchment.

Onexis pounded his staff down in anger. "No one's
good!" *Not even me.*

"My Chief, I'm confused. What does that letter say?"
Trovado asked, still staring at the ball of parchment on the
floor.

The Chief's eyes narrowed in anger. "Our race has
consistently been victim to the hatred from mortals who don't
understand the differences in magical races. Brannon
Broadwine holds the Ylewood and the Moiiralatta over my
head, like the mortals were the ones who did *us* a great favor.
Without the Verrativas, where would the mortal race be? I
will be respected; my voice must hold weight." *Tell him the
truth.* Onexis grabbed a hold of the horn around his neck.
"I--I need to admit to a crime. As you know, the Capital has
created specific areas for me to send and receive letters, and I
have always obliged to the arrangements that were set up
fifteen years ago. During those years, though, my
carelessness grew, and I became increasingly more arrogant."
Onexis looked up to the arched ceiling then back out the
window. "I went to retrieve a corresponding letter a fortnight
ago, and things didn't go as planned. Posing as a mortal, I
knocked out an old man and murdered a young boy in cold
blood."

Trovado let out a sigh. "Was this boy of noble birth?"

"A butcher's apprentice; he tried to kill me. It was--it was
the only option."

"Self-defense is not a crime, my Chief," Trovado said, patting Onexis on the back. "The mortal would have taken your life."

Onexis whirled away in anger. "He was just a boy! Too young to know anything! It wasn't his fault that he was educated to loathe all magical races."

Following Onexis as he paced around the room, Trovado seemed unsure of what to say to his Chief. "You've taken many mortals' lives in the defense of our race! Remember the tyrant? He didn't only have Oracles and Shadows at the battle of Stone Break Valley!"

"Killing soldiers is the way of war." Onexis spoke softly. "I took those lives fifteen years ago so I wouldn't have to in the future. So, I wouldn't have to today!" Tears welled up in the Chief's eyes. "I'm afraid there will be consequences for my actions, and you need to be prepared."

Trovado furrowed his brow in confusion and stopped following Onexis around Evore's chamber. "Prepared for what?"

The Chief halted in front of Evore's chest and traced his finger around the eye carved in its top; first the sun, then the moon, then the pupil in the middle. "If I am called to answer for my crime, I will do so. I regret my deed, but I cannot deny it. Your title of Rajihn will make you the Chiefling of the Verrativas, and you will rule until Evore comes of age."

Onexis opened the trunk and began to take out Evore's belongings, piece by piece at first, but then he started to grab at the items in handfuls, dropping them onto the floor next to the chest. When the trunk was empty, Onexis lifted his staff and placed it inside and fished around until he felt a tiny indent that fit the bottom of his weapon perfectly. He pushed down gently, revealing a circular opening on the side of the chest, which he bent down to and reached inside. When he pulled out the tiny orb, wrapped in a tree branch protective cage, Trovado gasped and almost lost his footing.

The ball itself was small enough to fit inside the Chief's palm, even with its tree coating, and seemed to be filled with a green smoke that swirled around, doing anything that it could to escape.

"My Chief, I hope I am mistaken." Trovado's voice quivered. "Please tell me that isn't what I think it is."

Onexis unwrapped the tree branches from around the orb and stared with his cat-eyes as the green smoke started churning faster and faster. "It is," he answered before he threw the ball down.

When the orb reached the floor, the impact made it crack down the middle as if it were an egg being opened on the brim of a pan to be fried. Within seconds, Evore's bedchamber was filled with a green fog that was impossible to see through, and every time either one of the Verrativas went to open their mouths to try and yell out to one another, the mysterious smoke rushed in, like a prisoner escaping through an open cell door.

The Chief of the Verrativas held his breath, keeping his sights out the window, at the trees. *The trees are more trustworthy than a man of any race, and when I'm gone, they'll watch over my people.* Trovado fell to his knees, his cheeks purple from the lack of oxygen, and Onexis watched his fellow Verrativa's yellow eyes close before falling down flat upon his face.

Suddenly the smoke dissipated, allowing Trovado to cough the life back into his lungs. Onexis casually glided over to his friend, whose eyes were still fearfully closed tight. *He thinks that he's dead. I remember the first time I used the Volani; I thought my life had come to an end too.* The Chief of the Verrativas lifted Trovado by his shoulders and helped him regain his balance. "I know what you're thinking," Onexis whispered. "Open your eyes, you're safe. Trust me."

The room was no longer Evore's bedchamber but a dank quarter with moss-stained stone walls and a brown marbled floor littered with beige specks. In the center was a rounded table carved from a thick tree trunk with red candles on either side, tiny orange flames dancing upon their wicks. A large golden chalice stood in between the two candles, towering over them like a castle would a pair of lowly shacks. Behind the table was a circular door with a large white ivory ring for a handle. With a painfully loud creak, the door opened slowly, and a creature who was nothing more than skin and bones skulked inside.

Shaking with each step forward, and with the assistance of a large curved cane which held a shrunken skull that grinned manically at its end, the hunchbacked man made his way to the table, cursing and muttering under his breath at everyone and no one. He wore a suit of absurd armor that was made up of skinny tree branches braided together around his blotchy torso that continued down to his thighs, with only a strip of leaves, moss, and mud to cover his private parts. Some of the branches had grown sharp thorns that dug into his skin, striping his body with thin lines of red, some of which were still wet, while others had become a hard crust that could have been scratched off. Around his neck, on an unraveling strand of rope, was an eye, a dried-out tongue, and a bloody ear, while a pair of emaciated forearms led to limp hands and boney fingers that were tattooed with an array of unrecognizable symbols, none of which matched in color. The helm that he wore was a Smiladon skull, its jaw clenched together, making it impossible to see the creature's face.

"How can I be of service, Chief?" He bowed to Onexis as deep as his hunched back allowed.

150

Trovado picked up his staff, charged at the being, and swung his weapon, aiming with the spiked top, but it went straight through the creature's torso as if the Verrativa was cutting through air. "I see we have a new visitor who doesn't fully understand Oracle magic. Do you really think I would reveal the true whereabouts of my lair?" The Oracle's cackle was high but faint. Every word sounded as if he was saying his last. "This is nothing more than an illusion, my friend."

"Don't you dare call me your friend!" Trovado sneered. "Coward."

The Oracle cackled loudly before interrupting himself with a violent fit of coughs. "You call me coward while you hide in the trees of a land protected by a monster of the sea."

"We banished your kind to Soarfrost! How did you escape?" Trovado's hands were wrapped around his staff as if he wanted to change it to the morning star.

"That's a good question for your Chief, don't you think?" While the Oracle's face was covered by the Smiladon skull, his tone sounded as if he was smirking. "I'm surprised you don't already know. Isn't a Rajihn second-in-command to your race?"

Trovado turned his attention to Onexis, his knuckles bone white as he gripped his staff.

He wants to kill me. Onexis kept his distance from Trovado but looked him directly in the eyes. "There will be time to explain everything. This is--"

"I know who it is! Syrah the Creator, architect for Zabkar Inwar."

Taking a step forward, the Chief of the Verrativas placed a hand on Trovado's shoulder. "He is our ally."

"Our ally? Oracles torched our homes and nearly brought our race to extinction. We are allies with the mortal race, you have committed treason! If this is ever found out--"

"The Moiiralatta will protect us," Onexis responded calmly.

"They--they took Buldoc's life at Stone Break Valley." Trovado looked down to the floor, and he bit his lower lip. "And you banished them! I heard you speak the spell," he screamed as tears filled in his eyes.

The shrunken skull on top of Syrah's cane looked as if it was laughing at Trovado's anger. "Do you really blame the Oracles for your Buldoc's death? Or do you blame the one who gave the command that separated you from him during the battle?" Syrah the Creator asked curiously, as if he didn't already know the answer. "Also, let me ask, have you ever wondered why the Chief of the Verrativas is constantly going out to forage when he has put his wife and child in charge of the task? You didn't reveal all of the contents of the last letter from Broadwine, did you?" he asked Onexis.

"Alright, that's enough," Onexis cut in before the Oracle could say anything else. The Chief shifted to Trovado. "Please, let me finish with Syrah alone." *It was my mistake to reveal the Oracle this way. It's no different than slicing open a barely healed wound.*

Trovado stormed out of Evore's chamber without a word, slamming the door behind him.

"Do you ever think about what comes out of your mouth? I'm not sure who you think you are, but as of now, I'm your only friend, and that means we respect each other." Onexis spoke in a low voice but he didn't need volume to show his anger with the Oracle.

Syrah opened up the shrunken skull's mouth and pulled out four vials and a pouch; two of the vials were filled, while the other two were empty. "I'm Syrah the Creator, the last free Oracle," he said, ignoring the rest of the Chief's tantrum.

"You know as well as I do that's not true," Onexis scoffed dismissively. "I need your help," he continued as his voice softened.

Syrah spread out the contents of the skull onto the table in front of him. "Help? Again? You came a month ago asking for a potion to rid your land of shy aconite and I told you it wasn't possible. Keep burning the plant, like I said. The Saige agrees, at least according to the letter from Broadwine." Onexis didn't need to see the Oracle's face to know he was smiling. "Tell me, though, instead of burning all of the shy aconite out of fear that Trovado will find some and use it to kill you or your family, why don't you just feed him to the Moiiralatta? Seems much easier to me."

Onexis looked out the window to see Trovado whipping his new morning star at a tree. *I'll never get used to his ability to read minds.*

"I know why you're here. You wish to see if the murder of Barnibus Trapp will be your downfall. Of course, you understand I can't cut it so cleanly." Syrah coughed. "You'll have to trim some fat if you'd like a taste."

The Oracle opened up the two vials and dumped them both into the large golden goblet. The sky-blue liquid from the first vial mixed with the deep purple from the second to form a swirl of colors as beautiful as a sunset. While the room was dark as the night sky, the skinny red candles gave off a strong glow, illuminating the chalice, like dim stars that surround their brighter moon. An onyx Coatus was wrapped around the stem of the cup, and a large green emerald shined as the beast's eyeball. Trilon was etched around the actual bowl with ruby red sapphires representing each realm's capital city. Onexis studied the goblet and saw the northern territory of Soarfrost and felt a chill creep from his lower back to his shoulders. *This is the only time I've seen Soarfrost acknowledged on a map.*

"I carved Soarfrost into the chalice after you banished my people to that snow-capped hell and we came to our--" Syrah stifled a coughed, "--agreement." The Oracle fiddled with the pouch's drawstring with one hand while he still held himself up with his crooked cane. "Tell me, Chief. Did the potion you drank to send my people to Soarfrost at least burn your insides? We spent years perfecting that recipe before Cellyadure finally figured out the last ingredient."

When Syrah lifted up the top of the pouch, two skinny brown legs crept out that were quickly followed by six more. The tiny brown spider danced awkwardly around the table, its beady eyes mirroring the chalice in a turquoise tint.

"This is the Fiddleback Spider. Its poison is deadly to mortals." He pet the insect's maple brown coat gently. "See the pattern here?" Onexis looked at the top of the spider's torso, which had two arches with three lines connecting them together. "In ancient days, they could play the fiddles on their backs to put their prey to sleep. Fascinating, don't you think?"

Onexis nodded in forced agreement. "What's the point Syrah?"

"These spiders are very valuable to my people's magic. We've used them for years. It was so hard to believe we overlooked them while mixing our banishment potion." He continued to stroke the fiddle marking as the spider raised its legs in ecstasy and began to click its dagger-sharp pincers together. "Unfortunately, they're endangered, but we've always made due."

Syrah laid his tattooed hand flat on the table top to feed the Fiddleback Spider, and the insect clicked appreciatively before elongating its fangs. It lifted its head and lunged forward to bite, but when the spider went to dig into flesh, the Oracle moved his hand as quick as a cat.

While the Chief wanted to look away at the Fiddleback Spider as it tried to pull its fangs from the table, he couldn't help but stare. Syrah grabbed the empty vial then yanked the spider's body up, leaving only the fangs stuck in the tree trunk table. As he placed its head over the vial and squeezed, the spider kicked all eight of its legs, as if that would stop its flow of black poison from filling the container. When he finished, the Oracle tossed the fiddleback carcass into the goblet and corked the vial.

"Seems extreme, doesn't it?" Onexis asked as he peered into the golden chalice and watched as the liquid consumed the spider like crows feasting on dead soldiers after a battle.

Syrah placed the vials back into the shrunken skull. "Does it intimidate you?"

"Not at all." The Chief's voice shook.

"Let me tell you this, Onexis, Chief of the Verrativas. There are no extremes when it comes to anything you love."

Onexis tugged at the horn around his neck. "And what does Syrah the Creator love?"

The Oracle grabbed onto his tree branch armor and stuck one of the thorns into his chest just below his left nipple, opened a new stream of blood, filled the other empty vial, and poured it into the chalice. "Fear," he croaked. As soon the blood joined the rest of the potion, it began to crackle and pop and thickened to a black mud in a matter of seconds. "So, when exactly are you going to do me a favor?"

"I did you a favor fifteen years ago when I didn't banish you to Soarfrost with the rest of your people," Onexis fired back.

The Oracle smelled the potion through the nostril holes of his Smiladon helm. "This is absolutely true, but what happens when I start to study how to release binding spells? What happens when the one who can wield the Frosthammer is revealed? I'm sure it will take time, but I'll figure out how to free all the Oracles and we'll take over Trilon once again. Your son never felt the heat of a firestorm, did he?"

Onexis didn't reply.

"Look at me, time stealer!" Syrah screamed, his voice raised with fury.

The Chief scowled at the Smiladon skull.

"If my people ever return, only one life will satisfy their thirst for revenge."

"What is it that you want?" Onexis growled.

"Now that's a good friend." Syrah's cackle had more life to it now. "Either you or your successor will have to be more careful in the future, so let's figure out a plan."

Onexis gazed into the goblet at the potion, which now seemed as if it was too thick to stir. "Something tells me that you already have one."

Syrah clapped his hands together. "Yes, such intuition! I will create more passages through the Iron Ash Tree, and this time they'll be all throughout Trilon. I'll even make an extra passage from Lake Gheller; one could come out near Soarfrost."

"Nothing near Soarfrost." Onexis's grip tightened on his staff. "And what exactly do I need to do in return?"

"No matter, then it will be a passage to the Rytys River." The Oracle shook his cane, and the vial filled with the Fiddleback Spider potion rattled inside the shrunken skull, as if its teeth were chattering. "As I told you before, Fiddleback Spiders are endangered in Trilon, but that's not true on the paths that have yet to be dug. After I'm done creating, and you start exploring, bring me back as much poison as you can carry, and a healthy number of carcassas from the smaller spiders."

Smaller spiders?

"Now, for what you actually summoned me to do..."

Syrah grabbed a hold of one the Smiladon's tusks with his left hand, the helm's bottom row of teeth with his right, and pulled the mouth open, exposing his wrinkled, sweaty face. The Oracle's eyes were set far apart and were a sickly green color, with milky white pupils. His nose was tiny and stuck up, with enlarged nostrils, which was his own doing from sticking jewels inside them during certain rituals, and his lips looked like fat wet snails that would crawl off his hideous face at any moment. Syrah had no hair that was at least visible through the opening of the Smiladon skull, but a patchy white beard clung to his cheeks and chin.

He struggled to lift the chalice even with both hands; his skinny tattooed fingers were like spider legs wrapping around its prey. As the Oracle drank down the sludge, his neck muscles pulsated with every gulp until there was nothing left. When he put the golden goblet back onto the table in front of him, Syrah closed his eyes as if to go to sleep, and the red candles died instantly. It only took a moment, but when the Oracle awoke, the flames ignited once again, and his eyes were stone grey, hiding his pupils, like a storm covering up the sun.

"The decisions you've made will haunt you," Syrah the Creator bellowed in a voice that wasn't his own. "Your demise comes from the south, but the boy will fly! The boy will fly high and leave you behind!"

The shrunken skull grinned at the Verrativa.

FORBATH: RELISS

CLANG!

"It's really quite fascinating," Prince Tycho said through heavy breaths as he swung his sparring sword. It connected with a thud to an old wooden shield and chipped away at the painted Lark. "According to *Magic: The Unbiased Facts* written by Quarlo Jomidë, the Verrativas aren't exactly invincible."

THWACK!

"Hold your shield arm higher, I can see the top of your chest! Jomidë writes that they can be killed or even wounded, but they will never die from natural causes, not even suicide."

CLUNK!

Tycho lunged in, but his opponent blocked his attack and returned with a cut of his own that the Prince danced away from. "Good! Think of your shield as a second weapon and you'll succeed. I remember my father telling me how much he loved Verrativas, and how we still continue to protect them today."

CRASH!

A strong slash from the Prince of Trilon split his opponent's shield in two, ending the match.

Taking off his rusted helm, Forym Quist wiped the sweat from his eyes. "Protect them from what?" he asked.

"For years, the Verrativas have endured attacks from the people of Trilon, who intend to wipe out their race. The person who kills the last Verrativa gains their gift."

Toby Vaino sprinted over to his Prince and handed him a skin of water when he noticed the sparring session had ended.

"Thank you, Toby, but next time, make sure it's wine."
Tycho laughed, spraying some water in the squire's face.

Toby licked his lips and ran the water through his orange
hair. "Thank you, my Prince. I'll see what I can do next
time."

"A joke, Toby. And call me Tycho, for fuck's sake!"

Tycho tossed the skin to Forym, who proceeded to guzzle
it down as two streams of water ran from each corner of his
mouth. When the Prince removed his half-helm, his dark
brown hair stuck to his forehead. After handing his
gambeson and helm to Toby, he slicked his sweat-soaked
hair back and began to walk through the courtyard while
Forym Quist lumbered behind him. Tycho turned and began
to backpedal.

"Toby, please make sure Symphony is saddled. I'm riding
later on today."

As Toby hurried to the covered parapet walkway, Tycho
smiled appreciatively and continued on to a winding stone
staircase that led to Larkmore's battlements. Forym halted at
the foot of the stairs like a dog waiting for his master's
command.

"Walk with me, Forym."

"Yes, of course, my--Tycho." The short-haired boy
walked as gingerly as his barrel-shaped body allowed and
met his Prince. The grounds of the battlements were grey
stone that had a number of blotchy white and green shit
stains from Akupara, the Coatus of Forbath. The three
Coatuses, better known as "the sisters", were tamed and
trained, but when Saige Lorrode created two surprises, the
Trainer's Guild was not prepared at all, which led to its
destruction.

From Lorrode Allwater's account, the Coatus eggs fell
from the sky like meteors and all hatched simultaneously.
Akupara and her sisters were wild at first and showed signs

of aggression to men when they were infants. King Tanwill realized the destruction they could have inflicted onto Trilon but still decided to have them trained instead of executed. The King's Cabinet sought after Vengar Stoneburner, who was found at the Tired Traveler, a tavern off of Dearborn Road. A lasting member of an ancient race known as "RoarCatchers", Stoneburner had the gift to speak with any creature as long as he held their blood in his Bellow. He came up with the idea to create custom horns to call each Coatus, while Lorrode constructed the instruments.

It took the Saige several attempts, where he experimented with different materials including a Smiladon tusk and a human bone, until Vengar suggested trying a Tantae horn. It took some convincing, but King Tanwill finally consented to purchasing a large quantity of the rare and controversial material from a merchant at the Euku Market, who claimed he "mined" the material himself. The salesman's lie didn't matter, though, because once the three Coatuses were tamed, they became loved throughout the three realms, leading the King to take the majestic creature as the symbol to represent Reliss.

Stoneburner was a hero in King Tanwill's eyes, which made his disgusting act of treason that much worse. He manipulated his rank and his gift to destroy Trilon, fully knowing the love that King Tanwill had for him. Because of the RoarCatcher, Prince Tycho not only had to watch his father whittle away to a skeleton, but he had grown a strong case of insomnia from wondering where and when the next attack would be. When Sir Ryker brought back the traitor, Tycho would be the one to take his life, and he wasn't brewing Silent Bite in anticipation of the execution. *I'll remove the traitor's head and drink wine from his skull.*

"Thank you for sparring with me so early, Forym," Tycho said as he walked side-by-side with the squire. The sun was the color of a pale ale and the sky was still red, but the Prince was wide awake, while Forym had barely been able to keep his beady eyes open, even after the sparring lesson. "I've been lazy with my training ever since Sir Ryker left to hunt Stoneburner."

Tycho looked out to Stone Break Valley, an open field of sickly green grass painted with yellow strokes and brown stones poking out sporadically, most of which were camouflaged by moss. Great cliffs that made Larkmore Castle look tiny in comparison anchored the Valley and occasionally sent down broken boulders, adding to the graveyard of rocks.

The morning sun kissed Prince Tycho's hair, accentuating the blood-red streaks as he removed his armor. "All of Trilon is mine, yet I've never felt more powerless in my whole life," he said with a half-smile to Forym, who seemed quite confused at this statement. "I haven't been myself since... since Lord Brannon and Sir Ryker left."

His father was affecting every aspect of his life, all except one. Meetings were clouded by the darkness that cloaked his father's existence, which caused him to miss most of what was said by Saige Lorrode Allwater, who had filled in as a transitory "King's Cabinet".

"Not only that, but Saige Lorrode has informed me that there is a feast set for tonight," he continued. "What it is to celebrate, your guess is as good as mine, but I'll need someone other than that crusty old Saige to accompany me at the high table." He turned and faced Forym. "I want you to join me at the high table for the feast tonight."

Searching for words, Forym made a face as if he was just told he was born a woman. "My Prince--"

"Tycho!"

"Tycho, I'm not exactly seen as high table-worthy," the squire mumbled.

The Prince of Trilon laughed at that remark. "Says who? I've seen you eat and drink your fill, and your appetite puts even Lord Lirum Rhygell to shame. If I say you're high table-worthy, you're high table-worthy. I will not hear any other objections. Unless you find a wench to stick your dick inside, I expect to see you there."

Forym began to chuckle. "Okay, okay, I'll start working on finding a wench."

"Excellent! More likely than not, we'd become bedding brothers, and I've always wanted a brother!"

Tycho started walking again, his brown boots scraping against the concrete. Tycho continued to walk through the battlements, passing cracked statues of Larks watching over the Valley, wings slightly spread as if they were getting set to fly off.

Forym opened his mouth, thought for a moment, then found his words. "Tycho, could I ask you something?"

The Prince nodded as he stared at Brannon's solar, which was the highest tower at Larkmour Castle.

"Why doesn't your father make a statement about Reaper or Stoneburner? Most of the people in Reliss know that it's doing the King's justice as it's said, but couldn't it be misinterpreted by others?"

Tycho furrowed his brow before making eye contact with Forym. "Misinterpreted how?"

"Well, your father... I mean, the King... I mean..."

"It's fine. Go." Tycho's voice hardened.

Forym scratched at his chin anxiously. "Well, your father has been missing for so long, people could think he went mad and just wants to destroy Trilon with Master Vengar Stoneburner and his demon Coatus, Reaper. What with Lord Brannon away in the west, it is… curious."

"Don't you dare give that traitorous piece of shit the title of Master." The Prince closed his eyes and began to rub his temple. "To think that anyone would believe that."

He knew at the meeting, right when Lord Brannon came up with the ploy, that it would never work. He knew that the people would eventually grow suspicious. All of Trilon would have rushed to the King's aide if he had made a statement that his father was poisoned by the RoarCatcher. Instead, he listened to Lord Brannon, a mistake he would not make again.

Tycho looked over to Forym, whose eyes were stuck on the blurry horizon past Stone Break Valley. "You couldn't possibly think that's true, could you?"

"It sure seems a lot more likely than the letter Lord Brannon sent out to every realm." Forym spoke like he had rehearsed the rebuttals to this conversation.

Tycho wrapped an arm around Forym. "To you, my friend, I will say, Reaper was not sent by my father at all."

His voice quivered, but his heart thumped in excitement. Finally, he was able to tell Trilon's secret, and sharing his burden that was eating at his insides.

"My father is not the King of Magic, he doesn't terrorize his people for entertainment, and he can defeat his enemies with troops of Knights." At first, his face was hard, just the way his father taught him to keep it when speaking with anyone, but tears began to stream down his cheeks, causing his stone-like composure to finally crumble. "King Tanwill is slowly rotting away, and I'll soon inherit three realms, when I've barely mastered a proper sparring regimen," he said through an unapologetic sob.

"What's wrong with him, my Prince?" Forym asked, sounding unsure if he should have.

Without a word, Tycho wiped his puffy eyes and began to walk again until he was under the tower of Brannon's solar.

"Some things are better to be seen." He grabbed onto the iron ring to the door and pulled, beckoning Forym to enter the tower with him.

"My Prince, I'm not sure if I should enter Lord Brannon's quarters without his--"

"Please come with me, Forym."

The Prince didn't command his squire; he was begging him to follow. He didn't wait for an answer but instead disappeared up a dark spiraling staircase that rattled with every step. Forym gulped and obeyed his Prince.

Higher and higher the duo climbed through the tower, with only small breaks in the walls every so often, that could have been seen as windows by some or breathing holes by others, to light their way up. While Tycho was quick on his ascent up, Forym was slow, unsure of where to step, and more than once he banged his body against the skinny rail or his head against the wall.

The top of the staircase opened up to an archer's window, so high up that it seemed almost a disadvantage. That is, until Tycho picked up from the floor a longbow which was almost as tall as he. He gripped the bow tightly and noticed that each end was equipped with a sharp blade.

"Only Brannon would have this," the Prince chuckled.

The bow was littered with jewels of sea foam green and a large onyx rock in the center that Tycho assumed assisted with aiming the weapon. After taking aim with the bow, he checked both blades by pressing his pointer finger into the steel. They were both dull from misuse, but Tycho pushed his finger on the top blade until it pierced his skin then wiped the blood on his black breeches and placed it against the wall near the exit.

"My Prince, are you sure it's okay that I'm here?" Forym asked as Tycho pushed the mahogany door and crossed the threshold to Brannon Broadwine's solar.

Tycho sucked the beads of blood from his finger that sprouted like a leak in a basin. "I'm the Prince of Trilon. If we wanted to shit in Brannon's bed then light the entire solar on fire, we could." He smiled as Forym's eyes widened at the glass cases and shelves overflowing with rare weapons and jewelry. "Plus, he's in Gojii, dealing with a suicide or something. I'm pretty sure foul play is suspected, but Brannon likes to keep all bad news to himself." Tycho reached into his breeches and pulled out the large silver key to his father's secret quarters. "No wonder he has so many wrinkles!"

Quist didn't respond, and when Tycho turned around, he saw that his squire was mesmerized by an eastern longsword that had its own individual case, set away from the rest of Brannon's collection, including the Ghordaan steel weapons.

"Do you like it?" Tycho asked as he glided across the Trilon map rug and wrapped his arm around his friend.

"Like it? I fucking love it." Forym's face blushed to an apple red. "Excuse me, I shouldn't speak so brashly."

Tycho clapped the large squire on the back. "Don't you mean, 'I fucking love it, *my Prince*'?"

The squire smiled widely, showing all of his teeth, and Tycho couldn't help but notice how different he looked. "You see the black and blue inlay throughout the blade?" He pointed at the large silver blade, its tip just short of touching the ceiling. "That's the mark of the Moondown Lands."

The sword was a strong silver and seemed plain from a distance, but a closer look showed dark blue and black lines that started on either side near the hilt. As the inlay made its way up the blade, both lines grew closer to each other until they met in the middle, intertwining like two lovers.

"My father fought with the same style of sword, and his before him. Everyone says that Ghordaan steel is the strongest, but I say, fuck that." Forym turned to Tycho and stared directly into the Prince's dark brown eyes. "Anyone who fights with a blade from Ghordaan is using enchanted steel."

"It gives them an advantage," Tycho said.

"It's cheating," Forym shot back passionately. "The swords from the Moondown Lands are forged with blood, sweat, and iron." He looked back to the greatsword. "Only blood, sweat, and iron. I'd like to see the smiths from Ghordaan work with unenchanted steel. I'd bet my tongue they wouldn't even be worthy of a sparring session. This, though..." He took a step closer to the sword, cautiously, as if his footsteps could awake it. "This is a true warrior's arm!"

The Prince had heard enough. He stepped in front of Forym and opened the glass case, lifting the sword from its wooden stand that held it up by the hilt. The Prince grabbed it with one hand like it was any other longsword but quickly realized how heavy it was. "Try it out!" he laughed, handing it over to Forym.

Quist's eyes lit up like flames glowing in a brazier when he wrapped his fingers around the hilt, and his wide smile looked borderline manic. "A weapon like this needs to be wielded with two hands," he said as he swung the sword slowly. The grip was the color of freshly fallen snow with matching grey-blue moonstones throughout the crossguard and pommel.

After a few practice slashes to a standing suit of armor, Tycho began to clap. "If the air was a soldier, he'd be dead," he chuckled. "When you're knighted, we'll have to take a trip to the forgery in the Moondown Lands."

"Don't you mean 'if'?" the squire asked. He carefully placed the sword back in its case as if he were putting a very large sleeping baby into a crib.

"When," Tycho responded. The beginnings of a scab had begun to form over his self-inflicted puncture wound that he bit into, reopening it. As the Prince sucked the blood from his finger, he fumbled through his breeches and pulled out the silver key once again. "Come on, Forym, it's time you meet my father."

King Tanwill's quarters seemed colder than the last time the Prince visited, almost as if the window was letting in a nighttime draft. Tycho opened the curtains, letting in the sun through a stained-glass window, and when he looked through to the sky, he saw it was the same color as the sea.

Grabbing his father's hand and kissing each gnarled knuckle, he felt his eyes grow heavy like clouds minutes before a storm. The Prince's lips felt dry as sand, but he still curled them into a smile and felt them crack.

"It's good to see you, Father." He looked to the side of his bed and saw a tiny nightstand with a half-eaten bowl of stew. "How--how are you feeling?"

"I'm feeling..." King Tanwill groaned, his dull, golden-brown eyes focused in on his son. "Old," he said, showing a mouth full of yellow teeth.

The clouds finally reached their capacity and the storm erupted, sending tears down the Prince's cheeks. "Better than the alternative." He smiled through puffy red eyes. It had been so long since he heard his father's voice that even three simple words brought on a happiness that no woman, alcohol, or possession ever could have.

Reality kicked Tycho in the head when his father spoke again. "Are--" He coughed loudly, bits of spit flying out of his lips. Tycho felt the drops splash onto his cheeks, mixing in with the trails of tears. "Are you Lorrode's apprentice?" The King arched his head up, revealing a fat leech, happily sucking away at his neck.

Tycho wiped the tears from his eyes and lifted the small clay bowl next to his father's bed. "Yes, and my Master has instructed me to feed you the rest of this." It was a hearty stew with carrots, potatoes, peas, and large chunks of meat swimming in a thick brown broth. "And if you don't finish, it'll be my head."

Nodding, King Tanwill slurped the stew as Tycho spooned it into his mouth. He put his boney hand up as a symbol to pause, chewed on a piece of meat, and closed his eyes to savor the meal. "Hard to believe we can get food this good now. Bunch of rebels, prowling through Trilon trying to take down the King of Magic and his evil minions." His cackle started strong but ended in a phlegm-filled cough. "Oh, the songs they'll sing when this is all over will make us legends."

"That's right," Tycho said as he filled up the spoon with more soup.

"Did Lorrode say if there were any tidings from my wife?" the King asked. "When we left, Lanlei's belly was so big that it looked as if a pin could have popped her. I hope to come home to a son." He closed his eyes again. "No, not just a son. A Prince. If you can believe it, my Lady still wanted to fight for the cause!" A smile formed on his face, creating a dozen more wrinkles around his mouth. When he opened his eyes back up, he looked over to Tycho and said, "If Allwater ever gives you a hard time, you come and fight for me." The King squeezed his son's chest. "Strong young man like you should be causing injuries, not mending them, especially since the older warriors like myself keep getting cut down."

Tycho wasn't sure how to feel about this interaction with his sire. On one hand, the Prince was grateful for the conversation, but the fact that King Tanwill couldn't appreciate the strong young man his son had become because of him put quite a damper on things. "I'll be sure to keep that in mind, my Lord."

That was when he noticed Forym lurking in the shadows near the door. The King did his best to sit up, but Tycho pushed him back down without any sort of rebuttal.

"Thorlak, my friend!" he said, grinning.

Forym walked up slowly to the King's bedside, knocking into the tiny nightstand.

"I knew you'd be fine after the battle at Hillrode, but not even a limp?" The King let out a loud single laugh. "Tell me, was it Lorrode's work, or are you really that fierce?"

The squire was lost for words. "I uh--well, I mean--"

"Ha! It must have been that pretty wench you met at the Swine! She had a pair of tits on her that you could get lost in, not that I have to tell you." He grabbed Tycho's bicep. "We were meeting with a Shadow who we had captured and turned. He was relaying information from Zabkar's camp, and all this fucker could do was show off his injured leg to any bitch who winked at him! What can I say, though?" King Tanwill's voice grew more horse. "He's standing while I'm in bed, injured by the great Cellyadure. Had to chase the piece of shit up Dearborn Road even after Brannon, Bekan, and Onexis advised against it. He killed six good men and hit me with a spell in Ghordaan, paralyzing my entire body. The Oracle was just about to end the rebellion when Onexis and Thorlak -- not Brannon, not Bekan -- stormed the town with an army of Verrativas, saving my life. I guess the effects of the spell haven't fully worn off yet, but I'm alive, so it's hard to complain," he said, closing his eyes. "Oh, any word from Xalvadore or Lirum? Did they get the reinforcements from Rutherfall?"

"No--not yet, my Lord," Forym said, playing along.

"What, did that Shadow drop you on your head? 'My Lord'? It's 'Tanwill the Triumphant'! What was the name you came up with again?" The King thought for a moment then yelled out, "Thorlak Thunder Clap!" Tanwill laughed, trying to playfully punch Forym, but stopped when Tycho pushed his arm back down. "Alright, it's time to rest again, but Thorlak, could you stay behind a moment?" he said, not even acknowledging his son.

Tycho left the chamber silently, whether out of anger or out of respect to his father, not even he could say, but he bit the scab off his pointer finger again when he sat down to wait for his squire in Brannon's solar.

His body sunk into the rich white leather chair and he leaned his head back to stare at the ceiling, a mural of King Tanwill screaming like a mad man, riding Akupara in a blue sky filled with flames. While it was a flattering picture of his father, it was wildly inaccurate, as Tanwill was shirtless, muscles rippling, and dark brown hair dancing behind him, wearing none of the Trainer's Armor. The King was also deathly afraid of heights and had to drink triple doses of Ulshaberri, a calming potion specifically brewed for him by Lorrode Allwater, every time he crawled between his guards to travel via Coatus.

The groan that came from the door to his father's chamber sounded like an old man's last, and for a moment Tycho thought the worst. Forym stepped out and closed the door, his eyes only focusing on his thoughts, when he saw Tycho. Without a word, he sat in a matching chair opposite of him.

For a few moments, neither of the teenaged boys spoke to one another nor even so much as shared a glance. The Prince still stared up at Brannon's mural, while Forym crossed his arms and closed his eyes as if to take a nap.

"I never knew my father," he grumbled, breaking the silence, his dark, beady eyes still closed.

"I'm sorry if that was... hard for you," Tycho answered unsurely. "I--uh--wasn't expecting that." He stood up. "I thought we'd maybe get a groan so to know he's still alive, but a fevered war story..."

Forym opened his eyes. "My grandfather told me my father did the same thing before he--"

"I know it's coming." Tycho didn't let him finish but sat back down in the chair. "What did he say to you when I left?"

Squirming in the seat like it was made of hardwood instead of imported leather, Forym bit his lower lip as if that would give him an excuse to not speak.

Tycho locked his fingers together and rested them under his chin, waiting for an answer.

"I'm supposed to tell Brannon and..." Forym squirmed again. "And no one else."

Tycho cracked his knuckles through his fingerless gloves. "I respect that. You're a man of honor, and they're rare." He smiled. "Your father sounded like a Knight of honor; that is something to be proud of."

"He most certainly was," Forym said sitting up. "I never got those kinds of stories from my grandfather. It was the first time I felt proud to be Thorlak Quist's son." He glanced back to the Moondown Lands sword. "It's crazy to think about how our fathers paved the way for us to be sitting here today. Without them, we'd be--"

"Dead," the Prince finished. "And we have to protect the life they created for us." He got to his feet. "Come on, we've still got a long day ahead of us."

They went to exit through the bookcase passage but decided against it because Forym was too tall to even crouch down and fit. For the entire walk back through the yard, Tycho couldn't stop laughing and poking fun at the fact that even Sir Ryker was able to use the secret entrance.

Before the two friends went their separate ways to their respective quarters, the Prince gave his squire's belly a playful squeeze and said, "Hopefully we can find a saddle to fit you!"

Forym slapped Tycho's hand away and picked him up over his head, spun him around, and dropped him down to go the granite floor. "Just remember me whenever your nose bothers you." He grinned, reaching out a baker's glove-sized hand to help his Prince to his feet.

Tycho's chamber was comfortably cooled by a late morning breeze blowing through an open balcony. He removed his sweat-stained under-tunic and splashed some cold water from a basin near his bed that he assumed was filled by Toby Vaino. The room was enormous, enough to sit five comfortably, if it wasn't for the ridiculous amount of chairs and chests placed with no pattern throughout the carpeted floor.

After kicking off his boots, the Prince made his way to his balcony to let the air kiss his bare chest. The view of Reliss always thrilled him -- a winding labyrinth of carts, shops, brothels, and apartments with the sounds of salesmen yelling out to the unexpected passersby. Screams of "PRINCE TYCHO!" soon overtook the salesmen as he waved to the chanting men and swooning women.

"Ready for round two?"

A faint whisper warmed his ear and began to excite him. Soft hands grabbed Tycho from behind before making their way down to tickle his stomach. The Prince whirled around to face a fair-skinned, freckled woman with emerald green eyes. Her hair was hidden by a robe, and when Tycho shoved her back into his chamber, she took down her hood.

Their lips locked as she began to tug on his hair, and together they fell onto the sky- blue silk blankets that covered the Prince's bed. Tycho gently untied her robe, exposing a pair of perky freckled breasts, and then the beast inside him ripped it off. When she moaned, he grabbed a handful of her hair and pulled hard. As he began to suck and lick her tiny pink nipples, the mystery woman grabbed at him through his breeches.

"Let me help, my Prince."

She untied his pants and took him in her mouth, but he felt nothing.

"Get on top of me," Tycho commanded sternly.

The girl bit her lower lip and climbed on top of her Prince. "As you wish," she said as she began to grind on Tycho's groin. Then she tried to slip the Prince inside of her, but still he felt nothing. Tycho grabbed her hips, trying to get himself hard, as frustration began to grow in his mind. "Give it to me, Tycho," she moaned, and it was all he wanted to do.

Taking her advice, the Prince threw her down next to him. This was what he needed, an ability to unleash his anger and frustration. Tycho felt her wetness flow as he took control of her body, and in that moment, he felt stronger than ever before. She kissed his neck and then followed it with a sharp bite. The pain sent a shiver down his back, like a falling star that erupted into an explosion of goosebumps. He pressed his forehead against his lover's and sighed, letting out all the warmth from their tangled bodies.

Rolling over to stare at the blank ceiling, Tycho inhaled deeply and exhaled slowly. "I'm sorry, my Lady."

The woman wrapped her naked body in Tycho's blanket and laid her head on his chest. "Are you bored of me?" she asked as she ran her fingers up and down the Prince's chest hair.

"Not at all." His tone was bordering on annoyed. "I've got a lot on my mind." He rolled out of bed, searched a nearby chest, and pulled out a short navy-blue robe. "My concerns are regarding my future, and clearly it's making me less of a man."

The woman walked over to Tycho, still wrapped in the heavy silk blanket, and they kissed once again. "Your future, or your *father's*?" Her raspy voice made Tycho want to rip the blanket off her body, but the words she spoke encouraged him to break down and weep once again.

"What do you know of my father?" He ran his hand through his lover's hair, long and black as ink with tips of green that matched her eyes. She was tiny, standing just below Tycho's chest, but he never felt as safe as in her embrace.

Her lips met Tycho's chest. "There are certain questions you don't want answered."

"Well, you haven't answered any of my questions, like what is your name?" Tycho's tone was teetering on annoyed now.

The woman playfully tapped him on the nose. "Oh, you don't need that. It's not like you'll be giving me yours."

Tycho wanted to laugh, wanted to be happy, but sadness won the duel for his emotions. "My father is alive, but he's not living," he said through reprised tears. Telling his secret for a second time was much easier than the first. "I wish there was just something I could do other than spoon stew into his drooling mouth. Trilon needs a King, and I'm not ready to be crowned. All we have is that pretty boy Brannon Broadwine with his fucking tapestries and parchments!"

"There's always something you could do." She kissed his nose and Tycho felt her long lashes dance provocatively along his brow when she closed her eyes. "You just need to figure out what that something is." Her lips were pouty, red, and tasted sweet as wine. When she bit the Prince's lower lip and grabbed at his manhood, his blood got pumping. "Let's try again," she said, dropping the silk blanket before bending over the bed.

Three knocks at the door sent Tycho into a mad scramble. He tied up his robe and yelled out, "Just a moment!" The great oak door felt twice as heavy as normal and seeing Toby

Vaino made the Prince want to scream and throw the squire from his balcony. "Yes, uh, come in, Toby." He looked over to his bed, carved from maple wood with a headrest that almost touched the ceiling, but didn't see his lover. "Sorry about the mess I... I couldn't sleep." The balcony doors were still open, and the protective bannister made of iron was tall enough to climb over, but the long fall to the heart of Reliss almost guaranteed serious injury if not death.

"No reason to apologize, Prince Tycho," Toby squeaked out.

This time Tycho didn't correct the squire but instead went to splash some more water onto his face from the faded wooden basin. That was when he realized how hungry he was. "Let me guess why you're here." He drank a small amount of water from his hands, which were locked together to form a very leaky cup. "You're here to remind me about the feast tonight." He smiled slyly. The room had grown dark since Toby entered, like the sunlight from the balcony was being blocked out by a wall.

Toby was dressed in a baggy, colorless tunic that fell almost to his thighs, and his black breeches had grass and horse dung stains with rips in both knees. "Not exactly," he mumbled. "Lord Aiken Pritchett said a rider from Lord Xalvadore's camp just arrived. The Corwin host is expected to arrive by nightfall."

The room brightened as sunlight flowed in, like a river breaking through a dam. "Lord Xalvadore? You mean Lord Xalvadore Corwin?" Tycho threw on a pair of yellow silk breeches and a tightly fitting black tunic with buttons that led up to his neck.

"Maybe a surcoat too? He is the baron of Aleru," Toby chimed in as the Prince hustled around his room.

Nodding, Tycho opened his largest chest near the side of his bed, a tall, toasted almond-colored box that was smooth as glass with a golden Coatus painted on top. The surcoat he chose matched his pants in color, and he finished off the outfit with short black boots.

"Why wasn't I made aware that this feast was in Lord Xalvadore's name?" Tycho said as he hurried down the castle hall with Toby.

"It says in Lord Aiken's notes that the feast was discussed in a recent meeting with you and Saige Lorrode. I've been copying all of his parchments upon his request."

Tycho turned down a candlelit corridor and opened an iron door to a staircase of chipped stone leading to a cellar. Toby followed. "Do we have enough food? Enough drink?" he asked as he coughed out a cloud of dust.

"Lord Aiken has been complaining that Lord Brannon didn't inform him of the feast in a timely manner. He would have flown the meat in from Xxafulok but there just wasn't enough time to set up a transaction, and it's not like we can get any fish from Yatorga. We had to go into the castle's stores, so they need to be replenished. Also, we're very low on alcohol."

Opening a flimsy door made of rotting wood, Toby allowed his Prince to walk ahead outside to the open air. They walked on a pale stone sidewalk adjacent to the castle's eastern wall. The walkway turned right, leading right through a bell tower, its base made of stormy grey stone that led to two red brick pillars connecting together at the top. In between the faded green roof and a platform large enough to fit only one was a brass bell that was so large that people in Aleru swore they heard its song.

Walking through the bell tower, Tycho and Toby continued until they came upon a stable where a black destrier stood outside fully saddled. While the old wooden pen was large enough to fit close to twenty horses, it was rather empty today with both Brannon and Ryker needing saddles for their respective journeys.

"Where's Forym?" the Prince asked the stable boys brushing the destrier's mane. "Where's the company that's supposed to ride with me?" he asked after he received no answer to his first question.

"The big guy came here about an hour ago, my Prince. He saddled Honeywheat himself and rode off," responded one of the stable boys, who couldn't have been more than ten years old.

Tycho ran his hands through his steed's mane then kissed her on the nose. "You won't disappear on me right, Symphony?" The Prince named her when he was just a young boy after concluding the white spot on her torso looked like a musical note. "Well, I can't wait any longer," he said as he mounted Symphony and grabbed the reins. "I'm late as it is."

"My Prince, you can't go out on your own!" Toby yelled out. "Please wait, I'll send a stable boy to find Forym and another to assemble the rest of your company."

Tycho's eyes narrowed as he applied pressure from his legs to Symphony, sending her into a quick gallop before crashing into Toby. He went airborne for a moment, the boy's arms and legs flailing as he hit the ground, his head bouncing off the walkway like a ball. The stable boys ran over to help the squire, but when they lifted him up, his body hung limp like a sack of potatoes, and his hair was more red than orange.

"He's dead," the youngest stable boy cried out.

"He ain't dead, shithead, just unconscious," another one sneered. "Come on, let's bring him to the Saige."

The two stable boys each grabbed Toby by the arm and dragged him back to the castle like he was a Knight who had just been unseated at a tourney.

Symphony kept going, and the Prince didn't stop her until he heard the rumbling of horse hooves coming from the western side of the city.

"Tycho!"

The Prince looked up to see Forym riding Honeywheat, a pony that was the color of her namesake. Men and women dove out of the way of the squire, and Tycho saw him even kick one or two to the street as he rode through.

Forym was still wearing his tunic from their sparring lesson earlier and was so out of breath that he was wheezing. "You can't..." He spat on the ground. "You can't leave the Capital."

"I'm the fucking Prince of fucking Trilon, I can do whatever the fuck I want," he said through gritted teeth.

Forym shook his head. "Tycho, there have been two deaths outside the Trainer's Gate, both of them Kingsmen, and they were--"

The common folk were all watching the encounter now, listening attentively. The Prince sighed and reared Symphony back towards the stables. "Now, what happened?" he asked as Symphony and Honeywheat both trotted next to each other.

"The archer at the western gate."

"Taro Geiz," Tycho said without hesitation.

Forym gulped as if he was trying to stop himself from vomiting. "The hole in his chest was so big that I saw right through him. There was another unidentified guard... his throat was cut to the bone."

"And what made you go there?" the Prince asked suspiciously.

Shuddering in his saddle, Forym made a face like he just drank a cup of spoiled milk. "I went to get a drink at The Fox and The Hound after we split up before. The King's Law was there feasting when a carrier came with a scroll, and they hustled out like they were told sickness was spreading through the tavern." He looked at Tycho. "I was going to follow them on foot, but we were so close to the stables, so I saddled up ol' Honeywheat here." He patted the pony on the neck.

"What could have possibly caused this?" Tycho asked. "Or, should I ask, who?"

"I'm not sure," Forym answered. "But no matter how you slice this meat, it'll still be rotten."

Tycho nodded in agreement. "Xalvadore's feast will have to wait, for his own safety. Quickly, my friend, find Lord Aiken Pritchett and have him ride out to meet Lord Xalvadore. Tell him to give the Corwin host gold, food, and to book a room for them at Ghordaan, the finest inn they have to offer. If the room that Lord Xalvadore desires is occupied, then demand the occupants to vacate their quarters in the name of King Tanwill."

Forym didn't balk at the task. "Anything for *my* King."

After watering Symphony and Honeywheat, Forym headed to meet Aiken Pritchett at the castle's stores while Tycho went to make sure his other squire was all right. Toby Vaino was a faithful boy but not the best fighter. In fact, he had lost every sparring match since he was named a squire for the Prince. Rather than embarrassing the boy by taking away his title, Tycho decided to make Toby a glorified errand boy, which he was not only quite good at but also allowed him to keep his sense of importance. More recently, Tycho had the squire shadow the Lord Steward, Aiken Pritchett, who held the position since his father came into power. The Prince's hope was that Aiken could groom Toby to someday take over the position so the transition could be seamless.

The familiar smells of Lorrode Allwater's laboratory wafted around Tycho's head when he entered, his vision blurred by different colored smokes billowing from different sized beakers.

"Coming to see if Toby Vaino is okay, my Prince?" he heard Saige Lorrode say through the smoke. "He's still unconscious, but 'twas only a blow to the head. No need to worry. He will have a headache, but I've been brewing a batch of sweet berry elixir that will cure that." Allwater stepped towards Tycho. "I trust you've heard about the death of the two Kingsmen who guarded the Trainer's Gate. Clearly, the Capital has been infiltrated."

"Er--yes," Tycho mumbled as he tried to sound confident.

Lorrode turned his back to Tycho and combined a red beaker with a blue beaker, which filled the lab with a vibrant purple glow. "Wouldn't you suggest sounding the bell to put all the Kingsmen in the Capital on high alert?"

Tycho nodded. "Yes. Wise words from a wise man." He spoke in his most Kingly tone but sounded half his age. "Thank you for your council, Saige Lorrode." Each word he spoke shrunk like the memory of a love lost.

"I would also advise you to leave the Capital, my Prince. Lady Rayne Blackwood can take you to Gojii where you'll be safe from the attack. Akupara will fly you to Pelegu and you'll return with Lord Brannon via Nyteah."

Tycho balled his hand into a fist. "If you think I'm abandoning Reliss amidst an invasion, you're mistaken, Saige Lorrode. This is *my* home…"

"My Prince, if anything were to happen to you with your father in his present condition, the Embray dynasty would come to an end before it could even begin. I say that with great confidence -- this course of action is one your father would approve." Lorrode didn't look at Tycho as he spoke but instead studied his new potion.

The purple glow in the room died when Tycho's rage came alive. He grabbed the vial that Lorrode's eyes were stuck to and hurled it into the other beakers, opening a storm of glass splinters inside the laboratory. "Your arrogance has removed yourself from my good graces, but after a comment like that, I wonder if it's your head that needs removal. You, who saw Stoneburner more than anyone except his students, yet had no idea of his true intentions to dementedly kill my father before setting off to destroy our world. The very fact that you would know which course of action *my* father would choose is such utter nonsense that I'm beginning to wonder if you even finished your schooling at The Mind."

Suddenly, the door at the opposite end of the lab opened, and Toby Vaino walked in, rubbing his head.

"Watch out, lad, there is some broken glass on the floor," Allwater said as Vaino's boots crunched on top of the broken beakers.

"Toby, m'boy, great to see you up!" Tycho said before Saige Lorrode had a chance to speak again. "I apologize for my actions before and hope you can find it in your heart to forgive me. If you're feeling up to it, I would love to give you a secret journey to go on, which would require flying with Lady Rayne Blackwood to Aleru." Toby blinked a few times, then smacked his lips together. "Saige Lorrode, please get my future Lord Steward some water."

The Saige walked past Tycho, his head down, and pushed through the door Toby came from just before.

"Of course, I forgive you, my Prince." This time, Tycho didn't correct the use of his title. "My head does hurt quite a lot, though. I'm not so sure flying on Akupara would be the best idea."

"A lot of Lords and Ladies call Akupara 'the Queen'. Do you know why?"

The creak of the door sounded like a sickly old cat when Lorrode entered the lab. Tycho snatched the goblet Allwater held and gracefully spun around the old Saige, stopping right in front of Toby.

Toby's eyes brightened up like stars when he saw his Prince in action. "I'm not sure I know the story true."

"Well, my friend, I know it true as sunrise," Tycho said, handing the clay goblet to Toby. "My mother, Lady Lanlei, was a great fighter. She was so great that she was even crowned victor in a tourney at Ghordaan. Could you imagine the headache she caused the Lord Steward? I mean, you do know what the Lord Steward of a castle is supposed to give to the crowned victor of a tourney, right?"

"Of course." Toby nodded his head while he finished his water. "A bouquet of roses, for the Lady of the tournament."

Tycho smiled. "You've been studying, I see. She couldn't give her *Lord* of the tourney a bouquet of roses, so the Steward provided a Tantae horn of ale." He began to laugh so loud that Toby felt obligated to join in. "She gave that horn of ale to my father, King Tanwill Embray. As great of a fighter my mother was, it did no good during the rebellion, as she was pregnant with me. I was born when the tides had turned in my father's favor, but one more battle had to be won."

"The Battle of Stone Break Valley," Toby said with excitement bubbling out of him. "The Rebel's Stand!"

"She died valiantly at the battle and put up a fight to the man who cut her down." Tycho ran a hand through his hair and then wiped his face. "Cellyadure was put to death by Lord Brannon Broadwine, and that day King Tanwill vowed to never love again. You see, because my father will never choose another to wed is the reason that Akupara is known as 'the Queen'. Wouldn't you like to help the Queen?"

Toby's orange hair seemed to be even brighter as he puffed his chest out. "It would give me great honor, my Prince."

Tycho spun back around to Allwater and clapped both hands together. "Saige Lorrode, please fly Toby to Pelegu to deliver the message to Lord Brannon."

Clearing his throat, Lorrode searched for his words. "My Prince, I'm not quite sure this is--"

"Thank you both for your assistance."

Lorrode opened his mouth, but Tycho turned around. "Yes, of course. Come on, lad," he said to Toby, beckoning him towards the door.

"Oh, and make sure you clean up this lab when you're finished making all the arrangements with Lady Rayne," Tycho said as he crunched down on a glass shard with his heel.

"As you command, my Prince."

With the old Saige and squire gone, Tycho turned to leave. This was his chance to fight, his chance to win, his chance to show he was worthy to carry King Tanwill's name.

He crunched a few more steps and stopped at the messy black table. Books were stacked upon books that were stacked upon more books, most of them the Prince had read before, either during his studies or when he was being healed by the Saige. However, at the bottom of the pile was a leatherbound book twice the width of any of the others on the table. Tycho began to rummage through them, like he was a pirate digging for treasure, until he reached the bottom. The covers were plain with no design whatsoever, but each corner was curled up and heavily stained as if they had been fully submerged in some sort of liquid. He flipped through the pages that were yellow with age and felt as if they would disintegrate in his fingers. Different spells and potions were listed alphabetically, and when he finished skimming the As, he paused at the B section.

The Burrato Bomb
8 Fiddleback Spider legs
1 Tantae horn
2 cups chalk dust
1 leech (filled with the blood of a living King)
2 Smiladon eyes
5 drops of the user's blood

¥ Grind up the Tantae horn and Smiladon eyes before mixing ingredients in the exact order listed above.
¥ Allow mixture to sit for 3 weeks in a location cold enough for it to freeze.
¥ Place mixture in a RoarCatcher's Bellow
¥ Burrato Bomb will explode on impact

Tycho closed the book and went to put it back but opened it once again before the covers could meet the parchment. The Burrato Bomb page was handwritten as if wasn't supposed to be published or even read. Glancing around the room to make sure he was still alone, he ripped the page out and folded it until he couldn't anymore. As he stuffed the parchment into his breeches, he felt the floor shake, and the bell's toll called out to him.

FORBATH: RELISS

When the bell cried out, chunks of debris came crashing down from the ceiling of the Iron Skull's lair. Below a fruit stand at the Euku Market -- which always seemed to be fresh out of fruit -- Kylan, Dink, and Manx sat in a quarter so cramped that calling it a dungeon would be entirely too generous. After the Iron Skull led the trio in through the Trainer's Gate, Dink was determined to go straight to the Guild and find the incubator, but the other two were able to convince him that a place to regroup was necessary. Without so much as a word, the Iron Skull led them through the twists and turns of Reliss to an overcrowded alley with stands flying ridiculously-colored flags on both sides. During the day, salesmen and women stood shoulder to shoulder, shouting their pitches over each other, making them sound like nothing but mindless blabbering to any prospective customers.

The "fruit stand" was set up in an area protected by darkness, sandwiched between the butcher cart that swore their meat was flown in by Nyteah from Xxafulok, and the fish market that claimed they had the last shipment of Yatorga fish. Needless to say, many people strolling the market paid no mind to the tiny stand, nor to the trap door in back of it that blended in with the sandy ground. After the Iron Skull opened the door, he beckoned the trio to enter down a rickety wooden staircase, half of which had been a recent feast for termites, the other soft and rotten. When all three were swallowed by the darkness below, he slammed it shut, killing any sort of visibility that had come from either moon or starlight.

For the whole night, Dink had been complaining that sitting around and waiting did more harm than good. After a couple of hours of uneasy sleep, he picked up where he left off -- that is, until the bell began to ring. Chunks of the dirt ceiling fell and broke over each one of the three's heads. Manx had tried to dodge the pieces but wound up somersaulting into a wall, giving herself a pounding headache. Kylan had removed her blood-stained vest that she borrowed from Manx and used it as a shield, which was not worth the effort.

The first time Dink got hit in the head, he grumbled a curse under his breath and went to sit in the corner near a cabinet that touched the top of the lair. "I fuckin' told you we should have gone right into the Trainer's Guild," he spat. His robe was covered in crusty black blood, but, unlike Kylan and Manx, he refused to take it off. "The great Iron Skull," he said, staring into a lantern that wobbled on a wooden stool, its tiny flame swayed as if it was also trying to dodge the falling clumps. "This is where he hides?" Kylan and Manx both looked at each other, unsure of who he was speaking to. "In a hole like a fucking mouse!" He kicked the side of the cabinet with the bottom of his boot, and the crash of broken glass from inside caused Kylan to finally jump to her feet.

"What's the matter with you?" she yelled. "One thing doesn't go your way and you have to sit in the corner and cry like a-... like a little... little bitch!"

Dink looked up past Kylan's dirt and blood-stained undershirt to her face and smiled. Her hair had once been a rich auburn with full curls, but now it was greasy, lumpy, and bloody. "You look more like a boy now than when you first came to Yatorga." He chuckled. "When you fucked everything up. A spoiled little pampered princess whose father has servants to feed him grapes then wipe his ass when he shits them out."

Dink slumped into the corner, grimacing in pain, his pale and gaunt face covered by a dirty beard that was showing more grey by the day. If that was the worst of his worries, he'd consider himself lucky, but the hole in his hand had begun to reek like dead fish, and a fever had overtaken him.

"I fucked everything up? I'm a spoiled princess? My father all but disowned me when he sent me to the Trainer's Guild, and Everlid is barely even a memory to me." Kylan's voice shook with the ceiling. "And not for nothing but coming back into the Capital wasn't *my* idea." She screamed so loud that her voice cracked.

Manx stood up and hugged Kylan as she sobbed, her tears making long streaks of blood and mud down her face. "Shhh, love, it's okay," the nomad whispered before kissing the girl's forehead. "Don't let anger steer you away from those who *do* care for you. Remember, without Dink, you wouldn't have a heartbeat."

"That's fucking right!" Dink said as he sat up.

"You shut your mouth!" Manx sneered. Her ripped undershirt now had only one sleeve after she used the other to rewrap Dink's wound, but other than that, she seemed to be in the best condition out of the three. "None of us want to be here, but it's a hell of a lot better than being caught by the King's Law. We need to stick together now more than ever!"

It took all of Dink's strength to stand, his eyes swimming in and out of focus, as he tried to keep his balance. "Stick together?" he slurred out as if he had spent the night at the Grateful Swine. "You're a fucking nomad, you'll sell us out the first chance you---"

Suddenly, the trap door opened, and a gust of fresh air flew in, hot and muggy, but it felt as cool as a ghost to the trio.

When the door shut and the loud thuds of someone coming down the stairs grew louder, they inched closer to each other, Dink pulling out his knife and Manx unbuckling her hookshot.

The Iron Skull was not only tall but thick, and even through his black coat that covered him from shoulders to ankles, it was easy to see his arms were roped with muscle. The staff in his hand matched in color with the rest of his outfit and stood as tall as he was, smooth without so much as a knot throughout. On top was a large ring that was wrapped in a layer of mystic blue. He eyed the company when he entered his lair, reached into his sleeve, pulled out a packed pipe, and handed it over to Dink.

"Graybill told me you were a smoker." He spoke in a gruff voice, one that sounded as if he too were an avid smoker. Reaching into his deep pockets, he pulled out a skin of water and a tiny sack that was covered in blotchy grease stains. He tossed the skin to Manx and the bag to Kylan and walked over to his cabinet, leaving a trail of deep prints from his boots and staff in the soft ground. "It's salt beef. Eat," he said to Kylan in a commanding tone. "You lot have caused quite a stir."

"Quite a stir? What exactly did you expect us to do, give ourselves up?" Manx cut in.

The Iron Skull never took down his hood let alone his mask, silvery grey with black netting on the eyes, nostrils, and mouth. Two crimson lines went over the forehead like wrinkles, and each cheek was decorated with a circle of gold. He looked to Manx but didn't answer her question, instead mumbling, "Ration the beef."

Three broken jars fell out of the rotting cabinet when he opened it, different colored liquids seeping into the ground. The Iron Skull reached in, grabbed a long match, and showed his anger by how hard he threw it at Dink. "Smoke," he said. "It'll help with the pain."

"How the fuck do you know I'm in pain?" Dink growled, his dagger clenched in his uninjured hand.

He took a step towards the Iron Skull when the uneven stool shifted, causing the lantern to slide just slightly to the right, making the left side of the chamber nearly impossible to see. A shadowed figure stepped out of the darkness wearing a cloak black as a shadow. Manx and Kylan jumped back but Dink just stared, his mouth open in astonishment.

"Saria?" he said as the figure removed her hood, revealing a head of black hair with green tips.

"Hiya, Dink," Saria exclaimed, her green eyes glowing like emeralds in the candlelight.

Dink furrowed his brow. "I heard you in the Swine, getting---"

"Fucked? I probably was," she giggled. "Not all of the Shadows are assassins, but we all steal. There's something exhilarating about posing as a whore, getting paid, then stealing everything from your client without him even noticing. Well, they all realize eventually, but by then I'm already onto the next." Saria pulled out a tiny burlap sack from her robes and began counting handfuls of gold coins.

The Iron Skull stepped away from the cabinet, holding a large jar with holes in the corked top. "Did you find out anything?" he asked Saria.

"Well, first these three fucked up the Capital even more than it already was. I'll blame the nomad," the Shadow said, chewing her lip.

Manx aimed her hookshot at Saria. "If it's already fucked, then one more dead wench won't mean much."

"Woah, hey, stop!" Dink yelled out, grabbing the hookshot and lowering it. "Whataya doing here, Saria?"

Saria scrunched her nose playfully and put her sack of gold away. "You know, just being me."

"Anything we didn't know?" the Iron Skull asked, ignoring Dink.

Saria reached into the bag of dried meat and popped a piece into her mouth. "Xalvadore Corwin is coming to Reliss," she said in between chews. "Well, he was. I don't even know now that the city is on lockdown."

"The city's locked?" Manx yelled out. "How are we to get out?"

Smiling with her plump red lips, Saria ran a skinny finger through Manx's hair, flicking off a strand of dried blood. "You can't expect to kill people right outside the Capital of Trilon and not face any consequences." The clumps of blood that were trapped in the nomad's hair looked like red flies caught in a spider web. "The bell doesn't toll to tell the time, you know."

"I won't hear this pointless bickering anymore," the Iron Skull said, slamming his staff onto the floor. "There's a quest at hand, and you've all shown you're less than qualified to fulfill it. Trust me, I'll voice my disappointment with Graybill."

"I was never a member of this quest, but you must be able to see that isn't fair. Under the same circumstances of being attacked by the enemy, anyone would have fought," Manx fired back.

Kylan's stomach dropped upon hearing her father's name. The man who was more a ghost than a father was coming to the Capital? She was a barter chip to him, the strongest way to keep an alliance with King Tanwill, a way to show his utmost loyalty. She wondered if Xalvadore Corwin was even coming to see her, but then realized that, after ten years, he probably didn't even remember who she was. "Ten years," she muttered to herself.

It was as if a dark cell was lit by a thousand candles at once, a true moment of clarity. When Kylan was at the

Trainer's Guild, she had created herself a calendar, one that she used to track sessions, seasons, and special dates. Since setting off on her adventure, she had obviously abandoned the practice, as her responsibilities were now quite different. However, special dates should never be forgotten, especially a girl's Nascense Day. Being that Kylan had trained at the Guild for ten years, Xalvadore Corwin and the rest of her family were coming to celebrate her Nascentem Feast, but it escaped her mind like a stranger's face in a dream. She didn't say anything about it but instead held back her tears and stood tall with her friend. "You certainly do a lot of scolding for someone who seems craven."

The Iron Skull looked at Kylan as if he was trying to intimidate the girl, but she scowled at him through narrowed angry eyes that seemed to surprise even her. "There are times to fight, and there are times to take a stealthy approach. When you're planning a heist on the Capital of Trilon, then it's better to use the darkness, not the sword. This, though, is a conversation that I should not be having."

"Yeah, well, what do you know about it?" Kylan's voice was turning into a weapon, one that she was becoming less afraid to wield.

The Iron Skull sucked in deep. "How do you think Graybill has that Coatus egg?" he asked as another clump of ceiling fell. "Saria, what's your plan?"

"I'd like to go back to the Prince," Saria joked, trying to break the tension.

Manx's eyes widened. "You were with Prince Tycho?" Her voice fluttered. "Now that's a man I wouldn't mind---"

"That's enough!" Dink yelled out. "Didn't you two hate each other two minutes ago? And what the fuck are you doing with that pretty boy?" Dink asked Saria.

Saria laughed at the question. "Discussing poetry, of course."

"I'm going to be sick. You---you've slept with him, haven't you?" Dink's voice dropped so low that it sounded as if he was going to start to cry at any moment.

Hugging him tightly, the Shadow kissed Dink on the cheek. "You know I've slept with others, Dinky."

"Hey, we call him Dinky too! Well, Dinky-poo..." Manx yelled out, wrapping an arm around Kylan.

Dink didn't even acknowledge the nomad. "I knew I was better than the rest." His eyes couldn't leave his boots. "But the Prince of Trilon..." he trailed off.

"Aww, Dinky! I'm sorry!" Saria went to kiss him again, but he pushed her away and pressed the pipe that the Iron Skull gave him in between his teeth. It was made from a walnut-colored wood with vines carved up the stem to the mouthpiece. The bowl was a skull with the tobacco stuffed inside its mouth.

Striking the match against the wall, Dink lit up the pipe, inhaled, and sat back down into his corner. "Fuck off," he said as wisps of grey smoke hovered around his bald head. A piece of debris fell from the ceiling and broke over Saria's headbut he didn't even look up. "Good," he spoke to the pipe.

"Stop this nonsense, none of it matters. Not now, not ever," the Iron Skull boomed, juggling three jars all labeled *Tantae Horns*. "Saria, I suggest you leave now and head back to Yatorga. I'm sure Graybill is waiting to hear from you."

"Like I'd leave when the Baron of Aleru is nearby," Saria said rubbing her head. "It's about time we had another big payday." She threw her hood back over her head. "It was nice meeting you two." The Shadow gave Kylan's arm a squeeze and nodded to Manx. "I'll see you, Dinky?"

Dink inhaled the pipe again and blew out a puff a smoke that would have put any chimney to shame. "Stay in the

Shadows. At least until you find another royal bone to chew. I'm sure the Prince has a dog."

"Grow up," Saria said awkwardly before stepping into the darkness.

Manx walked over to the lantern and lifted it up, giving light to the area where the Shadow stepped, and saw nothing but the moldy wall. "So, she really is a Shadow."

"She is," Dink said, flexing his injured hand. "She's also a whore." His tongue felt funny, like it was gaining weight with every word he spoke, but at the same time, his pain and worries seemed to be shrinking.

The Iron Skull walked over with the glass jar that had the holes all throughout the cork and knelt down to Dink. "How's the pain?" he asked as he smelled the wound through his netted nostrils.

"Got any ale?" Dink asked. "I'd fucking love a cold pint of suds right now."

Uncorking the jar, the Iron Skull reached in and pulled out a fistful of squiggling white threads. "Don't fight them, they have no interest in you, just the infection," he said as he placed the maggots on Dink's palm and the back of his hand.

As the bugs feasted at the puss and green flesh, Dink closed his eyes and puffed away on the Iron Skull's pipe. "You know," he said as smoke crept out his nose, "Normally I'd be fighting this, but right now I just..." He yawned. "...don't care."

"What did you give him?" Kylan said, partly holding back a laugh at Dink's apparent inebriation and a gag from the maggots eating away at the infection. Although the wriggling larvae were disgusting to look at, the sounds they made as they feasted were what really made her stomach turn. It sounded wet, like men sloshing slowly through puddles of mud, with an occasional ripping. They ate at a rapid pace, until Dink's pink flesh began to show once again.

Some of them burrowed inside the palm to stifle the infection near the bone, sucking up all that they could, then found their way back up, fat and full.

The Iron Skull continued to sift through the jars, never looking at Kylan, like a small child afraid of a fool because of the hat he wore. "It's a plant native of the northern region of Aleru, near the Fabled Peaks."

"The Fabled Peaks? Why would you travel all the way to the Mirrored Mountains? Who would ever venture so close to Soarfrost?" Manx asked, throwing her long strand of red hair behind her back.

"The plant is called whispering goldenglow. It's a natural sedative," the Iron Skull said, ignoring the nomad's question. He looked back over to Dink and noticed that the maggots had finished eating, so he picked them up in handfuls until the red hole was visible once again.

Kylan smiled as she watched the man who saved her life more than once snore away blissfully while his hand was being mended in the most disgusting way she had ever seen. "It looks a lot better," she said in a surprised tone. "Should we wrap it now?"

Reaching into his jacket pocket that seemed to be bottomless, the Iron Skull revealed a drawstring bag and untied it. When he pulled out the tiny brown spider with the line design on its back, Kylan yelped and jumped back to Manx. She was just about to stomp out the spider when she saw it crawl down Dink's arm to the hole in his hand. Ever so slowly, it began to spin a sticky web around the wound, protecting the swollen area.

After it formed another web around the front of Dink's hand, it crawled back into the small drawstring bag and the Iron Skull placed it back inside his pocket. "Now you can wrap it."

Manx ripped off her other sleeve and sat down next to Dink, unsure how tight to wrap the wound, her hands sticking to Dink's even as she grazed it.

"When he wakes, you three will make for the Trainer's Guild.-"

"Will he able to fight?" Manx asked, sounding afraid that Dink would never wake up.

The Iron Skull nodded. "You've left yourselves no choice but to fight, and a party of three is sure to fall."

"I wouldn't count the Crown as victors just yet," Manx said with confidence. She placed her left foot on the wall and began to stretch out. "We three have a lot of fight in us."

"Uhm, two," Kylan mouthed. "I'm not much of a fighter."

"I will join you then," the Iron Skull said without hesitation. "Know this, though: once we're done, none of you will be allowed back here. I will not risk my lair for this mission, and I can't have anyone follow you back to its whereabouts." His voice was stern like a father speaking to his first son. "What's your weapon of choice, nomad?" he asked Manx.

Manx arched her back and puffed out her chest, which was still partially stained with blood. "I'm the best archer in Trilon."

Pulling up the cabinet away from the wall, the Iron Skull revealed a leather quiver filled with arrows and a tiny bow. Within the body of the weapon were carved rosebuds, painted a milky white, weeping tears of blood that looked so real that Manx actually ran her finger down the stream to see if it was wet. The bow was about half the size of the one Manx left back in Craven's Bog, but once she nocked an arrow, the bowstring's strength became apparent. It grew so tense that she struggled to bring it back to her chin.

"Her name is Rose Thorn," the Iron Skull said. "Loose an arrow into the wall."

When she shot the bow, the arrow flew so fast into the dirt wall that only a bit of the shaft and the fletching of white and blue feathers showed. While she had to get used to the aim of the much smaller weapon, she nodded approvingly as to show that the speed would make up for her poor accuracy.

The Iron Skull reached into a scabbard tied to his midsection hidden by his long black coat and handed over a dagger to Kylan. "Here you are, girl," he mumbled more to himself than to Kylan. "Believe it or not, you're the most important person in this company."

When Kylan wrapped her hand around the hilt, it felt cold as an old man's death rattle, even though it was covered with sweat-stained cloth. The blade was almost yellow and wide at the base with a narrowed, curved tip.

"It's not Ghordaan steel," he almost laughed. "But the blade is made of a fang from a Smiladon pack leader. Not sharp, but it's strong, so try to slash your opponents with it."

He opened his jacket, revealing a rope necklace with a shrunken skull dangling from the end. It was faded with cracks all through the top and several teeth missing, and the ones that weren't were broken.

Counting to himself, the Iron Skull began to open the jars that were spread out on the floor, drinking some of them through his netted mouth and pouring even more into the shrunken skull's broken teeth.

Manx crept up behind him to see what he was doing and made a "tsk" of disapproval. "Do you have any idea how painful it is for a Tantae to have its horns removed?"

"Do you have any idea how painful it is to get stabbed by a Tantae?" the Iron Skull responded.

"It's just so offensive that people use an innocent creature's body parts like they're natural resources."

"My dear," the Iron Skull said as he opened one of the jars labeled *Tantae Horns* and sprinkled a pinch of the silvery powder onto the bottom of his staff. "If this offends you, leave this company tonight."

As he took off his necklace and tied it to the top of his staff so that the shrunken skull dangled inside the ring, Dink began to stir in the corner.

"Give him some of the beef, he needs his strength," he said as Dink yawned.

When Dink was finally up, and Manx explained the procedure that had been performed on his hand, the Iron Skull wasted no time. Kylan eyed him suspiciously as he slipped a tiny corked vial filled halfway with a wine-colored liquid into his sleeve before making his way up the rotten staircase. They heard the door squeak open slowly, then a yell of "All clear!" came from the darkness above them.

"Wait, a spider web?" Dink whispered to Manx as she crept up the steps, but she gave no reply.

The nomad climbed out to the open air and Dink followed, twirling his dagger with his uninjured hand. Kylan gripped hers awkwardly away from her body, like a father who held a son unsure if he came from his own seed.

"Stick with me, girl," Dink muttered to her.

Kylan still wore the pack that Graybill had given to her back in Yatorga, knowing she could fit the incubator inside.

"And remember, look for flesh; slashing at a man's armor is as useful as a cripple at a joust."

The great bell grew louder with each step, as if it were trying to warn the King's Law that intruders were coming. The last stand had a small pen next to it that seemed to be empty, until curiosity overtook Dink and he looked inside.

There were two long troughs, one filled with water, the other with a mushy, cornmeal-looking substance. That was when Dink realized it was a butcher's stand, where the buyer would pick out a pig they deemed worthy, then it would be slaughtered and cut to their liking. Business must have been good because there were no hogs in the pen, but then Dink heard a faint "oink" that was almost a squeak. He allowed Kylan to walk ahead of him to give him an extra look.

In the corner, shivering, was the runt of the litter. It had a snout that was covered with black spots and light hairs all over its chunky body, except on its head where it had a few brown strands. The pig's torso was tiny but its feet were oversized, and when Dink stuck his hand in the pen, it stumbled trying to come say hello. Just as he wrapped his fingers around the brown strands on the pig's head, he felt a strong gust of wind shoot past his back, through the sleeves of his robe.

The brightly-colored flags whipped and snapped, trying to stay attached to their poles. Kylan, Dink, and Manx froze in their steps as the Iron Skull bent down to one knee, muttering to himself, wind whistling through the large ring at the top of his staff. The shrunken skull began to spin, flipping upside down so fast that it became a yellow blur. When it stopped spinning, the blue wrap around the ring began to pulsate angrily, and the sky turned from a plum purple to a dire grey before opening up, sending an army of raindrops to attack the ground and turning sand to mud.

"Climb up to the top of the brothel," the Iron Skull screamed to Manx over the bell's song.

Manx unbuckled her hookshot with the leather quiver and Rose Thorn hanging over each shoulder. When she pulled the trigger, the harpoon pierced into the gutter of the skinny, black stone building that stood on the right side of the Euku Market. The rain seemed to fall faster after her feet left the ground, her eyes half-open, only granting her visions of wavy silhouettes as if they were the ghosts of the city's architecture. Between the bell and the storm, she couldn't hear anything else as she zoomed up. Trying to shake the rogue red strands of hair from her eyes, she passed a large stained-glass window with a skinny sill. Manx planted both feet on the windowsill to help propel herself, and the hazy roof was in her sight.

That was when the sounds of the ringing bell went silent, and the crunch of aluminum rattled through her teeth and down her spine. The brothel's gutter came lumbering down towards her, and just as fast as she was flying, she was falling with the weapon that she created zeroed in on her. If the nomad stayed her course, the harpoon would land squarely in her chest, and shifting to the left or right wouldn't help. Either way, she was free-falling to her death. The decision she had to make now was between dying on impact or with cold steel ending her midair. Her body grew strangely warm, as if she was seated on her rock near an open fire in Craven's Bog, even though every inch of her body was drenched.

Just as Manx saw the steel tip twinkle through the rain and was sure it would rip through her insides, the stained-glass window appeared out of the corner of her eye. She reached out with one hand, still holding the hookshot with the other, and her fingers slid down over the glass until they found the windowsill. The gutter continued to fall, just missing Rose Thorn and the quiver as it whizzed past her with the harpoon still lodged inside. When it hit the ground, she lost her hand on the hookshot, sending the weapon instead of herself to the watery grave below.

Silly as it seemed, but with her life on the line, she noticed every detail of the stained-glass art. Three women and a man were entangled with each other, while another man watched, drinking from a jeweled goblet, pleasuring himself. She had seen silk woven in Hillrode, stood on top of the Mirrored Mountains in the Moondown Lands, watched the Torch erupt in Ofrea, but this would not be the last thing her eyes allowed her to see.

Digging her nails and flexing her hands, Manx did anything to keep her grip. Swinging her other arm, she grabbed onto the windowsill with her free hand and pulled herself up. As she pressed her back to the window, her boots slipped, but she quickly regained her balance. In order to snipe a path for the others to get through, she needed to get higher, but without her hookshot, it was easier said than done.

Thunder raged and lightning lit up Reliss for a moment, and Manx thought she saw Dink and Kylan trudging through the streets. It was time to make a decision that would either kill or save her companions, and her calloused hands had enough blood on them. She turned around and planted each arm into the window's frame. The first kick into the glass caused her entire body to tremble. The second sent a shooting pain up her foot and into her calf. But with the third, she saw a crack open up on the masturbating man's face, like a single wrinkle.

Kylan couldn't see where she was going with the cold rain pounding the hot street, creating a haunting blanket of mist over the city. She kept walking, though, her hand wrapped around the hilt of her Smiladon dagger.

"Careful with that blade, girl!" Dink said as they turned down another alley of apartments, passing a green sign that hung on top of a thick iron banner connecting the two sides together. It read, "Honnek Way."

"Sorry," she whispered. "I thought the King's Law were swarming the streets."

After a few more steps behind Dink, she felt her legs tangle and fell flat on her face. Spitting out gravel and blood, she stood up and realized that a thin cord was wrapped around her ankles. She pulled on one side and heard the scraping of aluminum.

"Manx's hookshot," she exclaimed loudly.

Dink pulled the harpoon from the gutter and Kylan fished out the hookshot that was caught in a railing of an apartment staircase but undamaged.

"You don't think---"

"No." Dink didn't wait for the question. He looked at Kylan's leggings and smiled. "Those are the nomad's, right?"

Kylan nodded, realizing what he was getting at. She felt the waistline of the leggings and realized there was a small buckle and smiled back. "Can you reload it?" she asked as she clipped the weapon onto the loop, while Dink tried to stuff the harpoon back into the barrel.

After a few more tries, Dink was able to reload the hookshot. "Looks like you're one step closer to being a nomad." He made eye contact with Kylan and realized the smile was wiped off her face.

Dink turned around to see what she was looking at when a gang of the King's Law started down through the alley. Some had longswords, some had greatswords, and one had a mace.

"Let's go back!" Kylan grabbed Dink's sleeve. "Come on, we can just--"

"I want that fucking mace!" he said, pulling up his hood and flexing his injured hand.

Kylan shook her head. "Dink, there are way too many! We can't--"

Dink shook Kylan off and pulled out his dagger. "We can and we will," he yelled back. "We don't retreat, remember that. If we run, they'll catch us, and who knows what will happen." His face twisted with anger. "If we fight, I know what will happen. We'll live or die." He threw his dagger from hand to hand, clenching it with his injured hand, and his mouth curled into a demented smile. "But either way, I'm putting some of these fuckers in their graves."

The guard with the mace stepped out first and smashed his weapon and shield together. His armor was midnight black with a red crown etched in the center. Not a sliver of skin showed through his visor, and he stood close to a foot taller than Dink. The other guards flanked him on either side, but he held his mace up and they all froze, as if he had control over their every movement.

"I'll kill the old fat man, and then we'll all have fun with the bitch," he said loud enough so that not only his fellow guards could hear but Dink and Kylan as well.

Still smiling, Dink began to bob up and down on the balls of his feet. The rain had stuck his hood to his face, so his eyes weren't visible. "You talk too much, boy." He let out a chuckle. "See, that's the problem with the King's Law. You have fancy armor, fancy weapons, but the only weapon you know how to truly wield is that mouth." He twirled his dagger around. "How about you fucking shut it and come fight this old man?"

Thunder echoed through the alley and lightning cracked, cutting through the haunting mist. Then the guard charged with a yell, his armor clanging like an overpriced whore wearing too much jewelry. When the mace came down to where he thought Dink was, a clang of steel on stone overpowered the storm's song for a moment, and he realized his blow had gone directly into the street. The guard looked left, then right, but Dink was nowhere to be seen.

His sights were now set on Kylan, and, lifting his mace up to swing at the young girl, he took a step towards her, then was forcefully jerked back. Before he had time to realize what was happening, his visor was lifted up, and Dink introduced his dagger to the guard's face.

It felt like stabbing a grape when the dagger went through the guard's eye. As the blade continued, cutting through skull, brains, and skull again, Dink kept pushing until he felt the back of the man's helmet. The rest of the King's Guard stood in disbelief as their Captain fell, letting out a gurgling sob, before dying facedown in a pool of his own blood.

Dink looked up to the sky and opened his mouth, drinking in the rain. He stepped on the Captain's gauntlet and pried the mace from his iron-protected fingers, then barbarically slapped his own belly. He screamed as he brought down the mace to the dead Captain's head. Bits of blood and skull clung to the tip, and he flung the mess towards the rest of the King's Law.

"All o' you will suffer the same fate unless you let us pass. Let us pass and you'll all live to see another day. I'm sure y'all are lucky enough to have families; they'd rather show their love with an embrace, not a funeral."

"You mistake us for cowards," a voice cried out, though the rain made it impossible to tell who spoke. "We of the King's Law will never lay our weapons down to a criminal. You are outnumbered. In this case, we would normally accept a surrender, but since you murdered one of our brothers, a Kingsman, we will make an exception."

The King's Law began to close in on Dink and Kylan, outnumbering them ten to two. Kylan slashed at the air, hoping that would make them hesitate but it only made them trudge forward faster.

Dink pointed his new mace towards the guards and nodded, daring them to come. "You okay, girl?" he asked, never taking his eyes off the King's Law.

Kylan gave a single nod but clearly wasn't okay.

When the first man charged, Dink smashed him in the back with his mace and he fell to one knee, dazed. Dink continued to the others, leaving the man to get up on his own.

After shaking the cobwebs from his head, the guard saw Kylan and lunged with his longsword. Jumping out of the way to the right, she just missed getting her stomach opened, but by dodging the attack, she smashed her shoulder into the alley wall and struggled to keep her footing.

Kylan couldn't see the man through the mist but still saw the silver blade as if a ghost wielded it. It was time for Kylan to attack, giving a weak slash to the air, hoping to feel the connection of flesh or even armor. The miss made her uneven, and once again she stumbled into the wall. Sparks flew bright as stars when she ducked out of the way of a full-bodied swing, the blade slicing out a chunk of concrete instead of her head.

Whether the mist dissipated, or her eyes got used to her surroundings, she couldn't say, but Kylan noticed that her attacker wasn't wearing gauntlets, and a thin line of skin showed around his wrist. Before he was able to line up again, she slid down low, ripping her leggings, and slashed the guard's wrist wide open. When she jumped back up, she unbuckled the hookshot, her fingers slipping and fumbling with the strap.

The guard held his wrist as blood seeped out over his longsword. "No, please! A young lady like you shouldn't be here." Kylan had cut a vein, and blood seemed to gush out in unison with every breath he took. "I'll show you a way out of here," he whimpered, throwing off his golden helm, exposing a shaggy mop of brown hair to the storm.

"Fuck you," she sneered as she wrapped her finger around the hookshot's trigger. Right when she was about to apply pressure, though, he fell back, gave a few twitches, then relaxed. Kylan ran over and saw an arrow lodged into his chest.

"No one uses my hookshot," Manx yelled out as she jumped down from an apartment roof, tumbling before she hit the ground. "You alright, love?" she asked as she retrieved her arrow and tossed it back into her quiver.

Kylan handed over the hookshot and hugged the nomad so tight that she felt the air squeeze out of her. Kylan and Manx whirled around to see Dink standing above the rest of the King's Law, half of their heads caved in, the rest with arrows sticking out of them like flags of victory. Dink's head was covered with a squared half-helm that he had claimed as another prize of war, and his robe was ripped in several areas, bushels of chest hair poking through the holes.

Beyond Honnek Way where Dink stood was wide open, with paved cobblestones replacing the sandy streets from the Euku Market and the alleyways of apartments. Tall marbled walls enclosed the area into a circle, with a layer of smooth porcelain on top colored a pastel blue that was bright as a baby's smile on a sunny day. In the middle of the circle was a long rectangular stage made of aged oak that was stained a lighter shade of brown, but with the heavy rain it looked its original almost-black tree trunk color.

Dink spun around and smiled proudly, his crooked nose protected by the strip of cold iron from the half-helm. "Fuck the singers and the storytellers," he yelled. "Now that was a damn show for the ages."

"You'd be dead if it wasn't for me," Manx teased as she stepped through the opening of the circle.

Dink laughed and lifted his mace up, showing a pair of silver gauntlets he had also claimed for his own. "Let's not play that game now," he said as he walked over to Manx to embrace her. "Kylan, did you get that guy?"

Kylan followed behind Manx and gagged when she saw all of the dead bodies swimming in a puddle of blood, rain, and excrement. For whatever reason, she had a vision of the King's Law all standing and smiling as a singer performed on the stage when her two companions came in and slaughtered them, turning wives into widows, sons into criminals, daughters into whores. "I would have, but Manx got to him first."

"Always after the glory aren't you, nomad?" Dink said, turning back to Manx. "No matter. You'll pop that cherry soon." Dink put out an arm to hug Kylan but she didn't even make a step towards him.

"When we get to the Trainer's Guild, I have to find a Coatus horn too," she said, holding back a dry-heave as she stood awkwardly by the entrance to the circle.

Dink squinted in confusion. "Uh, right. Do you think you'll be able to find one?"

There was no reply. Instead, Kylan stepped out of the circle, dagger still clenched in her hand. The cobblestones narrowed back into a path that she stepped onto.

"Hey, what are you doing? Where are you going?" Dink yelled out.

"Come on, let's go," Manx said, hopping over a body whose breastplate was completely caved in. "The girl is just shocked, that's all," she continued after noticing the confused look on Dink's face.

They followed after Kylan down the cobblestone path and turned through a maze of rectangular hedge bushes that were all weighed down with rain to squares. While the storm had almost subsided, the sky was still ominously grey.

"What happened to the Iron Skull?" Dink asked Manx.

"I was about to ask you the same thing," Manx replied. "He told me to climb up the brothel and I never looked back."

"Coward just vanished after he made the storm start," Dink said uneasily.

Manx tried to ring some of the water from her long strand of red hair. "You think he..."

"I fucking saw him do it!" Dink yelled, clanging his two gauntlet-covered hands together. "Graybill never really told

me who he was, but the man practices magic. Dark magic."
When he looked back ahead, there was a gigantic enclosed
colosseum. "Is this the--"

"Trainer's Guild," Manx said, her mouth gaping in
astonishment.

It was made of smooth beige stone and stood so tall that it
even towered over Larkmore Castle. The stone that it was
made of felt so fine that Dink even gave it a few knocks to
make sure it wasn't glass. The archways on each of the five
entrances were painted honey gold, making them shimmer
off the puddles on the ground. Creamy white ivory pillars
held the building together, each one splashed with a
strawberry red. Story after story, it was strong, until the top,
where it almost looked unfinished. Part of the ceiling and the
top floor was missing, as if some hungry giant took a bite out
of it.

"So, this was your home for ten years?" the nomad asked
Kylan but received no reply. "I guess she's inside already,"
Manx concluded after a few glances around the Guild.

Dink fingered his mace in such a way that showed he was
hungry to use it again. "Let's go in after her then."

"We've got to stand guard for her," the nomad said,
nocking an arrow to Rose Thorn. "We're no help to her in
there anyway."

Dink nodded. Holding his mace with one hand and his
dagger with the other, he began to pace around the
colosseum.

"Thought I told you, grabbing a dead man's weapon was-"

"Yeah, bad luck," Dink finished, giving his new mace a
swing. "Don't gimmie that nomad gypsy bullshit."

The halls of the Trainer's Guild seemed to go on forever,
and Kylan wondered if the ascent to the top was always this
draining. Her feet scraped against the concrete floor that
wrapped around the building, coiling upward like a fighting

207

snake. Each floor looked no different than the last -- dark, unlit torches hung from the wall that would have guided her, and heavy wooden doors popped up every now and again.

When she got to the floor below the top, all the doors were numbered, and for the first time, memories from her time as a Trainee filled her head. She thought of the friends she made and the ones she lost, the times she cried all night hoping for a letter from her father or her mother, the woman who didn't put up any sort of fight when she was sent away from her home at six years old.

Number Five was her room, her home for ten years. For a moment, she thought about going in to retrieve her old possessions, drawings, diagrams, and, most importantly, her Coatus horn, but as Kylan went to open the door, she heard footsteps, slow footsteps.

"Kylan Corwin," a haggard voice called out.

When Kylan looked ahead, she saw a tiny old man limping down from the top floor.

"Only daughter of Xalvadore and Alma Corwin. Do you know who I am?" he said when he was in front of her.

Kylan looked the man up and down, from his tiny legs to his smoke-stained grey robes. "You're the Royal Saige, Lorrode Allwater."

"That's right," he laughed, and small wrinkles formed around his mouth. Once he closed his lips, the lines disappeared, and his skin was as smooth as a newborn's. Lorrode pivoted to the protective bannister on the opposite side of the wall and looked down below to the training ground. "You know, when I was informed about dead guards, I had a thought that a Trainee could be involved. Such a courageous bunch, I assumed one or more would return in a desperate attempt to stop Stoneburner. There were tales that the egg was destroyed along with the Guild, but 'twas as true as those that tell of Hyberina. *My* Coatus egg can't be cracked and fried for breakfast. It's more resilient than stone and will preserve the creature it holds for up to six months, even if it were to endure the harsh bitter temperatures of Soarfrost." He looked at her. "You, Kylan Corwin, are lit with the same fire as your Lady Mother. It's unfortunate that I'm the one who has to extinguish the flames."

That was when Kylan noticed the incubator in the Saige's hand, a small, red ring with an egg-shaped glass shell on top.

"My incubator will hatch the babe, *I've* unfortunately confirmed that much. I took it upon myself to collect all the Coatus horns as well, in case my hunch proved to be correct."

She was lost for words. Everything she went through couldn't end in failure. "What will you do to me?"

Lorrode traced his finger around the incubator. "How many members of the King's Law did you and your company kill?"

"How do you know I'm not alone?" she fired back quickly.

He smiled again and his laugh lines reappeared. "My dear, you are not a fighter. You're a flyer. Your world is above us in the clouds, not on the ground with the smells of steel and blood polluting your senses."

"At least ten," Kylan admitted.

"Ten?" He began to fumble at a chain around his neck. "Do you know the punishment for murder?"

Kylan didn't respond but she knew the answer.

"The punishment for murder is beheading, but the punishment for murdering a member of the King's Law..." He looked back out to the training ground, an empty field of sand filled with large ringed chains. "Let's just put it this way -- your friends will be caught, and they will be appropriately sentenced. You, on the other hand... Well, King Tanwill is a *just* man. I'm sure we can convince him that you were pressured into--"

"How about you tell me where the King is right now?" Kylan's question was only answered by the bell down below. "Shouldn't the Crown put all of their efforts into stopping my old Master? If you did, then my party wouldn't have had to slay anyone."

Lorrode inhaled deeply and exhaled. "The Crown *is* hunting down Vengar Stoneburner and the Coatus that he took for his own, the one Trilon is now calling 'Reaper'. The beast that *I* hatched. They will both be put to death."

"You're going to put the Coatus to death? It's an innocent creature that's only following commands from Vengar Stoneburner." Kylan took a step towards Allwater. "Kill the RoarCatcher but spare the baby Coatus. I could train her!" She had seen the babe hatch from her egg and fed her oysters twice a day because no other Trainees could. Then, one day, she was gone, like everyone else in her life.

"How could you think that's even remotely feasible?" The Saige's voice rose. "Now, come with me. Your family is staying at the Famished Frog in Ghordaan. I'm sure you know they're in the south for your Nascentem Feast. Since the city is on lockdown, I'll write a letter to Lord Xalvadore. I'm sure he, your Lady Mother, and your Lordling Brother will be happy to know you're alive and well."

He noticed the large cut on Kylan's lip from when she tripped over the hookshot. "I'll stitch that up too." Allwater smiled, put the incubator down next to him, and rested both of his elbows on the bannister. "Of course, you'll have to return the egg that you planned to incubate. The Guild will be disbanded, at least for the near future."

"What will happen to the other egg?"

Lorrode spat to the training grounds below. "We were ill-prepared for Reaper, and that was with the Trainer's Guild running. Though it may seem barbaric, hatching and executing the babe is the only logical choice, for the good of

Trilon. These are not the things the future Lady of Everlid needs to worry about, though. You'll be going home soon, to the Two Tower City where a different servant will be tending to your every need. I know how much you've longed to be with your family. Go home to Everlid."

Kylan looked up to the hole in the ceiling, and the moon was watching. Its angry red face gawked back, disappointed in her failure. She had sent her only friends to their deaths, and now she was set to go back to Everlid and live a life as a noble Lady. In a few years, she'd marry a man who would be presented to her like a roast at a feast, pop out a few children, and live happily ever after growing old and fat.

The Saige was right; she needed to gome home. Everlid wasn't her home, though. Kylan Corwin didn't need a fancy castle -- the *sky* was her castle!

When Kylan grabbed Lorrode Allwater's hair from behind, she kicked the incubator back out of the way. It surprised her how easily the skin cut when she ran the Smiladon blade over the Saige's neck.

His arms started to flail around as if he was drowning, but he stopped and tried to speak his last words.

Finally, he whispered, "Why?" as he slumped over the bannister, and Kylan grabbed at the chain around his neck and pulled it back, slicing deeper into the incision she made.

Putting her dagger in her mouth, the taste of blood excited her as she tried to unhook the chain. Her fingers felt numb, like they had been dipped in buckets of ice, but she finally found the clasp and ripped off the Coatus horn before shoving the Saige over the bannister to his death. There was a loud *splat* noise, and when Kylan looked below, she saw the mud had become a pond of blood.

She put on the chain, shoved the incubator in her pack, and wiped the Saige's small white hairs off her hands.

"I was always meant to fly."

FORBATH: RELISS

Symphony took a few unsure steps through the misty streets before she realized it was safe to trot. The bell's song had been playing for so long that it seemed an afterthought to Tycho as he and his party made their way to the western side of the city. Normally, when the Prince rode through Reliss, he was greeted with smiles, laughter, and chants. But now, his city was still, as if the fog was poison, deadly to anyone not wearing armor. Ten men had accompanied Tycho, though the only one he truly trusted was Forym.

While an invasion could never be convenient, this one was particularly ill-timed, as both Brannon and Sir Ryker had both taken the strongest of the King's Law on their respective journeys. Prince Tycho also had to make sure that his father was properly guarded, leaving only squires and the eldest of the King's Law for his company, half of which couldn't fight because of lack of experience, while the other had one too many duels with Father Time. Even so, if the Prince of Trilon was afraid, he never showed it.

After leaving Lorrode's laboratory, Tycho called a quick meeting between himself, Forym, and Sir Anurd Kincaid. He was lucky that Lord Bekan had sent the Knight over so quickly from Windrip, even though Brannon was not very clear on the terms he had discussed to get him to the Capital. While Prince Tycho wasn't so naive to believe that the Nightmare wasn't coming to Reliss out of the goodness of his heart, he knew that the discussion of his compensation could wait. Brannon had primarily been in charge of these matters since King Tanwill had been poisoned, and Tycho was glad for that. If there was one thing that the Prince had learned from living in the Reliss, it was that the more noble the Knight, the quicker he would be to take offense to something, and talks of remuneration could exasperate even the most humble of commoners.

Forym bolted right back to Larkmore Castle once he heard the bell's toll, which pleased the Prince. He knew that his squire was trustworthy, but once any man is deep in a drunken stupor, getting him to pull his pants up could cause a headache. Tycho was struck with a strong feeling of guilt when he asked the Lord Steward Aiken Prichett to bring Sir Anurd to Brannon's quarters, but without Toby, he had little choice.

When the Knight arrived, the Prince was shocked by how large he actually was. Sir Ryker had told him the Nightmare ate enough for three, but Tycho always took that as another one of the Battle Master's exaggerations. Sir Anurd was so tall that he had to even look down when he spoke with Forym, and so wide that he had to walk through the entrance to Brannon's solar sideways.

The Nightmare was already in his armor when he arrived, and Tycho wondered if the man had been wearing it in his sleep, which made a tiny grin curl on his lips. While the circumstances weren't particularly appropriate, there was always time for a quick joke, even if it was just to himself.

His armor was midnight black, and the rumor was that it was forged using volcanic rocks from the Torch in Ofrea. A long mane of thin hair matching in color to his armor covered the Knight's head, but that was only seen after Tycho commanded him to take off his helmet. Below his hair, a scar ran down the Nightmare's forehead, taking away a good deal of his eyebrow, but just missed the right eye. His top lip also looked like it had been split in two, but a long, grizzly beard, which Sir Anurd had dyed a bloody red, covered it up.

Tycho had recognized the mace that the knight wielded, a fabled weapon that Lord Bekan had used in the conquering of Zabkar Inwar. A single-handed mace known as Desire's

Rage and forged in the Moondown Lands, its head had tiny spikes made of Ghordaan steel throughout the club so to cut through armor easier. If the stories could be believed, it was said that the spikes had given the mace the ability to block against certain magical attacks. While the blacksmiths of the Moondown Lands were wary to work with any Ghordaan steel, they were also not so stupid as to refuse a request from Lord Bekan Atalay.

The plan that Prince Tycho had put forth was simple enough yet effective. First, the Nightmare would lead a brigade through the city towards the western end. With any hope, the Knight would take out most, if not all, of the intruders by himself. Best case scenario would be that the first wave defeats the enemy, with the worst case scenario being the Nightmare having to retreat. Tycho would then lead his team to reinforce the Nightmare and either join in on the battle or clean up the mess left behind and identify the deceased.

Tycho was confident in his plan, though he would have rather had the assurance of Lorrode Allwater, Sir Ryker Tygurnach, or even Brannon Broadwine. He thought that it was a plan that his father would approve of -- don't wait and let the enemy advance but hunt for them like the prey that they are.

It was a tactic that he learned from a story he was told as a young boy, when Tanwill had claimed Hillrode as a base village during the rebellion. The tyrant Zabkar Inwar sent in a small army of Shadows to try and infiltrate the town, but once the gate was breached, Tanwill sprang into action. His first wave was able to take out a majority of the Shadows, while the second allowed the future King to capture their leader. This would be a good idea, but with the Nightmare leading the initial attack, Prince Tycho had given in to the idea that there would most likely be nothing left of the enemy except brains, blood, and bones.

Just before setting out, Tycho sent Molte Holten as a scout to check how the battle was unfolding. When his team had made it to The Fox and The Hound, the prince commanded them to stop. The pub was tiny and could have been seen by some as no more than a log cabin, especially compared to the Grateful Swine in Yatorga. However, to those who drank at The Fox and The Hound, there was no other pub, even if the liquor had been running low recently. Right outside the flimsy misshapen door was a statue of a hound dog pinning down a pointy-eared fox carved from black stone. The detail was once precise, but time and weather had stolen the finer lines in the two stone animals.

Lying in between the statues was Molte Holten, wheezing so heavily that it sounded as if the stone hound was strangling him. Tycho hopped down from Symphony and crept towards the squire.

His team had mismatched and dented armor with half-helms, but Tycho's was a powder blue slashed with red flames throughout the breastplate that brightened when the moonlight touched them. The suit was a gift from Brannon, forged in Tulrose, and was an exact replica of what King Tanwill wore during his rebellion. Tycho's favorite piece of the armor was the great bascinet helm with curved horns on either side, and when Molte Holten saw the Prince walking towards him, his eyes widened as if he were looking at a creature from the depths of Soarfrost.

"Are you hurt?" Tycho asked, pulling up his visor.

When Molte realized his Prince stood before him, he tumbled off the statue and got down to one knee. "No, I'm fine, my Prince."

"I hope you're out of breath from the excitement of bringing me good tidings."

"My Prince..." Molte stuttered. His chainmail hood rattled, and his legs shook. "There was so much blood. They--" he panted.

Tycho grabbed Molte from his shoulders and lifted him up. "They what?" he asked, but all the squire could do was gasp for air. "They what?!" Tycho repeated, giving Molte a shake.

"They painted the western side of the city with the blood of the King's Law. We have to go back to Larkmore Castle now!" His voice cracked. "If we retreat now, we can still save some--"

The sound of Tycho unsheathing his longsword silenced Molte. "We aren't retreating. Go back and get the Nightmare and tell him he's to join the second attack."

Molte didn't move but instead stared at his boots. "My Prince, Sir Anurd has fallen. His brains are splattered all over Honnek Way."

There was a low rumbling from Tycho's team behind him before Forym screamed for everyone to shut up. The Prince hopped back up onto Symphony and clanged his blade against the stone statue as his horse trotted back and forth in front of the brigade.

"The mighty Nightmare has fallen," he yelled. "That fat fuck ate more food than all of you combined. Yes, I'm including you too, Forym. What did that get us? A Knight who was all bark, and when he tried to bite, his teeth fell out!"

There were a few nods of agreement and encouraging mumbles.

"I'd take each and every single one of you over that disgrace to Trilon! You all want to be fighters, you all want to prove yourselves, and, best of all, you're all hungry." He turned Symphony to face Honnek Way. "Let me tell you, men, the blood of your enemies is the best meal you'll ever taste." Tycho held his sword up and put his visor down. "Let's go eat!"

Unfortunately, Molte was correct in his assessment. The Nightmare was sprawled out across Honnek Way, his monstrous body nothing more than a steel boulder that blocked the street ahead. His armet had two visors but neither one protected his face, as the helm had crumpled in as easily as a sheet of parchment, splattering his thoughts and dreams all over the apartments.

Forym hopped down from Honeywheat and rolled Sir Anurd to the side so the brigade could make their way through, while Tycho examined the walls. He wanted to look away and be disgusted, but the bits of brain and bone that mixed in with the black blood was eerily beautiful to the Prince. It was if an artist used the apartments as a canvas to create some abstract work that most would never understand. Tycho wanted to be that artist. His eyes continued up through the mist and landed on the rooftops that were lit by the moon above.

That was when he saw him. Or it? A large, silhouetted figure stood on top of an apartment roof, staring down to the Prince's company, his trench coat snapping in the wind. The stalker's eyes were furious red embers that looked as if they could burn a hole through a man's chest.

"Who goes there?" Tycho cried out, causing Forym to look up.

"Archers?" Forym asked as he jumped to Tycho's right side, holding his shield up in one hand and a long axe in the other.

Were his eyes playing tricks on him? Tycho blinked, and all he saw was the red moon as it was being swallowed by grey clouds.

"N--no, we're okay," the Prince said. "Let's continue. It looks like the skies are going to open up again."

217

Madison Theatre had a full house of dead that Tycho counted to himself.

"Stay on your guard!" Tycho said as he rode Symphony through the bloody pools and broken bodies. "Forym, Molte, with me. Everyone else, stay behind and clear the area. If anyone comes through, arrest them in the name of the *King*. If they resist, kill them and taste their blood!" He tried his hardest to sound bold but judging by the lack of response from his team, he realized it didn't work.

Tycho and Forym rode side-by-side while Molte ran ahead towards the Trainer's Guild. Forym held his shield up but only had interest in protecting his Prince.

"We're so fucked," Tycho whispered.

"Fucked? Since when are you so negative?" Forym asked, much louder than the Prince.

"Did you notice anything out of the ordinary about the slain we just trudged through?"

Forym didn't answer.

"They were all King's men. Not a single enemy was killed, and they took out our best fighter."

Forym scoffed. "You're our best fighter, followed closely by me. What, because some liver-spotted old shit who can't wipe his own ass trained the Nightmare, he's the best?"

"Right, the best fighters that have never taken a life. Me and you combined have the same amount of kills as Toby Vaino."

Clanking his axe and shield together, Forym let out a single laugh. "Not for long, my friend."

Tycho was about to answer when Molte Holten sprinted up to them. "They're at the Guild. Two of them. One's an archer, the other is wielding a mace."

"Go back and get the rest of everyone!" Tycho yelled to Molte. "This is your time. You want to prove you can be a Knight? Show me now! When you come out of the path leading to the Guild, I want everyone in a V-formation." The Prince looked ahead. "And unsheathe your sword, damnit!"

Molte sloppily pulled out a shortsword and nodded. "Yes, my Prince!"

As he ran back to the rest of the brigade, Tycho looked over to Forym. "This is it." His voice shook, but whether from fear or excitement, he couldn't say.

"Punch me in the face," Forym asked in an evil voice that Tycho hadn't heard since he first met him.

"What?"

"I'm sorry," Forym answered. "I mean, punch me in the face, my Prince."

Tycho didn't think about it, even though his fists were both covered in steel gauntlets. He smashed his squire directly in the jaw, which was unprotected by the half-helm, and heard the crunch of his teeth.

Forym Quist spat out a bloody molar and screamed at the top of his lungs, "Let's rip out their souls and make them our slaves!"

With that, they both gave their mounts a kick and furiously rode forward to meet the enemy.

Tycho felt his anger grow and his anxiety subside. This was his time to prove who he was to his doubters. Brannon Broadwine, Sir Ryker Tygurnach, Lorrode Allwater... even his father, in a sense. Every single one of them treated him like a baby that couldn't be removed from his mother's breast... all except Forym Quist. Forym Quist followed him into battle, like his father followed Tanwill. Today, they would spill the blood of a common enemy together, making them brothers. It was a start of a new age, and years from now, the singers would tell of their bravery.

The arrow was zeroed in on his face as their mounts stepped onto red and grey pavers, and just when Tycho saw it through the slits in his helm, Forym blocked his vision with the shield. Molte was correct, there were only two standing near the Trainer's Guild: a nomad woman, and a fat older man who was oddly dressed in a grey robe but wore gauntlets and a half-helm.

"Stop in the name of King Tanwill," Tycho boomed.

The nomad reloaded her bow and the man held his mace in an attack stance, neither one of them giving a hint of surrender.

"Where's the rest of your party?" Prince Tycho asked.

They both looked at each other before the nomad answered, "It's just us." Her accent was thick and sounded like nothing Tycho had heard before.

The sounds of scraping boots and rattling armor was heard from behind them, and Tycho knew that Molte and the rest of the company were filling in behind them.

"You're surrounded. Lower your weapons, or face the consequences," Tycho said angrily.

"Either way, we die, Manx!" the fat man said. "Let me smash the great Prince Tycho's fucking face in like I did to all his men."

Tycho hopped down from Symphony and walked toward the fat man, the flames in his armor seemingly rising higher, like the anger in his head.

"You want to smash my fucking face in?" he said through gritted teeth. The Prince closed his hand into a fist, his longsword clenched in the other. Then he whirled around, punching the nomad in the nose before she could loose another arrow, causing her to fly backwards and smash the back of her head into the Guild wall. "You, who entered my city and murdered my men?"

Forym hopped down from Honeywheat and began to pace back and forth, never taking his eyes off the intruder.

"The penalty for murder is beheading or hanging. For you, though, I will make an exception. Your life is mine to take. Mine!"

"Bring it on, you fucking pretty boy! Let's see how many dents I can put in your shiny armor," the man answered.

The anger was a screaming kettle inside Tycho, but then he felt himself cool down.

Rain began to fall, in single drops at first, but then, with a rumble of thunder and crack of lightning, the clouds sent down their own attack.

He charged at the man, and when he raised his longsword and brought it down, the vibrations of steel on pavement went through his body. When his visor opened up and he saw the tip of a dagger, Tycho reached out and grabbed the hand that held the weapon. Whipping the fat man back around in front of him, he felt the twitch and snap of his enemy's shoulder dislocating.

"You'll have to do better than that!" Tycho yelled out as the man leaned against the Guild, his shoulder slumped like he was carrying a sack filled with anvils.

When the Prince charged for a second time, his sword connected with the mace, but the man dropped it as soon as they made contact. This was it, his first killing blow.

Tycho's eyes narrowed, and as he went to shove his blade into the intruder's heart, a girl ran out of the Trainer's Guild wearing a leather pack.

"Get her!" he yelled. "Get her now, Forym. Now!"

The moment's hesitation gave the fat man enough time to push Tycho, bend down, and pick up his mace.

They squared up once again, with Tycho having the upper hand. Out of the corner of his eye, he saw Forym tackle the young girl, who surrendered without a moment's hesitation.

The storm swelled but Tycho didn't even feel it. All he wanted to do was hurt this man -- no, to *kill* this *enemy*. Steel

221

on steel echoed, sounding sweeter than a choir of angels, and the two were locked up. Tycho pushed as hard as he could and heard the fat man yell out in pain. When they separated, the Prince ducked out of the way of a full-bodied swing and had a clear shot to bury his blade into the intruder's gut.

Just as he went up, the ground shook, sending everyone and everything falling into different directions.

"DIVIDE THE SKY!"

It seemed to come from above, as if the thunder were speaking to them and was so loud that a high-pitched buzz reverberated through the air when it was done.

A thin line opened around the Guild, cracking the red and grey pavers as if the ground were glass. Tycho stood up, even though his knees put up a fight. His head couldn't put a single thought together, and his eyes didn't allow him to see anything.

As his vision came back into focus, he felt a rumbling smash to his chest and was once again on his back, drinking in the rain that infiltrated his visor. He tried to take a deep breath, but his chest refused to expand, and when the Prince touched his breastplate, he realized that the middle had caved in from the mace blow.

Whether he came to his senses or it was a reflex, Tycho couldn't say, but he sent out a kick and felt the explosion of a kneecap from under his boot. The fat man dropped to the ground and the Prince rolled on top of him, finally able to rattle in a few coughs of air. He pulled up his enemy by the beard as if it were the scruff of a dog's neck and ripped off the half-helm he had taken from a King's man. It only took two punches to turn the fat man's face to a bloody ruin, but Tycho added three more. The Prince brought him up so close that he smelled the blood pouring from his broken teeth, and it was sweeter than any kiss. Still wearing his horned helm, he headbutted the fat man and stood up over him.

Tycho wanted to kill his enemy with his own weapon, the one that he used to rip apart the Capital, but when he lifted up the mace from the fat man's hand, he realized it was Desire's Rage and let out a scream. It was time to christen his blade, and, throwing down the mace, he began searching for his longsword. Scrambling, he finally found it and pointed it to the man's heart.

"I, Prince Tycho Embry," he wheezed, "sentence you to--"

A stream of lightning flew down like a hawk trying to snatch a rabbit, forcing Tycho to leap out of the way.

"Tycho!" Forym screamed, and when the Prince turned around, *he* was there.

The Prince hoped his eyes were playing tricks on him before, but he knew all along that they were being stalked.

He would have made the Nightmare look like a dwarf, and the mask he wore had a grin that matched the shrunken skull which dangled from the top of his staff.

The stalker stabbed the ground with his staff and wailed, "OPEN UP!"

As the shrunken skull's eyes lit bright red, the cracks around the Guild broke up, transforming into cavernous holes, and Tycho watched four of his men fall to the abyss below. He knew that this man, this monster, was the real threat to Reliss, and started towards him.

Without missing a beat, the skull-faced man twisted the top of his staff, releasing it from the base that was still stuck in the ground. The blade that he he revealed was a skinny katana, orange as a rolling fire that steamed as it cut through the rain on its way to meet Tycho's.

But the song of steel on steel never played, and there was no buzz in Tycho's hands from the hilt. When the Prince brought his sword back, the blade was black and limp. As the silver shriveled and fell to the ground like a dead tree branch, he realized it was the end.

223

The axe swing from Forym would have ripped open any other man, but not him. It was if he had eyes in the back of his head, and when the skull-faced man twisted out of the way, he kicked the squire in the lower back. He flipped Forym over with his boot and planted it in his neck.

Tycho flew back in tackling him, and for the first time, the monster was on the ground. Once again, the Prince felt like a child as the man pushed him off with ease. Tycho backed up cautiously, watching the burning catana for any sort of twitch, then he felt his boot step on steel.

Reaching down to the ground, he found Lord Bekan's mace, his chest feeling like it was about to explode. When Tycho stood back up, the taste of blood filled his mouth and snuck out of his lips. The pain in his upper body was so intense that every time he blinked, he thought his eyes would stay closed. All the Prince wanted to do was lay down and go to sleep. He would be better after a small rest, he was sure of it. The rain was still falling strong, but his insides were on fire, and with every passing moment, the mace in his hand seemed to gain ten pounds.

As Tycho swayed, trying to keep his balance, he took one too many steps back and felt his body fall backwards as the ground underneath him ended. The darkness below reached for him, and just as he was about to be consumed by the abyss below, he felt a strong push.

"I've got you, my Prince!" he heard from behind him. "For Trilon!" Molte Holten cried out, hopping over the endless hole, his shortsword gripped tightly.

The skull-faced monster's trench coat seemed to follow his every movement, as if it were a part of his body, and when he jumped up, Molte went to meet him.

Suddenly, Forym was behind him too, as well as the rest of the remaining King's men. That was when Prince Tycho realized they were willing to die for him. These were his people, and today would be the day he would die for them. He lifted his visor, spat out a mouthful of blood, and drank the rain. Pain subsided as he stormed forward.

It was as if Molte was an insect to their enemy as the skull-faced man swatted him away, his burning red eyes focused only on Tycho. His first attack was a full swing aiming to decapitate, but the Prince had anticipated it and ducked out of the way as steam danced over his head. When Tycho tried to counter with an upward blow, the mysterious man leapt back as graceful as a cat. Tycho wanted to follow up with a lunge attack, but he knew it would cause little to no damage without a blade. A mace was a power weapon made for contact, but the blazing katana would surely melt it like the longsword before. His best strategy was avoidance until he had a clear shot. However, after a quick thrust that tangled his feet after he sidestepped it, Tycho realized it was only a matter of time until they had to make contact. When the blade came up towards his heart, Tycho decided that the time to procrastinate was over. If today was the day he would fall, let his men see him die a fighter, not a dancer.

Everything froze around them, like they were fighting inside a painting. A blue haze colored Lord Bekan's mace and ran down the katana blade, stealing its heat. When the red glow left the eyes of the skull-faced man, Tycho screamed and a burst of energy pumped through his veins. Blow after blow he dealt, his enemy blocking every single one, but, still without the burning sword, they were for the first time on equal ground.

Tycho went in to crush the man's face to see if skulls could bleed, but with a loud screech, they were engaged. Yells of encouragement from his men gave the Prince his strength to push harder and harder until he felt the blade he was battling snap. All of his fury was behind him when he connected the head of the mace into the skull-faced man's rib cage, bringing him down to one knee.

"I, Prince Tycho Embray, sentence you to die," he said triumphantly to the hoots and hollers of victory.

Without looking up, the man that he had defeated reached into his trench coat and pulled out a tiny stained-glass apothecary jar. When it was uncorked, the pain that had been haunting Tycho returned as if it never left.

A Bellow?

"Burrato bomb!"

OFREA: TORCH'S BRAND

The thick grey plumes of smoke blossomed like flowers from the tip of the Torch, mixing in with the muggy morning air. It had been the same for a fortnight, causing rumbles of a full-fledged evacuation from Ofrea. Even after the members of the Brazier promised the Tsumari that they weren't in any danger, paranoia had infected the vast majority of the race. It had been fifteen years since the volcano erupted and rivers of lava flowed, covering the island and scorching the Tsumari and everything their race had built.

Relief was promised from King Zabkar, but then Tanwill Embray overtook the throne, cutting ties with almost every magical race. While Tanwill assured the Brazier that the Tsumari were still a part of Trilon, neither the King nor his Cabinet ever reached out to offer any aid. Even after complaining that raiders snuck onto their island right off of Yatorga to poach the ivory from their beloved and sacred Tantaes, they still were not given any help. The Brazier had planned an attack on the Capital, but how could they wage a war against three realms when their race was barely large enough to take over one? For fifteen years, the Tsumari rebuilt their home, trying to mend scars, knowing well that certain cuts were just too deep to heal.

Princess Rorah stared out her balcony window, watching as the white smoke swirled into the sky, turning deep reds and even darker blues to a creamy color that looked good enough to eat. Insomnia had plagued the girl of fourteen, and while her handmaiden, Tage, had brewed monthly batches of night's tea, sleep simply never came easy. A breeze blew from the Moiira Sea that brought soft wet kisses to her mocha skin.

The quarters behind the Princess would have been simple for a commoner in any of the three realms of Trilon, but the Tsumari never placed a high priority on materialistic goods. A hammock woven from fireproof rope was set in the center of the room covered in blankets and was large enough to fit three comfortably. Indigo and purple flames were painted on the walls with dancing silhouettes blowing horns and banging drums below. Near her balcony was a square bamboo table and two matching chairs that had small indents carved into each armrest, with candle flames peeking out from inside.

The door was made of clam shell with deep ridges, and when Tage crept inside, it creaked just like wood.

"I'm out here!" Rorah yelled without taking her almond-shaped eyes off of the Volcano.

"You need your sleep, Princess. It's too early for breakfast," Tage mumbled as she placed a tray filled with chopped up mangos, bananas, and a cracked coconut on the bamboo table.

The young girl laughed at that. "If I were sleeping, I wouldn't be able to watch the sunrise!" She pointed to the sky above the Torch. Princess Rorah wore a gown decorated with purple and yellow flowers and sat crossed legged on her balcony. Her hair was black as soot and tied down her back with a bright red braid that touched the floor.

Tage sat next to her dressed in a sand-colored top and skirt that showed her midriff. Her mahogany hair was short, barely covering her ears, and, unlike Rorah, had wrinkles etched in her face. "Sleep is important, Princess. You're too young to understand, but please trust me."

"Sleep is important if you're tired," Princess Rorah said. "Someday I'll be an old lady unable to get out of my hammock to see the sun, and I'll remember this view. When that time comes, I'll sleep."

Clearly frustrated, Tage stood and stepped back into the bedchamber. "Prince Jarreau won't like you coming and going all night."

Rorah sat down at the bamboo table and opened the coconut. "I'm not worried about Prince Jarreau." Her lips curled into a smile before she took a deep gulp of coconut milk. "All I care about is what's happening now." She sat back in her seat and popped a banana slice into her mouth. "And now, I'm hungry."

There was a groan from the pile of blankets on top of the giant hammock, and Rorah let out a squeal of delight, instantly forgetting her breakfast.

"Sama!"

She jumped up and pulled off the blankets, each one patterned with a different flower. Buried below was a reptilian-type creature the size of a calf with mossy green scales and a large, three-pronged plate on the top of its head. Each point narrowed into a pearl-colored horn, and while the Tantae's body was relatively tiny, her feet would have been able to crush any breastplate with ease.

Sama's eyes glowed orange when Rorah climbed on top of her, like two burning lanterns in the dead of night. She opened her rounded beak mouth, releasing a morning groan, and the young girl began to scratch under her pet's chin.

"Did you sleep well, Sama?" Rorah asked as she slipped in next to the baby Tantae. "Come cuddle with mommy," she said as she wrapped both arms around her pet. As Sama nuzzled up to Rorah's chest, the Princess felt her eyes grow heavy.

When Rorah felt the fuzziness of sleep draw closer, Sama wrapped her tree trunk of a tail around the hammock, and it felt warmer than any blanket. Soon the Princess felt the vibrations of her pet's snores and her eyes grew heavy in bliss. As they finally closed, the snorts from Sama seemed to hold on the lowest note without pause, and when Rorah opened her eyes, the Tantae was staring back at her.

"Princess!" Tage screamed over the horn blast. "Princess Rorah, you need to get up, right now." The handmaiden ran over to the hammock and with both hands tried to roll Sama's tail off of Rorah. After the third attempt, the Tantae growled and snapped at the woman, causing her to jump back.

"What's happening?" the young girl asked as she wriggled herself free from Sama's grip. "Where's my mother and father?" she continued, trying to sound fearless, but the crack in her voice told another story.

"They'll come for you, Princess. They'll come."

Rorah furrowed her brow. "And what about you?"

The window that led out to to the balcony was suddenly sealed with another seashell door that flew down like a guillotine. With the sunlight beheaded, Rorah, Tage, and Sama sat in darkness waiting for whatever came next. It only took a few minutes for Rorah's eyes to start playing tricks, but when they did, it was all that she could see.

When the candlelight from her chair touched the dancers painted on the wall, they seemed to come alive, and she began to imagine them playing for her. Their horns fluttered a high melody while the drummers snapped a driving rhythm. Faster and faster, louder and louder, the song rolled on, finally climaxing in a crescendo that ignited the candles in each armrest. The flames shot up then came crashing down like a wave before forming into a fiery portal.

The man that stepped out was short but had enough muscle for another twice his size. His dirt-colored hair was tied up into a bun, which only made the scowl on his face more apparent.

"Princess, please come," he said, holding out a calloused hand with layers of sand under each nail. His other hand was wrapped around an axe with a stone head that was sharpened just as fine as steel.

"Eji? What's happening?" Rorah asked. "Where are my mother and father?" She backed away towards Sama and Tage. The Tantae stepped down from the hammock and squatted, positioning herself to charge at any moment.

A frown formed on Eji's cracked lips, as if he was offended at the question. He was shirtless and had flames tattooed down his ribcage that were mostly faded on his sun-blackened skin. The skirt made of dried seaweed that was wrapped around his waist was held together by a rope, which had a number of tiny pouches attached to it. A deep scar started on the left side of his neck, went across his chest, and ended on his right side where it split his nipple in two. The left nipple was still fully intact and had a large yellow ring through it that caused it to hang unusually low. "Come with Eji now, no time."

"I'm not going anywhere without Tage and Sama," she protested, backing away even further toward the front door.

Tage hugged Rorah tight with her long skinny arms. "Go, Princess, we'll be fine. Eji will take care of you."

"I said I'm not going!" Rorah yelled as she clapped her hands together. The Tantae began to snort loudly, then roared in a pitch so high it could have shattered glass. "Attack!"

Sama looked back to the young girl, who snapped her neck back to the barbarian, and began to stamp her foot. When she charged at Eji, he threw down his axe and leaped up and over the baby Tantae, landing with a grunt. The Tantae's momentum drove her right into the door that led out to the balcony with two of her horns piercing it like a sword going through flesh.

"Princess, please!" Eji panted.

Tage screeched when Sama yanked herself free of the door. "Princess Rorah, stop this now! You know Eji!"

Sama lowered her head to strike again, but when she tried to buck, Eji used his lack of height to his advantage, positioning himself under the Tantae, and tackled her, taking out the bamboo table in the process.

Rorah huffed in anger. "Sama, come." With that, the baby Tantae stood and made her way to the young girl. "I'm sorry, Eji, I can't trust anyone anymore. Ever since the Torch has been smoking, everyone's been acting..." She threw her red braid over her shoulder. "...differently."

Eji wiped the sweat from his brow and licked his fingertips. "Eji is not hurt." He chuckled. "And never apologize, Princess. There is no shame in showing the fire that grows inside you." He put his hands up as he inched towards the Princess, but each step he took toward her was followed by a growl from Sama.

Clapping once again caused the Tantae to look back toward the Princess. When their eyes met, Rorah spoke in a much gentler tone. "Friend."

Sama trotted up to Eji, sniffed his hand, then rubbed her cheek against his leg.

"Peace," Eji whispered as he knelt down and hugged the Tantae. When he stood back up, Rorah saw that tears were streaming down his face. "Makes Eji feel good to say that word. Seems like we will not hear it for a long time," he mumbled.

Tage walked up to him and wiped his tears away and squeezed him tight. "Are we in danger?" she asked as her eyes too began to glisten with tears.

"Yes," Eji confessed. "Poachers came last night, and--" He began to sob. "The Brazier put their trust in me to guard the Tantaes and I let them down. Eji let the entire Tsumari race down. Now I must make up for my mistake."

As he picked up his stone axe, Rorah's head filled with questions. "How did it happen?" she asked.

Eji tapped the butt of his axe onto the floor in frustration. "Last night, a man came to Ofrea."

"A human?" Tage asked.

The nod Eji gave was filled with guilt. "Yes, a human."

"You let a human onto the island?" Rorah's voice swelled.

"He was all alone, and Eji should have taken his life, but the human was unarmed and in a rickety rowboat. Killing an unarmed man is no better than killing a baby."

Tage started to rub Eji's back, trying to comfort him. "Sometimes you need to make exceptions."

Eji cracked his knuckles. "This man shook Eji's hand and--" He seemed lost for words. "This man called Eji his friend. Said he was a rebel who wanted to see Tanwill dead. He wanted to form an alliance with us."

Rorah examined the man from head to toe. "Well, he didn't hurt you."

That made Eji tear up all over again. "The man said we should make a trade as a sign of our new friendship. All Eji had was a pebble bracelet, and the man had a big bottle of rum. Said it was even, and then gave Eji a hug. When the man left, Eji drank the entire bottle of rum. It was so tasty."

"I've seen you drink three bottles of rum then kill four men in the pits," Tage whispered as she stroked the barbarian's cheek.

Three thuds came from the butt of Eji's axe. "Eji was tricked. Eji was poisoned!" He grumbled through gritted teeth as his tears continued. "Now Eji must make up for his mistake. Please come, Princess."

"Well, can you at least tell us what he looked like?" Rorah asked in a softer voice.

Eji thought for a moment, searching through the catacombs of his mind. "No. The man wore a grey robe with his hood up." He stared at Rorah and then stomped his barefoot down. "His eyes!" Eji cried out triumphantly. "The man's eyes were the same color as that flower," he said, pointing to Rorah's nightgown.

"Lilac? The man had lilac eyes?" Tage asked, looking at the Princess's garment. "What kind of man has lilac eyes?"

"An evil one. One who can fool you with kindness," Eji growled. "Princess, we must go now, though there's no time."

Rorah shuffled her feet. "I'll go, only if you tell me where we're going."

Eji wiped the tear trails from his cheeks. "To the Tower of Dreams. The Brazier is holding a meeting about last night's attack." The man sounded as if he were reciting practiced lines.

"Will Prince Jarreau be there?" Rorah asked, trying to hide the excitement in her voice, though judging from Tage's smile, she didn't do a good enough job.

"He is already there. That is why we must hurry," Eji said. "We are late."

At that moment, Rorah knew that she had lost but took comfort in the fact that she would get to spend some time with the love of her life. While she had only seen Prince Jarreau enough times to count on one hand, they were set to be married, so she jumped whenever she got time to spend with him. Born a month apart, the Prince and Princess of Ofrea were the children of the head members of the Brazier. Unlike Trilon, which had a King and Queen who ruled with Barons taking care of each realm, the Tsumari ruled as a Republic, allowing more than one voice to be heard. Ofrea was split up into two parts, with the Torch dividing each area. The Red Reach was on the southern side of the island, where Gamuka and Lady Ah-Sula were the leaders. Torch's Brand was on the northern front, where Okawos and Lady

Haruah ruled. Both sides were joined together by Princess Rorah in the north, Prince Jarreau in the south, and a RoarCatcher who called herself the Big Eyed Fish.

Eji reached into one of the many pouches that were attached to his belt and pulled out a pinch of sand. "Do not be afraid, Princess. Put your trust in Eji." Closer and closer, he brought his hand to the candle that waited in the armrest of Rorah's chair until the flames grabbed him. While any mortal man would have pulled away in pain with charred black skin, Eji let the fire weave in and out of his fingers like he was being touched by a lover. The flame slithered up off the wick, quick as a snake, following the man's touch, and when it was eye level, he threw the sand in.

As the fiery door opened, Rorah stepped closer to Eji. She didn't feel the heat, but the roaring fire called to her, telling her to come forward. Eji disappeared into the flames, and Tage winced in pain for the man. When Rorah stepped in, she felt sand crunch under her bare feet. It took a moment for her eyes to adjust to the sunlight, briefly being blinded by a white blur.

She heard the screams before her vision returned, and with that the Princess was outside on the sands of Ofrea. As her eyes settled to the light from the sun, the smell of blood punched Rorah in the face. They appeared out of a bonfire on the Wick, which was the land between Torch's Brand and the Red Reach that led up to both the Torch and Tower of Dreams. It was the first time Rorah had been on the Wick outside of her carriage, and she fully understood why.

The Wick was a bare, red, sand-filled wasteland where many Tsumari who weren't affiliated with either The Red Reach or Torch's Brand dwelled. More often than not, they were rebels who openly refused to conform to any political agenda, choosing to view violence as the answer to any question.

235

A band of the barbarians hovered around their leader, who stood atop a mound of sand holding out a severed head. The leader had a shaggy head of tangled black hair. While it was long around the sides, his hairline had begun to recede, greatly aging him. He was shirtless but, unlike Eji, had a fat belly that was covered in stretch marks and purple veins.

"This is what happens when you join them!" he screamed as blood sprayed from the head onto the listeners below, who seemed happy to bathe in the sticky red water. "This man was our friend, and he betrayed us." The crowd responded with yells of agreement. "Last night, poachers came to Ofrea and butchered our sacred creatures and stole their ivory. This man said the Wick was too dangerous for his family and wanted to bring them to The Red Reach, forgetting the ones he called brothers and sisters."

The crowd of the rebel Tsumari began to chant, *"Duboz! Duboz! Duboz!"*

Eji had used the rally to his advantage and slipped past the crowd, but Princess Rorah stood frozen, disgusted at her people. She watched as Duboz stepped down from the mound of sand, his skirt made of splintered bones clanking together with each step. As the throng opened, Rorah got a glimpse into the circle and saw the body that the severed head belonged to lying naked in the sand, stained black with his blood.

"Bring the boy forward!" Duboz boomed as his followers continued to chant his name.

"Princess, we need to go!" Eji pleaded. "If we stay, we--"

Rorah shook her head. "No. I must stay. We must stay! Eji, we have to stop them!" She reached for Eji's axe, but he slapped her hand away. "How could you just let this happen, Eji? I had no idea that it was like this."

"This is how it is here, Princess. Since before you. Since before Eji. This is how it will always be. The Tsumari on the Wick hunger for blood. They're not like you."

The Princess stepped closer to Eji and he pulled her in close. "What about you?" she asked, but all he did was squeeze her tight to his body.

A scrawny, bald Tsumari stepped forward, his head littered with oozing infected cuts, and shoved a small boy in front of the leader.

"You're scared," Duboz said, kneeling down to the boy. "Why? We're your people," he hissed through rotten teeth. "What's your name?"

"Toprek," the boy answered, unable to take his eyes off his father's head, which still dripped from Duboz's grip. He had short, caramel-colored hair and a pair of grey eyes that his face had not grown into yet.

Duboz flung the severed head behind him and smeared the blood from it in his palm and wiped it on Toprek's cheeks. "I don't blame you. I blame your father and mother." He stood up, causing the splintered bones around his waist to rattle again. "Where is your mother?" Duboz asked.

"Father said that the poachers took her." Toprek's eyes began to well. "Father said--"

"You no longer have a father!" Duboz screamed to a swell of cheers. He put a fist up, silencing the crowd. "Every boy needs a father, though, so I will be him. Are you ready to be my son?"

Toprek nodded as urine trickled from his tattered shorts onto the red sand.

"Bring me fire!" Duboz bellowed and was handed a lit torch. "Will you obey your father?" His face twisted into a smile.

Once again, Toprek nodded, as his tears streamed down his blood-stained cheeks.

"Do you know what happens to a Tsumari when he dies, son?"

The young boy shook his head. "No."

"'No' what?" Duboz asked almost playfully.

Toprek's lips quivered as he searched for words. "No, Father."

Duboz laughed and his belly bounced up and down. "When a Tsumari dies, they are no longer immune to fire's touch." He brought the torch down to the decapitated body and touched the deceased with the flame.

As the skin began to crackle and bubble, the chant began once again. *Duboz! Duboz! Duboz!*

The dead man's back turned into one large blister that inflated then popped, spitting up white puss into the air. With that, Duboz brought the flame closer and the red raw skin began to char and blacken as grease glistened, dripping out onto the sand.

"Now, eat."

ALERU: EVERLID

Elmar Corwin drained his glass of red whiskey, poured another, and threw it back just as easy as the first five. Finally, the crick in his back was loosening up so he could lean into his leather seat.

Forbath was always exciting compared to Aleru, but the Coatus ride back on Akupara had taken a toll on the young man of twenty-five's body, or at least that was what he kept telling himself. His father, Xalvadore Corwin, the Baron of Aleru, had forbidden Elmar from drinking at all during the trip, out of fear that he would act out during his time at the southern realm.

A week before they flew out, Lord Xalvadore hosted the Broadwine family to try and secure a Clubsodon for the defense of Everlid. The party, however, went sour during the second course of the evening, when Lord Xalvadore brought up Forbath. Lady Mallory Broadwine began to sob uncontrollably into her pea soup. This was the first time the Lord and Lady of Tulrose expressed their displeasure with the Capital of Trilon.

"Trilon is now run by a King who never speaks to his people, and our son who holds more secrets than Soarfrost," Lord Tremaine Broadwine boomed. "And when Embray is angry, or finds it necessary to flex his muscles, he sends a RoarCatcher to turn towns upside-down with his demon Coatus, Reaper. Then our son, the Lead Confidant, has the audacity to send a letter informing us that our taxes will be raised? Both of them were stupid fucking rebels who never grew up, and it shows."

If that were the worst of it, the Corwins would have considered themselves lucky, but a very drunk Elmar had to cut in.

"Count your fucking blessings! You at least are in some sort of contact with your son." He burped. "My parents sent their daughter to the Capital and never bothered with her again. Do you have any idea how long ten years is? What does that decade buy you? A second-rate Nascentem Feast, then a goodbye for another ten long years. I've had the importance of my family shoved down my throat since I was in short clothes, and yet we've divided ours for the good of the three realms?"

That was when Elmar's mother, Lady Alma, excused herself, but not before hurling her wine glass against the wall to shatter.

Lord Xalvadore smashed every single bottle of alcohol in Everlid in front of Elmar that night. He was a lean man, with skinny arms and even skinnier legs, but had a temper that could make even the toughest warrior shake. Elmar, on the other hand, wasn't intimidated by his father and chose to laugh at his shiny bald head and the fact that he had a missing front tooth that gave him a lisp.

"Alcohol is poison, Elmar," Lord Xalvadore yelled. "I've seen the way Emerick Callowat acts. He was normal until he turned to the bottle. I will not have that in *my* family!"

"Right, you'll just ship your family away," Elmar sneered before getting cracked in the mouth by his father. He spit out a mouthful of blood.

Xalvadore puffed out his chest. "It's time you grow up and stop shoving that in my face. You're the future Baron of Aleru and Lord of Everlid, start acting the part." He wiped his bloody palm onto his breeches. "If your people know you're a drunk, then they know your weakness. Once they know your weakness, they'll know how to take advantage of

240

you. When they can take advantage of you, they will no longer be your people."

The night the Corwins returned from Forbath, Elmar went straight to his quarters.

Elmar sat alone at his mahogany desk trying to distract himself any way he could. The Sight's Tower always seemed cold to him, and he knew part of that was in his mind. When Elmar was little, he would imagine his quarters were an ice cave in Soarfrost, and he wasn't the future Baron of Everlid but an evil nomad conjuring powerful potions strong enough to kill every Oracle.

While he was surrounded by glass walls, giving him visibility to all of Aleru, he was an avid reader and chose to try and lose himself in his books rather than the endless landscapes. In total, he had five bookcases that were stuffed with literature and trinkets from every realm. The first book he pulled out was written by Saige Lorrode Allwater entitled *The Flight of the Coatus*. Elmar's sister, Kylan, left for Reliss when she was six to become a Coatus Trainer, which meant there was to be no communication between her and any member of the Corwin family, except for once every ten years. He had practically memorized Allwater's work for when he saw Kylan to celebrate her Nascentem Feast.

When his family arrived via horse and carriage to Hillrode, a journey that had lasted just over a fortnight, they were all quite weary. Rather than ride directly to Reliss, which Elmar preferred, his Lord Father decided to rent a room for a few hours to nap and freshen up. Xalvadore Corwin always bragged of his relationship with King Tanwill, yet no one in the Corwin family could possibly be seen as tired from traveling.

Elmar waited until he believed his mother and father to be fast asleep before he set out to find something strong to drink. Hillrode's local tavern was named White Mana, which, according to a local, served tiny slices of beef that were blackened until they formed a crispy outer crust, and a stout that could spring up chest hairs.

The charred crispiness around the meat at White Mana had a slight coffee flavor to it, which was complemented nicely by the stout. He had one beer while he waited for his meal of meat and garlic greens, a second to wash it down, and a third because he wasn't yet buzzed. As his head grew lighter, he began to look around the inn, which was clumsily covered with red and white banners. His eyes met his mother's at the opposite end of the bar, and he knew he'd be lucky to escape his father's secret dungeon for the next fortnight.

"Didn't your Lord Father forbid you to drink on this journey?" Lady Alma said in her hushed voice when she made it to Elmar's barstool.

"He did," Elmar responded coolly as he waved for the bartender. "But I rather enjoy disobeying his commands, like a dog who steals a honey ham from the dinner table."

Lady Alma had the same smile as Elmar's sister, and that was often his only reminder of Kylan. "Even a dog knows that it is in its best interest to sit and roll over, especially if it wants to gnaw on the bone."

"Oh, my dear mother," he answered with a somber tone. "I have never wanted table scraps."

The bartender placed another pint of stout in front of Elmar and left his hand out like a traveling bard. Elmar stuck a silver in his palm, and Lady Alma swiped the beer.

"To hear you say that brings me more joy than you will ever know," she said after a great gulp of the pint. "Is it fair to assume you've heard the news?"

"The news from where? I've heard that a Verrativa has infiltrated a western village, the Shadows are back in power, and that Lorrode Allwater used his scientific knowledge to create Reaper, so you're going to have to be a tad more specific."

Lady Alma shook her head. "This wasn't sung from a bard; 'twas told by Lord Aiken Pritchett."

Emar's eyes widened. "The Royal Steward? What couldn't wait until we arrived?"

Lady Alma placed her hand on Elmar's forearm, and he felt the iciness that could only come from a woman of Aleru. "Your father's friend has turned us away. Tanwill Embray decided that seeing our daughter for the first time since we handed her over to him wasn't important. When your Lord Father awakes, we will travel to Ghordaan. Try to see straight by then."

"What was the King's reasoning?"

"There is no reason worthy of hindering a family's ability to be whole for a single night," Lady Alma responded before waving the bartender down once again. "I'll have another bottle of cherry whiskey. A glass won't be necessary."

Elmar's head had pounded ever since his mother told him that. It even continued after he returned home. The worst part was that his mother was right, but Xalvadore Corwin thought nothing of it. The undying loyalty that his father had to King Tanwill was borderline nauseating, so much so that Elmar often wondered if there was something more to their relationship.

He breathed in deep, and the air tasted like ice, which reminded him of his favorite way to drink rye. *The Flight of the Coatus* was supposed to distract him, but all it did was make him angry. Angry that he had ever read this book, angry that his family was taken advantage of, angry that his father didn't see it, angry that he couldn't have a damned drink, and that anger made his head scream as if he'd looked directly into the sun. Chills crept up his back as he kept trying to push the headache away, but the frustration reached a boiling point in the cauldron that was his mind and finally spilled over.

The clinking of footsteps came from the glass staircase leading to his quarters after Elmar spiked the book.

"I have had enough childlike outbursts from your father, please spare me of anymore."

Alma Corwin stepped up into the room, walked softly over the floor, gave her son a kiss on the forehead, and placed a jug of whiskey on top of Elmar's desk.

"Besides, you're in a tower of glass; throwing tomes is not in your best interest."

"I have barely the upper body strength to lift this full jug of whiskey, what makes you think I can shatter an ancient tower that was constructed with Oracle magic?" Elmar said as he rubbed his eyes.

Alma opened the bottom drawer of the desk and pulled out a chipped crystal glass and a long match. "How can the two men in my life be so different?" she asked with a laugh.

Her sky-blue dress was embroidered with fluffy white clouds down each shoulder and tightly hugged her hips. While Elmar's father looked borderline emaciated, his mother was thick-bodied and homely. Whenever Xalvadore sent Elmar to bed without dinner, Alma would creep up into his quarters with a full plate, always trying to fatten up her son.

Elmar looked more similar to his mother than his father, with the same auburn curls and chubby cheeks. "We're not so different," he said as he unbuttoned a maroon-colored tunic, exposing his undershirt. "Father kills people, and I kill myself."

"Don't remind me," Alma mumbled as she opened the jug, took a swig of whiskey, and filled the chipped crystal glass. "You know your father, Emerick Callowat, and Tanwill were once best of friends. Savage killers and rebels that journeyed through Trilon to destroy their enemies, but afterwards..."

She struck the match against Elmar's desk and stepped to the middle of the room. Directly in the center was a large stained-glass bowl the color of murky sea water that was filled with skinny dead twigs. To the naked eye, the bowl looked as if it was levitating, but it was actually held up by a pedestal which matched the Sight's Tower's translucence.

"Afterwards, your father acted as if Tanwill did some great favor to him." Alma lit the twigs and watched as the flames were born. "He believed that we all owed our lives to Tanwill, that we must ask 'how high?' when he tells us to jump. If he thinks that I will let go this great insult from Tanwill Embray of denying us to be with Kylan for her Nascentem Feast, then he might as well believe the moon rises in the morning."

Elmar saw the hatred in his mother's eyes; whether that was toward the King of Trilon or her husband, he couldn't say. "And whatever happened to Emerick Callowat?"

"Lord Emerick used the bottle to dull his memories from the rebellion, and with your father as his commanding Lord, I'm sure you could imagine why."

Elmar let out a single laugh. "I'd like to meet this Emerick Callowat. We can have a drink and talk about the man who drove *us* to drink." He finished the glass and poured another.

"You and I both, baby," Alma said as she took the jug from her son and smiled.

"What?" Elmar asked, noticing the grin.

Alma took a swig from the jug. "Just thinking about her. Did you know that, when she was little, people used to call her your brother?"

"She did always look boyish, didn't she?" Elmar said, matching his mother's smile.

As she walked back toward the steps to leave, Alma Corwin turned around with tears in her eyes. "We'll see her again, and I'll make sure it won't take ten years."

The whiskey was aged in cherry barrels, and its melodious flavors of sweet and tart danced across his tongue. After the sixth glass, Elmar couldn't even taste the alcohol, which typically signaled he should stop. Tonight, though, he wanted to drink the whole bottle as a personal "fuck you" to his father.

As the whiskey traveled through his bloodstream and Elmar's head grew heavy, he decided to pick up another book. Scanning the spines as his vision doubled proved to be too difficult, and he settled on grabbing a small wooden figure that rested on top of the bookcase.

It was a present for his sister that Elmar carved when he still held the hope of seeing her at the Nascentem Feast. He gave it a long boomerang for wings, which allowed it to glide for a moment. While the Coatus could have been mistaken for a cat at a certain angle, he was proud of it, and used to dream of the day he'd give it to Kylan on her sixteenth birthday. He tossed the toy and it zipped around the Sight's Tower, and when it came back to him, he tried to catch it, but his reflexes failed him, and the boomerang Coatus came crashing down into the empty whiskey jug. It shattered on the glass floor, spreading porcelain shards around his feet.

For a moment, he wanted to grab one of the more jagged pieces and end it all. Elmar thought how easy it would be to just run a sharp edge over his wrists or throat but paused.

"Of course, you won't do it," he said to himself. How could he do that to his mother? What if Kylan ever came home?

The fire was really roaring now, crackling inside the dark blue bowl. Embers began to float up and down like tiny lightning bugs, and Elmar tried to count them when he realized how many there were. Higher and higher the flames climbed out of the bowl until they escaped and formed a burning portal so bright that Elmar had to shield his eyes.

After the flames crawled back into the bowl, a boy was standing in front of Elmar. He was tall and lanky with coconut-colored skin and a head of wavy black hair that fell to his shoulders. Elmar noticed he was armed with a pike that had a black spear on top.

When the boy blinked his eyes, Elmar grabbed the longest shard of the whiskey jug to defend himself but split his finger open.

"Like I even had a chance," he mumbled as he sucked the blood from his finger. "I'm going to assume this is a peaceful visit?" Elmar continued as he buttoned his tunic and stood up.

"I am Prince Jarreau of the Red Reach, and yes, this is a meeting of peace," the boy answered, placing his pike on the glass floor. He had an accent that made him slightly roll his Rs.

Elmar seemed almost impressed. "Pleased to meet you, Prince Jarreau. I'm Elmar Corwin, future Baron of Aleru, and unashamed alcoholic." He laughed. "I'd offer you a drink but I'm unable to keep a collection."

Prince Jarreau furrowed his brow, clearly not understanding Elmar's humor. "Thank you." He wore strange armor that had a tan, rocky front and a red back that was filled with curved spikes. His legs were bare but for the belt around his waist which held two large pouches.

"Is your armor a turtle shell?" Elmar asked as he knocked on the chest plate like it was a door.

"Yes, there are many turtles off the shores of Ofrea," Jarreau said, taking a step back, trying to get some distance between himself and Elmar. "Most of the Tsumari eat them."

Elmar gave a nod of approval. "What about the others?"

Prince Jarreau ignored the question.

"And no boots?" he asked, looking at the Prince's bare feet.

Jarreau swallowed, then shifted his turtle shell armor. "Tsumari's feet are stronger than any boot from walking on the sands of Ofrea."

"I've read that the Verrativas don't wear boots either. Is that a trait of all magical races?"

"No, Verrativas choose to not wear boots to be lighter on their feet," Jarreau answered quickly.

Scratching his uneven auburn beard, Elmar looked out to the north-most wall to the endless hills below. "So, my new friend, why have you traveled to the eastern realm?"

The Tsumari stepped up next to Elmar. "My people were attacked last night, and our sacred creatures were poached."

"Tantaes?"

"Right. I'm happy to hear you know about the magnificent animals that represent my race," Prince Jarreau said with a half-smile.

Elmar looked around to all the different bookcases. "I read a lot. A question for you, though, Prince Jarreau: Why not take this to King Tanwill?"

The question seemed to pain the Tsumari Prince. "We tried to contact the King, but we are only permitted to enter through a certain portal as per the request of Lord Brannon Broadwine. The Lead Confidant assured us it would be lit at all times, but--"

"It wasn't lit," Elmar cut in. "Let me tell you, there's something going on in the Capital, and when it gets uncovered, it will spell trouble for the current regime."

Jarreau seemed lost for words. "The Brazier thought it smart to seek you out before your father, given his--"

"Desire to eat the hearts of babies and wash it down with their mother's tears?" Elmar said, cutting off the Tsumari Prince again. "So, what do you want me to do?"

"Tell your father to tell King Tanwill we demand a meeting to discuss the defense of Ofrea," Prince Jarreau shrugged.

Elmar laughed. "I'll try, but my father didn't want to confront King Tanwill about his refusal to see his own daughter, so I doubt he would give two shits about the safety of your people."

The Prince frowned, showing his disappointment. "Thank you, my Lord. I will take your message back to my people." He untied one pouch and reached inside.

"Wait, what's that?" Elmar asked, turning his full attention back to the Prince.

Pulling out a pinch of red sand, Prince Jarreau held up the sack for Elmar to see. "It's sand from my land. We use it when we travel through the flames."

Elmar's pupils dilated. "So, I'm going to assume the other pouch is dirt from Everlid."

Jarreau went and picked up his pike but didn't say a word.

"How did you get dirt from our land?" Elmar asked but was distracted by Prince Jarreau's desire to attentively stare outside.

The Tsumari stepped back, towards Elmar. "Are you expecting any more visitors?"

"I was expecting to drink until I passed out, why do you--"

Everything was still over Everlid when Elmar looked out to see what Prince Jarreau was speaking of, but suddenly the blanket of darkness unraveled into flapping wings. When Reaper crashed through the Sight's Tower, Elmar was hit with a storm of broken glass. Black and purple feathers flew around Elmar's quarters, some of them catching fire, while others covered the floor.

Prince Jarreau had fallen down amongst the commotion and dropped his pouch of sand from Ofrea, its contents scattering all around. He found his ground but froze in place after seeing the Coatus's head writhing, trying to pull free. The bowl that kept the fire had been knocked over by the winged creature's long neck, which led all the way outside.

When the Tsumari grabbed his pike to attack, Elmar held a hand up. "No, it's okay," he coughed.

That was when Jarreau realized what the Coatus was trying to break free from.

Reaper's mohawk was purple but specked with globs of red. Its beak was shaped like a blade, but unfortunately for Elmar Corwin, that wasn't the only thing it had in common with a sword. Pinned against a bookcase, the Coatus had gone through Elmar's stomach, his entrails slithering out like eels.

"Just go," he yelled to the Tsumari. *If I can die with the smell of rebellion against whatever my father fought for in the air, and the taste of whiskey in my mouth, then I can die a happy man.*

Jarreau tried to grab a pinch of red sand that had spilled, but the Coatus shifted, causing everything to shake. He opened up the second sack tied around his waist, threw some dirt onto a black feather that had the tiniest hint of a flame hovering over it, and a portal opened.

Elmar looked at Reaper trying to break free from both the bookcase and the back wall. Every time the creature pulled, more blood poured out from Elmar's stomach, but it didn't hurt him. It was as if he was watching this torture happen to someone else. He patted the Coatus on the beak, and traced his fingers over the indigo stripes which were now slashed with red.

"Your sisters were a lot nicer." Elmar closed his eyes, licked his lips, and smiled. They still tasted like cherries.

GOJII: LEEFSIDE

Lord Brannon,

The moon is red.

Larkmour Castle has been infiltrated by a group of four, one of which has magical abilities that I haven't seen in fifteen years. The group entered through the Trainer's Guild, slaying both guards Taro Geiz and Mychael Theozeed in the process.

We were taken by surprise, and judging by the small number of enemies, they do not mean to take over the Castle. Instead, I believe they are on a heist mission, and as of now, their victory is imminent.

I am entrusting this letter to Toby Vaino, Prince Tycho's squire and Lord Aiken Pritchett's apprentice. Return when you are finished meeting with Lords Lirum and Emerick but know that you will likely return to a defeated city.

It is important that no one is aware of this defeat. Please make sure that no one else reads this letter or tells a tale of what happened in the Capital.

Regards,
Saige Lorrode Allwater

GOJII: THE YLEWOOD

A sharp gust of wind swept through the great oak tree, taking a number of leaves as prisoners. Evore stood on the roof of his tree hut, soaking in the morning, while cold air blew in every direction. It felt like hands were pushing and pulling him, doing anything to make the Verrativa fall. Heights still frightened him, even after making the Ironash leap, but he knew that the fear in his belly needed to be conquered, as Verrativas were one with the trees, their protectors. Evore could have very easily walked to the Moiira Sea to meet his father, but how much longer could he take the easy path? Now was the time to prove who he really was, no matter what that actually meant.

Evore wore a long, baggy green robe that he tied together with a rope that was woven by his mother. The garment was a gift from his father, given to him after the inking ceremony, but this was the first time he had worn it. It made him feel powerful, like any task was possible, just as his father told him it would. He threw the hood over his messy tangled hair that seemed to be growing more wild than long, looked below, and tasted hints of his breakfast. Closing his cat-eyes tight, Evore stepped closer to the edge, readying himself for the plunge.

He expected to feel frozen while falling, similar to the Ironash leap, but the ground seemed to bum-rush him. When Evore looked down, he spotted a large branch jutting out from the neighboring tree and was able to land on it silently. While the bark felt rough against the soles of his bare feet, it didn't stop him from running across. Sliding over the trunk of the tree onto the next branch, he was completely covered by green leaves. Everything seemed still, and all that Evore heard was the wind's whistle, calling on him to continue. For a brief moment, he wanted to sit down on the thick branch and enjoy the tree's protection, but that wasn't the Verrativa way.

The end of the long branch wasn't covered by leaves, and the wind began to bully him once again. Shifting his weight up and down, Evore realized he could use the branch to spring himself to the next tree. Taking two steps back, he leapt to the end and felt the branch go down slowly, then it shot up, propelling him even higher than his tree hut. This time, things seemed to slow down for Evore, so he decided to push himself. One flip, two flips, and the Verrativa felt more alive than ever before.

On his way down, just before he ran out of space, Evore grabbed a branch on the next tree and dangled there for a moment. He knew this should be the time for him to climb down and walk the rest of the way, but his heart urged him to continue. Searching for any sort of limb that could drive him forward, Evore's arms began to grow numb. That was when he noticed the brown vine that seemed to hug the mossy trunk. As the Verrativa swung back and forth on the branch, he could feel the sharpness of the bark dig deeper, as if teeth were sinking into his palms.

Evore let go of the branch when his hands were sticky with blood and reached out ahead, but before he had a chance to fight back, the vine was coiled around his arm like a snake. Thorns stuck into his sleeve as he swung around the tree, unable to let go. The third time around, nausea set in and he sent down a storm of vomit below.

After the vine's grip loosened, Evore was able to slip down a bit, but that made him level with another tree branch, and with no chance to slow his momentum, he was swiftly punched in the stomach. Though the vine let go, he was unable to hold on to the branch that stole his wind, and again he was falling. This time, Evore was ready, and felt his long nails slide out of his fingers. Stabbing the trunk with them, he swerved down to the ground, leaving a trail of ten scratches behind.

"How smooth!" Tawanie's voice caused goosebumps to spread over Evore's back and arms. "Thought no one saw you?"

Evore spun around to see her hop down from one of the smaller trees in the near distance. She wore a strapless green dress that Evore thought for a second was made from leaves. As Tawanie grew closer, though, it was clear that the garment was silk, like something his mother would wear. The dress was cut short, as if she wanted to flaunt her collection of cuts and bruises. Evore blushed as he eyed her thighs, though he wasn't sure if it was from her beauty or the fact that she saw him fall.

"I'm up here, mister," she said, lifting his chin up.

Her black hair was tied back messily, as if each strand put up a fight to stay restrained. Evore had never seen anyone style their hair like that before, but he knew he liked it.

"You were doing fine until the vine, that part is tricky." Tawanie smiled.

All he wanted to do was kiss her lips as they parted into a grin.

"Sorry." Evore's head finally reached his body from the fall.

"Sorry? For what? You didn't hit me when you puked!" The girl laughed as she took down Evore's hood. "The trick is to let go of the vine when all your weight is going forward."

Evore felt his cheeks flush. "Yeah, I got caught…" He checked his robe and fingered the tiny hole in the sleeve. "…on a thorn."

Tawanie smoothed out his hair. "That's okay. If we never fell, we would never know how to get up."

As she twined her fingers through Evore's curls, he closed his eyes in ecstasy, losing himself in her touch.

"Your hands!" she yelled out just before Evore was about to melt, and as she reached for his wrist, he quickly turned away.

"I'm alright, don't worry," Evore mumbled as he hid his bloody hands.

Pressing her hip into his, Tawanie stepped even closer to Evore, like she wanted to share a secret with him. "As you say," she whispered.

Evore tasted her breath, smelled her hair, felt her warmth, but didn't know what to do or even say.

"Where are you headed anyway?"

Evore finally built up the courage to look into Tawanie's eyes, deep seas of yellow that he wanted to swim through. "I'm meeting my father at the Moiira Sea." He nervously faked a smile.

"Aren't you afraid of the Moiiralatta?" Tawanie asked as she focused on Evore's mouth.

Though his father was surely waiting for him, the only thing Evore wanted to do was stay with Tawanie. "No, of course not," he lied, unsure of what she was even talking about.

She ran her hand down his side, tickling him, and Evore's throat clenched, but he didn't want to breathe. When Tawanie wet her lips, the 10-year-old boy's body filled with goosebumps. "I wish I had something to give you for good luck."

"I don't need any luck," Evore said, immediately regretting it.

Tawanie gave his hair a slight tug. "We can all use some luck."

With that, she leaned in and kissed Evore. He kept his mouth open at first, as if the moment would end if he made any sudden movements. No honey or berries could have compared to the sweetness Evore tasted when he finally closed his lips around hers. That was when Evore realized he could climb and leap from every tree in Trilon, but nothing could ever make him feel higher than this. Her kiss made him more empowered than the robes his father gave him, more accomplished than his inking ceremony, and more important than when he read the note from Lord Brannon Broadwine.

She pulled away, leaving a sting in Evore's lower lip from a playful bite. "All good pleasures come with a little pain, wouldn't you agree?"

The sky was still hazy with clouds the color of spoiled milk when Evore finally closed in on the Moiira Sea, though he only got glimpses of it through tall trees that stood over him. It was as if his protectors were watching the boy as he walked on the dirt path that grew softer and softer as he stepped closer to the sea. Though he decided to walk the rest of the way -- five miles of skinny paths past Lake Gheller that only got more confusing after the Ironash Tree -- the memory of Tawanie's kiss kept him determined. Evore expected the ghost-like clouds, as they were the same most mornings in the Ylewood, but the fog that led up to the Moiira Sea was practically blinding him.

When the path transformed into muddy grass and the trees split apart, the stench of something rotten wafted in the air. The strangest part was the sound he heard. Anywhere in the Ylewood, Evore could hear the chirping of birds and the rustling of leaves as they danced to the wind's song, but here was different. The silence that hung over this place was not meant for the living. All of the colors that Evore had known were vibrant; from the green trees he climbed to the earthly dirt paths he walked, everything in the Ylewood had healthy colors, colors that meant the land was kissed by both the moon and sun. Here, though, everything seemed to be ill. Even the grass looked as if it were on its deathbed.

"Quiet, isn't it?" he heard from behind him. When Evore turned, his father, Onexis, Chief of the Verrativas, stood, almost as if he appeared from the fog.

Onexis was dressed in a hooded, dirt-colored robe that ended at his waist. His breeches were the same color and covered with green grass stains and yellow patches. As the Chief approached, he used his staff to help with each step but had no limp. At first, Evore noticed he looked different but couldn't pinpoint what it was, until he realized that a thin shadow of a beard covered his cheeks and chin.

The Chief of the Verrativas opened up his arms, allowing for father and son to share an embrace.

"It is quiet, but doesn't seem peacefully quiet, like by the Overhang," Evore responded.

"That's because it isn't," Onexis said, wrapping his arm around Evore. "Come, son, let me show you something… but keep in mind, this is not somewhere everyone can step."

Evore nodded. "Only a true Verrativa, right?"

Shaking his head, Onexis got down to one knee. "Son, everyone here is a true Verrativa. Your mother, those who were at your inking ceremony, even Trovado's newborn is a true Verrativa. This area is meant for the leaders of our race. You do understand that someday you will be Chief, don't you?"

"Chief? Father, *you're* the Chief of the Verrativas. I could never lead like you."

Wiping some of the dirt from his pants Onexis stood once again. "You're right, Evore. You won't lead like me. You'll be better." The sadness in his voice was heavy as the fog that surrounded them. "Just step lightly."

They both walked so gingerly that their feet barely made indents in the path that lead to the Moiira Sea, and when Evore was a step away from it, his father pulled him back.

"What do you think?" he asked, looking into the sea.

The fog that filled the area was coming directly from the Moiira Sea, and it felt as if an icy hand grabbed Evore's face as he looked into the water. Lake Gheller was a bluish-green that was warm enough to swim in, but the Moiira Sea was black like a night's sky and seemed to have a thin layer of ice over it. Evore had spent many nights looking up and wondering how far the sky went, and when he looked down, he asked himself the same question.

"It's black," he said, confused.

"That's right. What does that color mean to you?" Onexis asked.

"What does it mean to me?" Evore repeated. "It means nothing to me, but it reminds me of nighttime."

Onexis made a crooked smile. "Interesting. But the night is filled with the light of the moon, right? The light that can heal us when we're hurt. The Moiira Sea is only black, and that means there is no coming back... That means death."

Evore nodded and mouthed the word "death" more to himself, but he knew his father heard. "So, why are you... Why are you showing me the Moiira Sea?"

"How many times have you asked me about the pact I made with King Tanwill? This is it. This is why I, along with the bravest group of people I've ever known, fought the mortal's war."

"You fought for the sea?"

The Chief of the Verrativas almost laughed. "It's not the Moiira Sea, Evore, but what's below. We need to be protected. Fully protected."

Evore frowned as if he had just heard the news of a death. "Why do we, father? Why do we need to hide from the mortals? We're a peaceful race... Why would they want to kill us?"

Onexis took a step back and pointed to the land beyond the Moiira Sea. "For fifteen years, we've dwelled in the Ylewood, and for fifteen years, I've watched mortals march to their deaths to try and take what we have. You do understand what we have?"

Evore squinted, unsure of the answer his father wanted him to give.

"We have life, Evore. Unlimited life. The only way it can be ended is if someone takes it! What happens when the last Verrativa dies?"

"The person who takes the life becomes a Verrativa, so our race can never end!" Evore answered triumphantly.

"You're right. Our race can never become extinct, but what that means is that someone can steal our gift and call it their own. It is our job to protect our people and make sure that no one takes what is ours."

Onexis made a scowl that Evore had never seen before. Through the fog from the Moiira Sea, he didn't look like himself, and for a moment, the boy wondered who this person was. The Chief of the Verrativas was a man who smiled, a man who told him that everything would be fine, but now, he had either put on, or taken off, his mask.

"Evore, today I have to do something to protect our people, and I want you to come." He reached into his pocket and pulled out two empty corked vials and handed them over to Evore. "I wish I could have given you a proper childhood, son. You should have been given time to grow and flourish into a leader, but instead I'm telling you about the politics of bloodshed. I led our people to battle so we could restart in a world where we're protected, but I am still paying the debts from my actions."

Evore stuffed the vials deep into the pockets of his robe. "I'm ready to help you, Father, but if King Tanwill gave us protection, why are you so worried?"

"Son, I haven't spoken to the King in far too long. The only contact I have with the mortals is Lord Brannon Broadwine, and he's a man I didn't even trust during the rebelli--"

"WEEEEEEEEE!"

The high-pitched scream stung Evore's ears, and when it dropped an octave lower, he felt them pop.

"OOOOOOOOHHHHHH!"

His eyes began to water, and as he wiped them dry, a pair of wings flapped across the Moiira Sea in Gojii, over the tops of the trees. Flashes of green and gold sparkled in the sunlight and made even the Moiira Sea glitter gently.

"WEEEEEEEEE!"

The Coatus roared again as it glided down, closer and closer to the Ylewood. She flapped her wings once, ripping out half a dozen trees as a child would pick daisies.

"OOOOOOOHHHHHHH!"

As the Coatus closed in on land, the trees that still stood swayed back and forth, until the trunks splintered and broke. Some fell backwards, causing both Evore and Onexis to leap out of the way, but the others crashed into the Moiira Sea.

When the icy water sprayed Evore's face, he shivered, both at the temperature and the stench. However, he couldn't help but be amazed at what he saw before him. The ground rumbled when the Coatus touched down, landing the final blow to any of the trees that still stood in a daze.

"Look, Father, it's Nyteah! She's actually here!" Evore yelled out, his voice squeaking with excitement.

Her torso was a forest green, with golden raindrop-shaped spots all throughout that gleamed like treasure. As the boy took a step towards the creature, his father grabbed him, his knuckles an angry white. The Coatus's neck was covered in thick feathers that were spiraled with gold rings, which continued to her wings, and although she was magnificent, what shocked Evore most was her size. A quarter of the creature's body was on the sloping hill of Gojii, her belly fully submerged with the water of the Moiira Sea.

The Coatus had a shorter beak, with only one stripe of indigo, and her green mohawk was so long that the top was able to be braided. Evore judged that her neck was only a bit shorter than the Ironash Tree and questioned to himself for a moment if she could make it fall just as easily as the rest of the forest.

At the point where her neck and body connected was an armored man who climbed down from a saddle made of boiled leather. As the man took his foot out of the steel stirrup, the Coatus positioned her neck as to make a bridge of feathers that lead to the ground.

"Lord Onexis?" he asked when his boot squished in the mud.

"I have no reason to respond," Onexis sneered, still holding his tight grip on Evore. "This is my land. How dare you enter it unannounced," he boomed. "Who are you?"

The man wore a silver cloak that was fastened at the neck with a compass pin. His helmet was as black as the sea he landed on and had two white crystals that gave him sight but completely hid both eyes. It was quite different from knight's headwear, as there was no visor, with only a few tiny punctures in the mouth area, and in the top of the forehead was a spike the size of a dagger's blade. With each step he took, a clink of steel followed, though under his cloak was a doublet and breeches made from the same boiled leather as the saddle he climbed from.

"Forgive me, my Lord, just following orders." The Trainer's words weren't muffled at all through the helmet. In

261

fact, it sounded as if he was speaking into something that altered his voice, making it unnaturally clear and deep.

"Answer the damned question, mortal!" Onexis screamed, his voice a fist of flames rising above a brazier. "Who are you?

It was as if the question offended the man. "Who am I?" he questioned. "My name is Roycroff Kaylee. I am the Trainer of Nyteah, Coatus of the western realm."

The Coatus seemed to recognize her name, as she started cooing and clicking after the Trainer said "Nyteah".

"Could she get some water? The Lady of the west is quite thirsty."

Nyteah seemingly didn't want to wait for Onexis to respond, as she dunked her head deep into the Moiira Sea and began gulping. When Nyteah came back up, she spat out a mouthful of water into the sky like a fountain. As Evore felt the icy water spray on his cheeks, he beamed and looked to his father but saw that his feeling of bliss wasn't shared. Onexis wouldn't look at Evore, nor the Coatus, but instead kept his yellow eyes glued to the Moiira Sea, as if he were waiting for something.

Roycroff started petting Nyteah with a gauntlet-covered hand, and that was when Evore's head filled with memories from Saige Lorrode Allwater's book, *Trilon: The History and the Magic of the Three Realms.* A steel tail covered the Trainer's back, which dragged behind him, and at the tip was an unspiked mace head. If Evore remembered correctly, Vengar Stoneburner created the back piece as a way to imitate and discipline the Coatus. The Master Trainer was against any sort of cruelty to creatures, which is why he chose the unspiked mace, always saying that violent acts are as contagious as a plague. "*An alliance between men is built on trust and respect; it is no different when forming one with a beast.*"

"And who gave you the order to fly down to my land?" Onexis sneered as he pushed Evore behind him.

"That would be me, Chief."

Attached to the top of Nyteah's torso was a large litter, one that could have fit ten comfortably. Evore assumed that he must have not noticed it with the commotion brought about by both Nyteah and Rycroff Kaylee. Onexis must have not noticed it either, judging by the anxious look that took over his face. The litter's roof and walls were camouflaged on Nyteah's body, sharing her green color with an inlay of golden ribbons, and when the door flung open, a rope ladder rolled out. A man climbed down and was followed by a young boy. The man walked over to Roycroff and whispered something, then turned his attention to Onexis.

"It is a pleasure, Chief." His salted blonde hair was greased back, showing a pair of eyes that were desperate for a good night's sleep. The man's doublet was made of rich purple velvet with red buttons down the center. A pair of tight-fitting breeches led to spotless, knee-high black leather boots, and a jewel-encrusted scabbard was tied around his waist.

"I wish I could say the same, Brannon," Onexis shot back as he stepped forward.

Brannon Broadwine frowned at the Chief of the Verrativas. "I had the courtesy to address you with your proper title, the least you could do is the same for me." He looked to Evore. "Ah, this must be Evore. It's been so long, you probably don't even remember me," he chuckled. "Maybe you should run along, young one. I'm not so sure this is a conversation your father wants you to hear."

Evore was about to respond, but his father cut in. "He can and will hear anything you have to say. Why have you come to my land? Who is the boy?"

"Which question would you like me to answer first?" Brannon answered calmly.

"Choose for yourself, mortal!" Onexis yelled back, his voice growing more horse by the word.

Behind Brannon, Roycroff climbed on Nyteah and the Coatus stretched. With one flap of her wings, she was airborne, and the second one brought her high above the Ylewood. She was gone with the third flap, and Evore closed his eyes, wishing he could have flown away with her.

"And where is the Trainer going?" Onexis continued with his attack of questions.

Reaching into his scabbard, Brannon pulled out a dagger and touched the point of it against his palm. "Roycroff Kaylee is a very busy man, some say the busiest in Gojii. He and Nyteah had many stops, but they were able to drop off me and my friend Toby here for a quick visit, but they'll soon return."

Onexis eyed the dagger in Brannon's hand.

"Chief, do you know who Lord Emerick Callowat is?"

Evore watched as his father nodded, still staring at the dagger.

"Oh, you do? I thought so. Supposedly, there was a suicide in Leefside, a carrier boy. But an old butcher, Adley Roundtree, swore it was a murder. Swore a time stealer killed the young boy, so Lord Emerick went to Rutherfall. Of course, Lord Lirum Rhygell had to get me involved, and the two demanded that *I* fly to Gojii. I had to convince both of them that the old butcher was lying and was in fact the murderer. I hanged an innocent man, and it was all because of you." Brannon tossed the blade down at Onexis's feet. "You left that," he scoffed.

"It was an act I wish I could--"

"Listen, I set up specific routes for you to send and receive my messages, to reduce the chances of any encounters. The plan is as sturdy as the foundation of a castle, but you went and ripped out a center brick!" Brannon continued. "The King has enough to deal with as it is." Brannon cleared his throat. "Did any more innocent townsfolk see you?"

"No, only the butcher and the carrier."

"So, the two men you've seen were both wrongfully killed. I thought Verrativas were the peaceful race." Brannon's voice raised. "If the people of Trilon figure out that you can enter their land with no issue, but they can't enter yours, what do you think will happen?"

Onexis looked over to the red-haired boy who stood next to Brannon. "Why is the boy here?"

Brannon clenched his hand into a fist. "What does the boy have to do with anything? Don't you understand? The people will eventually come after the Crown for giving you so much freedom, and if they were to somehow take us down…" He trailed off for a moment. "If they were to take us down, then they're only a Coatus ride away from restarting your race. You know as well as I do that the Verrativa race is not one adept at battle."

This man Brannon Broadwine spoke sharply as if words were his weapon of choice. Evore never spent that much time with his father, which he understood, because being the Chief of a race was a burden as much as an honor. It just seemed that, ever since that day at the Ironash Tree, the warmth that filled his father was hidden by a cloud of darkness.

When Evore was little, the Verrativa Chief called King Tanwill his friend, but now he couldn't help but wonder, was he lied to? Or was he simply being protected from the truth? All his father told him now was how the mortals wanted the Verrativas dead, constantly repeating himself. He seemed to pull himself apart about the deal he made with King Tanwill, but maybe he was searching for some assurance of his past decisions.

The stories that Evore had read of the mortal legends, Sir Bekan Atalay and Sir Ryker Tygurnach, were no better, with the two Knights always being depicted as heroic, fighting in tournaments or triumphantly defeating their enemies. After meeting Brannon Broadwine, though, he realized that there were truths buried beneath the songs and sword fights that the writers left out. This man, who was dressed in the fanciest garments, who was immaculately groomed, who made his grand entrance into the Ylewood, used all of these distractions to hide his true ugliness. If the mortals were anything like him, then his father was right to be defensive.

"Who are you to enter our protected land unannounced and verbally attack the Chief of the Verrativas? Whatever my father did or didn't do, it was with good reason." Evore couldn't believe it when the words spilled out of his mouth.

Brannon smirked. "Well, he certainly is your son, that's for sure. My dear boy, King Tanwill and I have done everything with good intentions for your race. The Ylewood was a gift from the King, which, I may add, is more land than any other Lord received for their efforts during the rebellion. Now, have there been a few rotten eggs over the past decade-and-a-half? Of course, but this land is more protected than the Capital! There is no hidden agenda; we just don't want any violence between races."

"If all of that is true, why can't we hear it from the King?" Evore asked.

"King Tanwill has done enough regarding these particular matters," Brannon's answer came with a strong tone of annoyance, like he was swatting away a persistent gnat. "And to be honest," he shifted his attention back to Onexis, "Between your recent actions in Leefside and the treasonist accusation in your most recent letter, you should consider yourself lucky."

"Please enlighten me as to why I should consider myself lucky," Onexis snapped back.

"Lucky I didn't arrive with King's Lawmen to take you away in shackles."

Onexis gave Brannon a look that could have killed an elderly man. "Why is the boy here?"

"This is Toby Vaino, squire to Prince Tycho," Brannon answered, clearing his throat.

"Well, I was his squire; now I'm more of a steward's apprentice," Toby answered, unsure of himself. His orange hair was greased and combed down the sides, covering both ears. A black lump stared at the two Verrativas from the center of the boy's forehead like a third eye, with a scabby pupil. He seemed uncomfortable in his black surcoat, which had a silver crown sewn on the chest.

"A modest boy, you see." Brannon laughed, giving the boy a slap on the back. "Toby Vaino is in constant contact with Lord Aiken Pritchett as well as Prince Tycho himself. He is a very important piece to the Crown and will now stay here as a token of our mutual understanding."

Onexis furrowed his brow. "Staying? We don't barter for respect with hostages, Broadwine."

Brannon fixed the collar of his doublet. "We prefer the term 'ward'. It's far less barbaric, don't you agree?"

"One can call a battle a dance, but that wouldn't change the fact that blood would be shed. We will not accept your hostage, mortal," Onexis grumbled as he paced back and forth.

"You're looking at this the wrong way, Chief," Brannon answered with a tight-lipped smile. "Evore, wouldn't you like a friend to grow up with? Someone to tell you stories about the Prince and teach you how to swordfight?"

The word "friend" echoed through Evore's head and awoke his soul. Maybe he had misjudged Brannon Broadwine. What if his only motive truly was to unite the Verrativas and mortals?

"Don't let him manipulate you, Evore!" Onexis wailed. "The Verrativas will not be swindled into any agreements! I'll figure out your plan. The question is, what will you do once you're exposed?"

"Ha! Oh, so high and mighty. You say that you'll expose me, but I believe I've already shown your true colors today, murderer. I just hope that your son doesn't also grow up to loathe those who help protect him."

Evore felt the anger rumble inside of him like thunder just before a storm break. "The trees are our protectors!"

Brannon shook his head with disappointment. "I can see we're not going to see eye to eye on these matters. Please do not enter our land, Chief, as per our original agreement fifteen years ago."

Onexis seemingly wasn't done arguing. "I'll stop when I speak with King Tanwill!"

"WEEEEEEEEEEEEEEEE"

The sounds of Nyteah's return shook the ground once again.

"You should really heed my advice and accept the boy," Brannon hissed.

"And what if I don't? You'll come flying back down again and scold me?" Onexis fired back, a hint of sarcasm mixed in his voice.

"OOOHHHHHHHHH"

"Something like that. Come, Toby."

When Toby Vaino faced the Moiira Sea, Brannon slipped behind him with such a silence that it would have impressed a Shadow, and he gave the boy a sharp kick in the back with his spotless boot. Toby tried to stop himself from falling into the Moiira Sea, both arms flailing as he fought to keep his balance. Leaning forward and standing on his toes, the boy was able to stable himself, but a few pebbles rolled over the edge, making a sound as quiet as a whisper.

"Get back, behind me, boy, now!" Onexis screamed, pushing Evore away as he lifted up his staff, but it was too late.

Two long, neon tentacles wrapped around Toby's calves and yanked him to the ground.

Toby flipped over and reached out both hands, his eyes swelling with tears. "I've never ever spoken ill of anyone with magical blood. I'll do anything you ask of me and more if you stop her. I'll--"

Before the boy could say any more, a third tentacle flew out, fleshy-colored suction cups latching onto his face parasitically and lifted him up. With the brutality of a blacksmith smashing his hammer against an anvil, the Moiiralatta brought Toby down right in front of Brannon Broadwine.

A graveyard silence followed as the boy was seized into the murky blackness, and after a few single bubbles rippled up, the Moiira Sea turned wine red.

Evore blinked a few times, trying to figure out if this whole day had been a dream.

"I--Why?"

He felt his throat tighten and his eyes grew heavy. How was it even possible to have felt so high and so low in such a short time span? The sweet taste of Tawanie's kiss was replaced with the saltiness of his own tears.

"How could you?" Evore sobbed, but as he narrowed his eyes towards Brannon, the tears flowed faster. "He did nothing wrong, you're a--a..."

"Monster? Yes, I suppose so, but let the boy's death be a reminder to you both of whose in--"

There was a snap like a whip and the sea monster's tentacle reached out again, this time grabbing Brannon Broadwine. As the Moiiralatta brought him up high, he reached into his doublet and pulled out a dagger. The blade never connected, though, as another tentacle appeared, grabbed the knife, and hurled it across the Ylewood.

Onexis held his staff up high. "NO!" he bellowed with a voice that felt louder than Nyteah's.

From the depths of hell, the Moiiralatta arose. Her bulbous head had purple veins running through it, twisting and turning like roads on a map leading to two curved horns on top the size of greatsword blades. The sea monster's face led to a snout shape, but instead of a mouthful of teeth, there was a black hole large enough for a man to step inside. As she stood up, more and more tentacles appeared until the Moiira Sea was barely visible.

Brannon squirmed, trying to wrench himself free from the Moiiralatta, but it simply tightened its grip, still staring at Onexis.

"We thank you for your protection but leave this one." The Chief spoke softly, but the Moiiralatta's eyes, two black abysses, showed it was still feeding time. "LEAVE HIM TO ME!" Onexis screamed, holding his staff up with an outstretched arm.

Suddenly, the Moiiralatta froze, its neon green skin glowing as Onexis brought his staff down. As the sea monster lowered its head, the Verrativa turned his staff to the left and right, and the Moiiralatta obeyed like a pet. He lifted his staff again, and the tentacle that held its prize mirrored the movement. When the monster placed Brannon Broadwine on the opposite side of the sea, it vanished underwater with a splash that drenched the man, whose face was now a sickly yellow. His blonde hair was no longer slicked back, and the purple doublet he wore was stained with slimy green goop.

GOJII: THE YLEWOOD

The smell of blood and fear hovered over the Moiira Sea like a ghost unable to let go of its past life. Onexis took a deep breath and stared at Brannon, who seemed determined to not make eye contact. *The air tastes like victory; let him remember this on his flight back to Reliss.*

"WEEEEEEEEEEE!"

Nyteah screamed as she came into sight, casting a shadow over the Ylewood, but Onexis didn't wait for her to land. As he turned and walked away, Evore stood frozen as a statute.

"Father? How did you--how did you do that?" The boy's eyes were still puffy, and his lips quivered on each word.

Without even a nod, Onexis stormed past Evore. "Follow me. Remember what I told you before," he said sternly but with a certain softness that only a father can speak with his son. *Is it still a smart idea to bring him along?*

Evore sprinted back to Onexis and eyed his staff cautiously. "Can I touch it?"

With a single nod, Onexis held out his weapon and his son patted it as he would a small animal.

"It just feels like a stick." His voice had a hint of disappointment.

"What were you expecting?" Onexis asked as they walked back towards the Ironash Tree.

"I'm not sure. I guess I thought it would have been at least warm."

Onexis tapped Evore on the backside with his staff playfully. "It's not a cup of tea!" He expected him to laugh, or at least smile, but the boy just kept walking, like a man being escorted to his own hanging. *Your family, everyone you know will be murdered, and you won't be able to do anything to protect them. If the mortal didn't say that...*

Evore let out a sigh and his voice cracked. "He did nothing wrong."

"The squire?" Onexis asked, knowing what his son meant.

"His name was Toby! Toby Vaino, and he died because of that coward!" Evore's voice hardened quickly. "Why didn't you save him?"

Onexis bit his lip trying to stifle a sigh of his own. "I tried, Evore. I really did. It all just happened too fast."

"You should have accepted him to be our ward. I would have!" Evore shot back.

"Evore, if we took the boy in, then we would have Brannon Broadwine dropping in on us as often as rain."

Throwing his hood down in frustration, Evore walked ahead of Onexis.

He still has so much to learn.

The cloudy morning had transformed into a warm afternoon, one that allowed the sun to shine even through the trees. Onexis thought about nature and how its purity could never be tainted or pushed to a certain agenda. An innocent boy was murdered moments ago, and yet the sun still beamed down on the Ylewood, impassively blanketing the land in its warmth.

As Evore continued ahead, Onexis dragged his feet, looking at the dirt that colored his toes. The single purple flower that had grown on the side of the path had six petals, same as all the shy aconite that Onexis had burned countless times. Seeing the poisonous flower sent him back to a time when victory didn't taste so bitter...

The sky had wept uncontrollably for a fortnight, welcoming Evore into the world with a storm strong enough to rust Ghordaan steel. Onexis had informed King Tanwill of Emery's due date, and even though he thought there was no way Trilon's ruler would make the trip to the west, he still let out the rope ladder that led up to his tree hut out of respect.

273

The hut had been dimly lit with candles that gave off fragrances of vanilla and honey. Emery sat up on an oversized feather mattress, nursing Evore, whose eyes still weren't opened. The curtains around their sleeping quarters were tied up with hemp rope as Onexis kept marching in and out, bringing in cups of tea, bowls of berries, and anything that he thought would help comfort Emery.

"Nex, he's not coming." Her words were barely louder than a whisper. "Come lay with your son."

Her voice will forever be my favorite song.

Onexis wrapped a second blanket around his wife before kissing her lips lightly, and as he cupped his hand over Emery's cheek, she grinned. Her skin felt soft against his calloused hands like a flower petal, but Onexis knew she was anything but delicate. Though Emery's eyes had deep black bags under them, the way that the candle's orange flames danced with their nectar color gave her a lively look.

"Can I get you anything?" Onexis asked as he tried to get Evore to hold his finger.

"No, I'm o--ahhh!" Emery winced. "Who would have known that a bite from a toothless mouth could hurt so much." She laughed as the flames continued to ripple through her eyes.

Onexis shared her smile. "I'm sure that means he's full. You need your rest anyway. I'll take him."

The rain fell so hard that it didn't even have a pitter-patter noise but instead a snake-like hiss. Dark shadows were painted on the walls, and the Chief of the Verrativas glared at them as if they were intruding on his family. He knew what he had told his people -- it was best not to procreate until the Ylewood was built up to his liking, but a Chief needed an heir. Besides, Onexis didn't need to explain his actions to anyone, as the savior of the Verrativas as well as the mortals.

If he wanted to bend his own rules, who was going to stop him?

No, I'm not a savior, not a hero. I'm just the only one that didn't hide.

Five years was a long time to hope that there were no new mouths to feed, and Onexis was sure that women were becoming mothers in secret, but he knew that the population needed to eventually be rebuilt.

Our people needed to be secluded from the rest of Trilon.

Mortals, Shadows, and Oracles were all different, yet they all yearned for the Verrativa's gift. It was always the same -- the Verrativas hid while the rest of Trilon hunted them down, like wild boars that were meant to be served at a feast with an apple clenched in their jaws. The truth of the matter was that Onexis regretted his pact with Tanwill Embray. He marched three quarters of the Verrativas, a race that was already dancing on the line of extinction before Tanwill's rebellion, toward death. The remaining quarter mourned their lost ones but rejoiced at the fact that they were now able to live on a protected land. It didn't even occur to the Chief of the Verrativas that he was now expected to build a fully functional society for a race that, for the majority of their lives, was in hiding.

Onexis never thought to ask about the crop growth in the Ylewood, but a single harvest only brought a few baskets of berries, six bushels of wheat, and three barrels of leafy greens. There was an abundance of purple flowers that were coated in a sticky golden sap in the far north, but he was certain they weren't edible. Still, the mystery flowers looked nice, so he had picked a handful for Emery and placed them in a clay vase on their dining table.

When Onexis lifted Evore from Emery's arms, he dropped the cloak of fear he was shrouded in and let his son's warmth radiate through him. It filled his veins with a euphoric feeling that he never thought possible, and for that moment, all of the Chief's decisions made sense. Lightning screamed in a blaze of white light after a stampede of thunder, and Onexis squeezed Evore tight to his tattooed chest, as if to shield him from the world around them.

A moment later, there were three knocks at the front door, and Emery grabbed her son, the flames in her eyes glowing once again.

"Just relax," Onexis had muttered as he threw on a white robe.

When he turned the knob, the door flew open, and four cloaked men, each carrying different sized bags, burst in, all soaked to the bone.

"Ever hear of a staircase?" the first and tallest man grumbled.

"Ever hear of being hidden in plain view?" Onexis answered with a smirk.

King Tanwill Embray pulled off a navy tunic and dropped it to the floor, while the other three followed, with the last also removing a Coatus Trainer's helmet. Tanwill wore a powder blue gambeson under his cloak that had leather straps tying in his oversized belly. Around his neck was a silver necklace that held a golden crown with tiny red rubies on each of the three points. His curly hair was maple brown with subtle hints of red throughout, and his chin was covered in a goatee that touched the middle of his throat.

Tanwill let out a hearty laugh and clapped Onexis on the stomach. "Always with the quick answers, this one! You could learn a thing or two from him, Broadwine." He pinched the Chief's sides and frowned. "Don't you eat?"

"It's been… err… difficult with our harvests, and Emery needed the extra nourishment, so I--"

"No matter!" Tanwill cut in, holding up a large burlap sack. "Tonight, we feast in honor of your son... Uhm, what's the little one's name?"

"Evore. We named him after my father." Saying his name filled Onexis with warmth again.

"Then we'll feast to Evore!" Tanwill said, walking through to the kitchen and leaving a trail of mud with every step. "Come on, you know Brannon and Lorrode. Oh, and this is Vengar Stoneburner, head Coatus Trainer." Tanwill froze when he saw Emery lying down with Evore and held his hands out. "Would you like to dine with us, my Lady?"

Emery pulled up blankets around Evore's body and shook her head. "No, I'm okay, I want to stay with Evore. But thank you, Your Highness."

"Ah, there's no stronger shield than a mother's love. We'll save you a plate and try to keep it down."

"It's quite alright, Your Majesty, have all the fun you like. Onexis needs to enjoy himself for a night," Emery answered warmly, making eye contact with Onexis while Evore continued to have a feast of his own.

Tanwill laughed. "Titles, titles. Titles are for books. My name is Tanwill, but if you insist on calling me something, I'll settle for The Most Handsome Mortal In Trilon."

He gave a playful wink before untying the ropes that held the curtains up, and with that, Onexis's family was shielded by two dark satin sheets that together showed a night sky. The two candles that were lit around Emery made themselves a part of the picture, as if the flames wanted to hide amongst the rest of the stars.

"You've got quite the wife there, my friend," Tanwill said, giving Onexis a light squeeze on the shoulder. "Make sure you protect her."

"Thank you, Tanwill." Onexis smiled back. "Though, I must say, Emery has protected me better than any weapon or tree."

"If only you could have written something for me to read to Lanlei when she was still alive. Maybe she would have wielded a bottle for Tycho rather than a sword and shield." King Tanwill chuckled but frowned as he rolled up his sleeves. "What the fuck is this?" His voice was a bark from an angry dog, and his party, who stood idle around the dining table, winced as he yelled. "This man just had a son; it's time to celebrate!"

Lorrode Allwater cleared his voice. "Erm, Your Highness, I suggest perhaps we remove that vase on the dining table before we start our festivities. It contains shy aconite, a type of flower that, if mixed with the right ingredients, can create certain poisons, including Silent Bite, Stranger's Tongue, and Chalkdust Torture." The smoke-grey robe wrapped around his squat body was identical to the one he removed earlier, only slightly drier.

"What's the meaning of this, Chief?" Brannon asked, curtly. "The King of Trilon enters your home and you greet him with poisonous plants?"

He wore a black doublet with thin yellow lines down each side. A line of yellow studs started at the chest and sectioned off like a fork in a road towards the left and right pockets. The Lead Confidant's blonde hair was shoulder length, and he wore a beard that hid most of his face. A thick golden chain that held a matching open eyeball hung only a little further than Broadwine's beard but was low enough to clank against the yellow studs on his doublet.

"There are Lords who would have your head on a spike right now," Brannon sneered as he slicked his hair back, paying no mind to the dollops of rain that fell from his greasy, noodle-like locks.

Onexis looked at King Tanwill, then Lorrode, and then at Brannon Broadwine. "Your Majesty, er, and my Lords, I assure you that I had no idea of the flower's poisonous nature. Those were picked during our last harvest, and I thought they would bring a smile to my wife. Nothing more, nothing less."

Brannon grabbed Tanwill by the elbow to walk him away from Onexis. "I knew this was an ill-advised journey, one that was poorly planned from the--"

"If you don't get your sticky hands off me, you'll lose them," Tanwill said, slapping Brannon's hand away. "If I say we're feasting in the name of Onexis, Chief of the Verrativas, and his son Evore, then you bet your ass I'm leaving here full."

At that, Brannon stepped back and gave a single nod.

"Chief Onexis," Saige Lorrode Allwater broke in. "I would recommend burning every trace of shy aconite. If you were to ingest the flower yourself, you'd be fine, as you know, but if someone else were to feed it to you, it would be another story. There are always rotten apples in every race, peaceful or not."

King Tanwill had heard enough. "You two spend all your time in the Capital, yet you don't understand common courtesies. You accuse him of wanting to poison his friend and then tell him how to run his lands?"

"Your Majesty, I was simply trying to protect the Chief," Allwater responded quietly.

"And I was trying to protect you," Brannon joined in.

"I didn't sign over the deed of this land to the Chief of the Verrativas so we can tell him how to run it," Tanwill roared. "And he didn't invite us over to poison me, so you two better show some damn respect. Without Onexis and the Verrativas, where would we be? Would either of you have recited the banishment spell and drank the potion that would

have burned your insides until you vomited up your lungs?"
There was no answer from either of the Kingsmen. "Onexis
came to my rescue when I went against Cellyadure in
Ghordaan. If he wanted me dead, there was no easier of a
time to let me die! Remember, you were too craven to
follow."

Brannon punched the dining table. "You were advised to
let the Oracle escape by your entire Cabinet. When will you
let that go?"

"I'll let it go once your racist views stop clouding your
judgement! Without Onexis, I wouldn't be standing here
today, and if I had fallen that day, do you really think the
rebellion would have continued?"

"I would--"

"That was a rhetorical question," Tanwill bellowed. "It's
been five years, Broadwine. Five fucking years! I'm
surprised the Chief even let us in with how we've ignored
him since the rebellion."

Onexis cleared his throat and cracked his knuckles. "I'll
light the fireplace."

After doing so, he grabbed the shy aconite to toss into the
flames, watching as the bouquet shriveled from a lilac to
black. *Was that flower always a few petals short?*

King Tanwill cooked everything himself, starting with a
thick pumpkin bisque that was topped with lightly toasted
almonds. The main course was a haunch of boar bathed in a
raspberry vinegar sauce, with roasted red potatoes and
applesauce. When Onexis informed the King that he had
never eaten any sort of meat, Tanwill replied, "Tonight you
will." It had been the greatest meal of the Verrativa's life.

Afterwards, the party sat around sipping on brandy while
Brannon brooded in silence.

"Thank you all for coming during this time of celebration for Emery and me." Onexis smiled as he held up his glass, which seemed considerably heavier than before.

Tanwill nodded. "Nothing like having a son, eh, Lorrode? Bah, who am I kidding, you're probably numb to it all now!" He laughed heartily as he untied his belt.

Onexis let out a chuckle of his own. "I didn't realize Saiges could wed."

"Well, we aren't permitted to marriage, but certain loopholes allow our order to--"

"Fuck whores!" Tanwill cut in. "The Saige has more bastards than a dog has fleas!"

"But I give them all my name," Lorrode said as he grimaced at the mouthful of brandy he drained from his glass. "My bastards are a gift to Trilon." He let out a phlegm-filled cough. "Tell me, Chief, you've had harvest issues here?" He addressed Onexis though his eyes were focused on the jug of brandy.

"Yes, every harvest had just been enough to get by with rationing," Onexis answered. "Maybe our fortunes will change soon."

Lorrode swallowed another glass before answering. "It is possible, but highly unlikely. I know that the Oracles brewed a potion that made any ground fertile, but no one has ever been able to, err, replicate it."

Syrah always knew that I'd need him.

"And if things don't change, we can supply you with enough food to fatten up every Verrativa," Tanwill burped out, his eyes closing. "Wait, our gifts!" he said with a spontaneous burst of energy. "Vengar, you go first. I'm going to close my eyes." He passed some wind and his sudden jolt of life fizzled out like an ale that had gone flat.

Vengar Stoneburner, who didn't take a bite of food or a sip of alcohol during the entire feast, stood up and limped over to

Onexis. He was the smallest of the group, with the top of his head barely reaching Lorrode Allwater's shoulders. Some said he was the last RoarCatcher, an ancient race that were wiped out by the Oracles well before Zabkar Inwar ruled. RoarCatchers viewed all creatures as their only allies, which was the main reason they were tragically defeated during the Battle for the Mirrored Mountains.

His dark skin was filled with deep wrinkles that looked as if they were drawn by hand, and the only hair he had came from the white whiskers that hung from his nostrils. Vengar's torso was so skinny that it looked like it belonged to a malnourished child. Still, there was a mystical strength to him. The tunic that reached his thighs was the color of fiery peppers, and his tight breeches were black as coals. Around his neck was a thin rope that held three tiny horns, one golden and filled with different colored jewels, one bone-colored, and one that looked as it were made of ice. The RoarCatcher's second necklace was his Bellow, a corked stained-glass apothecary jar. Thick lines of black cut red and purple diamonds onto a background of twilight blue.

"Chief Onexis, thank you for allowing me into your home." Vengar croaked like a frog. "Typically, I wouldn't make such a voyage, as I oversee all three of Trilon's Coatuses, but because of the inclement weather, King Tanwill thought it was best for me to fly Akupara tonight."

"Thank you for joining us, Lord Vengar. How are the three Trainers fairing?" Onexis answered with a smile.

Vengar cleared his voice as best he could. "They're doing well so far. Of course, there have been problems since Saige Lorrode and myself found a way to train the Coatuses, but all together, they've been adequate. I started a Guild to teach future Coatus Trainers, and they're learning surprisingly quick."

"A Guild? That's fascinating. Have there been any standout students?"

Reaching into his tunic, Vengar pulled out a tiny drawstring bag. "Lord Xalvadore Corwin's daughter has only been a student for a month, but she's catching on faster than most. I will say that her pugnacious nature may hold her back."

He opened the brown bag and pulled out a bone-colored horn.

"This is my gift to you, my Chief. If you are ever in dire trouble, don't hesitate to use it, but only if it's absolutely necessary."

"Thank you, my Lord. Your concern for our protection means a lot to me and the entire Verrativa race." Onexis bowed to Vengar and placed the horn in his pocket. "May I ask you about the jar around your neck? It seems oddly familiar."

"Ah, your familiarity to my Bellow is no surprise. This allows me to speak with creatures as long as it holds their blood," Vengar said before his face dropped and his tight-lipped mouth unweaved into a frown. "The Battle of the Mirrored Mountains was where my race was defeated by the Oracles. They stole the deceased RoarCatcher's Bellows and used them to create Burrato bombs."

A light flashed in Onexis's head and he saw an explosion of body parts in the back of his mind. *My memory is my hell.*

Next, Brannon Broadwine stood and placed a velvet sack on the floor in front of Onexis. "Chief Onexis, I've brought you two gifts." He spoke through gritted teeth like he was a child who didn't want to share his toys. "First is a doublet for the rare times you need to cross the Moiira Sea and receive a letter from King Tanwill. I know there will be a system set up to hide them in specific areas and thought it'd be better to be... what did you call it before? Hidden in plain view."

283

Once again, Onexis bowed, but just as he was about to thank Brannon, he pulled out his second gift from the sack. "This is a dagger from my personal collection, forged in Ghordaan with a Clubsodon bone hilt." He handed over the dagger without making eye contact.

Holding the blade never felt right, even then.

Onexis ran his finger over the blade, searching for the words to say to the Lead Confidant. "Thank you, Lord Brannon. I hope that I'll never use it for more than a decorative piece, but I take solace in knowing I'll be properly prepared in case I do."

Lorrode Allwater dragged his presents over in a sack that matched his grey cloaks. The stack of books the Saige took out one by one included vivid descriptions of their contents and writers, including the ones he wrote. Even after Onexis thanked him, Lorrode continued. "A man may be a fierce warrior or a superior blacksmith, but books can save him just as much as a weapon or trade."

"Yeah, until the warrior cuts his throat, or the smith gives him a hammer to the face. Let's see a fucking book save him there," King Tanwill grumbled as he awoke from his nap.

Lorrode gave a final nod and the King stood, his curly hair falling over his eyes.

"Come, Onexis, I want to give you my gift alone."

Grabbing the grease-stained burlap sack, King Tanwill wrapped his arm around Onexis and together they walked back towards the front door.

"Listen, Nex, I'm sorry about Brannon. We've..." He rubbed the sleep from his eyes. "We've seen a lot of shit. Shit that he can't get over."

"It really is all right and understandable. Hopefully, after this meeting, his views will change," Onexis answered, keeping an eye on his sleeping quarters.

"My gift to you was the feast and the Ylewood, but to Evore..." Tanwill reached into the sack and pulled out a hooded robe. "From Hillrode. I had it fashioned after yours for when he's older."

Onexis felt his eyes fill up, and when he blinked, tears trickled out. "Thank you, Tanwill. I hope he'll be a better leader than me."

"A better leader? Even after all these years, you're still beating yourself up over the deceased Verrativas? It was a war, Nex. You did the right thing."

I did the right thing.

"Someday, Evore and Tycho will be friends as we are, and that would have never happened without you. Remember that, Nex, because I'll never forget."

There was a sudden cry from beyond the night sky curtain, but Tanwill didn't turn. It was as if the King of Trilon didn't hear the scream.

"Father!"

Onexis first noticed King Tanwill's goatee drip down, with the rest of his face following after. Before he knew it, everything around him began to melt, like his vision was nothing more than a sheet of wax.

"Father!"

All of the sweet smells of honey, vanilla, pumpkin, meat, and brandy were the next to be stolen, no different than a sword from a dead man. *Those were the smells of happiness.*

The hiss of rain grew louder, higher, transforming to a blood-boiling scream.

"BURRATO BOMB!"

His body tensed, bracing for an explosion, but it never came. A bitter taste coated the Verrativa's mouth when he came crashing down to the floor, which was soft with the puddles of his memories. Grabbing at the thick globs, he tried to stand, tried to yell, tried to breathe. Pale light erupted from everything around him, stinging the Chief's eyes as if salt water was being poured into them, and for a moment he was blind.

"What happened, Father?" Onexis heard Evore say, and even though he still couldn't see, he knew the episode was over.

"N--noth--" Onexis tried to speak, but a mouthful of mud came out instead. "Help me up, please." He choked out the four words, and as Evore grabbed a hold of his arms, grey blurs formed around him. Still spitting, he rubbed his eyes, but that made them sting even more, as his palms were also covered in mud.

Evore wiped his father's eyes clean and tried to knock off some of the muck that was caked on his robe. "Father, something happened. Please tell me."

The grey blurs started to grow darker and taller and finally blossomed into trees. "It was nothing. Let's just go." Twisting his arms around, Onexis struggled with his robe, finally conceding and pulling it off. "To the Ironash Tree," he muttered, tossing his muddy garment behind them.

Evore tried to give him support while walking, but the Chief of the Verrativa pushed him away, only using his staff for assistance. For the rest of the walk, neither father nor son acknowledged each other, let alone spoke.

Finally, Evore broke the silence just as they arrived to the Ironash Tree. "Father, something happened to you. You were writhing around in the mud. How could you possibly expect me to believe that was nothing? I may be young, but I think after today, I deserve to know."

Physical pain is temporary; mental pain is forever.

"Evore, let me tell you something, and always remember this: Your decisions will light the torch that you will hold through life. If you question your decisions, then you'll spend a lifetime in the dark."

286

With that, he tapped the trunk of the Ironash Tree three times and beckoned Evore to enter first. The darkness below called to Onexis, told him to come inside and hide from his life, and he welcomed it.

While the Ironash Tree had always been symbolic to the Verrativas, it was Syrah the Creator who transformed it into an underground sanctuary. After the Oracle was able to convince Onexis to spare him from banishment to Soarfrost, he promised to make the Ylewood even more formidable than it already was.

"The Moiiralata can protect the Verrativas from attackers on foot, but what would happen if, say, your friend Tanwill Embray goes back on his word? Trust me when I say this, time stealer -- there is no safer place than underground."

The Chief always used the Ironash hideaway as a cover, a destination for celebration and ritual, and now he had another use for it. *I will find out what happened to my friend.*

"Do you see that?" Evore asked, pointing ahead. The dirt path below was a mile to the sanctuary, but halfway down, there was a strange glow coming from the right wall. Normally, the walk was shrouded in darkness, but the shimmering glow gave the skinny corridor some much-needed visibility.

Onexis pushed Evore to the side and began running toward the glow. Directly in the center of the wall was a hole that was large enough to walk through, covered in a strange white film. Onexis pushed it with the end of his staff, but it wouldn't break and went bouncing right back into place.

"What should we do?" Evore asked nervously.

A skinny blade sprouted from the tip of Onexis's staff after he twisted the top and bottom in different directions. It cut through the barrier easy as parchment, but the sticky substance cocooned the weapon. Evore's eyes widened at the weapon fearfully but didn't bother asking any questions.

When Onexis stepped through, he realized where the light was coming from. Spider webs plastered the walls like sticky, webbed tapestries, each of them pulsating as they illuminated the enormous lair. At that moment, he wished that he had given Evore a weapon of his own. *Why didn't I give him the dagger?*

"Watch your step, and stay as close as possible," Onexis whispered as he crept through, the tree branches tattooed on his torso glowing from the mysterious webs.

Reaching to the end of his staff, the Chief went to clean it off from when he cut his way into the new passage and was kissed by the blade. A drop of blood bubbled up from his pointer finger before he felt any pain, and that was when the familiar pitter patter of rain began.

Rain? Underground?

"What is--Father!" Evore screeched, pointing up to an army of spiders scampering down the webs from every direction. The arachnids all began to click their pincers, sounding like they were greeting the Verrativas in their native tongue.

Onexis scanned the sea of spiders that kept growing deeper and noticed that none of them had fiddles on their backs. They were all larger than the ones Syrah showed Onexis, with grey furry bodies and skinny stick legs. Beady red eyes zeroed in on their prey, stepping closer and closer until Onexis and Evore stood back to back. The first one to attack went for Evore's calf, but he was faster and leaped into the air. When he landed, he planted both feet into the spider, cracking it open like an egg with a hearty crunch, and when the yolk came pouring out, the rest of the spiders snapped in unison.

Surprisingly, the spiders all backed away and climbed back up the webs, leaving their deceased sibling behind.

"Is this what the vials are for?" Evore asked, staring at the crushed spider.

"Yes, but we need to find a fiddleback, which none of those were," Onexis said, looking everywhere for another opening.

Then, he noticed it. Climbing the webs would be inevitable, but on the opposite side of the lair was a hole larger than the one they entered through.

"Over there!" he yelled, darting through the den.

The spiderwebs were stickier than honey covered in sap, and when he grabbed onto them, it took all his strength to let go. When he did, though, there was a clicking sound once again, this time a much deeper one.

The spiders either gathered reinforcements, or...

"Evore, get back, now!"

From the hole came two long legs the size of icicles in Soarfrost. Next, two pincers began to chew around the hole, making it larger. The spider that appeared was so fat, it had to use four arms to squeeze through. It landed and the ground trembled, scattering the dirt into the air like it too wanted to get away.

When everything settled, the spider bent down low enough to show the Vertativas the cream-colored fiddle mark stamped on the back of its brown body. Twelve coal-stone eyes circled around its head, giving it vision in every direction, and after two blinks, the rest of the spiders filled the walls, readying themselves for a show.

The Fiddleback Spider rubbed its front two legs together like a Lord readying his fork and knife for a feast, and then started to click its pincers. Circling around the lair, it continued to click, receiving unison responses from the small grey spiders. Finally, the fiddleback came to a halt, blinked at the Verrativas, and stomped a leg down, causing Evore to fall. A number of spiders pitter-pattered down from the wall and wrapped themselves around Evore, serving as his chains.

"I will kill every last one of you," Onexis howled as he stared at the look of utter fear on his son's face. "I'm telling you right now, by taking my son, you have declared war in my eyes. Release him. Release him and we will leave."

The Fiddleback Spider gave three clicks, and another swarm of chains were wrapped around Evore.

"So be it."

Onexis held his staff out and positioned himself to attack. This was to be a battle between the Chief of the land above, and the Master of the hell below. He dug the balls of his feet into the dirt and began sprinting towards the fiddleback.

As the giant spider bent over to dig its pincers into Onexis, he used his staff to pole-vault himself into the air. Landing gracefully on the back of the insect, the Verrativa couldn't help but smirk, and he brought his staff down, to end the fight.

Just as the blade started to penetrate, the fiddleback bucked, sending Onexis across the den to smash against the spider-filled wall.

Standing up, his back covered in guts and tiny bits of grey fur, he charged once again and lunged with his staff. This time, the fiddleback crossed its front legs and blocked the attack, driving Onexis back. Now it was time for the spider to attack, and with lumbering speed, it grabbed the Verrativa and held him against the wall. Paying no mind to the dozens of tiny spiders that were killed by the maneuver, the fiddleback snapped its pincers, trying to rip apart the Chief at the neck. Onexis held up his staff lengthwise, though, leaving the spider to just chew on bamboo. Pushing as hard as he could, the Verrativa was able to move his enemy back far enough to plant one foot firmly on the wall, and he launched himself free.

This time, he led with a lunge attack, and when the fiddleback went to block it, Onexis swung the butt of his weapon around, taking out one of its many eyes. The spider's shriek could have shattered glass, but it quickly got back into fighting position. Onexis knew his tactic angered the fiddleback, and now that it showed to be susceptible to feint attacks, he had to take advantage. Still aiming with the butt of his staff, he led with a downward thrust for another eye. As the spider crossed its arms to block, the Chief followed through, purposely bouncing his staff off the ground. Leaping up, he caught it mid-air and came down with full force, slicing off the Fiddleback's front right leg. A geyser of blood sprayed from the wound, painting Onexis as well as the rest of the lair. The spider squealed while it writhed around in pain, and in that moment, Onexis felt his heart grow heavy. *One of us had to lose.*

The Fiddleback clicked its pincers together slowly, the same way a warrior would speak his last words. Then, all the spiders on the walls began to rhythmically click together. Two of the larger ones crept off the walls to climb on top of their leader and took their positions. With one holding down the frets of the fiddle mark and the other fingering the strings, Onexis began to realize victory was not his.

At first, their song sounded like scraping bones and rattling teeth. It grew so loud that Onexis thought his eardrums were about to burst. *This is the song of hell.*

The spiders continued their lullaby, and slowly Onexis felt his troubles float away. He looked over to Evore and saw that all the fear had completely left his face. Some of the spiders had even crawled down to wrap him in a white blanket. As the Fiddleback Spider rose, the song grew sweeter, softer, and for the first time in his life, he felt safe. Dropping his staff, he watched a group of spiders form a blanket around his legs, then his waist, then his chest, and then his neck.

This is my favorite song...

ALERU: EVERLID

The sky had transformed from an angry red to a dark bruise purple as night fell upon Aleru. It was the third and final day of Elmar Corwin's celebration of life, and Lady Alma was finally able to be alone with her son. She had spent the better part of three days toasting glasses with different families from all three realms, receiving their condolences with gratitude. The Lady of Everlid wanted more than their words, though.

Her home was once known as "the two tower city", and she wondered how long that name would stick now that there was only one left. The Twilight Tower was built by her grandfather, Lord Elmar Staley, and was constructed not as a place of worship but as a memorial for every fallen Staley. Lady Alma took each step up to the temple where her son was on display two at a time, her feet hidden beneath a long, midnight-black gown. The dress had a lace trim and an open back, which she covered with a silk white shawl. Elmar had purchased the garment for her while they were in Hillrode before learning the news of their sudden refusal to attend Kylan's Nascentem Feast.

There were three hundred steps in total that led up to the entrance, which was anchored by twin pillars made of Tantae ivory. The rest of the sanctuary was maple brown marble kissed with streaks of white. When Alma was younger, she always thought the great temple looked like it was covered in snow, giving it a stark feel even during the summer months.

She remembered the last celebration of life ceremony for her family as if it were a fortnight ago. Like Elmar, her father Lord Avner and brother Sir Ereck were unable to be presented with an open casket. Her entire family had died because of Tanwill Embray and his unquenchable thirst for power. Even her mother, Lady Launa Teabrook, sliced her own wrists, unable to cope with the loss of her husband and first child, because of him.

The Oracles used to cast firestorms from the Sight's Tower, a deal that labeled the Staleys as supporters of the King of magic. Many would whisper that Lord Avner secretly practiced the spells and potions of the Oracles, but the truth was, their bond was built with intimidation. Zabkar had arrived to Everlid with Cellyadure and Syrah the Creator and said they would have the Sight's Tower, or the Staley name would end. On the contrary, if he agreed, then he and everyone that lived in his lands would be protected. Lord Avner had always said that there was nothing more important than family, and his pact with Zabkar Inwar showed that. "Family is air, and without air, there is no life."

It took two months before Tanwill showed up with his host. They had scouted the area and waited until Zabkar sent the smallest group of Oracles to cast their firestorms. Tanwill led a force that included Bekan Atalay, Xalvadore Corwin, Emerick Callowat, and Lirum Rhygell into the tower, defeating the Oracles in less than an hour.

Brannon Broadwine met with Lord Avner afterwards to try and convince him to join the rebellion. He cited how the King of magic may have promised safety and land to the Staley family, but with the Sight's Tower, Inwar had the ability to end families from each of the three realms with ease. Their final negotiations included a marriage between Alma and Xalvadore Corwin, who was to be assigned the position of Baron once the war ended. Broadwine agreed to this on the condition that Lord Avner guaranteed he'd give the cause his entire force, including his squires, who were training at The Blade.

No one wanted to see the Lady of Everlid wed to a craven, but the betrothal was already documented with King Tanwill as well as Lord Avner's seal. Sir Raylon Tarbuck, the Battle Master of The Blade, even pleaded to have a duel for Lady Alma's hand, but King Tanwill refused the match. When Lady Alma married Xalvadore, it was well known that she had no love for the westerner, who held a small keep outside of Pelagu before joining Tanwill. At one point, Corwin was seen as a potential candidate to lead a rebellion against Inwar due to his known disdain for magic. It was said he would even set up traps to catch Verrativas and execute them in the town square as entertainment for his people. While most of Trilon had a strong hatred towards the Verrativas, and many tried to put an end to the magical race to gain their powers, this presentation was widely considered cowardly and in poor taste. Corwin wouldn't even kill the Verrativas once they were captured, leaving that task for his castellon.

The inner walls of the Twilight Tower were lined with rows of candles, and the ceiling was a peaceful purple. A golden velvet carpet with navy vines embroidered around the edges lined the second set of marble stairs up to the coffin. Her deceased son was protected by a gate of wild flowers, and once Alma reached the top, she picked one.

"You weren't supposed to leave me, baby boy," she whispered, placing the stem of the flower behind her ear. Her curly auburn hair was braided behind her back and tied at the center with a single black ribbon. "You weren't supposed to leave me alone," Alma continued, curling her hand into a fist. "Who am I going to drink with now?" she asked, cracking a smile. "When your father told me Kylan was to join the Trainer's Guild, I refused. I didn't eat for a week and lived off of wine and hatred. They never allowed visits or even letters to the Guild, so for ten years I had to just pray to the God of Wine that my daughter would come back to me. I'm not sure if she's dead, but if she is, that means I didn't say goodbye to either of my children. Your father always said I was over-dramatic, but what would he know? He didn't have his entire family ripped apart by one man. When your grandmother committed suicide, Tanwill came to Everlid and prepared a feast, and your father ate everything that was put in front of him." She closed her eyes. "You were supposed to be my rock. You were the one who kept me going, with your wits. You were the only one with a mind worth a damn around here."

Just then, the door to the Twilight Tower opened, and in entered Xalvadore Corwin. He wore a silver jerkin that had an extended fur collar. The buttons were brass circles, and his breeches were a charcoal black.

"Finally get time with our son?" he lisped. "It's a shame things had to happen this way," he continued, his voice bouncing off the walls.

"Yes, a shame that my son was murdered. It's a shame that we haven't seen our daughter in over ten years." Her eyes narrowed into balls of fire as she spoke. "It's a shame that the Coatus didn't kill you."

Xalvadore Corwin's face grew red with rage. "I would have gladly given my life if it meant that I could change places with our son." Sweat dripped down from his shiny bald head as he climbed the steps. "Tanwill's gone mad. We said it would happen after he refused to execute the Coatuses."

"'We'?"

"Yes, we. I used to speak of this with Lords Emerick and Bekan. When the rebellion began, it was about defeating the King of magic and the Oracles. It was about putting an end to magic once and for all. The things we saw Inwar do to our homes? Tulrose still isn't fully rebuilt, you heard it straight from the Broadwines. Inwar made King Tanwill watch his mother butcher his Lord Father before hanging herself, all because she drank a drop of liquid. Power like that shouldn't exist."

Alma crossed her arms, unmoved by Xalvadore's tale. "Tanwill Embray and Brannon Broadwine stole their weight in gold from the Oracle camp at The Mind."

"To feed the hungry! Unless you practiced magic or settled an arrangement with Inwar, any man, woman, or child could have been butchered like a boar," Xalvadore yelled, his chest puffed out.

"That's why my family bent the knee! They knew they couldn't win, and our lives were more important than our pride." Alma spoke quietly and turned her back on Xalvadore. "Then you all came along and made my every breath a misery."

Xalvadore grabbed Alma by the arm and spun her back around. "King Tanwill's rebellion saved the human race! It's just that once the Shadow got involved, our leader changed. The Shadows were our enemies, just as much as the Oracles, but Lord Brannon insisted on turning one of them. The plan went from killing Inwar and every single one of his followers to banishing them all to Soarfrost with a spell. The Shadow was able to get ahold of an Oracle tome, but a human couldn't speak the banishment spell without ending their own life. He then suggested that we join with the Verrativas and have one of their kind speak the spell because time stealers can only be killed and cannot… ahem… die on their own terms." He looked at his son's casket as his eyes began to water. "I should have seen this coming then, but I was blind. We told him all three Coatus eggs should have been destroyed right when they fell from the sky. Instead, he teams up with a RoarCatcher and has the demons tamed? The next thing I know, my family is turned away from the Capital! We should have just stayed. I knew madness had taken him when we were refused! He would have never attacked us in Ghordaan. Of course, he and Stoneburner would strike once we were back in the east."

Alma frowned. "You thought he was prone to madness since the eggs fell from the sky, and still you sent our daughter to be a Trainer?"

"It was either send her or Elmar." Each word grew longer until he began to sob. "I couldn't give up my firstborn to him, in case all my paranoia proved to have merit."

"So, let's take our revenge then. We will gather forces from Aleru and then Gojii. Lord Lirum Rhygell will fight with you, I know he will."

"King Tanwill was always the most skilled battle tactician and will have Lord Bekan Atalay's forces," Xalvadore responded hesitantly.

The Lady of Everlid bit her lower lip. "Are you saying that your fear of this man is greater than your love for our son?"

Xalvadore cracked his knuckles and moved even closer Alma. "What would you know about love?" Corwin continued wiping the tears from his eyes. "He would have had his wits about him if he weren't inebriated. If you loved our son so much, then you would have never introduced him to the vice that put a strangle on your life!"

"Oh, do you mean drinking? It's actually necessary for anyone who spends an extended period of time in your presen--"

CRAAAH!

Xalvadore slapped Alma in the face with the back of his hand. "Our son is gone, as is our daughter." His voice was as cold as stone. "From now on, you will show me the respect that I deserve. There will be no gathering of forces, is that understood?"

Alma didn't respond, so Xalvadore cracked her again, this time giving her a fist to the kidney. She fell down to one knee and began to lightly wheeze.

"I said, is that understood, wench?"

Once again, the Lady of Everlid didn't respond, so Xalvadore kicked her in the stomach, causing Alma to drop to the floor. She laid face down in front of her son, gasping for air, her eyes alive but dead inside.

Xalvadore flipped Alma over with his boot and stood over her. "I am the Baron of Aleru, and when I ask a question, I expect a response." His mouth twisted into a smile as he stepped between his wife's breasts, like she was a trophy from a hunt. "I believe that you've had enough. Just remember, my Lady, always answer any question that your Lord asks of you." He looked once more at his son, nodded, and turned to head back down the stairs.

Alma latched onto Xalvadore's boot just as he began to walk, and at first, he tried to wretch himself free, but her grip was too strong.

"What do you thin--?"

With a twist of his ankle, Xalvadore Corwin went toppling over, face first down the marble stairs. Alma stood up, still wheezing, but she couldn't have been happier. Before strutting down the stairs, she looked back to Elmar and blew a kiss.

"Rest easy, baby. Mama will be okay."

She walked slowly down the stairs, stepping directly onto the velvet carpet that was now littered with dark red smudges.

"Oh, this won't do," she said softly. "This carpet was my Lady Mother's and now it's stained with your blood."

Xalvadore was sprawled out halfway down the stairs with a cut above his eyebrow and another on his chin. Alma helped him by pushing him again and watched as he rolled until he reached the bottom of the staircase. She began to chuckle when her husband wiped his cuts and gaped with wide eyes at the sight of his own blood.

"Ho--how dare you?!" His voice cracked as he tried to sound hard.

"How dare I? How *dare* I?" Alma wailed, giving Xalvadore a swift kick in the side. "I've sat and held my tongue while you overtook my land and abused or exiled *my* family. You would have never given your life for Elmar because you would no longer be able to--" She gave him another kick. "--impress your King."

"I--I--I'm the Baron of--"

"You're nothing. This land is Staley land; remember that, craven. From now on, I will be in command of Everlid, and you will be my puppet. You can't go to your best friend now, can you? You know everyone listens to you because you're married to me. The Staley family is the rock. You're nothing more than the snow, and now it's time for the sun to come out again."

Xalvadore coughed. "I'm sorry, my Lady." He whimpered like a hungry puppy.

"There will be a gathering of forces, is that understood?"

"Yes."

"We will discuss this later in more detail, when you're in a better frame of mind." Alma smiled as she stepped over Xalvadore and exited the Twilight Tower.

The night air kissed Alma's face as she walked through Everlid, which now was unnervingly tranquil. She breathed in deep as the wind swirled and wondered if these gusts were her family trying to speak, voicing their approval of what she had just done. While the strikes from Xalvadore still stung, there was nothing that could bring her down right now.

Although Everlid was known as the two tower city, a great majority of it was taken up by rolling hills. Alma continued walking on a path that took her to the top of a particular mound where she could overlook the main strip of the city. Beyond that was the city gate, and beyond that was the Rytys River.

If legend could be told, Rytys, a Umenyonga from Hybernia, the world above Trilon, created the river with his shovel. The Umenyongas were a race of Giants from a land which had never been seen but were talked about since the age of the Frosthammer. Rytys fell from Hybernia and had to take refuge on Trilon. The Giant was tired of walking to the Gulf of Azure when he was thirsty, which was quite frequently, so he dug out a river to satisfy his laziness.

Alma remembered going to the river to gather water with her Lady Mother, filling up bucket after bucket. Lady Launa would always tell her to fill up a few extra buckets so they could dump one over Lord Avner and Sir Ereck's heads while they slept. Late-autumn frost covered the bottom of her dress, and she wondered how long it would take for the Rytys River to freeze. When Alma went to gather water with her mother after a harsh snowstorm and saw that the river was frozen over, she began to cry that they wouldn't be able to provide water to Everlid. Her Lady Mother kissed her tears away and took out two pairs of ice skates from her pack.

Handing Alma the ice skates, Lady Launa Teabrook said, "Remember this, my wildflower. When faced with a problem, just do what makes you happy."

Alma smiled at the thought and was grateful that, although Tanwill Embray took her family, he could never take her memories, those which she treasured more than all the gold in Trilon.

The path down the mound divided into two sections, one that led to the city gate, and the other towards her father's quarters, which had been usurped by her husband. When Alma was a girl, she would always visit her Lord Father in his quarters, and no matter how busy he was, he would always make time for her. Whether it was for a chat or a pre-dinner meal that they called "linner", Alma was always the center of his universe.

Lord Avner's favorite linner was hard-boiled eggs with a side of crisp boar bacon, and Alma tried to prepare it for him at least once a week. Her father would give her twelve boros to pay for a dozen eggs, and one day she realized that the peddler had been shorting her by one. When she informed her father, he was incredibly calm with his approach. He told her, "You gave him your business and he took advantage. Never let anyone take advantage of you." The next time she went to buy eggs, she paid the twelve boros, and proceeded to smash every egg that the peddler had in his cart, other than the dozen for her father. When the peddler said that Lord Avner would hear of this, Alma smiled and said, "Don't worry, I'll tell my father myself." Without so much as a grunt, the peddler saddled up his horse, hopped into his cart, and was on his way.

Xalvadore had two grey stone walls built when he took over Lord Avner's quarters. Sandwiched between them was an iron gate with railheads as long and sharp as broadswords. The Baron of Aleru said he would use them to mount the heads of those who committed acts of treason, but as far as Alma saw, they were bare, and even glistened in the moonlight.

"M'lady Alma!" She heard a voice from behind her. "You shouldn't be wonderin' around on yer own so late at night!"

Alma spun around to see Sir Geremy Vaino hustling towards her, his armor clanking with every step. He wore a white breastplate with two black towers etched in the center. His helm had two visors, one to protect his eyes, and another for the rest of his face. He opened up both visors, showing a pair of pale blue eyes and a bushy orange beard.

"It's so cold, m'lady, please take my cape." Sir Geremy removed his cape, crimson with a white fur collar, and wrapped Alma in it.

The cape brought her a warmth she hadn't felt in a lifetime. She looked to Sir Geremy's side and saw no sword. "You're not armed, Sir?" she asked, confused.

"Of course I am, m'lady," Sir Geremy responded, grabbing the hilt of a greatsword that was strapped to his back. When he unsheathed the blade, Alma felt her body tingle with excitement.

"That isn't a Knight's sword," she whispered. A breath of warm air snuck out from her mouth into the cold night.

Sir Geremy nodded. "You're right, m'lady, it isn't a Knight's blade in Everlid, but in the Moondown Lands, it's quite common." He held the greatsword with two hands. Its hilt was specifically molded for his grip. "The blade itself is reflective and has blinding ability if the sun hits it just so."

Alma glared at the sword and was able to see her red cheeks inside the blade.

"May you let me pass to my fa-- my husband's quarters?" she asked, brushing her hand against Sir Geremy's bicep.

"But of course, m'lady."

Alma gave his arm a squeeze through his chainmail before he sheathed his greatsword. He wasn't a large nor muscular man but grabbing a hold of him sent another wave of warmth through her body. "Thank you, Sir."

He unlocked the gate with the largest key on a ring of over ten.

"Will you be accompanying me on my walk?"

"Aye, m'lady, as I would with Lord Xalvadore, if it pleases you." He spoke like he had practiced the lines in front of a mirror.

The path turned into white gravel that crunched under their feet, then opened up to a dome-shaped building. It was an earthy brown with a rounded roof and covered in a blanket of frost.

"I'm sorry for your loss, m'lady. No one should have to bury their baby."

"Thank you for your kind words, Sir. Tanwill is a rabid animal, one that needs to be put down." Alma spoke with harsh coldness in her voice.

Sir Geremy opened the oak door to a room lit up by a roaring fire. "You speak of treason, m'lady. You speak of *our* King, the man who knighted me."

"What family do you serve, Sir? Or, what family were you serving when you *became* Sir Geremy?" she asked, stepping into the office. It had a table made of glass in the center and a portrait of the two towers behind a backdrop of a setting sun. The flames reflected off the glass table, giving the room an orange tint that was almost as vibrant as Sir Geremy's beard.

Sir Geremy followed the Lady of Everlid inside, his voice tied to his tongue. "The Staleys, sixteen years ago, when I was just a boy of fifteen. I've served yer family through the rebellion and even fought alongside the Knights of Rutherfall."

"You fought beside my father, then."

"M'lady..." His voice grew heavy. "I was your father's squire when he fell."

Lady Alma shut the door and sat in her father's glass chair. "Are you going to weep, Sir?" she asked, shifting back and forth on the plump red cushion. There were a number of documents on the desk that Alma balled up and threw into the fireplace without even giving them a glance.

Sir Geremy removed his helm and placed it on the marble floor. His eyes had heavy bags under them, and he had a head of hair that fell past his shoulders. "M'lady, Lord Avner was like a father to me. I trained with Sir Ereck at The Blade. We were as close as brothers."

"Lord Avner and Sir Ereck were my father and brother," Alma cut in, pounding the desk with a fist. "Lady Launa Teabrook was my mother. Elmar and Kylan were my children, and while I'll never see them again, I will kill the man who took them from me. If you truly serve the Staley family, then you will assist me."

"M'lady, how could I be of--"

Lady Alma put up a single finger to hush the Knight. "You must call upon Lord Tremaine Broadwine. Half of the host he commands are Knights of Rutherfall. If we could find a way to rally all the Knights of Rutherfall, we can rid Trilon of the Embray name."

"M'lady, I would like to bring in Lord Xalvadore to have his input," Sir Geremy responded.

"You craven. You claim to serve *my* family but need an approval for *my* orders from *my* husband," Lady Alma roared, her face growing redder with each word.

Sir Geremy shook his head. "I understand your frustration, m'lady, and I can't imagine the pain you've endured. What you're asking me to do, though, goes against everything a Knight stands for. A Knight without honor is like a sword without a blade -- useless. Our rebellion against Zabkar was about protecting the innocent, not about vengeance."

"Then fight for the innocent, Sir Geremy. Take my son out of the discussion and the fact remains the same that Tanwill and Vengar Stoneburner are taking out cities with Reaper!"

When Sir Geremy heard Alma's words, all the color drained from his face, and he looked ten years older. Unsheathing his greatsword, he got down to one knee. "I, Sir

Geremy Vaino, will continue to fight for the Staley family, will give my sword to you, and, if needed, my life for your cause."

Lady Alma was just about to tell him to rise when she heard a faint scratching. Her eyes darted around the room, looking for the source, but she saw nothing.

"Maybe it's the fireplace?" Sir Geremy asked when he heard the noise.

"That's not it," Alma responded. She moved closer to the portrait and the scratching became louder.

"Careful, m'la--"

"Hush!" Alma hissed as she pushed into the portrait.

It began to slowly separate from the middle, cutting the two towers in half. The inside was lit up by the fireplace and revealed a tiny dungeon that was occupied by one prisoner. Fully naked and shackled was a young, brown-skinned boy with a tangled mane of black hair that helped hide the fear in his eyes.

"What's your name, young boy?" Alma asked as Sir Geremy sprang to her side.

"Prince Jarreau of Red Reach," he responded with a voice desperate for water.

"Ah, a Tsumari Prince then," Alma said with a smile. "Sir Geremy, please fetch our guest some food and drink. I'm sure he has a lot to say."

ALERU: CLAY HARBOR

"It's too bloody cold here," Sir Ryker Tygurnach grumbled, shifting back and forth on a wooden stool that seemed to groan every time he breathed.

Lord Bekan's laugh was short and gruff. "You're a Knight of the south; this isn't cold."

"*You're* a Knight of the south!" the Tiger growled. "And not for nothing, but maybe if you stayed in Ghordaan, your bloody home, maybe we wouldn't be in this situation."

Since setting out from Reliss to hunt down the RoarCatcher outlaw Vengar Stoneburner, he had lost all of his company to desertion. The Tiger was well aware that, to fulfill a task such as the one bestowed upon him, lives would be taken, but he always assumed that it would be death's doing, not some whispering Lordling. Sir Ryker had explained to the Knights of Rutherfall that their mission was to capture Vengar Stoneburner and take down Reaper, as it had grown mad.

Lord Brannon had commanded Sir Ryker not to speak of the King's poisoning to the Knights of Rutherfall, as to preserve its secrets like buried treasure. By leaving out this detail, the Knights all grew suspicious, and most wondered where the King was during all of this. Some seemed to believe that King Tanwill had grown obsessed with punishing his so-called enemies, and the Knights of Rutherfall were cleaning up his mess. Sir Ryker felt his face grow tomato red when he had to tell his brigade that Vengar Stoneburner had stolen a sacred heirloom from the King. The snickers and sneers made him realize it'd be easier to sell them a bag of cow shit.

It started on Dearborn Road, when the toll tower leading to Yatorga was ripped down. A story brewed that King

Tanwill was unhappy with the collector because he was pocketing levies and summoned Reaper to take the man's life. When he addressed the rumor to the entire camp, Sir Horace Pommel, one of the first squires that the Tiger had taken on, stood up and asked, "Have you spoken with our beloved King recently?" Horace was always an arrogant squire who would talk down to the stable boys, degrade women, and demand free drink at every southern inn. After Traetark the Blind was being transported from Gojii to Forbath for trial in front of King Tanwill, a group of Shadows led a rescue mission into the Capital. The squire stifled the attack, killing three enemies, and captured another who later escaped, but King Tanwill believed his acts of bravery were enough to be knighted, and Horace Pommel became Sir Horace Pommel of Piklorha.

Sir Horace's real issue with the King started when Reaper took out his keep on Piklorha. He was convinced that the Coatus was sent by King Tanwill, who was outraged at the fact that Pommel shared a bed with Lanlei Embray prior to her death. "On the eve of the battle at Stone Break Valley, Her Highness asked me to warm her bed. Tanwill must have never gotten over the fact that the Queen was bored with his fat ass." Of course, everyone called him a liar, but Pommel held strong with his story. "Please, when I was a squire, I walked in on her and Brannon Broadwine. I'm sure if she were still alive, both of us would still be having fun with her." After that, things were never the same in the camp.

It was the perfect picture in the Tiger's mind, one that the authors and singers would paint for generations after he was gone. Ryker could even see the smile on Bekan's face as he watched an army march in formation up to his keep at Windrip, trumpets blowing, and drums booming. Instead, he was miserable at Menya Sandaime, a noodle house.

Pushed against opposite sides of the establishment were two long mahogany tables, both of which had white porcelain borders. The table by the front door had a view of Clay Harbor, a town that was immaculate in every sense. Whether it be their sales carts or inns, cleanliness was as important to Clay Harbor as a cunt to a whore.

The Tiger had spent four days in Clay Harbor, even though he only planned on staying one. He had rented a room at the Red Oak Inn, putting his company up, but when he awoke after the first night, the men he thought could be trusted had abandoned him. Where they had all gone, he had not the slightest idea, but Sir Ryker still had to make the trip to see his old friend for aid. When he was saddling up with the plan to ride up the Frostway to Windrip, a saddle boy handed him a letter to meet Lord Bekan at Menya Sandaime in three days. Tygurnach had never been to any sort of noodle house, nor was he completely positive of what a noodle even was, but after three nights, Bekan arrived at Clay Harbor, mumbling that they needed to meet where there were "less birds to sing songs."

His stool creaked again, and he gave it a swift kick with the back of his boot. The surcoat Sir Ryker wore was crimson red with midnight black sleeves that could be seen through his chainmail, and Ripple was sheathed. His handlebar mustache had formed into a bushy salt-and-pepper beard that was littered with bits and pieces from earlier meals. A scar on his cheek was never noticeable while he had the mustache, but it showed with a beard because hair wouldn't grow over it

Lord Bekan, who sat on a stool next to Tygurnach, cleared his voice. "If it were up to me, I woulda cracked open the three Coatus eggs and fried 'em up with some butter. No fucking RoarCatcher would have poisoned Tan, because no RoarCatcher would have been in the Capital."

"You shouldn't have left, then," Sir Ryker said with a heavy heart.

"Had to, Sir. When Tanwill took the throne, he was aided by a Shadow and a Verrativa."

Ryker nodded. "Well, an army of Verrativas…"

"Nevertheless," Lord Bekan continued, with an apologetic wave, "Without magic, Tanwill would have lost. The rebellion was, to me, about ending magical races, not being selective with them. The Trainer's Guild, the fact that he still called the Verrativa Chief 'friend' after the rebellion ended, and how he allowed a RoarCatcher to give itself the title of 'Master', made me realize that the royal court would never be *my* home. I even passed on Desire's Rage out of my family because the weapon was forged with Oracle magic." Lord Bekan narrowed his grey blue eyes. "But still..." His voice was like ice, smooth but bitterly cold. "I will help catch the filth that poisoned my friend and King."

Sir Ryker was ashamed that he had come alone, without the Knights that were hand-picked by Lord Bekan to protect the King. "If only the Knights of Rutherfall shared your sentiments."

"I picked every single Knight of Rutherfall after they finished their training at The Blade. 'Twas one of my responsibilities to make sure the lot shared my sentiments."

Lord Bekan was still thick with muscle, even in his old age. Thin grey hair streaked with with white was tied behind his back in a braid tighter than a rope. His navy doublet had a white mace sewn on the chest, and his velvet cape matched in color with a layer of bushy bear fur around the collar.

"My Knights are no fools, though. Maybe they're right in thinking this goose chase is a farce. Tan didn't go mad, but I'm beginning to wonder if the RoarCatcher was really the one who poisoned him," he said, glancing around, taking note of the three other commoners who sat at the opposite table.

"What makes you wonder that?"

"Why would the RoarCatcher give up a cushioned position at the Capital of Trilon to be an outlaw?"

Sir Ryker twisted his moustache with intrigue. "Who would be outside of their mind enough to do that? Tanwill doesn't even have an acting King assigned. After he goes, Tycho takes over, and it's not like Tycho would ever think of--"

Bekan dismissively waved his hand once again. "No, no, of course not. The way I see it, though, is if it was the RoarCatcher, he would be sending all the Coatuses to destroy our world, not just Reaper."

The Tiger scratched at his beard, causing crumbs to fall onto the table in front of him. "Your mind is as impressive as your achievements. "

"Don't have a stonemason build a statue for me until I figure out who the culprit is." Bekan signaled to the cook through the tiny window that looked into the kitchen. "The RoarCatcher leaving was timed perfectly. It's almost a little too perfect."

A pot-bellied man peered through from the kitchen. "M'lord?" He was dressed in a white undershirt that had as many rips as grease stains. His long hair was black without even a hint of grey, which matched the patch he wore over his right eye.

"*My* Lord. Don't sound like a drunken pirate, you already look like one. Now, two bowls of noodles in spicy broth, extra beef."

"My Lord, the serving girl will be around to take your order--"

Bekan reached through the window and grabbed the chef by the collar of his shirt. "I didn't ask you to take our order,

I'm telling you to." His face had no wrinkles except for deep crow's feet that appeared when he scowled. "Two teas as well, with a shot of bourbon in each," he muttered, shoving the man back through the kitchen.

"Still have that temper, I see. You're like a kettle, a little too much heat makes you scream." The Tiger laughed as the one-eyed chef handed him a steaming mug.

Smacking his lips together after a sip of tea, Bekan turned his stool around to face Clay Harbor. "I simply can't stand those who don't address their superiors correctly, especially when they're in the business of serving others." He took a second sip and placed the mug behind him. "I trust you've heard about Everlid."

Ryker followed Bekan's lead after draining his mug, with the stool squeaking in pain. "I know the Corwin boy was found in two separate pieces."

He watched people make their way through town, some on horseback, others carrying wheeled carts on their own. Clay Harbor was so tiny that it could have doubled in size and still fit inside Reliss with room to spare. Even so, those who passed by Menya Sandaime seemed to be working twice as hard as anyone in the Capital of Trilon.

"They haven't reached out for aid just yet, but I'm sure they will once they're done grieving. Reaper destroyed the Sight's Tower, which I'm sure led to a number of injuries and maybe even deaths. Your timing is impeccable even if your company isn't," Bekan said with a sly smile. "If we're lucky, Reaper is still lurking around the east, but we'll have a better idea once we go up."

"Go up?"

A tan and slender girl slid up to the old warriors with a tray that held their bowls of noodles. "My Lords, two noodle bowls with extra beef." Her left cheek was a ripe plum, purple and plump.

Bekan eyed her up and down, so Ryker did the same. Her hair was long and black as a storm. "Thank you, my Lady." Bekan smiled at her, taking note of the filthy gown she was clad in. "No slippers?" he asked, trying to meet her gaze.

There was a loud crash of pots and pans from inside the kitchen, but it didn't break Bekan's concentration.

"I don't like them much, my Lord. I prefer to go barefoot." The girl's voice was so soft it almost seemed like she didn't want anyone to hear her. Still, she didn't raise her eyes to meet Ryker or Bekan.

"In this cold, girl?" Tygurnach asked before tasting a spoonful of soup. The salty broth warmed him up right away, but he eyed the thin noodles and chunks of beef that swam in the foggy pool. Reaching for his fork, Ryker was confused to find two skinny sticks instead. "What am I supposed to do with these?" He picked up a stick in each hand and tried to lift out the noodles, but it slipped away and splashed back into the broth like a fish escaping from a hook. After a second attempt, he threw the sticks down and reached in the bowl with both hands.

The serving girl bowed to step away, but Bekan grabbed her by the arm lightly. "My Lady, do an old man a favor and smile."

She inhaled deeply after another crash echoed from the kitchen, closed her eyes, and smiled. The girl's mouth was a ruin of splintered teeth and bloody gums. It sent a shiver down the Tiger's back, but Bekan's icy expression remained unchanged.

"Please sit, my Lady," Bekan said, emotionless as he stood from his stool. He took his enormous cape off, draped it around her and grabbed his bowl of noodles. "Here, eat. Enjoy yourself for a little while with my good friend Sir Ryker. He's the Battle Master for the King!"

Tygurnach looked up, his beard soaked with broth, noodles trickling through his fingers. "Where are you go--"

But it was too late. Lord Bekan punched the swinging door that led into the kitchen. It started with a blow to the chef's round stomach, causing him to fall to the floor.

"So, you like beating little girls?" Lord Bekan screamed, kicking the man in the chest, once, twice, then the third landing in his ribcage. "I like beating fat, disrespectful cooks."

Ryker watched attentively through the window with the serving girl and looked just in time to see a smile curl on her lips. The one-eyed chef reacted by reaching behind him and grabbing a nearby frying pan. He swung with all his might, connecting with Bekan's right forearm. A lesser man would have paused, but when the Lord of Windrip was blood drunk, there was no stopping him.

"I'll say this," he said, giving the chef another kick, "For a craven, you sure can take a beating!"

At the opposite end of the kitchen was a cauldron boiling with broth over a red-hot brazier. Bekan's appetite must have grown so strong that he decided to take a break, but not before stepping on the chef's face with his steel-tipped boots.

"Oh, would you shut your mouth?" Bekan commanded as the man let out a scream loud enough to shatter glass.

Searching for a pewter bowl, he chuckled at the cauldron and cracked his knuckles.

"How's the soup, Sir?" he asked loud enough for the Tiger to hear through the window, even over the screams from the chef.

"It's good. Hot and salty."

"And how about you, my Lady? Is the soup to your liking as well?"

"I like the noodles!" The serving girl's voice was bubbling with excitement like she enjoyed what she was watching.

Bekan took a swig from the bowl as he walked back to the chef, whose nose was pouring out blood thick as syrup. "They didn't lie. This is some delicious broth. How long does it take to cook?"

The chef didn't answer but tried to sit up, but Bekan pushed him back with his boot.

"No, no, no, you're not going anywhere."

"What's the matter with you? Look at the bitch's eyes!"

Bekan ignored the chef's request, but Ryker didn't. He glanced over to the girl and was able to catch a glimpse of her eyes. *Yellow...*

"You know, I was actually going to pour this hot broth all over your body, scorch your skin, and leave you with burns as a reminder." Bekan's voice was still icy, even with the broth in his belly.

"And now?"

"Now..." Bekan said, kneeling as the steam from the bowl rose up into his face, masking his features. "Now I see that it's your soul that needs to be taught the lesson."

He ripped off the chef's eye patch like a bandage, exposing a socket that looked puffy, red, and glazed with white puss, as if a new eye tried to grow back but couldn't open. There was a sizzle when Bekan poured the broth over it, and the scream that followed could have awoken the dead. A moment later, the chef was still, and Bekan stepped out of the kitchen with his face still cold as stone.

"Tell me what you're doing here, and *how* you arrived."

The serving girl smiled shyly, brushing the bear fur collar of Bekan's cape against her cheek. This time she didn't hide her Verrativa eyes at all. "I suppose you would die trying to do what I did. You'd have to be underwater for significantly longer than your mortal lungs could handle. Still, I can't reveal the secrets of my race, so kill me if you must."

"I would never kill a girl, even *if* magic flows through your blood," Bekan fired back. "Even so, my King made a pact with your race, which means killing you would be considered treason."

"You should return back to the Ylewood, girl," Sir Ryker said between gulps of broth. "We don't need to tell you that it's not safe here."

The Verrativa smiled, then licked up the bit of blood that trickled from her gums. "The lack of safety is what excites me!" Her voice was aggressively defiant. "When I was captured, that man told me he would keep me as a prisoner until my race was taken out. Then and only then he would take my life and become immortal."

"And now you're no longer a prisoner," Bekan growled. "So, go back the way you arrived, and we can pretend our paths never crossed."

"I'll return to the Ylewood when I please," the Verrativa said as she continued to rub the fur collar of Bekan's cape against her cheek. She reached around the garment and then realized it had a bear-faced hood. Pulling the hood up shielded her cat eyes just enough where they weren't visible. "A life that has no end is pointless if you're not living."

Lord Bekan watched as the Verrativa turned to leave Menya Sandaime. "Find shoes," he yelled with a hint of concern as she crossed the threshold.

Sir Ryker stood up from his stool and let out a full-bellied burp. "Surprised you let her go, my Lord."

"You've uncovered my weakness, Sir," Bekan responded. "Let's get moving," he said as the ice returned to his voice.

As warm as the soup made Sir Ryker feel inside, the breeze that blew outside made him feel just as cold, with a bite that froze the snot under his nose.

Bekan remained unfazed by the cold, even without his cape. "My wagon is right over this way." He grimaced with each step, walking with a heavy limp towards a cart made of polished wood that was covered by a bear skin roof.

"Your limp is getting worse, my Lord."

"I hadn't noticed at all," Bekan answered sarcastically through gritted teeth. "I have a Saige, but he can't seem to heal me correctly. Makes me wonder why I keep the pompous little shit around."

The Tiger watched Bekan limp, his ankle turned inward, and it sparked a memory that had haunted him for years. Though Tygurnach was a part of King Tanwill's Cabinet, there was a time that they fought on opposing sides. Zabkar Inwar gave him power that he only dreamed of, but it was at the cost of both his honor and morality. Because of intel received by a turncloak Shadow, Tanwill employed a siege tactic cutting off food supplies from Yatorga and weaponry from Ghordaan. When the tides finally turned and Tanwill's victory was becoming more of a reality to Inwar and his armies, the Tiger was ordered to meet the rebellion at Stone Break Valley in a battle that would later be known as The Rebel's Stand.

Leading a garrison, Sir Ryker was clad in armor silver as the sky before dawn, with a helm that had a blood-red visor. There was no mistaking Lord Bekan in the midst of battle, his armor black, the color of nightmares, and his helm fashioned after a Smiladon head with great steel fangs. The attack came at night, so he was camouflaged fairly well, even with the spells that were being cast by the Oracles, which flashed lights of green, white, red, and purple. With Desire's Rage, he ripped through his foes, breaking their bodies, crushing their skulls, ending their reign. Zabkar thought ahead, though, and set up bear traps all through the rocky terrain, knowing very well that the best way to stop a melee fighter such as Lord Bekan Atalay was to use his aggressiveness against him.

Even when the steel jaws of a trap closed tight around Bekan's ankle, he didn't stop. With his thirst for blood seemingly unquenchable, he revealed a crossbow that was built into his gauntlet, loaded it with arrows from a tiny quiver that hung over his back, and began to fire. After some time, though, he was overpowered with the number of Oracles that swarmed around him like locusts. The white light of a paralyzing spell hit Bekan, and Sir Ryker yelled out, "That's enough!"

Ripple was clenched tight in his fist, but she felt different, as Cellyadure had placed an enchantment on the blade, making her light as a feather. He heard a nearby voice say, "Typical, he wants all the glory," but ignored it. The Oracles all watched him with delight, skinny little creatures not even clad in armor for battle but burnt brown moleskin robes with shrunken skulls dangling from their necks, staffs, and swords. They parted, allowing him to step right up to their pinned Lord, and he saw Bekan's grey-blue eyes through the steel Smiladon fangs. "My Master."

"Come now, Tygurnach," Bekan said, not showing the slightest sign of pain in his voice. "I really thought we had come to be friends before you left me to follow Zabkar Inwar and his band of hooligans."

In that moment, Ryker knew what he had to do. He lifted up Ripple, stepped back, and tore into the Oracles around him, painting their brown robes red. When Ryker turned back around, though, Atalay had his crossbow aimed at him. When the arrow pierced a part of his neck that was unprotected from armor, the world went cold.

Ryker pulled out the arrow and saw that it was drenched in not only his blood but a thick purple casing. His heart felt like it was going to burst, and then everything grew bright, like the sun had risen. Sir Ryker had left his Master-turned-friend's side for money, but gold and silver couldn't erase the things he saw while fighting for Zabkar Inwar's cause. During the day, they would hunt for "flesh", and the night was time to torture their catches, all to benefit the Oracle's magic. He deserved to die; he was no better than them, and when his knees gave out, he mouthed the words, "I'm sorry..."

"Here, take the bow." Bekan tossed a wooden longbow from out of his cart before stepping down with one of his own. It was overly polished with finger grooves carved into the grip.

Ryker took aim and loosed the string, feeling the vibrations when it thrummed back into place. The quiver that Bekan pulled out with him held well over a hundred arrows, but he had no trouble throwing it over his back.

"Got any poison-dipped arrows in there?" Ryker asked playfully as they walked through Clay Harbor.

"We're not trying to spare Reaper's life." Bekan's response was just as cold as ever.

"Why didn't you do it? Why didn't you kill me the day Tanwill won?"

Bekan didn't make eye contact with Ryker as he spoke. "You were young and stupid, Sir. I saw what you were capable of before you left me, and knew you'd be valuable to Tanwill."

"I immediately regretted my decision. To this day, I still can't speak of the things he ordered me to do."

The Tiger might as well have said nothing from the response he received back from Lord Bekan, so he decided to fully take in the sights and sounds around him.

If Reliss was midnight, then Clay Harbor was sunrise. If Reliss was a man on his deathbed, then Clay Harbor was a newborn baby. The cobblestone streets were carefully

319

carved into a pattern of diamonds and painted delicate purples and blues. Buildings made of logs that had sliding screen doors that seemed impossible to lock were on the right side of the street, while the left had a tame forest of skinny trees. It was like nothing he had ever seen, the trunks such a light brown that they were almost white, and their leaves pink with sunny yellow buds. Living in the south only permitted him the smells of garbage, but Clay Harbor's fragrance was floral and fresh, and when he breathed in the air, it seemed to clear his lungs.

When the cobblestones lost their color and their design faded with dampness, Sir Ryker knew they had arrived at the Coatus Port of the east. Other than a tiny shack, the area was empty, with the only sounds to be heard coming from the water that splashed against the wooden beams that held everything above the Gulf of Azure.

"You should see when a Coatus is scheduled to arrive. The people of Clay Harbor are so damn polite, you'd think they were trying to rob you. Maybe that's the southern Knight in me." Bekan laughed as he threw down the quiver from off his back. "The truth of the matter is, when people fly into Aleru, Clay Harbor is the first town they'll go through, and maybe if they think the people of the town are nice enough, they'll stay to spend their money."

"All of them are nice? What about the one-eyed chef?"

"What one-eyed chef?" Bekan fired back without hesitation before knocking on the shack door, almost leaving a dent on the rotten wood.

The door opened so fast that it almost flew off its hinges. "This had better be--"

Lord Bekan gestured to the man. "Gripley Rotoro, Trainer of Syaestra, but his name really should be 'Grumpy'. I'd ask you to invite us in, but I don't think we'd fit!"

Gripley Rotoro wore his silver Trainer's cloak, but it was covered in salt stains, and Ryker wondered if they came from sweat or because he lived by the sea. His nose was abnormally large, and either he wanted to bring attention to it, or he simply didn't care because of the mask he typically wore, but through his septum was a bronze ring the size of a bracelet. His hair was short on top and a rich turquoise color the same as his eyes. The sides of his head were shaved clean and tattooed with red stars in a zigzag pattern.

"My Lord, I apologize, if I knew it was you knocking, I wouldn't have been so abrasive." Gripley bowed, then got down to one knee. "I hope you can forgive me."

"You see?" Bekan said to Ryker. "I don't care how you look, but if you show me respect, I'll reciprocate." He placed his hand on Gripley's shoulder. "Of course, of course, don't even think about it. Now, rise, my good man, we need to fly."

Gripley stood up and breathed a sigh of relief. "I'm flying to Forbath tomorrow. Can it wait until then?"

"Absolutely not. This ride needs to be only us three, no exceptions whatsoever," Lord Bekan said, the ice flowing through his veins once again.

Gripley chewed his lower lip, pondering for a moment, and then looked at the Tiger. "Sir, you're a member of the King's Cabinet, right?"

"I am King Tanwill's Battle Master, yes," Tygurnach responded, puffing his chest out, proudly. "Why do you ask?"

The tattooed Trainer stepped back into his shack and emerged with a rolled up piece of parchment. "I was told that this is addressed to the entire King's Cabinet. Though I'll be flying to Forbath tomorrow, by the decree set by King Tanwill, my duty is to give this to the first member of the King's Cabinet I meet while in possession of this document."

He handed the letter over, and Sir Ryker snatched it like a dog that was being fed a table scrap.

He ran his finger down the parchment, pausing at the wax seal. It was a blob of blue stamped with an imprint of two towers. "Everlid," he said to no one. "I wonder, could they be asking for aid from King Tanwill?"

Bekan took note of the seal. "I couldn't tell you, Sir, nor can I see the document until the entire King's Cabinet reads it, then a majority gives consent."

It was admirable that the Lord of Windrip was so honorable even in a time of turmoil, but Ryker needed his old master's guidance. When Sir Ryker broke the seal, he inhaled deeply and began to read. Once he realized what the document was declaring, each word became a hammer pounding at his chest, with the word "war" delivering the final blow. "This is…" He couldn't even think of what to say. "This explains where the Knights of Rutherfall went."

"Please say no more, Sir. I've already heard too much," Bekan pleaded. "Now, Gripley, could you please call Sy--"

"Bloody Tulrose?" The Tiger roared in anger, ignoring Bekan. "Brannon Broadwine is from Tulrose, for fuck's sake! How could they ever think about signing th--"

Lord Bekan's icy eyes melted with flames of anger. "Sir Ryker, that is enough, I'll hear no more! Do you understand?"

Sir Ryker rolled up the letter and stuck it inside his surcoat. "Yes, it is understood, my Lord."

Bekan's nod was the same that he had given before he shot Ryker with the poisoned arrow. "Gripley, please call Syaestra, we're going up. It's past time we end Reaper's reign."

"My Lord, couldn't we try an alternate route? We rode up Dearborn Road from Forbath to Aleru. Couldn't we do the same up the Frostway?" Sir Ryker asked nervously.

"Your tactic did not work in the south, Sir. What makes you think it will work in the east, a realm known for its mountain ranges as much as its cold temperatures? We'll be able to see everything from the sky."

Tygurnach wiped a handful of sweat from his brow. "Perhaps there is a tower we could ride to and then climb?" His cheeks were flushed red like he had drunk his fill.

"What's going on here?" Bekan snapped with his whip of a voice. "Are you saying you rode from the south to the east and now you don't want to fly to try and find Reaper?"

Staring at his boots, ashamed, Ryker frowned. "Yes, I--I have a fear of flying, my Lord."

"Go inside, Gripley, let me and my friend speak for a moment," Bekan commanded the Trainer, and when door to his shack closed, the Lord of Windrip began to pace up and down the deck of the port. "You fear flying? I think you mistake what fear is, Sir. Fear can cripple you, yes, that's true, but only if you let it. Trust what I say to you, Sir Ryker, because I too took an alternate route years ago, and it blacked out the sun that lit my life. I know my son Rean has been rightfully labeled a craven, but it's my daughter that no one, myself included, ever speaks of.

"When Zabkar named himself King of Trilon, I sent Rean to stay and train with Emerick Callowat in the west. I figured if I couldn't convince the boy to be a fighter, maybe he and his son, Atrius, could. The truth is that I had no use for an heir that didn't want to fight for what was his. Madison was everything to me, though, and it was like Zabkar and the Oracles knew that. As soon as I sent Rean and his host off was when the collections began. Oracles, Shadows, and sometimes even Knights would come for monthly payments, whether it was crops, steel, or gold depended on the mood they were in. They would tell me it was the price of holding land in the south, and unless I wanted firestorms to rain down, I'd better not put up a fight. I didn't, not even when they punished me for being light on my payments, and in their eyes I always was. Fear sucked away at me, like a damned leech. It got so bad that Zabkar even ordered his Oracles to put a paralysis spell on me in my own keep. I assumed they were there to rob me of everything I had, and they did. Madison was nine, and I was forced to watch as they beat her unconscious. The sound of steel from outside was like a song from my mother, and when Tanwill Embray broke down the door with Brannon Broadwine and Xalvadore Corwin, the fear that plagued me was replaced with ice. That was the day I joined Tanwill's cause, though I'll admit it was far too late. My fear didn't cost Madison her life, but it ruined her mind. She awoke a mute, unable to develop mentally, even after all these years."

He paused for a moment, collected his thoughts, and then narrowed his grey-blue eyes, sending a chill down Ryker's spine.

"Fear is an enemy, and you don't compromise with enemies; you conquer them."

The horn that Gripley Rotoro blew to call Syaestra looked like an icicle, and all of his breath produced a high pitch hum. He stopped after a half a minute, gasping for air. A moment later, the clouds broke.

"CLII CLII COOOO! CLII CLII COOOOO!"

The Coatus sang as she flew down from the parted clouds. Not only was Syaestra the youngest of the three sisters but also the quickest, and just as fast as she appeared, she landed. Her diamond-shaped feathers were a pale blue and covered in snowy white swirls.

"Hello there, girl!" Gripley called out after putting on his Trainer's mask, a bucket of frozen fish in his hand.

When Syaestra saw the Trainer, she flapped her wings in excitement, and galloped over to him, scratching the port surface with her talons. The Trainer tossed up a fish into the air, and she caught it in her long beak which had a veiny pouch like a pelican's, as her eyes, two stones of onyx, closed in ecstasy.

"Bah, they forgot to remove the fucking litter," Gripley complained as he threw his armor on, his voice now an octave lower due to the mask. "She's such a sweet girl to me, but she hates my crew! I wonder if they tried to take the litter off and she refused them." He giggled like a little girl. "Well, no matter now."

The litter was tiny, much smaller than the one Ryker had seen atop of Akupara. It was fashioned after the buildings in Clay Harbor, made of thick logs with two sliding doors, one on either side. Inside there were two rows of benches, with chains attached to their bases. Bekan put the large quiver in the space between the benches, and Gripley fastened in the two old warriors, wrapping the chains around their shoulders.

"What are the chains for?" Sir Ryker asked with a flutter of uncertainty in his voice.

"Sir, Syaestra has tendency to not only fly fast, but she's been known to go upside down from time to time. We lost two to broken necks, another five fell out, and on a different occasion, the shipment we were carrying to Aleru was spilled over the Rytys River." It was as if the ugly Trainer enjoyed making the Tiger feel anxious.

Lord Bekan nocked an arrow before they even went up, but Sir Ryker just gripped the chains wrapped over his shoulders so tight that he felt his palms grow sweaty.

It was not a smooth ascent; Syaestra took two balancing steps before shooting up into the sky with reckless abandon. Tygurnach felt the noodle soup slither around in his stomach, and with that the rosy color in his cheeks was replaced with a shade more fitted to a ghost. His ears had popped, replacing his sense of hearing with a whistle that could have driven him mad. He decided if he couldn't hear anything, there was no point to seeing anything either, so he closed his eyes tight.

Only after the third time Bekan grabbed at his arm did Ryker open his eyes. He mouthed a few words to him, but the Tiger didn't hear a thing until he stuck a finger in his ear, which lessened the whistle that plagued him.

"I said, are you all right?"

"Never better, old friend," Ryker lied, reaching into his surcoat to make sure the document Gripley had given him earlier was still in tact.

"We're almost at the Mirrored Mountains, I think that's where we'll find the beast," Bekan said, handing Ryker his longbow, which he had completely forgotten about.

It wasn't enough that he had to conquer his fear of flying, but now he had to go up and kill a Coatus, a task that had never been done before. After that, and only after that, he had to deal with the letter that was written by the Baron of the east.

When they arrived at the Mirrored Mountains, Lord Bekan slid open his door and immediately gasped. "I see the beast! I see Reaper!" He loosed an arrow and took another from the quiver. "Well, what the fuck are you waiting for, summer? Open your door and fight, dammit!"

The wind fought back as Sir Ryker slid open the door, and when it was open, the bite of cold air put some life back into him. The world seemed so perfect from this far away, like he was looking at a picture in a storybook. Then, his eyes caught the Mirrored Mountains, the jagged snow-capped points that divided Aleru from Soarfrost. They descended lower, and as they got closer, the sunlight hit the rocks in such a way that gave justice to the name of the mountain range. The entire party was blinded for a moment, but that was all Reaper needed.

Without so much as a growl, Reaper was upon them, crashing into Syaestra's body, sending arrows all over the litter. Lord Bekan fired another arrow, connecting in the beast's neck, but it bounced off and fell below to splash into the Rytys River. Reaper shot back up, but Syaestra dodged the attack, corkscrewing around the black demon. Syaestra darted down while both Ryker and Bekan fired arrow after arrow with no effect. The impact from the two Coatuses crashing into one another sent the entire quiver below, leaving both warriors with one arrow each.

Bekan was quick to loose yet another arrow, but Reaper dodged it, turning to one side with ease like a giant pendulum. Flying over Syaestra, it eyed Sir Ryker, his bow aimed and ready. Going in for the kill, Reaper opened its beak to grab the Tiger but jerked back as he shot an arrow into its open gullet. It made a hideous gagging sound and coughed up a glob of blood. In that moment, both Tygurnach and Atalay thought the battle was won, but when Reaper looked back up, the arrow that was fired down its throat was peaking from its beak. It sucked in air, and with a loud thrum of air, shot the arrow back. Ryker leaned back, and Bekan followed, and the silver blur flew through the first door of the litter, and out the other.

Ryker thought back to what Bekan told him before they took off. *Fear is an enemy, and you don't compromise with enemies, you conquer them.* He wrenched himself free from the chains that protected him and unsheathed Ripple. The wind screamed, told him to sit back down and take the defeat. This time he wasn't going to listen. This time there would be no alternate route.

"What are you doing, Tygurnach?" Bekan screamed as Ryker stood and steadied himself.

"Conquering the enemy," the Tiger growled back with Ripple held high. "FOR TRILON!"

He leapt from the litter and plunged the blade deep into Reaper's neck, dangling his legs, kicking as he tried to climb atop the beast. Warm blood rained down on him, tasting like sweet red wine, and the enemy writhed in pain, flapping its wings, trying to choke out its last breath of life. Ripple cut straight through Reaper's neck, and by the time the Tiger realized it, he was falling.

Down he fell, taking the plunge into the Rytys River. Underwater, everything was silent, peaceful, and the water was so cold that it burned him, but he felt alive. No longer was Trilon a slave to the Coatus called Reaper. No longer did the three realms have to live in fear. No longer would Sir Ryker Tygurnach take the alternate route.

The splash from Reaper's lifeless body broke the silence, blocked the sun from above, while the Tiger swam up. It was as if the beast was the size of the river. He tried to find an opening, but it was no use. Reaper was everywhere, falling down to the watery grave below, and she was determined to bring Sir Ryker too.

FORBATH: YATORGA

Build back the city
It's what we'll do
Build back the city
Until we're through
Build back the city
Brick by brick
Build back the city
It won't be quick
Build back the city
Where Shadows can hide
Build back the city
We will survive

Yatorga was alive. The faint heartbeat that it had after Reaper's demolition had steadied to a healthy tick. First, the houses were built back up, and next were the shops. While the fish had yet to return to the waters surrounding Yatorga, its people now had the coin to rebuild their homes.

Graybill had called a citywide meeting to remind everyone to do their part in the rebuild and specifically instructed every fisherman to continue their trade even though their efforts may seem futile. He concluded by telling the fishermen that whoever caught the first fish would be graciously rewarded if it was brought to him alive.

Atrius Callowat followed Graybill through the market strip as men and women sang together while they worked. Their hammers clanged in rhythm with the song, which put an extra pep in everyone's step.

"How about this, my friend?" Graybill asked Atrius over his shoulder. "*This* is Yatorga!" The hood of Graybill's cloak was down, but his tangle of long black hair covered his head just as well. "I hope you're just as proud of this as I am," he continued, his lilac eyes beaming with excitement.

"I suppose so," Atrius answered with a slight hesitation. Unlike Graybill, his hood was up as they walked through the streets.

"You suppose so?" Graybill said, spinning around with open arms. "Our home is back!" He laughed heartily.

Just then, Porter, who was carrying a stack of bricks from one side of the market strip to the other, stumbled and fell. Without a second thought, Graybill glided over to him casually and lifted him up with the same effort as if he were helping up an infant.

"Be careful, you're going to have a busy night at the Swine," he said with a wink.

Porter glowed, slapped his big gut, and pulled up his breeches. "Don't you worry, Graybill. I'ma make sure every shop is fixed and everyone's bellies are filled with booze." The bartender was so happy that even his scarred eye seemed to shine as he spoke.

"Fantastic. Make sure you save a pour for me!" Graybill answered with a slap on Porter's sweaty back.

Porter nodded and wiped the sweat from his brow. "You know I love gettin' ya drunk, boss!" His words were filled with love and admiration, but they were ignored as Graybill had wrapped an arm around Atrius.

"Tell me what's running through your mind, my apprentice." Graybill's words were weighed heavy with concern. "This city is thriving because of *your* accomplishments."

Atrius stared at his feet as they walked down the market strip. The voices of some singing, some laughing, some cursing, clashed together, creating an unintelligible hum. "I'm happy for the city, but what I did was--"

"Wrong, yes, but you did what needed to be done to survive," Graybill answered matter-of-factly.

The smells of a burning brick oven fluttered through the air and was greeted with a cheer from a crowd around the baker's stand. Atrius tried to ignore the commotion as he spoke.

"I understand that, but I still wish I didn't have to do it." His voice was shrinking with each word.

"*We* did it, together. Remember, I will *never* ask you to do something that I wouldn't do. The raid was what it was, and now it's done. The buyer will be picking up the last shipment soon and then our hands will be washed clean."

Atrius looked at his hands like they were still dirty with Tantae blood, then hid them away in his sleeves. "Right," he said quietly.

It wasn't until recently that he began to dislike his red robe but knew it would have to do for now. The red cloak was the symbol of a Shadow apprentice, and once training was completed, it would be traded in for a black one. Graybill had told Atrius that the red cloak was a garment that would garner respect, unlike the roughspun tunic he wore when he showed up to Yatorga.

As far as Atrius could tell, the red cloak had just brought him more ridicule and chores. When he walked into the Swine in his tunic, every Shadow had bought him an ale, and when he fell over, they picked him up and filled his belly with bread and fish. Now that he wore the red cloak, he was thrown dirty smallclothes with nothing more than a "wash it, sunshine." That's what they called him, and whether it was because of his blond hair or red cloak depended on whom he asked.

His cut from the raid was significantly smaller than the rest of the party, and while Atrius expected that, what he didn't expect was to use almost all of it on drinks for the Shadows. Still, he didn't complain to Graybill, as that wouldn't have helped him in the slightest. The Shadows were a family, and Atrius wanted to remain with this one, unlike his first.

He thought about his past life and how fast it all changed, like fall freezing to winter. The dreams haunted him for months before he said anything to his father. Faces of men would visit him while he slept but wouldn't speak, nor even look at Atrius; instead they just breathed long, frosty sighs. Sometimes it would be the next morning, sometimes it was a fortnight, but every single one passed. At first, Atrius thought it was a coincidence, as most of the men would march on the Ylewood, which always meant certain death because the Moiiralatta was undefeatable. Unfortunately, his father had not realized this yet, as he still devoted a great amount of time, resources, and lives on attempting to infiltrate the sacred land of the Verrativas.

When his mother, Lady Perine Biznowaty, appeared in his dream, Atrius finally told his father, and this was met with hearty laughter. After Lady Perine's eyes closed, Lord Emerick became obsessed with "cleansing Atrius's magical blood", no matter the cost. Emerick Callowat had gotten his hands on an Oracle tome, which contained a spell that would rid Atrius of his magical abilities, if he indeed had any. The problem, however, was obtaining the ingredients necessary to brew the potion for the spell. Emerick substituted a crushed up Fiddleback Spider with a tarantula, and Smiladon blood with a house cat's. The dreams continued, and Lord Emerick allowed the madness of cleansing his son to take over.

Emerick Callowat had put up notes at every inn and tavern through Gojii asking anyone who understood magic to help his son. This brought on a slew of gypsies, nomads, and failed saiges, all of whom claimed they could help Atrius. Each failure added another head onto the spikes of the Sycamour Gate, and the Mayor of Leefside had all but given up. That was, until Atrius's savior showed up. The man hid his identity behind a mask, and even when Lord Emerick asked him to show his face, the Iron Skull refused.

"Try a bite," Graybill said, shoving a warm pretzel in front of Atrius, bringing him back to Yatorga. "There's no salt, but even with its lack of seasoning, a brick oven pretzel is better than any orgasm you'll receive from a woman."

Atrius took the pretzel and bit its soft, fluffy center. While he couldn't say if it was better than an orgasm from a woman, it still put Atrius's worries on hold, at least for the moment.

Graybill looked up to the sky as he wiped a few crumbs from his goatee. "The buyer will be here soon. Come on, Atrius, it's time." His carefree stroll picked up, and Atrius was shocked at how he had to almost jog to keep up.

The Grateful Swine was oddly still in the early afternoon. When the inn wasn't filled with cheers and laughter, it seemed haunted, empty for a reason.

"It's dead here," Atrius said, taking down his hood.

"Everyone's still working, and that's a good thing. Think of their spirits when they see the sack of gold we'll come back with!" Graybill almost screamed in excitement. "Dink and Kylan will be back soon too, and that means our plan can go into its next phase."

Atrius furrowed his brow. "What will I be doing for the next phase?"

"Oh, my good, good friend, you'll be on your way to Soarfrost by the time everything goes into motion. Don't you worry about a thing." Graybill lit a number of candles around the bar, but no any of the lanterns. "I'll be back shortly with the merchandise, so please stay outside in case our guest arrives."

The sky was true blue and cloudless. Atrius wondered what Graybill saw in the sky that made him hustle so much but was sure he had good reason. There was a low hiss of some sort of insect in the distance that must have just hatched from a cocoon and was taking full advantage of its freedom. Atrius wanted to hatch from his own cocoon and do as he pleased, but every time he brought that issue up to Graybill, all he got were promises and pleads of patience.

Just as soon as Graybill left, he returned with a slam of the door and a red velvet sack slung over his shoulder. "Beautiful day, isn't it?"

"Sure…"

Graybill looked at Atrius and gave a frown that said he knew his apprentice was still troubled. He put the sack down and pulled out a pipe from the pocket of his robe. "You hear that?" he asked, striking a match against the Grateful Swine.

"All I hear is that bug buzzing around," Atrius answered.

Graybill exhaled a cloud of grey smoke and his lilac eyes looked back to the sky. "A bug?" The buzz grew louder, and from out of the sky came a tiny speck that moved steadily towards Yatorga.

Atrius squinted to try and make out what was flying their way. "What the fuck is th--"

"I do believe you should be asking, *who* the fuck is that, and to answer your question, that is our buyer."

Slowly, the buzzing speck began to take shape. The first thing Atrius saw was the shine in the sky, like a great golden comet. Wing-shaped blades spun underneath the machine, propelling it forward, and a large sun-colored balloon held it up.

As the brass body of the ship came into focus, Graybill wrapped his arm around Atrius. "Cherish this sight, my friend, not many get a chance to behold it."

The buzz had transformed into a whipping, and Atrius felt the propellers slap him in the face with wings full of air. His eyes began to water just as the ship was landing, and that's when the entrance inside was visible. It was a brass Coatus head with eyes made of glass stained red. The rest of the machine matched in color and material with a band of steel around its perimeter.

It was as if the Coatus made of brass and steel saw where it wanted to land, and the blades below it began to slow. Their guest had arrived, landing with a gasp of hot steam and a loud clunk that seemed to shake all of Trilon. At first, it was impossible to see inside the ship when the Coatus head slid down, but as the smoke cleared, a man appeared, sitting on a tiny leather seat between a large hand crank and a chain lever with a granite handle.

"Well, are ye gonna help me out?" he asked, holding out both hands.

Graybill stepped in front of Atrius and grabbed the man's hands and began to pull.

"Not so fast! Not so fast!" he yelled out with a voice that sounded like a child's. His feet were fitted into two pedals that he lifted out of delicately. "Come on now, hurry up," the man said impatiently.

"I trust that your journey was pleasant," Graybill said after lifting the man out of his ship.

"My journey? My journey was a storm, my dear boy, but I'm hoping to see a rainbow now that it's over."

Atrius couldn't believe who was standing before him. He was half the size of a normal man, with a great bushy brown beard that had three tight braids, each of which were tied together by purple ribbons. His navy-blue top hat was almost as tall as him and had a velvet stripe right above the brim. The man had almond-shaped eyes that were a light brown with a slight green tint. A bright pink coat covered his tiny body, which had a number of opal buttons down the center and charcoal black flowers embroidered on either arm.

"You're Daymon Stringfellow!" Atrius yelled out in excitement after finding his voice.

"Aye, that be me, m'lad" the Halfling Bard answered with a deep bow. Atrius followed his bow and noticed the man's boots had golden laces.

Graybill smiled warmly and lifted up the sack filled with merchandise. "Would you like to go inside to conduct business?"

"Inside? The dust from those ridiculous tapestries will make me sneeze until I'm blue in the face! Besides, your establishment is still lit by candles, correct?"

"Yes, yes, it is. We find that the dim atmosphere of the Grateful Swine gives a sort of cozy feel that our patrons have grown accustomed to," Graybill answered politely without a sign of anger or discomfort.

Stringfellow scoffed. "Please, you Shadows like the dim light for a reason, and it's not to snuggle. We will do the exchange here, so I can see what I'm buying."

"As is your right, my friend," Graybill said. "But what about a toast to seal our business? Surely we need to go inside for that. Atrius would happily pour us a--"

"Your persistence is getting annoying, Shadow," Daymon shot back as he reached into his jacket. He pulled out a silver bottle and popped the cork off. "It helps with the dizziness when I fly," he said after a deep drink.

Graybill reached out for the bottle, and the Halfling Bard started to laugh. His laugh was deep and jolly like it belonged to someone three times his size.

"You'll get a sip after we're done with business." The Halfling Bard eyed Atrius. "Here, lad, have a swig. You're no Shadow yet," he said taking note of Atrius's red robe.

Atrius took the bottle and glanced over to Graybill, but he was staring at the ground. "What is it?

"I'll tell you this, you won't find it in Yatorga!" Stringfellow said with a burp. He reached down and snatched up the red velvet sack.

Graybill cleared his throat. "What about the gold?"

"Do I look like I don't have the gold? I'm a very sensitive man, which means I'm easily offended. I don't conduct business with anyone who steps over the line, and right now you're dancing upon it."

Graybill nodded. "Right you are, and my apologies, I never meant to--"

"I'm a very busy man, Graybill. Not only do I have to bring this merchandise to King Hayao, but I also have to perform for court tonight."

Atrius almost dropped the bottle that the Halfling Bard handed him. "I'm sorry... King Hayao? You mean, the King of--"

"Hybernia," the Halfling Bard answered with a wink. "Drink that before it goes flat, lad." Stringfellow opened the bag and held it to his face. "Smells like blood, Shadow," he grumbled.

"Well, I'd say--"

"You'll say nothing. I've offered your wide-eyed apprentice the drink of my people twice and he still hasn't so much as smelled it. Are you both trying to disrespect me?" Daymon pulled out a silver-white horn from the bag and spat on the ground.

"Drink it, Atrius. Please." Graybill's voice quivered as he watched the Halfling Bard examine a Tantae horn that was just as tall as him.

Atrius nodded, and without even giving it a sniff, gulped down as much as he could. The bubbles caused him to belch right away, and then ice grasped his tongue tight, freezing his whole mouth.

"You and your group of misfits butchered these beautiful creatures for their ivory. Tantaes can have their horns removed humanely, so they can grow back naturally. Instead, you hacked them off, still leaving bits of their skin attached," the Halfling Bard screamed as he rummaged through the sack, and that was when Atrius began to feel light-headed.

Atrius's vision began to fade in and out. Ice had traveled through his mouth and down his neck, and he soon found it hard to breathe. Graybill said something, but his voice sounded miles away. His arms were now frozen and, unable to speak a word, the ground rushed up to him. For a moment, Atrius laid on the hot pavement, staring up at the blue sky, but slowly the color faded to grey, and then he closed his eyes.

A moment later, he was in a world that was all too familiar. It was black, too dark to tell if his eyes were open or closed.

"What's wrong with me," he screamed at the top of his lungs. "Who the *fuck* am I?"

All he wanted was an answer. Was he doing the right thing? Should he listen to Graybill and travel to Soarfrost? Was he meant to be a Shadow or something else? There was a pale light behind him, and he knew what came next.

"If I don't look, I won't know who will die," he said to no one.

The light grew brighter around Atrius, and then the sound of a hammer smashing a chain rattled his teeth.

"Please, help," he said, dropping to his knees.

Atrius closed his eyes when he felt tears trickle down his face, and when he opened them, Graybill stood before him, letting out frosty breaths...

The first thing that brought him back to reality was the smell of Graybill's pipe smoke. The dim lights of the candles came into focus, and Atrius realized he was in Graybill's office propped up in a chair.

"I would have brought you to your quarters, but the Halfling Bard told me to sit you up straight." Graybill sat across from him in his leather throne, both arms folded over the table that divided them.

"What happened?" Atrius asked, wiping his eyes clear.

Graybill puffed on his pipe. "Well, you passed out after drinking... whatever you drank."

That reminded Atrius of his dream. "I saw you."

"Hm, really? Well, we're all going to die." Graybill's response was oddly smooth and dismissive. "We're going to have to visit our first buyers, by the way. The Halfling Bard refused the ivory because of the violence that was used to obtain them."

Atrius put his hood up. "So, we didn't have to do what we did?"

Smoke billowed from Graybill's mouth before he spoke. "Yes, we did. Like I said, our first buyers will surely take the merchandise off our hands."

"Don't you care that I saw you in my dream?"

Graybill leaned back in his seat and stroked the wooden Smiladon on the left armrest. "Do I care that I'm going to die? Sure, but what should I do, curl up in a ball? No. I'm a Shadow, and I'll continue to be one until my death rattle echoes through the Grateful Swine." He reached for a bucket underneath the table and placed it in front of Atrius. "It wasn't all bad today, my friend," he said with a grin.

Atrius peeked inside and saw a tiny salmon swimming back and forth.

"This little fish will bring us all the way back."

Atrius held up the bucket and watched the pink blur swim through the murky water. "I understand how an ivory raid can help, but this little fish won't be able to feed both of us, let alone a whole city."

Graybill puffed on his pipe for a moment, pondering his next words. "Atrius," he said, stalling. "I've been holding quite a secret from you for some time. Do you know how King Tanwill *won* his rebellion?"

"Sure, a Shadow gave him the necessary information to end Zabkar's reign."

"Almost correct," he answered with a grin. "A Shadow did aide Embray's rebellion, but he didn't just give 'information'. This is the true story, the one that your father wouldn't tell you. The one that you won't hear in the songs. A Shadow gave Brannon Broadwine an Oracle tome. In that Oracle tome, there was a spell that, if spoken, would banish anyone to Soarfrost. Now who do you think that Shadow was?"

Atrius shrugged. "I always assumed he was dead."

"Almost correct again, my friend. According to you, I will soon be dead, but I am still very much alive." Graybill put his feet on the table in front of him and crossed one boot over the other.

These words were wind swirling around Atrius's head. "You're the Shadow turncloak?"

"Oh, my friend, I don't consider myself a turncloak at all. I'm more of a rogue," Graybill responded coolly.

"No, you committed treason. You fought for one side but helped the other side win."

Graybill put his pipe on the table. "I never switched sides, good boy. I just saw a chance to put my plan into motion and

I took it," he said with a grin. "All I did by helping Tanwill win his crown and his glory was create a temporary placeholder. Everything I've done was with a different ruler in mind." He held his arms out. "And soon the fruit will be ripe for the picking."

"What else did you do?" Atrius found it hard to ask the question because he wasn't sure he wanted to hear the answer.

"Before I say anymore, I need a favor, if you will. Go all the way upstairs to the last door on the left and show the guest inside that fish." Graybill pointed to the bucket and reached into his pocket. "Here, you'll need this," he said, tossing a large silver key towards Atrius. "Oh, and make sure he *doesn't* eat it; I'm sure he's hungry."

Atrius caught the key and stuck it in his pocket. "Who's up there?"

Graybill took a long deep drag from his pipe. "I wouldn't want to ruin that surprise."

The Grateful Swine had filled up since Atrius was unconscious. Songs rang through the bar while Atrius walked upstairs with the fish, not making eye contact with anyone or anything. His focus was on who could be behind the last door on the left. The words "Hey sunshine, buy me an ale" were shouted, but they went right through him like the smoke that was blown at him.

The last door on the left was forest green and had a large golden doorknob directly in its center. When Atrius stuck the key into the lock, he heard the rustling of chains.

"I've been keeping it warm."

The words were tired, and when Atrius opened the door, he saw what seemed to be a skeleton. The room reeked of ruination, with only a single candle to give vigil. There was a small window that cut out any natural light, with bars made of steel. Shit decorated the walls, and in the center was a pile of hay where a man sat, his arms and legs chained together.

"You see? I've been sitting on the egg the whole time." His voice was bitter, each word having more resentment than the last.

Atrius gagged trying to speak. "What--" He felt his stomach churn. "I was told to bring this fish to you." He held up the bucket, unsure if he wanted to cross the threshold.

"So, you're Graybill's new pet," he said with a laugh. The man's skin was brown, but dry and pasty. His long white beard was stained so dark in certain areas that it almost looked dyed. He was naked, with only a thin layer of skin to cover his bones, and by the looks of it, that too would be gone soon. Atrius noticed the turquoise Coatus egg the Iron Skull had stolen from Reliss, nestled underneath the expiring prisoner.

"I'm no pet. You're the one in chains!" Atrius stepped into the chamber and squinted at Graybill's prisoner. "Who are you, anyway?"

The man started to chuckle, then he spit a mouthful of blood onto his haystack. "It wasn't so long ago that King Tanwill trusted me with his life. Now look at me." He shook his shackled arms. "If I lose any more weight, I'll be able to slip out of these."

Atrius stepped closer, slowly, like a child would towards a dog who may bite. "Your necklace," he said when he saw the stained-glass jar tied around his neck. "You're a RoarCatcher," he continued.

"An' you say you're not Graybill's little pet? Why didn't he tell you he had a prisoner? Why didn't he tell you what he's done to Trilon?"

The questions echoed through Atrius's head as he stared at the naked prisoner. "Who are you?"

"I'm one of three RoarCatchers in all of Trilon. I'm the one who tamed the beasts so you lot could survive with 'em. Of course, you just use 'em. My name is Vengar Stoneburner," he said with a look of shame.

Atrius almost dropped the bucket he held when he heard the truth of the prisoner's identity. "So, Graybill kidnapped you to put an end to your destruction."

"You're either incredibly loyal or incredibly stupid, and there's no way anyone can be loyal to a Shadow."

"I'm going to be a Shadow," Atrius shot back.

"Is that what he told ya? Heeyeahh, lying comes as easy to Graybill as breathing, remember that." Vengar Stoneburner shifted back and forth on the turquoise Coatus egg. Even in his starved form, he looked strong, like he could knock out anyone if an arm was freed. "I should have known Graybill and Brannon's ties were still tight."

The smell of shit and vomit hung around Atrius's head like a swarm of gnats. "They're working together?"

"Just as they did during the rebellion. The *great* Lord Brannon Broadwine poisoned our King with Silent Bite, and I fell for the bait, like that fucking fish you're holding."

Atrius looked in the bucket and saw the salmon was now swimming in circles. "Bait for what?"

Vengar shook his shackles again. "I should have never told Broadwine I took blood from the babe." The RoarCatcher saw the confusion on Atrius's face and sighed with annoyance. "If I have blood from an animal, I can speak to them, or control them. 'Twas done with all the Coatuses in Trilon, except this one, of course." He looked down to the egg. "The baby has been listening to me, that is true, but not to my nor King Tanwill's orders. Once again, a Shadow is too cowardly to even command with his own voice. He has to use Stranger's Tongue."

A light breeze blew through the barred window and it smelled of salt. For a moment, the smell of shit was overpowered and Atrius was able to think clearly. Graybill wanted him to see Vengar to show what he's fully capable of. The question now was whether or not Atrius was going to play his game.

Atrius reached into the bucket and pulled out the salmon. Squirming in his hand, he smashed the fish's head against one of the window's steel bars. "I'm going to help you." He tossed the dead fish at Vengar, who caught it with his bound hands.

Vengar ripped into its stomach with his teeth and his eyes rolled back with ecstasy. He looked up to Atrius and gave a small smile as the fish's guts clung to his beard. "You're not a Shadow, boy, you're the light."

"What can I do, though?" Atrius asked as the anxiety bubbled in his stomach.

The RoarCatcher swallowed as if his next words hurt more than his imprisonment. "My Bellow," he croaked. "Take it. Take it and leave."

FORBATH: DEARBORNE ROAD

"Somethin' wrong with the soup?"

The innkeeper was a frail old woman whose face was covered in wrinkles and blotchy liver spots. Her sunken cheekbones were anchored by a veiny, crooked nose that sprouted white hairs from both nostrils. Each of her steps came with a heavy limp that she seemed determined to ignore by walking up and down the inn, refilling steins, taking away dirty plates, or collecting payments.

"Need salt?" She let out a cough that sounded closer to a death rattle before wiping a handful of bloody phlegm onto her already stained apron. "Aye!" the innkeeper yelled, putting a hand on her hip. "I'm talking ta you, ya filthy gutter rat!"

The girl sat alone, eyeing a bowl of murky brown soup as a thin layer of grease began to congeal on top. She looked up at the old innkeeper and blinked before realizing she was supposed to speak.

"It's--" The girl gave the soup another stir. "It's fine, thank you." The tunic and leggings that she wore were a size too big and smelled like they were in desperate need of a wash.

"Y'alright girl?" the innkeeper asked, showing a few chipped stalactites that dangled from the cavern that was her mouth. She took note of the patron's muddled black hair and her emaciated physique. "Don' look too good, if you don' mind me sayin' so. Girl your age shouldn't be lookin' like an ol' skeleton," the innkeeper said while affectionately rubbing the young girl's forearm. "Come on, girl, why don' you tell Mother Eden what's botherin' ya?"

Looking up from her bowl, the young girl pulled her arm away and faked a smile. "I'm okay," she said, her voice quivering lightly.

"Now, now, girl, there's no reason to fib, at least not to an old woman," Mother Eden continued, sitting down onto the chair across from the young girl. "Feels good to take a load off," she said, exhaling. Tied around her neck with a thin hemp rope was an apothecary jar made of stained glass that the young girl eyed suspiciously before tasting the soup. "When someone says, 'I'm okay', I hear, 'I'm broken.' So, speak, my dear. I may be hard of hearing, but Mother Eden can still listen."

I murdered a Saige after he tried to reunite me with my family. "I made a mistake is all," she said quietly. *Every person I've ever gotten close to has abandoned me.* "I'm also lonely." Kylan's emerald eyes welled with tears.

"Bah, sweet girl, if things continue a'way they're goin', a lot more people gonn' be lonely too. An' mistakes are a part o' life, like eating an' sleeping. Don't get too down."

Kylan ate another mouthful of soup, this time noticing the bold flavor of garlic and onions in the broth. "What do you mean, 'a lot more people are going to be lonely'?"

Mother Eden stood up with a creek from her bones like a rusty hinge. "War, my dear." The old woman's voice was a sad song from long ago. "I 'memba the last one, an' the one b'fore that. Wars always make lonely folks."

"What do you mean war is coming?" Kylan asked, wiping a tear streak off her cheek.

"Xalvadore Corwin is gatherin' men from Aleru. If ya can believe the tales from my patrons, then he's even recrutin' Gojii and Forbath warriors to fight for 'im."

The words pierced Kylan's heart like an arrow. "Wh-- what? Xalvadore Corwin is going to--"

"War, girl. It's always the same," Mother Eden scoffed. "A quarrel starts, and the only way ta end it is with blood. If ya' got Corwin and Embray togetha' in 'ere once again, I'd make them come to an agreement without blood, without makin' lonely folk."

"Once again?"

"Oh, they were always in 'ere during their rebellion. Tanwill Embray, Brannon Broadwine, Xalvadore Corwin, Lirum Rhygell, Bekan Atalay, all knew this was a safe place to meet. The Tired Traveler never supported Inwar or his band o' failed Saiges." Mother Eden spat on the floor of packed soil. "They were all such dear friends, it's a shame."

The Tired Traveler was a tiny inn right off of Dearborne Road that had been serving mead and mulled wine well before Zabkar Inwar came into power. It had only one innkeeper during that span, Mother Eden, who was said to have built the establishment herself. It wasn't a large inn nor sturdy, as the foundation was made of logs rotten from time, while all repairs were done with straw and mud.

Mother Eden had no bar in the Tired Traveler but instead a few round tables, which were given an ample amount of space between so as to prevent eavesdropping. Each table had a candle built into the center, and those tiny flames were responsible for lighting the entire ground floor.

Those who said the Grateful Swine was unsavory had never stepped foot into the Tired Traveler. It was known that the Grateful Swine was a haven for the Shadows, but Mother Eden's inn was different. The Tired Traveler openly welcomed outlaws offering the privacy and safety they often needed. Through the years, Mother Eden served every type of criminal there was, and not once did she refuse her cup or bowl, not since the Oracles were banished to Soarfrost. Mother Eden's only condition was that whoever entered would have to eventually tell her when, where, and what crime they committed.

"Why would Lord Xalvadore attack the Capital?" Kylan asked, staring into her bowl of soup.

347

Mother Eden swallowed before she spoke and lifted Kylan's chin, meeting her green eyes. "The King sent Reaper to the east to destroy the Sight's Tower. The Lordling is dead."

Kylan bit her lip. "You mean Elmar?"

"The one that stayed in Everlid," Mother Eden said, now looking directly into Kylan's eyes. "Who are y--" Her concentration was broken by a dog's bark. "Oh damnit, git outta 'ere," the old woman screeched at a tiny brown hound that made its way into the Tired Traveler. The floppy-eared dog yipped playfully before Mother Eden grabbed a broom that laid against the wall to shoo it out. "Damn dog thinks I'm stupit," she muttered under her breath.

"Can I take this to my room?" Kylan asked, lifting her bowl of soup.

A visibly distracted Mother Eden stared out the open door of the bar. "Take it upsta-- oh yes, I suppose that'd be okay, dear. Jus' make sure you bring everythin' back down, okay?"

Kylan nodded. "Yes, of course, I'll do that." Her voice cracked as she spoke.

The stairs groaned with each step, like an old man being woken from a deep sleep. Upstairs was a thing of nightmares, with ghostly white walls and thick wooden doors black as coal that each had rusted iron handles. Staring down the hall was a Smiladon head mounted on a mahogany shield. Its eyes were removed and replaced with candles that Mother Eden kept lit at all times, which made the beast seem alive again.

The door pushed open with all of Kylan's weight to a chamber that was no larger than a closet. There was a tiny nightstand with a candle on top that was running out of wax. Next to it was Kylan's pack and a pouch made of muddy leaves. She reached into the pouch and pulled out a fingerful of the black dye that Manx had mixed for her.

It was still embedded in her brain... the screams, the smells, the blood. To call what happened at Reliss a battle would discredit every battle in history, but Kylan and her company reigned victorious. The Burrato bomb put an end to most of Prince Tycho's host, all except him and his biggest squire, who used his strength to get the heir of Reliss out of the way of the explosion.

The monster who hid his face behind an iron skull protected the trio with some sort of magic. They were in direct line of the Burrato bomb's wrath when he screamed a spell and the flames passed around them, scorching all their "enemies". The smell of burning flesh still lingered in her nose, even though it had been close to a week since they escaped. Kylan hadn't been able to eat meat since the day she saw skin, muscle, and fat melt clear off bones.

She remembered the heat too, that rose so high it woke Manx from her unconscious state. The trio met, hugged, and began to limp back the way they came.

Dink stopped in his tracks, blood pouring from his face. "Go on without me!"

"Fuck yourself!" Manx yelled back angrily.

Dink shook his head. "Meet me at the Tired Traveler."

Kylan and Manx stood defiantly.

"Why are you two still here? Go, now! I'll meet you there, *I promise*."

Kylan sat down on the straw-filled mattress and kept eating her bowl of soup, ignoring the chunks of meat that swam amongst the grease. She sat back and felt a sharp pain prick her side. Reaching under the pillow, she pulled out the Smiladon fang dagger she used to murder Lorrode Allwater. No matter how she looked at it, she couldn't play the innocent little girl anymore. Some girls grow up to be wives or innkeepers, but she had grown into a murderer. This was her life, her burden, and for good or bad, it was the only life she had. *By cutting the Saige's throat, I cut any ties with my family.*

She closed her eyes tight and tried to remember her brother Elmar but couldn't even picture his face. His death wasn't sad to her, nor was the fact that her father was marching on the Capital. They didn't care about her, so why should she show any emotion towards them?

It happened without hesitation, but Kylan Corwin began to sob uncontrollably. No one cared for her. No one knew if she was alive or dead. At one point, she thought her family was the problem, but now she understood it was her. She was meant to be alone, forever.

Manx had traveled with her up Dearborn Road for a mile before leaving. She made a hair dye of mud, blackberries, and a drop of Kylan's own blood before setting back to Reliss. Kylan began to cry when the nomad told her she was going back for Dink, but the tears didn't faze her.

"You'll be fine, love. The innkeeper will try to convince you to tell her your crime, but you mustn't," the nomad whispered as she smeared Kylan's hair with the homemade dye.

"He told both of us to meet him at the Tired Traveler," Kylan objected. "Can't--can't we just stick together? Please?"

The nomad kissed her forehead. "I promise I'll be here tomorrow."

She said that seven days ago. Manx could have been arrested or even killed by the King's Law, but that was doubtful. Dink, on the other hand, was most likely dead. All she wanted was to see *them* again, the only people who made her feel special.

Wiping her eyes dry, Kylan sat up and clenched the dagger tight. *Did they lie to me? Could I have possibly been that great of a burden? Did they plan to leave me from the beginning?*

Kylan was lucky to still have enough silver coins from the toll collector who was crushed by Reaper to pay Mother Eden, but she needed to start thinking about work. She already proved to be a capable burglar, but that was debatable. The whole point of being a burglar was to get away with little to no damage. Kylan not only had to kill a royal Saige, but she also would have been arrested if it weren't for the Iron Skull.

Nevertheless, she successfully stole the Coatus incubator. That made her look over to the pack on the nightstand and remember why she was here in the first place. *Was I always meant to fly?* Graybill sent her on this mission a lifetime ago to do *his* dirty work, with no regard for her well-being. She wondered if Dink had the same realization, and that was what made him desert the company. *We should have never split up, I can't be on my own, not now, not ever.*

Just then, there were three hard knocks on door, and for just a second, she pictured Dink and Manx crossing the threshold with their arms open for a group hug.

"Yes?" Kylan yelled out as she hid the dagger under her pillow.

The door flew open, and two men dressed in full armor entered, followed by a very annoyed Mother Eden.

"Y'see? One girl wit' black hair. You asked aboutta group of two girls an' a man. The youngest wit' red hair, not black, ya' donkeys."

"Shut your mouth, innkeeper," grumbled the first man. He wore a gold-plated half-helm with a matching breastplate. The gauntlets he wore were gold as well, and his shield had a large crown etched in the center of a black border. A longsword hung from his hip, sheathed, like some sort of fancy decorative piece. "What's your name, girl?" he asked Kylan with a voice as sweet as vinegar.

The question seemed to catch Kylan off guard. "My name is Saria," she answered.

"Saria, you say? That's a whore's name. You a whore?"

Unsure, Kylan let out a squeak. "Er--yes, I'm a--I'm a whore."

"Hmph, that makes sense then," the first man said, removing his golden half-helm. His hair was a long, tangled mess that was oiled with sweat. It was once a black color but time had dusted it grey. "Well, me and my good friend here are members of the King's Law. Prince Tycho himself sent us after some outlaws. You see a nomad or a girl around your age recently?"

Mother Eden stamped her foot in outrage. "I already told ya' two," she screamed.

"Quiet, ya ol' hag," the second King's Lawman fired back. He was dressed in a silver half-helm and breastplate. His broadsword was gripped in his right hand while his left held the same shield as the Commander. "Let us do our job so we can get to arresting the rest of the scum in your shithole." The black cape he wore signaled his status as an Officer of the King's Law.

"The King's Law are a bunch o' failed squires who take their anger out on the less fortunate. Only difference between a King's Lawman an' an outlaw is, an outlaw didn't have no rich father to buy 'em a job!" Mother Eden screeched as she left the room.

The Commander stepped closer to Kylan and gave half a smile. "Hello, m'lady. I am Jerell Tennysion, Commander of the King's Law, and this is Lord Nolyn Whitworth, a rising Officer. May we ask you some questions?"

Kylan thought for a moment but nodded her head yes without saying a word.

"Did you accompany a bald, bearded man to bed within the last week?"

"'Course she did, Commander," Nolyn Whitworth sneered. "Problem is, she probably had at least ten in the last week."

"Calm yourself, Lord Whitworth. Remember your training."

Kylan shook her head as her hand reached out for her dagger. "No, I haven't seen any bald men this week. None." She wrapped her fingers around the hilt.

"And what are you reaching for?" Jerell Tennysion asked, grabbing her hand.

With a thud, Kylan's dagger fell to the floor, and the Commander unsheathed his sword.

"That wasn't the smartest move," he said, pointing his blade towards Kylan's neck. The sword had a pale, off-white blade and a golden hilt with a large ruby in its center. His face was a leathery orange color that was magnified by the candlelight. "I'm sure you're frightened, dear girl, trust me, we understand. We of the King's Law are here to protect, not to instill fear." He kicked Kylan's dagger across the room and smiled a mouth of perfectly straight white teeth. "Protecting does create stress, though, and we often go days without seeing our wives."

Nolyn Whitworth stepped closer, his half-helm still hiding part of his face. "Some of us don't have time for a family."

"So, m'lady," Commander Tennysion continued. "How much would it cost for my Officer and I to have a good time?"

"Bo--both of you?"

"I'll give you a hint. It's less than one boro."

Kylan furrowed her brow. "There's nothing less than one boro."

"Exactly!" Officer Whitworth broke in.

With that, the Commander of the King's Law shoved Kylan down and climbed on top of her.

"No!" Kylan screamed and tried to kick but she couldn't move her body. Jerell Tennysion's breath reeked of mutton, which made her gag as he brought his face in closer. He kissed her once on the neck, but Kylan refused to give in. "I said no!"

He pulled down the top of her tunic, exposing her shoulders, then dug his perfectly straight teeth into the skin near her collarbone. The pain from the bite caused tears to trickle from her eyes once again, but this time she said nothing. *This would have never happened if we stuck together.*

"I didn't ask for tears, whore," Tennysion said as he planted himself between Kylan's legs. He unstrapped his fauld and began to pull down his breeches and Kylan closed her eyes.

"Commander, we have a problem," Whitworth said in a hushed tone.

Kylan's pack was open, as was Manx's container, exposing both the Coatus incubator and hair dye.

"What's the probl--" Commander Tennysion's words caught in his throat when he saw what was on the nightstand. He smudged Kylan's hair and a lock of her auburn shimmered through like the sun peaking through a sky of rain clouds. "You--"

Just then, taking advantage of Jerell Tennysion's shock, Kylan punched her attacker in the throat. He gasped with a look of terror, and blood began to pour from his mouth onto Kylan's face. This was her life now, the life of a murderer. *I already killed the royal Saige, why not the Commander of the King's Law?*

When Kylan slipped out from underneath Commander Tennysion, she noticed the arrow through the back of his neck.

"You're all right, love." Manx smiled from the threshold of the door. The nomad nocked another arrow into Rose Thorn and loosed it at Officer Whitworth.

Nolyn Whitworth blocked the arrow with his shield and charged towards Manx, who stepped back into the hall. He lunged with his blade, and the nomad collapsed to the floor and swung her legs around, knocking Whitworth down, but he recovered with an upward thrust of his blade.

Manx spun out of the way, and that was when Kylan rushed out to join the fight. She leapt onto Whitworth's back and tried to cut his throat, but he dropped his shield and grabbed her by the neck. He began to squeeze and chuckled as Kylan dropped her dagger.

"Say goodbye, girl," Whitworth said through his half-helm.

Kylan felt the cold steel of Whitworth's gauntlet tighten, and her vision began to blur. She heard Manx yell something but couldn't make out what. *He's toying with me.* She kept hoping Dink would come from behind and slice his throat, or Manx would put an arrow through his face, but it wasn't going to happen. *This is my life, and I say it isn't ending.*

Whitworth started to lift his blade to deliver the killing blow, and for just a moment, Kylan's eyes swirled into focus.

The kick from Kylan was fueled by anger and landed squarely on Nolyn Whitworth's swordhand. She felt the officer's grip loosen when he dropped his sword, and that gave her just enough air to kick again. Using both feet, she pushed against Whitworth's chest, but he wasn't giving so easily. He slammed Kylan against the far wall next to the Smiladon head, and she felt her ribs struggle to protect her insides.

Thinking quickly, she reached toward the Smiladon head and pulled out a candle from its eye. Nolyn Whitworth completely forgot about Kylan when she kissed the flame to his cape. The dim hall glimmered for a moment with an eruption of fire as the officer whirled around in a panic, trying to extinguish the fiery inferno attached to his back. Kylan grabbed his broadsword from the floor, and when Officer Whitworth spun toward her, she buried the blade into his chest. Falling backwards, the flames died with Officer Nolyn Whitworth like a dog that couldn't live without its best friend.

She dropped the sword and looked for Manx, but the nomad had disappeared yet again. Kylan found her dagger and ran back into her quarters to grab the pack that held the Coatus incubator.

Downstairs was filled with members of the King's Law, all armed with swords and arrows. Kylan saw Manx on both knees, her arms shackled together, and she knew it was over. The stairs sounded disappointed as she walked down them, but not a word crossed her lips. Her face was covered in blood, her hair was a tangle of black and auburn, and she held both items that guaranteed she would rot in a cage for the rest of her life. Even so, she didn't cry nor beg for forgiveness. Instead, Kylan looked around at the scene she had created and laughed.

EPILOGUE

FORBATH: RELISS

The beer was a deep brown and sour as vinegar. Vengar Stoneburner sat at the bar of The Fox and The Hound, sipping his nightly pint alone, as always. *What I would do for a stein of honey mead.* There was a healthy buzz in the tavern, one that made it quite difficult for Master Stoneburner to go over his notes from the day's training, but he persisted, nonetheless. He took a sip from his goblet and felt the ale drip from his moustache onto the cedar wood bar. His patchy white beard was only a few weeks old, but the length was already bothering him. In certain areas, like his moustache and chin, the hair was thick and full. His cheeks, however, were covered with coarse wisps that made him feel like a brittle old man.

Vengar Stoneburner always felt safe in The Fox and The Hound. Well-known as a King's Law tavern, the establishment never brought any thieves or nomads, but it also never brought a single whore. He was in love many moons ago, before the Battle for the Mirrored Mountains, but when Stoneburner joined Tanwill's cause, he had to say goodbye. *Saying goodbye blackened my heart, but my honor turned it to steel.*

King Tanwill had put an end to the man who destroyed Vengar's race, and even if he was saying goodbye to his family, he owed the mortal his service. The law that said a Kingsman couldn't have any romantic relations was created by Zabkar Inwar, but most of Trilon thought it to be outdated and unnecessary. King Tanwill, not wanting to offend his people, edited the law so any Kingsman could do as they please -- unless they were a part of his Cabinet. This, of

course, didn't include anyone from the Embray bloodline, so
his son, Prince Tycho, could continue his dynasty. The
Trainer's Guild was another story altogether and allowed
Guild members to see their loved ones once a decade for a
Nascentem Feast. His partner had told him that no two
people could form a relationship if they couldn't watch the
lines darken on each other's faces. She also hated the idea of
helping mortals to create slaves out of the most magnificent
creatures Trilon had even been gifted. *I never wanted to say
goodbye.*

His tunic was the color of a sour apple, with milky-
colored breeches that looked significantly different than the
King's Law uniform that the majority of the tavern wore. He
was proud to stand out, just for the unlikely event that a
whore was to stroll on in. *Gold and steel aren't the key to
getting a woman into bed; it's giving them something they've
never had.* While prostitution was legal in Trilon, there was
a noticeable lack of traffic in The Fox and The Hound. This
was due to the tendency of the King's Lawman to take certain
unwanted or desired liberties, but in Vengar's tunic, he
wouldn't be mistaken for one of them.

The Fox and The Hound was an all-wooden tavern, and
that was apparent not only to the eye but to the nose as well.
Most taverns or inns reeked of booze or puke, but The Fox
and The Hound gave off rich, piney scents. Vengar would
have thought it would have smelled like steel, as the walls
were decorated with shields and swords from fallen members
of the King's Law, dating back to when Tanwill began his
reign. *These aren't shields, they're tombstones.* There were
arched windows on both sides of the tavern, which gave the
area a vibrant glow during the day, one that accentuated the
earthy aromas. In the front of The Fox of The Hound was the
thick bar that stretched from end to end. A large fireplace

was positioned near the back, with three wooden benches crowding it.

"Can I getcha anothuh?" the bartender asked as he cleaned out a pint glass with a dirty rag.

Vengar lifted his eyes from his notes and shook his head. *A different human is pouring my drink today.* "No, no, thank you, m'lord," he answered.

"Oh, I'm no Lord, Master Stoneburner, jussa man tryna pour a few drinks to pass the time."

"Sometimes I envy you bartenders. No concerns except an empty glass," Vengar said. The human was tall, close to seven feet, and skinny as a twig. He had close-cropped, white-blond hair and a grin that showed not a single worry line. "What shall I call you then?"

"Call me Chatou, Chatou Mulbody," the bartender's voice rang heavy with pride.

Vengar took another sip of ale. "Mulbody, eh? Where does your family come from, Chatou Mulbody?"

"My family is from here," he said as he poured another pint and handed it to a patron. "My Lord Father and brother both fight for the Knights of Rutherfall, though, as I will someday."

Rutherfall was known for their Knights, and rightfully so. Each realm was required to supply a certain amount of highly skilled squires every year to The Blade, which was a training Guild for fighters. After the five-year training program was complete, Lord Bekan Atalay would knight each squire, turning boys into Sirs. Only the best fought for Rutherfall, though, and they required high marks in every either course to even be considered by the Lord of Windrip.

"Have you had the pleasure of meeting Lord Bekan?" Vengar asked, with a raise of an eyebrow.

"Lord Bekan, no, I have not. My father tells me--"

"That there is no better Lord in all of Trilon, I'm sure. Do yourself a favor, m'boy, stick to pouring drinks. Let your mind grow rich with stories, not with ghosts. Let your back grow weary with age, not from carrying armor."

There was a slam of a stein onto the bar that almost made Vengar leap up from out of his skin.

"Gimmie another, Mulbody," Lord Jerell Tennysion said with slurred words. He swayed towards Vengar and stared at him with one eye closed. "Whatta you tellin' him, Master Stoneburna?"

His breath smelled so strong of booze that Vengar thought of lighting a match to see if he could breathe fire.

"This boy--" Jerell reached across the bar and grabbed Chatou Mulbody by the shoulder. "--is a fighter. 'Sides, whattya even know about fighting? Seems to me, you spend most of yer day cleaning up giant bird shits," he said with a hearty laugh that transformed into a cough.

Vengar looked the man up and down. He wore his King's Law armor and a silver cape embroidered with a golden crown over his shoulders. His skin was as orange as the sun at sunset on a summer day, which made his teeth look unnaturally white. "I fought in the battle for the Mirrored Mountains, m'lord," Vengar responded coolly.

"Aye, and you lost!" Jerell picked up his stein and slammed it back down onto the bar. "Fill it up, Mulbody. I'm the fucking Commander of the King's Law!"

A rage filled Vengar's head like black smoke, until he had to open his mouth to let it billow out. "Oh, I've tasted defeat, but your memory is hazy from the ale you keep swilling! Did you forget the Coatuses and *who* harnessed them?"

He shifted back and forth from his seat and Tennysion placed a hand on his sword's hilt.

"Oh, please, spare me your attempt of intimidation. You and I both know you can't pull a hair from my beard, because your head would then become a decoration for King Tanwill." Vengar watched as his words whizzed through Jerell Tennysion's head.

When the Commander of the King's Law didn't respond and turned his attention back to Chatou Mulbody, Vengar knew he had won.

"So where is Mirlo tonight?" the Commander of the King's Law asked Chatou as he sipped his now-full stein.

Chatou used the rag he was cleaning with to mop some of the sweat that glistened on his forehead. "Mirlo is performing tonight, at a ceremony for his brother, Toby. The boy is becoming a squire for Prince Tycho."

With a laugh and a snort, Jerell Tennysion puffed his chest out. "Oh, of course, to sing and dance for his brother, the future Knight. Let me--" He paused to let out a hiccup between words. "Let me tell you, once he's knighted, Toby Vaino will move up to be Prince Tycho's Lord Protector, and Mirlo will still be singing songs for a boro."

This time, Vengar didn't interject but instead sipped his ale and lowered his eyes to his notepad. The parchment was wet from ale, which dampened some of the ink, causing it to run, but still Kylan Corwin's name was easy enough to read. Not only was she able to feed and take Akupara on a walk through the Guild, but the baby Coatus also showed no aggression towards her. *The baby is strong like Akupara, and Xalvadore Corwin's daughter has shown zero struggle with commanding her, unlike the rest of the trainees.*

He then remembered what King Tanwill had told him: if any trainee goes above and beyond and shows any potential of becoming the baby's trainer, do not waste any time in telling him. "Day or night, Stoneburner. I don't give a fuck if I'm on the shitter, just tell me." *He treats me like his slave. Soon he'll be calling for me to wipe his ass.* Vengar's reports had begun to give the King anxiety recently with the hatching of the fourth Coatus.

The King's Cabinet had begged Tanwill to crush the two eggs that Saige Lorrode Allwater created with a secret type of science, but he wouldn't hear it. Because of the dangerous experiment without Tanwill's consent, Saige Lorrode was voted out of the King's Cabinet, which Embray reluctantly agreed to. He believed that his friend's scientific achievement shouldn't be destroyed but embraced. His Cabinet's concerns had merit, though, as the Trainer's Guild had six deaths and eight injuries, two of which included dismemberment, since the fourth egg hatched. If things continued at this pace, there would be no trainees left by the end of four moon turns.

Stoneburner paid Mulbody a silver piece, which was more than double what the ale was worth. "Just consider what I told you, lad. You're supposed to live your life, not fight through it," he said, readying himself to climb down from his barstool.

Before Stoneburner turned around towards the exit, he felt a blow of cold air flutter across his back. The hairs on the back of his neck stood up as he felt icy breath whisper to him.

"Vengar Stoneburner," the voice said, causing him to shudder from his head down to his toes.

"Who wants to know?" he asked, without turning to meet the voice. The Fox and The Hound was a sweaty mess of a bar, but whoever stood behind him brought winter's bite.

"Just a fan of the *last* RoarCatcher," the voice continued.

Vengar cleared his throat. "I'm not the last RoarCatcher. Get your facts straight."

"Well, for all intents and purposes," A hand groped for his groin and squeezed tight, "You are." The grasp on his

362

manhood caused it to grow, and Stoneburner let out a slight moan.

He spun around to see his admirer, but there was just the King's Lawmen laughing and singing. Lord Nolyn Whitworth had jumped on top of a bench near the roaring fireplace for a seemingly dramatic effect to the story he was telling his fellow Kingsmen.

Of course, I just imagined that. Oh, how my brain wanders when I've drank my fill. He grabbed at the back of his neck and it felt cold as steel. *There's no way this is part of my imagination, though.*

The barstool Stoneburner sat upon toppled over when he hurried toward the exit, but he made no attempt to pick it up. There were a few angry words directed toward him that carried way above his head, so he paid no mind to them. Right now, all Vengar Stoneburner cared about was leaving the bar and returning back safely to the Trainer's Guild.

The threshold opened up to a world blanketed in darkness, one that seemed to put the city to sleep, which became more apparent as Stoneburner got further away from the bar. Stars pierced the veil that was the night sky, giving a glimpse to the world above Trilon. There was a direct path from The Fox and The Hound to Honeck Way. This would take him directly back to the Guild, where he could further study his notes before creating tomorrow's exercise regimen for the trainees.

"My notes," Vengar said to no one. "I forgot my fucking notebook!" He began to sprint back toward The Fox and The Hound, his Bellow swinging back and forth from his neck like a pendulum.

Once Stoneburner picked up his pace, he tripped over something on the path, but regained his balance before falling. Reaching down, he picked up his notebook, and looked toward The Fox and The Hound. He opened the book slowly, as if opening it normally would release a curse upon him. Nothing seemed out of the ordinary at first, with the RoarCatcher's diagrams of armor and taming tools intact. However, when Vengar flipped to his notes, Kylan Corwin's name was circled everytime it appeared in blood red.

"So, Alma Staley's daughter has shown potential?" the voice asked from behind with words of ice.

"Alma Staley and Xalvadore Corwin's daughter, yes, she has, to say the least. The girl has an incredibly close bond with the babe, almost motherly," he responded with clenched teeth.

The voice's laugh pushed Vengar from bitter cold to numb. "Xalvadore Corwin is as spineless as a roach. An anti-magic, power-drunk coward is not the girl's father. His blood may flow through her veins, but she is Alma Staley's daughter."

"Whatever you may say. I'm admittedly not too fond of the man myself, and I've never conversed with Lady Alma; only seen her in the Capital." The coldness that flowed through his veins began to warm as if they were pumped with tea water. *What magic is this?*

Silence took over the night, one that had the grip of death. That was when Vengar noticed the shadow that was created by The Fox and The Hound. *It's just a different shade of black to most, but to some, it's a shield, it's a weapon, it's another dimension.*

She appeared from thin air, stepping out of the darkness into starlight. "Vengar Stoneburner, the man who has yet been able to harness the creatures that could kill us all at any moment," the tiny woman said as she stepped closer to Stoneburner. Removing the hood from her cloak, she revealed a face as pale as the stars and flowing midnight black hair.

With each step from the stranger, Vengar felt the warmth grow inside of him. "I've harnessed all of the Coatuses. Three out of the four are active members of a thriving society."

When the woman reached his boots, she continued onto Stoneburner's toes. Once he felt her breath warm his, her eyes of emerald green were clear, as well as the tips of her hair that matched them.

"I meant the ungifted, the ones who loathe *our* existence. Couldn't you just put some of their blood in your screamer and work your spells?" She batted at the jar around his neck like a playful kitten.

Vengar stopped the momentum of his necklace and stepped back, causing the woman to do the same. "It's called a Bellow, and no, I can't. A human is far more complicated than a creature. I've always thought it to be the hatred laced in their minds, like some sort of shield within their blueprint."

"So, you've tried to control a human?" the girl said, locking eyes with Vengar, a great sense of eagerness and desire in her stare.

He scowled at the woman. *I would never speak of my magic to a Shadow.*

"Oh, please, you can't still be salty over the Battle of the Mirrored Mountains," she continued.

"My entire race was destroyed from the battle. The Oracles stole my fallen brothers' and sisters' sacred relics used to communicate with our allies and turned them into weapons," Vengar hissed, seething as he clenched his Bellow tight. "I lost my life after that defeat! Who do you think you are to dismiss the extinction of my race?" His anger was wrestling with the ecstasy he felt from the Shadow's warmth.

The girl blinked as her lips curled into a devious crescent moon smile. "I know who *I* am, Vengar Stoneburner. *I'm*

Saria, and magic is the flesh on my bones, the air in my lungs. I thought the same of you."

There was a loud crash from inside The Fox and The Hound that caused Stoneburner to jump. He shook his head and looked back to Saria. "Magic is my blood. If you think otherwise, then you're--"

"I do think otherwise, Vengar Stoneburner. You're no more than a pet to the unenchanted, the humans, the racists. Is it really so honorable to fight for the people who see you as less than them?" Saria's voice was powerful and sensual, one that grabbed at Stoneburner's groin as much as her hand had.

The Shadow is right. I'm all but spat upon by everyone I come across, and without me, Trilon would be nothing more than a graveyard. "What are you proposing, Saria? Or are you simply here to haunt me?"

Saria grabbed at Vengar's beard, sending a sharp, exciting bolt of pain through his body. "Come with me for the night, be with those who will appreciate you. Say 'fuck off' to the King and embrace the pleasures that you deserve." She opened her cloak, revealing her naked body. The Shadow was a sunrise after a century of darkness, a feast he craved after being starved for too long. Stoneburner reached out to Saria and grazed her stomach with the back of his calloused fingers. With a kiss on the lips, she reached for his coffee-colored hands. Placing them on her freckled breasts, she pulled him back *into* the shadows. When Vengar was hers, Saria covered him in her cloak, blowing out the starlight.

Their lips stayed locked in the darkness, and Stoneburner let passion take control, giving in as a prisoner to the moment. *Lust can get you just as drunk as ale.* Right or wrong, it didn't matter, consequences were mere fables for the weak-minded and scared. This was what he craved, what he needed, and when their bodies twined together, he felt a connection grow as if they were roses blooming after winter's hibernation.

It didn't take long for Vengar Stoneburner to feel the Shadow's thorns, though, as her lips began to steal his air. He opened his eyes wide, but they failed to aide him, only showing endless black. The ground below began to soften, and Vengar wondered if a storm had opened up. Saria continued to kiss him, scratching at his scalp with her dagger-like nails. Pain and pleasure mixed together, creating a potion of ultimate bliss, and the RoarCatcher hoped the Shadow had an unlimited supply.

Their feet were no longer on the ground, whether it had disappeared, or had they flown from it, Stoneburner couldn't say, but either way, he wanted it to continue. Saria's body stayed steady as they traveled through the shadows, but Vengar was trudging through quicksand.

Stoneburner felt as though he could continue this for an eternity. *She can have my eyes, my air, my body. I was never this alive when they were mine.*

However, *all good things end*, and the RoarCatcher was punched with a fist of fatigue. A glimmering orange glow surrounded them, and he wanted to strangle it until it too joined the crepuscule. Then, the ground rushed up to meet Stoneburner, causing him to fall out of Saria's grasp. Gasping for air, Vengar laid flat on his back, staring up at the same star-filled sky as before, but he wasn't in Reliss. A lantern stared at the RoarCatcher as it hung from a thick wooden pole, like some sort of fiery monkey.

"You're certainly a clumsy one," Saria said, tying her cloak back around her body.

"Where…" Vengar tried to stand but was only able to make it to his knees before vomiting up sour ale and bile from the pit of his stomach.

The Shadow reached out a hand to help him up but he ignored her, still trying to heave up his insides. Finally, Stoneburner held out his right hand, and Saria lifted him up gently. The world was spinning as he tried to regain control of his vision, but he fell back into a great wall of grey ashlar.

"Where have you taken me, Shadow?"

The air was still muggy, like in Reliss, but the smells of salt and fish danced their way into his nostrils. *Of course she would take me to Yatorga.* His vision came fully into focus after a few deep breaths, and that was when Vengar realized it wasn't a wall he was leaning against, but an inn.

"You brought me to another tavern? Certainly seems counterproductive, wouldn't you agree?"

Saria grabbed a hold of his shoulders and closed her eyes before whispering an inaudible spell. The words seemed demonic, like they were conjured in the flames of a hell. *These words were forged in the land lost in frost.* Instantly, Stoneburner felt like his normal self, or as normal as he had pretended to be for the last fifteen years.

"You don't listen, do you? I brought you here to remind you what it's like to be around the gifted. These are the people who will treat you like a King, Vengar Stoneburner." Saria's emerald eyes glinted when the flames from the lantern met them.

She needs to be careful with her eyes; a lesser man would try to mine and sell them to a jeweler.

"You'll have fun here. Just make sure you save some energy for me," Saria whispered as she locked fingers with Vengar and led him to the front of the tavern. There was a strip of market stands that led up to the inn, all of which had colorful banners and signs. They swayed in the light breeze, like waves that had lost the ocean.

The great tavern stood tall over the shops, an alpha dog to the pack of Yatorga. No sign hung over the entrance, nor were there any windows, but a smiling pig was carved into the oak door.

This is the Grateful Swine; I should know, the damned ungifted always mention it in their glory tales from the rebellion. Brannon Broadwine met with a Shadow who gave up the Oracle tome. The potion for the banishment spell would have rotted out anyone's insides, but not a Verrativa. Chief Onexis is the true hero of the RoarCatcher race.

Just as Saria put her hand on the door handle, there was an explosion of laughter, and a stocky bald man burst out from the Grateful Swine, a pipe clenched in his teeth. His beard was a dusty orange mess that was matted and stained from ale.

"Ah, look who it is! Wha… what… whaddya say?" the man said with slurred words. He struck a match against the side of the Grateful Swine and kissed the flame to the bowl of his pipe.

"Dinky! I say you have perfect fucking timing," Saria said, embracing him. "This is Vengar Stoneburner," she continued, locking arms with the RoarCatcher.

"You fuckin' shitting me? Vengar Stoneburner? Ain't you never 'sposed to leave the Capital?"

He's right, what am I doing here? I need to go back, I've abandoned my post. I'm a deserter.

"He isn't supposed to, but he's not obeying the King tonight. Ain't that right, Master Stoneburner?"

She's right, I deserve this night. Fuck the King, fuck them all.

The Grateful Swine was alive with merriment, and when Vengar sat at the bar with Saria, everyone turned to greet him. Tapestries hid the walls as if they were protecting secrets within the ashlar.

"Stay here a moment," Saria said with a nibble on his ear. "I know someone who's been dying to meet you."

A vibration crawled through his chest, rattling his bones, and Vengar reached for his Bellow. The stained-glass jar pulsated with his heart, beating to the same rhythm, a drum of anxiety. *There's a creature in the tavern, one that I can speak with. I wonder what it would have to say.*

"Ayy, RoarCatcher," the gruff voice of Dink called from behind Stoneburner. "Pleasure 'avin you here." He grabbed a hold of Vengar's shoulder and kneaded it like he was prepping to bake him. The man, Dink, wore a grey, baggy robe with deep sleeves and seemingly deeper pockets. "Let's 'ave a drink. Didn't any of these cheap fucks get you a drink yet?" he yelled out with his eyes squeezed close, more to himself than to anyone at the bar. "Porter! Get *my* good friend, Vengar Stoneburner, a whiskey--"

"That won't be necessary," another voice called out, and the throng cleared the way.

The man whom Saria returned with wore a matching robe and had lilac eyes so beautiful they could put any woman or man to sleep.

"I will be buying *Master* Stoneburner his first drink at our establishment."

His voice is no louder than the fluttering of a hummingbird's wings, yet an entire bar cleared the way for him as if he were a Umenyonga.

"Porter, my dear friend. Please pour Master Stoneburner a pint of sour apple ale with as little foam possible."

Porter was obese and wore a shirt that was a size too small. There was a scar that ran across his left eye, a pink earthworm that prevented him from opening it. "We're running very low on the sour apple ale, Graybill. We--"

"--need to give our friend the very best ale we have, and the sour apple ale is the best."

There was no rebuttal from Porter, but when he placed the pint in front of Vengar, he muttered something about "not going to steal more this time."

Graybill grabbed the pint and smelled it. His hair was braided loosely and fell to the middle of his back. Pepper-black with a few hints of salt, his goatee matched in color and in length. He took a sip of the ale and smacked his lips together. "The sour and the sweet mix together harmoniously, like two lovers."

Saria, who stood with Dink now behind Vengar and Graybill, yelled, "Don't get him too drunk, I don't want any problems later!"

"I'll get the next fuckin' round," Dink chimed in.

Vengar nodded to Graybill. "Thank you... Graybill, was it?"

"Yes, and it's pleasant to hear you not call me 'Lord'. I've always admired your race, as what you did for Trilon."

Stoneburner couldn't help but laugh. "I have enough of titles and genuflects back in Reliss. Tonight is my night to remember what it's like to be with the gifted. There is no RoarCatcher race anymore, my friend. As for what I did for Trilon, 'twas no more than creating slaves for the ungifted."

"No, no, no, you didn't. You *saved* us all, Master Stoneburner." Conversation in the tavern began to pick up again, and deep in the back there was the delicate voice of a lute. "Yes, it is true that you aided the ungifted, but don't forget about the gifted. We would have all died, the Verrativas included, if the Coatuses weren't tamed. You're a god to whoever practices magic. Please, drink from my cup." He held out the pint that held the sour apple ale, the imprints of his lips still fresh on the brim.

"Get your fucking hands off of me, Dink!"

Vengar spun around just in time to see Saria slap the chubby drunk in the face. Cackling, Vengar turned back to take the pint. The ale tasted and smelled exactly like a sour apple, so much so that Vengar expected a crisp crunch after his sip.

When he put the pint down on the bar, he noticed a floppy-eared hound at his feet. "You shouldn't have done that, Master Stoneburner," the dog said to him as he continued through the crowd of people.

"Delicious, isn't it? Brewed with fresh apples, but unfortunately our fruit supply is running dry. That isn't a real problem for a Shadow, though. The issue is knowing when to strike." Graybill's mouth twisted into a smile. "Pass me that pint." Vengar did without even thinking about it. "Do you have any weapons?"

"No," Stoneburner responded, unsure of why he did.

Graybill's grin grew. "Give me your Bellow."

Vengar obeyed without a moment's hesitation.

"Thank you. Wouldn't want you to break this." The Shadow placed it gently into his pocket.

That's mine. The Bellow is my life.

"Now, smash your face against the bar as hard as you can."

Appendix

List of characters in *Trilon: The Flight of the Coatus* (alphabetical order)

Acconi -- Verrative smith who lives in Halftop Hills

Adley Roundtree -- Butcher in Leefside

Aiken Pritchett -- Lord Steward of Reliss

Alma Corwin -- Wife of Xalvadore Corwin; Mother to Kylan and Elmar Corwin

Anurd Kincaid ("The Nightmare") -- The only Knight to be fully trained by Bekan Atalay

Atruis Callowat -- Graybill's apprentice

Avner Staley -- Descendent of Deryk Staley

Bekan Atalay -- The Lord of Windrip; the former Lord of Ghordaan

Big Eyed Fish -- A RoarCatcher who is a part of the Brazier

Brannon Broadwine -- King Tanwill's Lead Confidant

Broddi Trap -- Butcher apprentice and carrier boy from Xxafulok

Buldoc -- Trovado's son who died during Tanwill Embray's rebellion

Cellyadure -- An Oracle

Celux Abale -- The King of Forbath before Zabkar Inwar's invasion of Trilon

Chatou Mulbody -- Bartender at the Fox and the Hound

Daymon Stringfellow -- The Halfling Bard

Deryk Staley -- The King of Aleru before Zabkar Inwar's invasion of Trilon

Dink -- An older mortal man who is associated with the Shadows

Duboz -- A Tsumari who resides on the Wick

Edwyrd Hendryx -- Prince Tycho's squire

Eji -- A Tsumari

Elmar Corwin -- Son of Xalvadore and Alma Corwin

Emerick Callowat -- Mayor of Leefside

Emery -- A Verrativa who is wife to Onexis and mother to Evore

Ereck Staley -- Brother of Alma Corwin

Eron Sichel -- Once the mayor of Yatorga, he was tricked and poisoned by Razzo Klessen

Evore -- A ten-year-old Verrativa; Son of Chief Onexis and Emery

Forym Quist -- Prince Tycho's squire and friend

Gamuka -- Tsumari leader of The Red Reach

Geremy Vaino -- A Knight of Everlid; Toby Vaino's father

Graybill -- The current leader of the Shadows

Gripley Rotoro -- Syaestra's Trainer

Honeywheat -- A pony in Reliss

Horace Pommel -- Knighted Lord of Piklora

Jarreau -- Tsumari Prince of The Red Reach

Jerell Tennysion -- Commander of the King's Law

King Hayao -- King of Hybernia

Kylan Corwin -- A Coatus Trainee; daughter of Lord Xalvadore Corwin

Lady Ah-Sula -- Tsumari leader of the Red Reach

Lady Haruah -- Tsumari leader of Torch's Brand

Lanlei Embray -- A fierce warrior who was supposed to be Queen of Trilon

Lanoria -- Trovado's wife

Launa Teabrook -- Alma Corwin's mother

Lirum Rhygell -- Baron of Gojii

Lorrode Allwater -- The Royal Saige

Madison Atalay -- Bekan Atalay's daughter

Mallory Broadwine -- Lady of Tulrose; Brannon Broadwine's mother

Manx -- A nomad who is especially skilled with a bow and arrow

Mirlo Vaino -- A bartender and bard in the south; Toby Vaino's brother

Molte Holten -- Prince Tycho's Squire

Mother Eden -- Owner of the Tired Traveler

Mychael Theozeed -- Guard in Reliss

Nolyn Whitworth -- Officer of the King's Law

Okawos -- Tsumari leader of Torch's Brand

Onexis -- The Chief of the Verrativas

Opoku Darkwa -- A resident of Leefside

Perine Biznowaty-- Atrius Callowat's mother

Porter -- A bartender at the Grateful Swine

Quarlo Jomidë -- Writer of *Magic: The Unbiased Facts*

Raylon Tarbuck -- Battle Master at The Mind

Rayne Blackwood -- Akupara's Trainer

Razzo Klessen -- A Shadow who took over the city of Yatorga years ago, using Stranger's Tongue

Rean Atalay -- Bekan Atalay's son who fled Yatorga, the city he mayored, after it was attacked by Reaper

Rorah -- Tsumari Princess of Torch's Brand

Roycroff Kaylee -- Nyteah's Trainer

Ryker Tygurnach -- The Royal Battle Master, who was knighted by Zabkar Inwar

Sama -- Princess Rorah's pet Tantae

Saria -- A Shadow

Sermi Blackwood -- A Guard in Leefside

Symphony -- Prince Tycho's steed

Syrah the Creator -- An Oracle who specializes in portal and path creation

Tage -- Princess Rorah's handmaiden

Tanwill Embray -- The King of Trilon

Taro Geiz -- A Guard in Reliss

Tawanie -- A young Verrativa girl

Tela -- A Smiladon and steed to Bekan Atalay

The Iron Skull -- An associate of the Shadows, he is a man who has strong magical abilities

Thorlack Quist -- Fought beside Tanwill Embray during the rebellion to overtake Zabkar Inwar; Foryn Quist's father

Tidas Rhygell -- The King of Gojii before Zabkar Inwar's invasion of Trilon

Toby Vaino -- Prince Tycho's squire

Toprek -- A young Tsumari

Traetark the Blind -- A pirate who was captured by Emerick Callowat

Tremaine Broadwine -- Lord of Tulrose

Trovado -- A Verrativa who holds the position of Rajihn

Tycho Embray -- King Tanwill's son, the Prince of Trilon

Vengar Stoneburner -- A RoarCatcher that helped set up the Trainer's Guild

Waliu -- Trovado's infant son

Xalvadore Corwin -- Baron of Aleru

Zabkar Inwar -- Once the King of Trilon, he was defeated during a rebellion led by Tanwill Embray

BARONS

A Baron is the overseer of a particular realm who reports directly to the King. When Tanwill Embray rebelled and took the throne, he appointed Barons for Gojii and Aleru, but not Forbath. Embray believed that the role was unnecessary in the south, as he could take on the title.

Lirum Rhygell -- The Baron of Gojii who resides in its Capital, Rutherfall. He played a major part in the rebellion against Zabkar Inwar, which included defeating a horde of Oracles to convince Lord Bekan Atalay to join their cause.

Xalvadore Corwin -- The Baron of Aleru who resides in its Capital, Everlid. He is married to Alma Staley, whose family was knowingly on good terms with Zabkar Inwar during his reign.

COATUSES

A Coatus is a winged creature that has a scaly torso, feathered wings, an oddly long neck, and a beak that is typically striped with a sunflower yellow and an indigo blue. Originally, there were three Coatuses, known as "the sisters", each one taking care of their own realm,

Akupara -- The Coatus of Forbath. She is said to be larger than Larkmour Castle and has been nicknamed "the Queen". Rayne Blackwood is Akupara's assigned Trainer.

Nyteah -- The Coatus of Gojii. Her torso is forest green with golden raindrop-shaped spots all throughout. Roycoff Caylee is Nyeah's assigned Trainer.

Reaper -- A Coatus that was created using science by the royal Saige, Lorrode Allwater. She has black feathers with splashes of purple.

Syaestra -- The Coatus of Aleru. She was the last to hatch, making her the youngest of the three sisters. Syaestra has diamond-shaped feathers which are a pale blue and covered in snowy white swirls. Gripley Rotoro is her assigned Trainer.

CREATURES

Clubsodons -- Native to the east, Clubsodons are covered in scaled armor, which
can be as strong as stone and just as heavy. This creature is large enough to carry up to four with provisions. Their clubbed tails are primarily used for defensive purposes. Most of the Clubsodons perished during Zabkar Inwar's reign, as Syrah the Creator would use their natural armor to build barricades or their tails for battering rams. Tulrose is still guarded by the few remaining Clubsodons.

Tantaes -- These are the creatures of the Tsumari and can only be found on Ofrea. They're the size of a cow with mossy green scales and a large, three-pronged plate on the top of their head. Tantae ivory is incredibly valuable, which has created a poaching problem in Trilon.

Smiladons -- Sabre-toothed cats that were used as a means of land transport. Certain men and women used to ride Smiladons, specifically in battle. There were some who chose to have their companions domesticated, allowing them into their homes. Most of the Smiladons disappeared when the Coatus eggs hatched, and those that remained fled into hiding when Reaper crashed into Yatorga.

GUILDS

A Guild is a educational association where those would go to learn a specific skill. Typically, if one is allowed to join a Guild, their family is well off and has a good relationship with the King. With the Blade being the only exception, Guilds are outrageously expensive.

The Blade -- Location and the name of the training Guild for fighters. After a five-year training program, Lord Bekan Atalay would knight each squire who completed the necessary requirements and assign them to whichever town or city he pleased. The elite would be sent to Rutherfall, where some could stay, but others would sell their services to High Lords outside of the city. Every year, each Realm is required to supply a certain number of squires to The Blade. Sir Raylon Tarbuck is the Battle Master of the Guild.

The Mind -- Location and name of the Guild for educating Saiges. There are many failed Saiges, as the work is quite demanding. The first Oracles were members of this Guild who didn't complete their training

The Trainer's Guild -- This Guild is located in Reliss and teaches future Coatus Trainers. While the Trainees are in the Guild, they must wear silver hooded cloaks. The three Coatus Trainers wear armor that includes a steel tail that has a clubbed mace. Master Vengar Stoneburner is the head of this Guild.

HIGH POSITIONS

Battle Master -- The head armorer in a city, town, or Guild. Knighthood is a requirement of this position. Often, such as with Sir Ryker Tygurnach, a Battle Master is in charge of both squires and Knights. They are also required to annually choose which squires to send to the Blade.

King's Law -- The keepers of peace in Trilon, who are often squires that never rose to knighthood.

Mayor -- The lead political figure of a city or town in Gojii, Aleru, and Forbath. In Gojii and Aleru, a Mayor reports to their Baron. Forbath is different, as the Mayors of the city and towns in the south report directly to the King's Cabinet.

Saige -- A Master of healing. Saiges are also known to have an appetite for experimentation and often use the knowledge gained at the Mind to create potions, and other devices.

Steward -- A position in towns and cities that is typically assigned to someone of noble birth. Stewards are in charge of day-to-day operations. These responsibilities include food store, town upkeep, and any event coordination.

MAGIC

While certain inhabitants of Trilon are born with "the gift", others choose to study and practice in order to gain abilities. Magic is generally looked down upon by mortals who believe that it can only be used against them.

There are also a few locations that have been enchanted by or a specific magical spell.

Enchanted locations:

Craven's Bog -- The southern swamp was a hideaway spot used by Zabkar Inwar. Syrah the Creator built a secret passage from the swamp to Reliss, and Cellyadure enchanted the area, making it impervious to any other magical spells.

Soarfrost -- An area of Aleru past the Moondown Lands. It was once where the Oracles practiced their magic, making it an enchanted land filled with failed experiments. Onexis, Chief of the Verrativas, banished Zabkar Inwar's host to Soarfrost using an Oracle spell. Shadow apprentices take a pilgrimage to Soarfrost without use of magic. Once they arrive, their cloaks are enchanted by the Oracles.

The Ylewood -- The land where the Verrativas live. The Ylewood was given to Onexis, Chief of the Verrativas, by Tanwill Embray as an offer to aide in the rebellion. The area was uninhabited before Embray took over as King because of the belief that the Moiiralatta would devour or enslave anyone who entered the land. The truth is that the sea monster protects the Ylewood.

Magical Races:

Oracles -- Their magic is reliant upon the mixing and drinking of potions. The Oracles were the first followers of Zabkar Inwar. While their abilities are strong, their magic requires a great deal of stamina. Their spells and recipes are written in tomes.

RoarCatchers -- This race was once seen as glamorous, given their ability to speak with and command all creatures. They trained Clubsodons, Smiladons, and even brokered deals with the Tsumari for Tantae ivory. Their ability comes from their Bellows, and their magic is that of blood. RoarCatchers wear Bellows, which are filled with the blood of all the creatures they can communicate with. The Mirrored Mountains was their home before it was taken by Zabkar Inwar after he gained allegiance from the Oracles.

Shadows -- Known as assassins or thieves throughout Trilon, the Shadows can use and manipulate darkness. While they do learn magic through training, their full abilities are unleashed when their cloaks are enchanted in Soarfrost.

Tsumari -- Members of this magical race are born with their abilities. They cannot be harmed by fire and can also travel through flames using the dirt from the land of their desired destination. They live in Ofea and have to deal with poachers that try to butcher Tantaes for their ivory.

Verrativas -- The immortal race of Trilon. The Verrativas are born and can live forever, given they aren't killed. They cannot die from old age, suicide, or sickness. However, they can be slain or poisoned. Once the last Verrativa life is taken, the power of immorality is passed on to whomever committed the deed. This prompted the entire race to stay hidden in the trees of Trilon for years. The Verrativa's gift garnered jealousy, causing the highest of Lords and lowest of servants to take their lives with zero remorse.

ABOUT THE AUTHOR

Dave Capp was born and currently resides in New Jersey with his partner, Amanda Jean, and their cat, Tormund. As a young boy, he drew inspiration from the works of JRR Tolkien, Jim Henson, and Shigeru Miyamoto.

He graduated Siena College in 2010 with the dream of becoming a novelist. This is his debut novel, which will be first in a series within the Trilon universe. Dave considers himself a connoisseur of coffee, noodles, and theme park rides.

When Dave isn't writing, he enjoys cooking, going to concerts, and complaining about the New York Giants

To learn more about the author:
Twitter @Thinking_Capp
Instagram @ThinkingCapp

Made in the USA
Middletown, DE
04 September 2019